THE LETTERBOX

Layton Green

To my mother, for everything

This is a work of fiction. Names, characters, organizations, places, and events are either products of the author's imagination or are used fictitiously.

Cover design by Sammy Yuen.

Interior by QA Productions

THE DOMINIC GREY SERIES

The Summoner

The Egyptian

The Diabolist

The Shadow Cartel

The Reaper's Game (Novella)

OTHER WORKS

The Letterbox

The Metaxy Project

Hemingway's Ghost (Novella)

Praise for the Dominic Grey Series

"Relentless." —*Publishers Weekly*

"A blend of action, history, anthropology, thrills, and chills, all delivered with a mature, polished voice. I am eager for more from this author."
—Scott Nicholson, bestselling author

"One of the top ten books of the year."
—*BloodWrites Mystery Blog,* on *The Summoner*

"Layton Green is a master of intellectual suspense."
—JT Ellison, *New York Times* bestselling author of *Edge of Black*

"*The Summoner* is one of those books that make you want to turn on all the lights in your house and lock the doors . . . [t]he settings are authentic and you can feel and smell the countryside . . . [t]his is a wonderful read for those who enjoy both suspense and action stories." —*Seattle Post-Intelligencer*

On *The Egyptian*: "Stirring and imaginative . . . both the characters in the story and the reader are in for a wild ride."
—Steve Berry, *New York Times* bestselling writer of *The King's Deception*

"I do believe Layton Green has moved into my top 5 author category—not an easy feat to attain!" —*A Novel Source*

"The confines of a page are not enough for Layton Green's writing. His work begs to be translated into 100-foot high IMAX images, rendered in 3D, and given a score by Hanz Zimmer." —*Biblioteca*

On *The Diabolist*: "A well-crafted and exciting thriller with a pair of interesting protagonists . . . and a charismatic villain who makes our skin crawl." —*Booklist*

"This is what you get when you combine Indiana Jones with Ludlum's Jason Borne . . . A must read for all you lovers of conspiracy theories, thrillers and mysteries alike!"
—*Baffled Books*

"Layton Green is an absolutely brilliant writer." —*Everything To Do With Books*

"Green's debut *The Summoner* was such a great read, I was hoping that he'd duplicate his literary excellence. In his second book, *The Egyptian*, Green exceeded my expectations."
—*BookPleasures.com*

"Favorite book of the year so far." —*A Novel Source*

"Layton Green has written a tale with supernatural and political undertones that unravels with ever increasing suspense . . . The book is plain terrific."
—Richard Marek, former President and Publisher of E.P. Dutton

"An awesome read . . . . The writing is polished and evocative, the subject matter fascinating, the characters intriguing, and the pace non-stop. Spooky and occasionally metaphysical, *The Summoner* harkens back to *The Serpent and the Rainbow* in its ability to convincingly portray seemingly paranormal events in a realistic (and therefore even creepier) manner." —*BloodWrites*, Mystery Pick of the Week

"[T]his book is above and beyond in its narrative, its cohesiveness, the depth of its characters and the quality of the writing. This is one of the best books I've ever read for Odyssey Reviews." —*Odyssey Reviews*

"Green writes like a dream."
—Melody Moezzi, award-winning Author, *Haldol and Hyacinths*

"[C]alls to mind such series as Jason Bourne and Indiana Jones, with supernatural/religious overtones thrown in. I recommend *The Summoner* to anyone looking for a suspense-filled journey into a unique—and at times, terrifying—culture that'll keep you guessing." —*Bookhound's Den*

"Yes, I did put TWO Five Stars up there . . . giving Green's *The Summoner* Five stars and Five stars alone downplays how I felt about this book." —*1000+ Books To Read*

"Dan Brown is pretty good at what he does and I don't begrudge him his success, but when it comes to interesting characters embarking on a thrilling exploration into the dark world of cults, religions and magic Layton Green does it SO much better."
—*Nylon Admiral Reviews*

"Layton Green kicks things up a notch and delivers a novel that should, if there's any justice to be found upon the shelves, make him a household name. *The Diabolist* is a dark, intelligent, spellbinding novel . . . I cannot recommend this one highly enough."
—*Beauty in Ruins Reviews*

"Green's *The Summoner* proved his great talent. *The Diabolist* ensures his place at the top of crime fiction: his number 1 place. Unbelievably good, unbelievably intricate, unbelievably Green." —*The Review Broads*

On *The Diabolist*: "[A] story that will move you to the edge of your seat."
—*Seattle Post-Intelligencer*

"The Gallic provinces, too, were pervaded by the magic art, and that even down to a period within memory; for it was the Emperor Tiberius that put down their Druids, and all that tribe of wizards and physicians."

(Plin. Nat. 30.4) (Latin)

Dartmoor, England
Three Months Earlier

The odor of waterlogged peat filled the air. Lucius Sofistere drew his coat tight, his eyes roving the mist-enshrouded worksite as the geologists labored to extract a tarnished silver container buried deep beneath the fen.

The moors were different at night. The silence, unnerving during the day, became deafening after sunset. Tendrils of fog caught the moonlight, turning the moorland into an eerie, dreamlike tableau of hidden menaces and imagined dangers. The fog didn't hide him, Lucius realized—it hid the moors.

He was used to eccentric clients in the world of high-end antiques, but this was extraordinary. *Discretion is paramount*, the voice on the phone had said. *No public officials, no reporters*. This alone was not unusual; many high-end collectors preferred the shadows, preferred to keep their Rembrandts and Egyptian artifacts to themselves, to hoard and worship in the privacy of their homes. And while this was a private dig, Lucius knew that governments had a way of making claims on significant pieces, regardless of the letter of the law.

No, the strangeness of the request had come in the collector's insistence—a mere forty-eight hours prior—that Lucius travel immediately across the Atlantic to this godforsaken expanse of moorland. As soon as the container was unearthed, Lucius was to carry it home and wade through the quagmire of history.

Reconstruct the past.

Discover its origins.

At last one of the geologists approached, cradling a silver container the size of a fattened briefcase. The geologist moved his scarf low enough to reveal the tanned, creased face of someone used to working in the elements.

"Fresh from its grave. I was paid to knock the dirt off and hand it straight over."

"How'd you know something was down there?" Lucius asked.

"Sensors picked it up about a month back," he said, ignoring Lucius's real question: *Why look here, in the middle of this wasteland?*

The geologist gave the moors a nervous moment of attention. "We went deep. Judging from the soil samples beneath the bog, this thing's been down there, untouched, for a long time. A *very* long time."

Just as Lucius moved to take it, the geologist muttered, "I saw something."

"Excuse me?"

"In the pit, during the extraction. When I was down there by myself."

When the man turned to face him, Lucius saw a haunted look in his eyes, a ragged mixture of fear and disbelief.

A grim smirk lifted the corners of the geologist's mouth. "Do you believe in ghosts?"

Lucius was disturbed by the man's behavior, but not enough to delay the job. The geologist had been working all night and was probably delusional from exhaustion. "I believe," Lucius said, "that fog and lack of sleep can play tricks with a man's mind."

The geologist chuckled with the edgy, disingenuous type of laughter used to break tension. "That's what the others said." He shrugged and handed Lucius the silver container. "It's all yours."

Lucius placed the vessel inside a leather carrying case. As he was walking away, the geologist called out to him, his voice still unbalanced. "So I don't get a look at it, then?"

It wasn't Lucius's place to inform the team, so he remained silent, intent upon the narrow path leading to his car. Following the footpath through the dangerous terrain required his complete attention, and he didn't look up for the entirety of the journey.

As soon as Lucius was out of sight, another figure, clad in a hooded white robe that merged into the fog, turned from his hidden vantage point and strode in the opposite direction.

Deeper into the moor.

NEW ORLEANS
The Present

-1-

I breathed deeply as I walked, enjoying the perfumed night air and languid pace of Uptown New Orleans. My best friend Lou and I had arranged to meet at Maison de la Voyageur, our local café, and after crossing St. Charles Avenue under a canopy of brooding oaks, I soon reached the familiar block of the Garden District where Maison lay nestled between a hookah lounge and an art gallery.

I spotted Lou in the corner. He was short and round and had a cherubic face, topped by the wispy blond hair of a newborn. I ordered an espresso, and Lou removed his stumpy legs from the chair opposite him.

"Have you banished the foul beast of work yet?" he asked.

"I wish."

Joining the pack of Camel Lights on Lou's table was a threadbare Princeton backpack, a coffee mug from Tulane law school, and a stained paperback. "So what's the grand plan tonight?" he asked.

"You mean with my life, or after I finish this espresso?"

"Is there a difference?"

I'd been planning to quit my job for years and could never seem to do it. I was a young attorney at a large firm, and things looked good on paper.

But at some point I found myself disillusioned with what life had to offer—and not just life at the firm. As the Chinese say, the mirror is the most powerful weapon one can wield, and when I looked in the mirror I saw a wind-up toy, at first unrelenting in its naive march through life, but with a battery that was winding down, stumbling in a circle with no way to recharge.

I had money and security but no soul, and was left with the constant nagging feeling that there was something else out there.

Something *more*.

"It's hardly grand," I said, "but I might try for an adjunct gig at the law school. Maybe take the Foreign Service exam."

"You're thinking of all those wide-eyed coeds who can't help but have a crush on the noble young prof who walked away from a life of luxury."

"You watch far too much television," I said.

"I'm down to eight hours a day. 'Oh, Aidan, I love those cowlicks in your soft brown hair and those dimples when you smile, your piercing blue eyes and—'"

I tried not to encourage him with laughter and failed. "Let's go to St. Joe's. I need a drink."

"Twist my arm," he said. "But I have to go somewhere first."

"Where?" I asked, surprised. Lou never had anywhere to go.

"A consulting job."

"At nine o'clock at night?"

"Some guy who owns an antiques shop wants me to come in after hours to look at a piece. Thinks there may be some type of obscure language on it. Come with me. It should only take a minute, and we can walk to St. Joe's from there."

I knocked back my espresso. "Sure."

The night air was as humid as a sauna. A few blocks later we found Antiques and Objets d'Art tucked away in the middle of the Garden District, on a deserted side street branching off Prytania. Lou pressed the buzzer, and I heard the click of a latch.

Dimly lit, the store possessed a subtle elegance. Richly framed paintings adorned the walls, lush carpets covered the floor, and it lacked the clutter of most antique shops. In addition to the typical period pieces, I noticed a number of macabre items scattered about the room: a six-foot-tall totem decorated with hair and animal skulls; intricately worked African figurines with deformed faces; a collection of golden masks whose vacant stares seemed to follow me around the room. Some of the paintings depicted fantastical scenes I would have expected to find gracing the walls of an occult shop in the French Quarter.

I cast an uneasy glance at Lou. He shrugged as two people entered the room through the rear of the shop.

The first was a tall, well-dressed man with an aristocratic face. Streaks of brown accented a thicket of gray hair. He entered cradling a wooden box, and as he looked up his weathered eyes gleamed with vitality.

"Mr. Sofistere?" Lou asked.

"Good evening."

"This is Aidan, a friend of mine. I hope you don't mind if he joins us."

"Not at all."

The shop owner didn't sound like a native English speaker, though his hint of an accent was oddly neutral, as if he had worked to scrub away all traces of the original inflection.

After he shook our hands, an attractive young woman stepped forward. She was slender, with mocha-colored skin and East Indian features. Wavy black hair framed her face, and she wore tan slacks, a silver choker, and a black spaghetti-strapped top. An assortment of colorful wooden bracelets adorned her right wrist.

"Asha manages the shop for me," Mr. Sofistere said. "As you can see, we specialize in objects of a more esoteric nature." He turned to Lou. "Which brings us to the purpose of my call. I understand you're knowledgeable in the history of Indo-European languages?"

"I am."

Mr. Sofistere stepped closer and held up a finely crafted wooden container the size of a shoebox. The lid of the box had splayed edges and was covered in lines of flowery design.

"I should begin with a bit of background," he said. "This letterbox, as we have come to call it, was unearthed by a dig in the Devonshire moors of

England. I've had the box examined and it dates to approximately first-century A.C.E."

"How was it preserved?" Lou asked.

"Sealed inside a silver container. Do you notice how the edges of the top are splayed, almost like tiny feet or wings? The style is distinctive to wood carvers in Southern Russia and the Baltic region. It was often used on pagan religious pieces." He wagged a finger. "But there's no evidence of this style outside the Baltics until centuries after the letterbox was made."

"That sounds like a puzzle," Lou said, his distracted tone evidencing his lack of interest in the history of wood carving in England, the Baltics, or anywhere else. "What's a letterbox?"

"Simply a name we've given it, since we don't know what else to call it."

"Isn't letterboxing some type of game?" I asked. "I seem to remember reading about it."

Mr. Sofistere paced in front of the totem. "Letterboxing is a hobby that started in England over a century ago, a treasure hunt for a small box or container. The owner of the box places a small prize inside, hides the box in a remote outdoor location, and makes up clues to find it. Nowadays, clues are usually posted on the Internet."

Lou flicked a wrist. "What does letterboxing have to do with this piece?"

Mr. Sofistere let his gaze fall on the relic. "In 1854, a traveler ventured into a remote region of the moors of South West England. As he was making camp for the night, he was shocked to find a cairn a few feet from the shore of a fen. Even more surprising, he found a bottle underneath the cairn, and inside the bottle he discovered a pile of ashes and a calling card. The name on the card was James Perrott."

Mr. Sofistere had an engaging voice, and I found myself leaning in to hear the story. I noticed Asha doing the same, though I assumed she'd heard it before.

"A local paper published the story. The idea of placing calling cards in remote locales caught the public's imagination, and the hobby of letterboxing was born."

Lou shrugged. "Okay?"

Mr. Sofistere smiled a smile of secrets. "On Perrott's calling card was a peculiar symbol drawn in ink—" he moved closer and held up one side of the letterbox "—which looked exactly like this."

One of the two longer sides of the box revealed a carving: four irregularly spaced vertical lines topped by a longer, wavier marking.

"Given your specialty," Mr. Sofistere said to Lou, "I was hoping you could provide some insight."

Lou took a long look at the box, eyes narrowing with focus. "That's nothing with which I'm familiar."

Mr. Sofistere looked away, disappointed.

"Does it open?" Lou asked.

Mr. Sofistere lifted the lid to reveal an immaculately smooth interior. Although empty, I had the impression that something belonged inside.

"Was that why you contacted me?" Lou said. "I'm sorry I can't be of more help."

"That, and the smaller markings on the other side."

Mr. Sofistere turned the box over, and Lou drew a sharp breath. He looked at Mr. Sofistere, then back at the box. "Those aren't random markings—those are runes."

Mr. Sofistere frowned. "Runes?"

"Characters forming ancient alphabets, sometimes reputed to have magical properties, often derived from modifying existing characters in order to facilitate carving on wood or stone. In layman's terms, runes are simply words. In ancient languages."

Mr. Sofistere gave an impatient wave. "Yes, yes, I know what runes are. But these aren't any I recognize."

"Those are Ogham runes," Lou said slowly as he studied the box. "Of which there are less than four hundred known surviving inscriptions."

"I've never heard of Ogham."

"There are almost seven thousand languages either spoken today or recently extinct. Not to mention the untold number of dead languages." Lou began pacing and waving his arms. I'd never seen him this engaged. "To be fair, compared to the number of spoken languages, there're only a handful of writing systems. I can't read this right now, but it's Ogham all right." Lou put his hands on his hips with authority. "First century, you said? That's earlier than any known Ogham inscriptions. This is a remarkable find."

"What exactly is Ogham?" Mr. Sofistere said.

"The alphabet of the insular Celts."

"Didn't the Celts utilize the Latin alphabet?"

"Only after the arrival of Christianity. Before the fifth century, the Celts were mainly an oral society, but among the Celts on the British Isles—or the insular Celts as they were called—a writing system called Ogham was used."

"If you're right," Mr. Sofistere murmured, "this could be an immense aid to the study of this piece."

"I'm right."

Asha peered at the runes. "You're sure you don't recognize the same marking that was on Perrott's card?"

Lou reexamined the larger symbol. "Nope. It's not Ogham."

"Can a translation be arranged?" Mr. Sofistere asked, a trace of eagerness creeping into his cultured voice.

"Of course. I'll need a few days to find the books I need."

He handed Lou a check. "Then let's meet at noon on Saturday and see what the letterbox has to say."

-2-

Lou and I walked the few blocks to where St. Joe's stood at the corner of Magazine and Joseph Street. A window covered by iron bars and burgundy drapes complimented the Gothic doorway, and we stepped into the shadowy confines of a bar that could only exist in New Orleans.

Catholic symbols inundated every inch of real estate: crosses of every shape and size, religious artwork, chalices suspended from the ceiling, replicas of saints and the Virgin Mary. The irony of St. Joe's, the religious décor hovering over the inebriated masses, always made me introspective. I think I viewed God in the same way I viewed relationships: I believed in the possibilities, but had never known faith or love, never *felt* them.

We wandered to the enclosed patio in the back. "So how's Fredda?" I asked.

Fredda was Lou's latest obsession, a professor of German literature he had met at Rock and Bowl. He fumbled with a cigarette. "Fine."

"Called her yet?"

"It's all about timing."

"Really?" I said mildly. "It's been two months."

Lou was pudgy and blond. I was tall and slender with a head full of dark hair. We joked that if joined, we would make the perfect male.

"Where's Veronica?" he shot back. "I haven't seen her around."

"Ancient history. She wants to make partner, I want to ride a motorcycle across Southeast Asia. The great tragedy of adulthood: you can't enjoy life without money, and you can't enjoy money without a life."

"That's why I have the perfect career plan," he said.

"What's that?"

"Winning the lottery."

I chuckled. "Getting tired of being the most overeducated temp on the planet?"

"I'm a professional linguist. Sometimes. Maybe I'll take your class, get back to a government-subsidized lifestyle."

"Nice plan. A PhD in linguistics, a law degree, and then back to happy hour at The Boot and intramural soccer."

"I've accepted the fact that happiness is comprised of doing the things that give you simple pleasure. I smoke, read bad novels, drink cheap rum, watch TV, ogle women, criticize the masses, and practice my languages."

I could only shake my head, realizing the brilliance of his comment while failing to grasp its place in my reality.

My thoughts drifted back to Mr. Sofistere's shop and the letterbox. "What's a cairn, anyway?"

"A pile of rocks stacked to commemorate something. Could be as small as a grave marker or as big as a tower. In ancient times they were assembled for sepulchral or religious purposes."

"Weird that someone preserved an empty box in silver and buried it in a bog next to a grave marker," I said.

"Weird that Sofistere is obsessed with the thing and runs an antique shop stocked with a bunch of creepy occult artifacts."

"Yeah," I murmured. "That too."

The next day was Saturday. When I showed up at Maison to browse through yet another what-to-do-with-my-life book, *What Color Is Your Parakeet* or some such, I was surprised to find Asha seated by one of the windows, this time in a red-and-black-patterned kaftan top. She noticed me, closed a magazine with a modernist building on the cover, and asked if I wanted to join her.

I ordered a black coffee and took the next table over. "Not at the shop today?"

"It's my day off."

It struck me as oddly coincidental that she just happened to be at my favorite coffee shop the day after we met. That was what being an attorney for too long did to you, though: made you overly analytical and suspicious.

Then again, it didn't mean I was wrong.

"I've never seen you here before."

"No?" she said, seemingly unconcerned with the coincidence. She noticed the book I was carrying. "Looking for a career change?"

"Yeah."

"What do you do?"

"I'm an attorney."

She met my gaze with an earnest expression. Her eyes were dark brown and enormous, almost too large for her face. "What happened?"

I liked her response. It wasn't the typical, *Oh, you must have something better lined up*. Her question was posed in a commiserative tone, implying, *What's taking you so long to leave your soul-sucking job?*

"I won't bore you with the horror stories," I said. "Sometime after the fifth missed Christmas, I decided it was time for a change."

"*Almost* decided."

"Yeah," I said, with a chuckle. "I guess that's right. And you? You don't sound like a native of N'awlins."

As she smiled at my overdone local drawl—I was from a middle-class suburb in Cincinnati, the only child of a third-grade teacher and a professional chef who worked opposite schedules—I took a better look at her features. High cheekbones and a pointed chin accentuated a narrow face, and a silver stud accompanied the dimple in the side of her nose where the curve began. Her ears were small but came to a point at the top which, combined with her petite stature, gave her a pixie-like appearance.

"I was born in India, lived in Zambia in my early childhood, and then did penance in Iowa. I went to college in London and moved here a few years back."

"That's quite a journey. How'd you end up working for Mr. Sofistere?"

"I studied architecture in school. After graduation, I found this job and fell in love with the city."

Those decisions didn't seem to add up, but I decided not to cross-examine her on our second meeting. "It's rare to find someone who truly enjoys what they do."

"I suppose I'm lucky for that." She flashed a wan smile that hinted at layers unpeeled. It also said, *That's enough about me.* "Mr. Sofistere was excited by Lou's discovery," she said, and I could tell by an undercurrent of energy in her voice that she was, too. "He hasn't been able to make heads or tails of the letterbox since he acquired it."

"Maybe a translation will help."

"Why don't you stop by and see what turns up?" she said.

I had always been attracted to mysteries and puzzles, the stranger the better, and I was curious to see if Lou could translate the runes. Still, I paused for a beat, trying to discern if she was being polite or actually wanted me to come.

Or maybe she had another purpose.

"I might just do that," I said, in a neutral voice.

We talked through another round of coffee. Though she didn't seem to know anyone, including the barista, my suspicions were allayed by her genuine manner and our conversation, which had a nice organic flow.

That, and I was self-aware enough to know that my attraction chipped away at any doubt.

"It is *alive*," I said the next morning as Lou, disheveled and groggy, joined me on the porch of my shotgun house. He lived in Mid-City and used the streetcar or bus for transportation. Whenever he tied one on Uptown, he often crashed on my couch.

As Lou smoked, I eyed the decaying cemetery brooding across the street. It melded with the neighborhood like a sinister Starbucks, accenting the architecture as much as the twisted oaks dotting the streets or the banana trees concealing the courtyards.

"What time is it?" Lou asked.

"Eleven."

"Got any pancakes?"

"No," I said.

"Why the hell not?"

"Have another cigarette."

"O–" he yawned "kay."

"Don't forget your appointment."

"I shan't."

"Mind if I tag along?" I asked. "I'm curious about that translation."

"Curious about the translation, or about what Asha might be wearing?"

"Both."

Just after noon we stepped inside the dim interior of Antiques and Objets d'Art, the solid door closing behind us like the sealing of a tomb. We were greeted by Asha's smile and the austere countenance of Mr. Sofistere.

Lou reached into his backpack and brought out two worn textbooks. "Books on rune systems, including Ogham."

Mr. Sofistere led us to the rear of the shop, where the letterbox rested on a table beneath an oil painting of a Gothic church rising out of a swamp. Lou set his books beside the letterbox, took a long look at the runes, and began flipping pages.

Mr. Sofistere gazed intently at Lou as he worked. I walked over to stand beside Asha.

"Do you think he'll be able to translate it?" she whispered.

"If anyone can, it's Lou. He's a whiz with languages."

"I wonder what it says. My guess is a family name."

We waited for long minutes as Lou pored over his books, the same rare look of engagement lighting his face. I shifted and leaned closer to Asha, who had her hair pulled above her head and was wearing a pair of snazzy white slacks with a V-neck top. She did the business look well.

"Have you heard of the new restaurant that opened a while back on Magazine?" I asked. "Sambor's?"

"No. Is it good?"

"I don't know. Want to find out?"

Before she could respond, Mr. Sofistere walked over to us. "Asha tells me you're an attorney. Might I ask with whom?"

"Toureau Dagmon."

"A very distinguished firm. In fact, I'm a client of theirs at times."

That surprised me. I thought I knew all of the firm's local clients, especially recurring ones.

He stopped to readjust a tribal mask hanging on the wall. Gaping holes in place of facial organs lent it a ghoulish appearance. "How would you characterize your collection?" I asked, trying to probe as judiciously as I could. "You carry a lot of pieces I haven't seen in other antique shops."

When he turned, his gaze had turned piercing. "I have an interest in acquiring pieces that are believed, by those who have faith in such matters, to embody and perhaps even house the spiritual realm."

I wasn't quite sure how to respond. "Are you implying that some of the objects possess some type of . . . mystical . . . property?"

"I don't claim to speak for the beliefs of others. And mysticism is often in the eye of the beholder, is it not? I like to think of my collection as an insight into the meeting of the human experience with the concept of the divine." He flashed a disarming smile. "I'm a dealer of antiquities. Each of my pieces is a cultural and artistic treasure in its own right."

Lou sprang out of his seat, keeping one hand on the page and tracing the runes on the letterbox with the other. "It seems to match. And here's another . . . ."

He fell silent again, looking back and forth between the letterbox and his books.

"So it's just a matter of locating the rune in your textbook, finding the translation, and constructing the sentence?" I asked.

Lou gave a tragic sigh. "It's a *bit* more complicated than that." He returned to the book. "Hold on, I'm almost done."

As we waited, Asha approached beside me and whispered, "Seven-thirty tonight? Pick me up here?"

"Great," I whispered back.

After a short spell, Lou looked up again. "It's four words, loosely translated."

Mr. Sofistere took a step closer. "What does it say?"

Lou slowly closed the book. "'The Path of God.'"

"Loosely translated?"

"Ogham doesn't have prepositions. *God Path* would be a more literal translation."

Asha swallowed as her gaze rested on the letterbox. "The God Path? What does that mean?"

"How should I know?" Lou said. "I'm a linguist, not an oracle."

Mr. Sofistere was also staring at the letterbox. "As I suspected, this piece has religious significance."

"Why would you suspect religious significance before knowing the translation?" Lou asked.

"Most ancient objects without practical utility were used for religious purposes," he said distractedly.

"Ah." Lou stood. "I suppose that's it."

Mr. Sofistere seemed to snap out of a trance, and handed Lou another check. "You've been a tremendous help. Do you think you could locate the surviving examples of Ogham, to see if there's any mention of this piece?"

"Gladly."

Lou and I murmured our goodbyes and left Mr. Sofistere hovering over the letterbox, his eyes fixated on the inscription.

-3-

When I returned to Antiques and Objets d'Art that evening, Asha appeared in the doorway wearing a black cocktail dress. Her wavy hair fell just past her chin, stray bangs teasing her eyes.

"I'm dressed okay for the place?" she asked. She had a coltish habit of holding her hands delicately in front of her body when she talked.

"Perfectly."

I breathed in the balmy air as she took my arm and we strolled to the restaurant. Sambor's was located near the corner of Prytania and Constantinople, among the grandiose houses looming above the streets like miniature colonial castles.

After a cocktail, the hostess led us into a dark-paneled interior that looked like a parlor in a French chateau. Comfortable spacing separated the tables, while candlelight illuminated the room with a soft glow.

"It's so warm and cozy in here," Asha said with a smile. "I like it." Her smile, when she let it, consumed her face. It was her best feature and betrayed an openness to the world.

After we ordered, I said, "So you went to college in London? I lived there my last year of university."

"Where?"

"South Kensington and then Tufnell Park."

"That's quite a change in fortune," she said. "Isn't Tufnell a bit rough?"

"Rougher than South Kensington. After graduation I stayed on and bartended, which included claiming a couch in Tufnell Park." I took a piece of bread. "Tell me about yourself."

"What do you want to know?"

"What do you want to tell me?"

She gave a half-smile, and I said, "Do you like New Orleans? What brought you here?"

"A lot of things about the city make me happy. The beautiful buildings, the levee, the slow way the locals talk, the little white hats the servers wear at Café du Monde." She fingered the stem of her wine glass. "So why don't you like being an attorney?"

I took a moment to respond, letting her know that I knew she was avoiding questions about her past. "How much time do you have?" I said. "But you know, I never blamed the job, I blame myself for being in the wrong place."

"Most people don't like to admit that. They want something to blame."

"There were also those two dirty words: *student loans.*"

Her eyes moved to a group of socialites at the bar, some of them arched backwards with forced laughter, others swirling drinks and roaming the bar with raptor eyes. "At some point you have to be true to who you are. No matter the cost."

"I agree," I murmured. "But first you have to figure it out."

We ordered dessert and more wine, discussing our shared loves of Russian literature, ethnic eats, and the city's abundance of atmospheric coffee shops.

We also discovered a mutual interest in the supernatural, though mine was limited to my bookshelf and my Netflix subscription. She confided that she read her horoscope daily, the Chinese and Indian versions as well as the Western, and was intrigued by psychics, magic, palm readers, tarot players, and anything else that hinted at a paranormal signature. Her eyes got a faraway cast during our discussion of such matters, her voice possessing an intensity which reminded me of the look on Mr. Sofistere's face when he was staring at the letterbox.

When we finally looked up, the restaurant had emptied except for the staff. "We should let them close," I said.

"Let's. I need to walk off some of this meal."

We took the streetcar to the French Quarter, then made the trek to the

Marigny. I led her into a jazz club. The place was dark and smoky, not too loud. A pretty, throaty girl maneuvered through Nina Simone.

"Warm and cozy again," Asha said. "You're doing well tonight."

"This place is one of my favorites."

Her eyes lingered on the musicians. "Jazz can be so lonely and sad."

"But it's a celebration of life through those things."

"What's to celebrate about that?"

"The bittersweetness of it all."

"It's not that I don't like jazz," she said. "I just think it's sad. Do you consider yourself a sad person?"

I thought it an odd question, and she asked it like it was perfectly normal. As if wondering if I were part of the club.

"I wouldn't have before. I don't know anymore. In the last few years . . . maybe."

A smile played at her lips. "You're a little young for a mid-life crisis. Or maybe attorneys have them early?"

"I was just so busy I never stepped back to consider the big picture."

"That big picture's a killer." Her grin widened, and she looped an arm through mine. "Don't be sad tonight, ok?"

I leaned back and drew her close. "How could I be?"

"I don't know," she said lightly.

We fell into a comfortable silence, and I grew conscious of a tingling running down the arm she was holding.

"Did Mr. Sofistere say anything about the letterbox after we left?" I asked, wondering if Lou was going to have any more income this month. I also had to admit that the bold claim on the inscription—the God Path—had stuck in my mind.

"He disappeared into the back room for the rest of the day," she said.

"What do you think the runes mean?"

"Who knows? Some ancient religious mumbo-jumbo, I suppose."

"You don't believe in God?" I asked, surprised.

"I don't know that, either." Her eyes left the room again, like when we were discussing the occult. "It's as if my mind wants to believe, but my heart or my soul or whatever you want to call it can't *feel* it."

"I know what you mean," I murmured, though I hadn't meant for the conversation to turn so weighty. "But you're superstitious, and with all the horoscopes and zodiacs—I just assumed you believed in God."

"I think I like those things because they're harmless, a bit of blind faith I can have without investing too much."

She hesitated, and there was something distant in her eyes, a separation not just between me and her, but between her and the world. "I really want to believe in something," she said quietly.

"Who doesn't?" I said.

We let the jazz caress us, and the room contracted. She entwined her fingers into mine.

"I believe in life," she said.

I gave her a quizzical look.

"I believe in this bar we're in, in the music that's playing, in this city. I can touch and see these things, and they make me happy. So I believe in them."

"It's good logic."

"I'm not talking about logic. I'm talking about feeling." She looked away, then turned back and smiled. "Let's dance for a while."

We stood next to our table in the corner, holding each other as we swayed to the reality of the music and each other. Our mouths lingered side by side, and I felt the hotness of her breath.

When our lips finally met, soft and sly, I supposed I believed in life, too.

We left the club and trekked towards the streetcar along the quiet fringes of the Quarter. New Orleans has a nocturnal energy, a preternatural life after darkness sets in. She took my arm as we walked in silence, turning down a side street that led to Canal. The iron gates of the contiguous homes and shops created a tunnel-like effect.

Halfway down the street, Asha stopped and turned. "What was that?" she asked.

"What was what?"

"I thought I heard something. It sounded like footsteps."

I turned to look down the desolate street, silent except for the faint shouts coming from Bourbon.

"It's too quiet here," she said. "I know it's the Quarter, but let's get back to the crowds. We can take Bourbon to Canal."

"Sure."

We walked to the next intersection and turned left, taking a street that would intersect with Bourbon. As we turned the corner, we both stopped. This time I had heard it. Footsteps accompanied by a scraping sound, as if one heel was dragging along the pavement, coming from the street we had just left.

A street I had just canvassed with my eyes and knew was empty.

"It's probably a stray dog," I said as we hurried away. The Quarter was relatively secure, but New Orleans is never the safest of cities, especially at night.

"Let's just get to Bourbon."

We could see lights at the end of the street. The dragging sound stopped for a moment, and then picked up again, faster. I could have glanced behind me, but something compelled me not to, an irrational fear of the unknown. We held hands and rushed forward, just short of a run.

Heart thumping inside my chest, we reached the end of the street, the chaos of Bourbon drowning everything behind us. We stumbled into the press of the crowd and stopped to catch our breath, only then turning to look.

The street stood silent and empty, the only sign of movement the night breeze against my cheek.

-4-

After a lingering kiss outside Asha's apartment building on St. Charles, she said she had an early morning, but would like to see me again.

On my way home, my mind lingered half on the softness of her lips and half on the scraping footsteps in the French Quarter. As unnerved as I had been, there were lots of weird occurrences in New Orleans, and by the time I got home I had consigned the memory to the graveyard of the city's quirks.

The next morning, after a pot of chicory coffee, I took the streetcar downtown to resume sorting through the crush of contracts, addendums, briefs, motions, discovery requests, and other documents that comprised my life as a corporate litigator. The day flew by, and before I left I decided to inquire about Lucius Sofistere.

I knew exactly who to ask. The adjoining office belonged to Prentice Meyer, a junior partner in project development and finance. Prentice put together deals around the world to build everything from office towers to power plants.

I stepped into his office overlooking the sweep of the Mississippi, and Prentice swiveled in his chair. His stick-like, pallid limbs poked out of the bespoke suit and huge Rolex like they were just visiting, rather than inhabiting. Prentice wore more dollars to work every day than most people drive to work in.

"Señor Aidan, what a pleasant surprise! I've missed your sunny but aloof disposition lately."

"I've got a ton going on."

"Do you?" He crossed his legs and said, as if I hadn't even spoken, "I've had a depressing day. I've got a new case, a favor for a partner involving faulty construction of his brother's house. How pedestrian can you get?"

I rolled my eyes, but he wasn't paying attention. Prentice was once assigned to work on a pro bono landlord-tenant dispute, and rather than go to magistrate court for a day and mingle with the masses, he had paid his own client the disputed two thousand dollars.

"My last case involved turnkey construction of a world-class hotel by a Hong Kong financier." He sniffed. "Residential contracts probably have consumer protection laws to deal with, or some nonsense."

"At least you still have your penthouse and hordes of young associates who worship you."

"The rest of our associates are sheep. They don't have your spirit, Aidy. Or your blue eyes."

Prentice had been unabashedly hitting on me—and making me laugh—since the day I started. He was a brilliant lawyer, and his ridiculous, over-the-top commentary possessed an honesty that I appreciated. Most people at the firm would tell you what you wanted to hear and then stab you in the back. Prentice said whatever he wanted and then stabbed you in the chest.

He also made it a point to know everything about everyone at the firm. "Have you ever heard of Lucius Sofistere?" I said.

Prentice looked at me oddly. "Where'd you hear that name?"

"Just came across it."

"He's been a client of the firm for some time. I don't know much about him, except he's dripping in class and style, and deals only with Marcus Arnoult."

Marcus Arnoult was a crafty trust and estates lawyer whose practice consisted of handling the estates of wealthy clients. The joke was that Marcus could hide a stack of gold ingots in a piggy bank.

"I know he owns a successful antiques store," Prentice continued, "but he must have other interests. And in this town, you know what that means."

Prentice meant organized crime. I agreed with his earlier assessment, since Mr. Sofistere struck me as someone who came from money. I wasn't buying the organized crime angle, however. He was too refined and didn't fit the profile.

Then again, you never knew.

"Be careful with whom you consort, Aidy. Lucius Sofistere might just turn you into a proper man of the world. No more doing lines of coke off the backs of young stevedores in your Range Rover."

"That's what you do, Prentice."

"Oh, that's right. I almost forgot."

"But thanks for the advice."

"Don't mention it. If you find out what else Sofistere has his sticky fingers into, be sure to let me know."

"Of course," I murmured.

-5-

The next Saturday, Asha and I met for coffee and then spent the day at the New Orleans Museum of Art. In each room we chose a favorite painting in secret, then tried to guess which painting the other had chosen. What I didn't tell her was that she gravitated towards one of two extremes: the most colorful painting in the room, or the one with the most soulful representation of angels.

After the museum, we had dinner at Jacquemo's, caught a brass band at the Maple Leaf, then went back to her place and watched the sun rise.

The last few weeks of summer passed much the same way. Conversation came easy and we loved to do the same things, whether sneaking into a midnight ghost tour, trying new restaurants, or just exploring the city.

While we spent long hours in each other's embrace, we had yet to consummate the relationship. My desire at times threatened to overwhelm me, but the drug of mental connection was a new and exotic one, and one that I was savoring.

Yet I was also aware—and wary—of the times at dinner when she seemed to mentally check out, or when things got heated late at night and she would suddenly push me away and, with a detached look, claim exhaustion, only to call first thing in the morning to ask about my dreams.

Of course, this only made her more desirable. Both sexes have a sixth sense for reticence and pursue it relentlessly.

The question was, did her moments of distraction concern *me*, or something else?

* * *

A week later, Asha invited me to dinner at her apartment, a one-bedroom on St. Charles. New Orleans was a beautiful and mysterious place, but even Uptown had plenty of crime. I gave her props for living alone.

Her building was very New Orleans: in need of a paint job, but oozing charm and architectural details. Asha answered the door in a dark brown, floral-print dress that blended nicely with her skin, and then led me to the combination living and dining room. Her furniture consisted of a knee-high wooden table, a floor strewn with colorfully embroidered pillows, candles of all shapes and sizes, a pair of oversize Klimt prints in glass frames, and a bookshelf full of Sufi poetry and travel guides and New Age literature.

I inhaled the aroma of freshly ground spices wafting from the kitchen. After dropping off a couple of tasty appetizers, she delivered the entrée, a coconut shrimp curry.

"I'm impressed," I said.

She sat with her legs tucked under her, both feet pointing to one side. "I have a proposition for you, and wanted to butter you up."

"I'm not quite ready for marriage."

She threaded her arm through mine, then leaned in close. "You don't think I'm marriage material?"

"Of course not. You can't support me."

"Gigolo."

"Tease."

She took a sip of chardonnay. "How would you like to go with me to Croatia?"

"Excuse me?" I said. "What's in Croatia?"

Her eyes were bright and playful, and she squeezed my arm. "Mr. Sofistere's hit a dead end with the letterbox and decided to send it to an expert in Dubrovnik."

The curry was delicious. "Dubrovnik's supposed to be beautiful," I said, "a medieval city right on the Adriatic. But why does he want us to take it?"

"He's busy and doesn't need to be there for the examination. He asked me if I would mind going, and suggested I take Lou in case more translation was needed. I told him I'd feel more comfortable if you went as well. So," she said a little guiltily, "I need to ask Lou also."

I took a long swig of beer. "That sounds like an expensive bit of research."

"I'm pretty sure that's not an issue. You'll see what I mean when you see his house—he wants us to swing by before we go. Plus, if the letterbox turns out to be a unique cultural piece, as Mr. Sofistere suspects, then it'll pay for our trip many times over."

"Is it safe to carry this thing around?"

"Hand deliveries are common practice in the antique world; he doesn't want it lost or jostled by some transport company." She peered up at me. "So can you take a week and come? I think a little change of scenery would be good for you."

I leaned back and palmed my beer, looking her in the eye and saying nothing. It was all very peculiar. "What's the date?"

"We'd be leaving next Friday."

I looked away. "Oh."

"Bad week?"

"There's no way I can get free that quickly."

"How much notice would you need?"

"A trip like that? A month or two, at least."

We sat in silence for a minute, and when she started eating again, all I could think about was how much I wanted to drop everything and go with her. Have an adventure and see something new.

The next day, I had never felt more trapped by my job, more dispirited about the rest of my life. The workday seemed to last an entire year and I couldn't sleep that night. The thought of going to Croatia tugged at me so strongly that it became a physical companion, an itch I couldn't scratch.

I asked for a two-week leave of absence, and the firm refused my request. I lessened it to a week, and they still wouldn't budge.

So I quit my job.

* * *

Later that evening, I met Lou at Maison and told him about my resignation.

"You're joking."

I couldn't stop grinning. My lips had been stretched wide, my head buzzing with newfound freedom, since I'd walked out of the managing partner's office.

"You're not joking," Lou said. "I can't believe it. You actually have a pair. So what's the plan?"

I told him about Asha's offer. His eyebrows lifted even higher. "And long term?" he asked.

"Ask me when we get back. You're coming, right?"

"Are you serious? Getting paid to travel is right in line with my career plans."

Asha was thrilled, both for me and the trip. She told Mr. Sofistere right away. The next day he invited all three of us to his house for an evening cocktail. He owned a monstrous stone mansion in the Garden District, the landscaped grounds enclosed by an imposing wrought-iron fence.

A middle-aged butler with sallow skin and pendulous eyelids answered our knock. He gestured with an open palm for us to follow, and Lou and I exchanged a glance. Firsthand experience with true wealth can be unsettling.

The house lacked natural light, and I peered at the original paintings hanging in the foyer. Wide hallways branched out from the immense balustraded staircase, and the foyer continued teasingly behind it. It was the kind of house you wanted to walk through and explore.

A house that kept secrets.

A grandfather clock dominated the sitting room, accompanied by four antique chairs gathered around a claw-footed wooden table. After Mr. Sofistere entered, dressed impeccably in a gray pinstriped suit, the butler served a Cabernet Franc and a Sancerre.

"Thanks for inviting us," I said to Mr. Sofistere. "Your house is stunning."

He tipped his head in acknowledgment and made no mention of my career change. "I wanted to ensure your preparations have gone smoothly," he said. "Asha, I just sent an email with Dr. Fleniken's address."

"What's his field?" Lou asked.

"He has joint degrees from Harvard in biblical archaeology and religious history. His specialty is locating, retrieving, and categorizing religious objects, and he's known for seeking out and acquiring pieces no one else can or will. After your translation and given the lack of information on the letterbox, I thought he should take a look." He hesitated, his lips parting in a mysterious half-smile. "Although he's respected and well known in certain circles, Dr. Fleniken is a bit unconventional. He—well, you'll see."

"Wouldn't it be easier to have him come here?" Lou said.

"He prefers not to," Mr. Sofistere said, offering nothing further.

Lou shrugged. "The Ogham translations I gave you didn't help?"

"Unfortunately, no."

"There's something I've been thinking about," Lou said. "How did you connect the larger symbol on the letterbox with the one on James Perrott's calling card?"

"A colleague I consulted in London was familiar with Perrott and the history of letterboxing. He made the connection and confirmed it was the same marking."

"Did anyone ever ask Perrott why he left his card under that cairn?" I said.

"Perrott claimed he wanted to see if anyone would ever find the bottle, and that the marking was his personal signature." Mr. Sofistere's eyes, dark and thoughtful, met Asha's before he continued. "That same colleague of mine uncovered a curious article in the archives of the British Museum. The article was published in 1856 by the local paper in Chagstead, the town closest to Perrott's estate, and claimed there was no evidence Perrott had ever used that symbol before. Moreover, no gentleman of the time who used calling cards would have inked his signature on a calling card. He would have had it engraved." He paused as if coming to a decision. "The letterbox was found buried beneath a body of water in the moors called Cranmere Pool—the same place Perrott left his card."

Lou whistled. "So Perrott's calling card was found a hundred and fifty years ago in the English moors, and this box here, buried more or less since the time of Christ, was uncovered a few months ago in the same location, and with the exact same marking."

"Correct."

"That's quite a coincidence," I murmured.

Asha didn't seem surprised. Mr. Sofistere probably hadn't wanted her to disclose certain details before he trusted us.

The butler returned to whisper something in Mr. Sofistere's ear, and Lucius's jaw tightened. "I apologize, but something has come up. You'll have to excuse me." He picked up an envelope off a side table and handed it to Asha. "Travel expenses. Let me know if you require more."

"Thanks again for the ticket," I said slowly, thinking how strange the whole affair was.

"My pleasure. I'm glad you're both accompanying Asha. Traveling alone is never a good idea."

"Anytime," Lou said magnanimously, as if he was the one who had supplied the free ticket.

Mr. Sofistere stood. "Good evening, then."

He shook mine and Lou's hand and embraced Asha, then disappeared into the depths of his house.

-6-

Since leaving the firm, part of me felt buoyant once again, full of hope and promise. Unencumbered, fresh.

The other part of me felt that somehow I had failed, and not just because of my dimmer financial prospects. Life's questions still lurked beneath me like the bottom of a dark lake.

The day before our departure for Dubrovnik, I walked alongside Bayou St. John, one of my favorite places to reflect. I saw the sluggish green water as a microcosm of the world: change and movement, a parade of colors and smells, a complete tactile experience with the mystery of the unknown lurking just underneath.

Yet what was really down there? Did the world's army of distractions exist solely to divert our minds from the fact that from dust we came and to dust we shall go and that nothing, no matter how glamorous, could change that fact? Were our entire lives a desperate grab to manufacture significance?

I wanted to do something before my time came. I wanted to find meaning, I wanted to fall in love, I wanted a glimpse of the puppeteer.

Metaphorical or not, the inscription on the letterbox kept rising to the forefront of my thoughts.

The God Path.

I didn't know if a trip to foreign shores would provide any insight to life's questions, or to the enigmas surrounding Asha's past and the letterbox.

But I was ready to find out.

* * *

That night Asha and I ate dinner in the French Quarter, then met Lou at Lafitte's Blacksmith Shop, a dive bar near the Fauborg Marigny. Lafitte's was one of the oldest bars in the country. Paint had never graced the wooden rafters, the stone floors remained pitted and uneven, light eked out of candles stuck in sconces and demijohns.

We slipped into a craggy wooden booth and enjoyed the buzz of anticipation before a journey. Asha had one arm draped over her handbag, which contained the letterbox. Since we were leaving in the morning, she had carried it home.

She turned to Lou. "So what's your theory on the runes?"

"That whoever made the box was under the same mass delusion as the rest of the religious world." He snorted. "I truly don't get it. Ninety percent of mankind still believes in the tooth fairy."

"Why are you so fanatical about your non-belief?" Asha said. "Isn't that the same as religious zealotry? They're both a belief system."

"My belief system doesn't need to invent answers to life's big questions. Don't you know that truth is always stranger than fiction?"

Asha smiled sweetly. "My sentiments exactly. We have no idea what's out there."

As they continued to argue, I noticed a figure in a hooded white robe lurking in the street outside our window. Except for the shadowy outline of his face beneath the cowl, I could see only wrists and supple fingers protruding from his sleeves, like the legs of a spider feeling around a corner. A mottled burn scar covered the back of one hand.

In any other city, I would have checked the news for escaped mental patients. But New Orleans was a magnet for bizarre characters and weird occurrences.

However, the man's appearance wasn't the only reason he had caught my attention.

I noticed him because he was staring right at us.

I didn't think the others had seen him, and I peered back uneasily through the glass, remembering the dragging footsteps from a few weeks ago. The robe, erect posture, and hands crossed in front of his body reminded me of a medieval cleric standing gravely before an altar.

Lou nudged me. "Hey. We're leaving."

I sensed the man's eyes following us out the door, and I looked for him as soon as we stepped outside.

As with the footsteps, there was nothing but the breeze.

I felt foolish and said nothing to Lou or Asha. The man was probably a drunken straggler from one of the Quarter's costume parties.

We made our way towards the streetcar, taking a detour because Asha wanted to walk through Jackson Square. A cornucopia of occult practitioners occupied the square at night: black-garbed magicians, tarot readers, palm readers, and others, hawking and practicing their crafts directly in front of the alabaster spires of St. Louis Cathedral. Instead of repelling each other, the two factions seemed locked in a symbiotic embrace of darkness and light.

As we ambled through the square, I felt Asha close to my ear. "I feel like some of these people are looking at me," she said.

"What're you talking about?"

She grabbed my arm and whispered, "Over there." She pointed at a hunchbacked crone perched behind a tarot table on the sidewalk. "She was staring right at me."

"She's not now. Are you sure?"

She hesitated. "And that man by the church, with the swords."

After casting a surreptitious glance around the square, she shrugged and kept walking. As we reached the edge of the low wall ringing the square, she gasped and drew back. I turned and saw a small hand holding Asha's wrist. The hand was protruding from a cheap, glossy black shirt and belonged to a young boy sitting on the wall. I moved to help Asha, but she held me back.

The boy was about twelve years old, thin and pale. Lank brown hair framed limpid eyes. He was a striking figure in a tragic way, and less overtly commercial than the other occult practitioners, as if this was how he looked and dressed all the time, not just at night in Jackson Square.

"Why'd you grab me?" Asha asked softly.

"You have a presence."

Lou snorted. "Get a new line."

Asha didn't respond. I had been watching the boy, but when my gaze traveled to her face, I was taken aback.

Her face had gone as pale as her brown skin would allow, and her eyes looked like twin headlights from an oncoming car, huge and intense and filled with an inexorable energy.

"What did you say?" she whispered.

The boy's eyes flicked to Asha's purse, then back to her face. I noticed he didn't have any cards or gimmicks, no sign proclaiming his skills or powers.

He released Asha's arm, but she edged closer. "Do you read palms? Auras?"

The boy looked up at her. "I read other things. I'll tell you more, but could you give me something small? I'll take whatever you want to give."

This was a common strategy among the street entertainers: people often gave of their own accord more than they might have paid up front, after their interest was piqued.

"C'mon Asha," Lou said, "it's just a scam. It's getting late."

Asha fumbled to take money out of her purse. The boy pocketed the bills and took Asha's hands in his own.

"What do you sense?" Asha asked, her eyes locked on him. "Is it me?"

The boy reached towards her purse. His hands hovered over it for a moment, at the spot where the letterbox bulged outward. He swallowed and inched his hands inside, then drew back as if bitten by a snake. With a wild look he jumped off the wall, backed away from Asha, and sprinted into the crowd.

Asha was rooted to the ground, shocked. Lou started laughing. "Check your purse, Asha. He just saw you pull money out of it, and we all stood here and watched him. I'll bet my next translation fee you're missing something."

She hesitated, then opened her handbag and held the letterbox for a long moment, before handing it to me while she riffled through her purse.

"There's nothing here," she said slowly. "But I think I cleaned it out already. I can't remember."

Lou rose up like a peacock. "You see? Those people will rob you blind."

"He's a kid out here by himself," she murmured. "He can have my money."

Lou walked off shaking his head. I gave the letterbox back to Asha. "You okay?" I asked.

She forced a smile. "Sure."

We caught the streetcar and returned Uptown. Lou exited after a few stops, and Asha settled her head against my shoulder.

"You want to talk about it?" I said.

"There's nothing to talk about."

Oh, there was something to talk about.

The conductor called out her stop. She rose.

I said, "Want me to come in for a while?"

"It's late, and we're leaving early. Thanks, though."

"You sure you want to be alone?"

"I'm fine. I'll see you tomorrow. I'm excited about the trip."

She kissed me, let our fingertips linger, and then exited with a small crowd of people. By the time the streetcar crept out of sight, I had seen her unlock and enter her building, clutching her purse to her chest.

After the streetcar dropped me off, I shuffled home, unable to stop thinking about Jackson Square. The part I couldn't shake was the look on Asha's face when the boy told her she had a presence. It brought back an unpleasant memory of the last time I had seen a look like that, when I had attended a trial in law school of a man accused of murdering his wife. He swore to his innocence, and had an airtight alibi that got him off, but whenever he talked about his wife he got a look of pure obsession that made me think, whether he had murdered her or not, that he would do just about anything where his wife was concerned.

I walked home and cracked a beer. I realized how little I knew about Asha's past. My own history was a quick and easy read, unworthy of translation, and I had assumed she felt the same about hers.

Now I wasn't so sure.

I finished my beer and went to lock up. As I was closing the blinds to the front window, I saw a glimpse of white in the darkness. I peered outside, at the cemetery across the street.

And saw the same cowled figure I'd seen outside Lafitte's.

He was standing a few feet back from the first row of headstones, pallid robes gleaming in the darkness. As before, he was facing in my direction.

I whipped the blinds shut and stood with my hand on the cord, mouth dry and heart thumping in my chest. I didn't know whether to call 911 or the mental asylum.

Clutching my cell phone, I got my nerve back and reopened the blinds, telling myself I was a grown man and this was my neighborhood.

The cemetery was empty.

I checked the doors and windows and fell into a troubled sleep on the couch, thoughts of boy mystics and dragging footsteps and figures in white robes crowding my dreams.

DUBROVNIK

-7-

On the way to the airport, I told Lou and Asha about the figure in the white robe.

Lou laughed. "New Orleans gave you a parting gift. That or you might want to lay off the sauce."

"I was sober by the time I got home."

"Whatever," he said. "My sixth-grade science teacher was a voodoo priest. Forget about it."

Asha said nothing, her eyes roving nervously to her handbag.

After a long flight, we arrived just after dawn at Zagreb, the capital of Croatia: a quaint, manageable city founded sometime during the last Ice Age. I took comfort in the fact that an ocean separated us from whoever had followed me home from Lafitte's.

Although attractive and hospitable, Zagreb seemed subdued, as if the Balkan Wars had left a pall of sobriety hanging over the city. We caught an overnight bus to Dubrovnik, and I woke to the Adriatic sparkling on my right, stretched out like a vast blue canvas.

A series of icicle-blue lakes dotted the countryside, and the bus began a gradual climb until we were traveling atop a seaside ridge. Little green islands poked out of the Adriatic like floating forests, sprinkled with stone cottages and lighthouses.

Around noon the bus started to descend. At the bottom of the cliff, a thick stone wall enclosed a medieval town poised right on the Adriatic. The morning sun glinted off the terra cotta rooftops, the city a peeled onion below.

"Dubrovnik's gorgeous," Asha breathed.

We grabbed our backpacks and walked through a handsome stone gate. A broad marble thoroughfare led into the city, lined with buildings crafted from the same smooth, dun-colored stone. Asha had booked a hotel on an island just offshore, so after dinner we caught a ferry to a cluster of pine trees that marked the edge of the island. A minibus carried us to a clearing dominated by a four-story hotel.

We dropped Lou off at his room and stepped into our suite overlooking the Adriatic. Asha purred when she saw it.

She dropped her backpack and flopped on the bed. "I'm spent."

"So what's the agenda?" I asked, propping open the balcony door to hear the lapping of the waves. "What time do we meet the expert tomorrow?"

"Not until six."

"Listen, Asha, how much do you know about Mr. Sofistere?"

"What do you mean?" she asked.

I took off my boots and sat beside her. "You've never wondered where he got his money?"

"I always assumed it was family money."

"Then why bother with the antique store?"

"I . . . guess I never thought about that."

She looked away when she said it, which made me think that she had, indeed, thought about it. "And the religious pieces?" I pressed. "Why the obsession?"

"Obsession's a strong word. Some people gravitate towards Chippendale furniture, some like French Restoration. Mr. Sofistere specializes in hard-to-find religious esoterica."

I backed off. It was obviously a touchy subject and we were both exhausted from the journey. She showered and joined me on the bed, resting her head on my chest. "I think I'll sleep right here."

I ran my fingers through her hair, and she coiled her arms around my waist. Moments later I heard the rise and fall of her breath. The last thing I saw before closing my eyes was the letterbox resting on the bedside table, the cryptic runes illuminated by the moonlight spilling in from the balcony.

We woke to an unseasonably warm morning. After spending the day lounging on the white-pebble beach, we cleaned up and headed to town to find Mr. Sofistere's expert. Dubrovnik's twisting side streets and tightly spaced shops gave the city a charming, maze-like feel.

The directions led to a narrow storefront situated at the end of a side street, right at the base of the wall. Two flags hung from the balcony, flapping in the late evening breeze. One bore the familiar colors of the United States, while the other consisted of a yellow and white field bearing a pair of crossed keys, set below a tiara. The sign above the entrance read JAKE'S.

"Maybe Dr. Fleniken lives on the second floor," Asha said.

"The papal flag?" Lou said, gazing at the crossed keys. "Someone outside of Rome actually flies that?"

We stepped inside. In sharp contrast to the sophisticated galleries of Dubrovnik, the left side of the store housed a jumbled collection of cheap Americana, everything from Elvis T-shirts to movie posters to model pickup trucks. The other side showcased an assortment of crosses, bibles, prints of famous religious art, and other spiritual memorabilia. A large portrait of the pope hung in the center of the wall.

Lou surveyed the empty store with a disdainful eye. "What kind of idiot owns this place? It's like a cross between the Mall of America and the gift shop at the Vatican."

"The same idiot who thinks you need a lesson in manners," said a voice with a pronounced Southern drawl.

Faded jeans and worn black boots materialized from a swinging door in the back, followed by a cowboy hat, a white T-shirt, and the tip of a cigarette dangling insouciantly from pursed lips. The owner of the ensemble was a tall and lean man around forty, stubbled, handsome in a rugged way. Auburn hair spilled to his shoulders.

Lou's mouth hung open, and I worked hard to suppress a laugh. The owner had good ears.

"Excuse my friend," I said, stepping forward. "We're supposed to meet someone here this evening and we're a little early. We'll wait outside."

"At least someone's got some manners." He held out his hand, which I shook. "Dr. Joseph J. Fleniken. Call me Jake."

Lou looked like he had just witnessed a mute person speak. I, too, had been under the impression that our renowned scholar of religious artifacts would not look like an adult Huckleberry Finn and work at a dollar store.

A small, forced smile curled the corners of Asha's mouth. "I'm Ashritha Rana. This is Lou, our translator, and Aidan's our attorney."

"What do we need an attorney for?"

"Hopefully nothing," I said.

He chuckled. "I guess we've got some business to dispose of. C'mon back."

He flipped the sign to CLOSED and led us to a far more orderly back room. A wooden desk dominated the center, and books and other objects lined the walls: a collection of weathered tomes, artifacts, and religious icons with none of the cheap and generic feel of the trinkets out front.

Framed diplomas hung on the wall, and I glanced at a few of the books: *Archaeology and the Religions of Ancient Israel; Christian Iconology; History of the Vatican Councils; The Sacred and the Profane: The Import of Monuments in Ancient Religion.*

Dr. Fleniken was a bit more sophisticated than he was letting on.

"You had dinner?" he asked. "I have some beer and crackers."

Or maybe he wasn't.

"I could use a beer," Lou muttered, staring at the Harvard diploma. "I suppose I'll have to settle for a Budweiser."

"I don't drink cheerleader beer. I have some cold *Pivo* in the back."

"Croatian beer?" Lou said. "What happened to your patriotism?"

"What happened to yours? Who doesn't like Elvis and movies?"

Jake pulled up three chairs across from the desk, then returned with a cooler of beers and plopped in his seat. "So let's take a look at this pile of wood. I'm curious about anythin's got that old goat intrigued."

Asha took out the letterbox and handed it to Jake. The box had taken on an unsettling anthropomorphic presence. I couldn't shake the feeling that the little wooden feet were legs, and that something was watching us from beneath the lid.

Jake turned it over, pausing as he looked at the bottom and then again at the runes on the sides. "What do we know so far? Lucius told me where it was found and the age."

"Why not send a fax?" I asked.

"Does this look like Office Depot to you? A fax won't show the texture of the wood, or a purposeful imperfection, or weight or dimensions or all those tiny little details that can flesh out the history of a piece. So, like I said, what else?"

"That's about it," Asha said. "Except for what Lou figured out, which might impress you."

"I'm not impressed by shit."

Asha paused half a beat with her mouth open, then said, "Do you see the symbols on the side of the box? No, not the larger one, the ones below it. Those are Ogham runes."

Jake's lips pursed. "That right? You sure, Commie?"

Lou looked even more surprised than Jake. "You know what Ogham is?"

"The alphabet of the insular Celts. Before St. Patrick converted the heathens during the reign of Pope Sixtus III."

Lou stared at him. "I'm impressed you're familiar with Ogham."

"I've studied plenty of Celtic pieces. I don't know anything about the language, just who used it. You translated it yet?"

Asha traced a finger along the runes. "The runes translate more or less to 'God Path.'"

Jake grunted. "Any idea what the larger marking is?"

"It's definitely not Ogham," Lou said.

We gazed at the letterbox as Jake rubbed at his stubble. "Well, the piece isn't Christian."

"How do you know?" Asha said.

"I know. Are you positive the Ogham translates to God in the singular and not the plural?

"Yeah," Lou said. "Why?"

"The Celts were still pagan at the time. Monotheism didn't even reach the British Isles until Pope Anicetus."

"Which was when?" Lou asked in exasperation.

"Second century A.C.E."

"After the box was made. How do you reconcile that?"

"I can't," Jake said. "Somethin' ain't right in the henhouse. Did any other monotheistic cultures use similar runes?"

"Ogham runes were distinct, isolated, and indigenous to the Celts," Lou said. "I'm *positive* those are Ogham."

Jake turned the box over and frowned at it. "Odd, isn't it? I've never seen anything quite like it."

A thrill passed through me when he said that, though I was sure the box would turn out to be something mundane, a new classification from the so-and-so dynasty, or the blank-and-blank age.

Still, who was that man in the white robe? And why had the boy in Jackson Square run away?

Asha's expression turned inquisitive. "What about the flowery decorations on the top?"

"Looks superfluous to me." Jake turned the box over again, holding it at arm's length. "Got to admit I'm puzzled. I agree with Lucius—I've a gut feeling this is a religious artifact, or a container that once housed one. Of course, the runes mention God, but even before that, I had a feeling about this box. And my instincts are good. I've seen more religious objects than the Commie's seen Twinkies."

Lou started to retort, but Jake pressed on. "Nope, the runes don't make sense. This thing's just plain queer. It's as queer as that hobby letterhumpin' Lucius told me about." He set the box on the desk. "There's also one large problem with this piece."

Asha leaned in, and I found myself joining her.

"The Celts had firm class separations," Jake continued. "They basically operated on a caste system. No one who wasn't a Celtic priest would have ever made, used, or inscribed upon a religious object. And according to the Ogham runes and my gut, this is a religious object of some kind."

"So what's the problem?" Lou said. "A Celtic priest obviously made it."

"The problem is, the Celtic priests had a strict prohibition on committing their knowledge to written form. Not a one of them would have dared inscribe what you're telling me these runes say." He folded his arms and looked at us. "Friends, there *are* no Celtic religious inscriptions from that time period."

-8-

After Jake's proclamation, we regarded the letterbox in silence. A nearby church bell announced the strike of the hour.

"I need a cigarette," Jake announced.

"Music to my ears," Lou said. "Let's go outside."

Jake opened his pack of Camels. "Why do you think this place is called Jake's? Light that coffin nail."

Lou lit up and blew a few elongated smoke rings. "I'm beginning to think this relationship might not end in a felony."

"What's the next step?" Asha said.

"There's not much any of you can do at this point," Jake said. "Leave the box and I'll study it overnight. Let's meet tomorrow for dinner."

"Is that enough time?" she asked, surprised.

"Enough time to form an opinion. I'll cross-reference the location where it was found, the style of the box, the Ogham, the marking, and a few other things. If nothing turns up, I'll have to get crafty."

We grabbed dinner in Dubrovnik and returned to the island. Lou retired to watch television, and Asha and I found ourselves on the balcony. Clouds floated by in the moonlit sky, and Asha pointed out creative interpretations of their shapes.

Eventually we slipped into more comfortable clothes. She sat on the bed behind me and laid her head on my back, arms encircling my waist. Her jasmine perfume mingled with the brine on the breeze, forming a heady union.

"Will you make me a promise?" she said softly. "It's something I've been thinking about for a while, but I've never found the right person to ask."

She moved in front of me and brushed away a stray bang. There was a sad, intense light in her eyes.

"What is it?"

She interlocked our hands. "Promise me you'll do it before I ask."

One of the many reasons I found this a bad idea was my college roommate's girlfriend, who asked me to keep a secret and then coyly told me she was sleeping around on my roommate.

I broke that promise once, and didn't want to do it again. "I never do that. Personal rule."

"Please," she whispered. "For me."

I was again very aware, despite our flirty declarations of what kindred spirits we were, of how little I knew about this woman. But as she looked at me with those huge and earnest eyes, I wanted to believe she wouldn't ask me anything that I could not, or would not, want to promise.

I wanted to break my self-made rules with her.

So I did. "I promise."

"Thanks," she murmured.

Her eyes, no longer far away, burned into mine. "If you die before I do, I want you to haunt me."

I would have laughed if she hadn't looked so serious. "Haunt you? That's the promise? Why?"

"I want to know if something's out there," she said, almost nervously, "and I'd want you to be the one to show me. I'd know we made this pact and that you're trying to comfort me."

Her request had a mortal gravitas to it, like we were a ninety-year-old married couple or trapped in an underground mine. It made me feel closer to her, but also uncomfortable.

"Is there something you want to tell me?" I asked.

"Only that I'll do the same for you."

"Um, thanks."

She took my hand. "So you'll do it?"

"Sure. I promise, Asha. If it's within my power, I'll do it."

"Thank you," she said.

We held each other without moving or speaking for what seemed like a lifetime, tingling with an undercurrent of energy. Finally we sank to a sleeping position, and I could feel her breath on my cheek, our shared space an intoxication.

I never knew why we didn't make love for the first time that night. Perhaps because in that moment, the space between two souls was as close as it was possible to get, and neither of us wanted to break the spell.

Or perhaps it was something else.

The next day Lou took a paperback to the beach, while Asha and I decided to explore the island before our meeting with Jake. A path began where the hotel's private beach ended, and we followed it into the forest. The soft pine needles created natural conduits through the woods.

The climate kept the forest dry and free of noisome daytime insects, lending the woods a preternatural calm. We walked for a spell and decided to take a break when the forest opened into a clearing punctuated by a huge tree stump.

"That's odd," Asha said. "That looks like an oak stump. And these are oaks ringing the clearing. I haven't seen anything besides pine in this forest."

I shrugged and sat beside her.

"How funny was it when Lou realized Jake was Dr. Fleniken!" she said. "I was biting my lip to keep from laughing. The look on Lou's face—"

She had a soft but unrestrained laugh that often, as it just had, turned to tears. Eventually she laid her head in my lap, and I stroked her hair. Her eyes closed and I leaned back on my elbows.

I reveled in the stillness of nature, amazed at how quickly my past life had become a diminishing shadow. Instead of rushing to make a midnight deadline for a partner, there I lay, relaxing with Asha in the middle of an island forest.

For the first time in a very long time, I felt fully in the present.

I tilted my head back to yawn, and thought I saw something moving through the trees. Probably a deer.

As I turned back to Asha, I saw it again, out of the corner of my eye. I whipped my head around and saw a man standing just outside the clearing, partially hidden by the trees.

A man dressed in a hooded white robe.

-9-

I stilled. He stood there and watched us, not moving or speaking. Was this some kind of sick joke, taken *way* too far?

It didn't feel like a joke. Although he hadn't made any threatening moves, I had the gut feeling his presence was not benign. Just as I was about to stand and confront him, I heard the rustle of a branch. I twisted around. Another man in a white robe stood behind me, opposite the other, watching me in the same impassive manner. I scanned the clearing and saw two more, all dressed in similar garb.

Four robed figures standing equidistant from one another, faces cowled in shadow, forming a square around us.

"Asha," I said softly, looking at each of them in turn and sending a telepathic message to leave us the hell alone.

The bizarre tableau continued for moments that felt like hours. They did nothing, standing still as sentinels, continuing to stare. The encounter felt like a macabre silent movie reeling away, with Asha and myself as the star victims.

I called Asha's name again. She began to stir.

Realizing they weren't going away, I felt around for sharp stones, knowing we had no chance against all four. I wondered if they knew we didn't have the letterbox, and decided to tell them straightaway. That was the only thing I could imagine this was about, though the thought of that sent a chill coursing down my back.

Before I could speak, one of them took a step forward. Out of the corner of my eye, I saw another move in unison, and a glance confirmed the other two had done the same.

Adrenaline poured through me.

"Asha!" I said, shaking her awake.

The cowled figures took another step forward, slow and methodical, as Asha blinked and sat up. Terrible scenarios flashed through my mind. I pulled Asha to her feet at the same time I heard people speaking behind us. I whipped around to see a group of tourists sauntering through the trees, carrying on in loud voices, unaware of the scene unfolding in the clearing.

When I opened my mouth to cry out, I realized I could no longer see the robed figure standing in the direction of the tourists. I quickly scanned the trees surrounding the clearing.

They were empty.

The new people turned out to be a Spanish tour group. We hung on their fringes until we could see the hotel, and I told Asha the full story. She looked as shaken as I felt, arms hugging her chest as she peered into the forest.

I'd seen these robed figures three times now. Who were they, and what did they want? How had they followed us to Croatia, and disappeared into the forest so easily?

What would have happened if those tourists had not shown up?

"We should tell Mr. Sofistere," I said.

She started towards the front entrance. "I don't think he needs to be bothered with something like that."

"Really?" I said, catching up with her. "I sure would, if I were him."

"It was probably just a prank. He would only worry."

"It's gone beyond a prank."

She stopped and turned, squeezing my hand. "We'll be more careful and let him know if it happens again. Promise. Let's get a swim in before we meet Jake."

My response was to stare at her back as she walked to the elevator. I thought she'd be traumatized, maybe question whether or not we should continue our stay in Croatia.

I informed the hotel about the encounter and asked them to call the police. I didn't know what else to do, except avoid solitary island forests.

And find out what secrets Asha was keeping.

We met Jake at the plaza in front of St. Blaise Cathedral, a beautiful domed edifice near the end of the avenue that led to the ferry dock. I was wearing gray cargo pants, hiking boots, and a black linen shirt. Jake showed up in the same clothes as the day before, looking as if he hadn't slept.

A full moon bathed the ivory-colored cathedral with a soft luminescence. Candlelit tables filled the plaza, spilling over from the restaurants surrounding the square. After spotting a free table, I ordered a bottle of wine and a plate of fresh sardines. I needed to put a little alcohol between myself and what had happened in that clearing. I was itching to discuss it with Lou and Jake, but wanted to see if Asha would bring it up.

Jake palmed his beer and nodded towards the church. "A fine monument from Pope Clement XI, wouldn't you agree?"

"What's with you and the popes?" Lou asked, his dated Princeton sweatshirt and khaki shorts in marked contrast to the well-heeled Europeans surrounding us.

The first time I had met Lou, at a law school function in the French Quarter, he was wearing a pair of old bowling shoes. His idea of dressy involved tucking one of his newer T-shirts into a pair of shorts.

"I'm Catholic," Jake replied.

Lou snorted. "I'm from New Orleans and know lots of Catholics. None of them date architecture according to which pope was in office."

"I give credit where credit's due."

I saw Lou scowl, and I cringed.

"Credit?" Lou said. "To the popes? For what, the retardation of civilization? The Catholic Church is a doctrinally flawed, pedantic den of pedophiles. The concept of God is for children and peasants."

"Is that the best you can do, Commie? Something started something, regardless of what you believe. If you think otherwise, I'd sure as Christmas like to hear you or anyone else explain it to me."

Lou's voice rose. "Just because I don't have the answers to the universe at my fingertips doesn't mean I have to invent a theology to get through life."

People at the surrounding tables were staring at us, and I put a palm out. "I appreciate both of your insights into the creation debate, but I don't appreciate ruining a beautiful evening. Grab a smoke, and let's discuss the letterbox."

They both lit up. The nicotine and the reproach seemed to calm them. Jake cleared a space on his side of the table, reached into his backpack, and took out the letterbox. Asha's gaze fell on the wooden relic. She was wearing a golden-brown cotton dress, and a choker with a silver ankh attached. Her hair was drawn back, accentuating her cheekbones, and I had noticed every man glancing her way as we arrived.

She fingered the ankh. "Did you find anything?"

Jake ran a hand through his hair. "I researched all night long, and nothing about it makes sense—not the date, the location, the Ogham."

Asha peered at him over her wine. "So what now?"

"There's a few tests I'd like to run, some colleagues I want to consult—"

I heard the sound of breaking glass, and a shout arose from a few tables over. I spun and saw two swarthy boys in rags running towards the church, one of them clutching a handbag. The youths created a wave of destruction as they careened through the tight space.

Jake cursed and sprang out of his chair, quick as a cat, then started wading through tables and patrons—but in the opposite direction from the thieves. I realized he was chasing after a full-grown man, as tall as Jake and with the same skin tone and threadbare clothing as the boys.

"The letterbox!" Asha said, pointing at the man. I noticed our empty tabletop as soon as she cried, "He has it!"

Pandemonium reigned. I squirmed through the crowd and sprinted down the main street, trying to follow Jake.

I was losing ground; he was *fast*. Steps behind the man he was chasing, Jake closed the gap with a burst of speed, taking the thief down with a lunging tackle. By the time I got there, Jake had one of the man's arms twisted behind his back, pushing his face into the pavement.

Asha arrived a few seconds later, Lou huffing along behind her. The letterbox had fallen a few feet from the thief. Asha shoved through the crowd to retrieve it.

Jake yelled at the man. "Why'd you take that? Who are you?"

The man responded in a language I didn't understand, and two policemen rushed over. Jake kept lobbing questions at the man, who kept babbling. Jake yanked him to his feet and threw him at the policemen in disgust. "Lock this gypsy up."

As the policemen carried him away, Jake muttered, "Why steal an old wooden box? That's not their style."

Asha gasped. I turned to find her staring at the letterbox with her hand over her mouth. One of the wooden legs had split down the middle.

"It's cracked," she said. "Mr. Sofistere's going to kill me."

Lou eased the letterbox away from her with a curious expression. When he turned the box over, a faint glow seeped through the ruined bottom.

"What the Devil's that?" Jake said.

Asha and I crowded in. "There's a layer of gemstones set into the wood beneath the base," she said, dismay morphing into curiosity. "It must have been a false bottom."

As Jake gently peeled off the thin layer of wood comprising the base, he uncovered a surface of hundreds, if not thousands, of miniature crystals imbedded into a second wooden underside. The stones looked alive, shining like tiny beacons of light.

"How about that," Jake said.

"Do you have any idea what it is?" Asha said, breathy with excitement.

"Not a clue." Jake pulled a small magnifier out of his pocket. "But let's take a look."

Lou chuckled. "You carry a magnifier? How old did you say you were?"

"Quiet, Commie. I look at a lot of ancient texts. Sometimes the print's small."

Jake moved the lens around the letterbox. He paused on one spot and gave a low whistle. "It's hard to tell, but it looks like there might be some kind of pattern here."

"Do you have any way to enlarge it?" Lou asked.

Jake looked up, eyes gleaming. "Let's go to the shop."

We paid our bill and rushed to Jake's place. After herding everyone into the back room, he set the letterbox on his desk. When we viewed the stones in the incandescent light, they stopped glowing.

"You do realize," Lou said, "that a light source drowns the illumination from crystals? Moonlight works okay, complete darkness is much better."

Jake muttered a reply and killed the lights. Lou was right; the illuminated crystals jumped out in the darkness, though the wood bottom still looked like a jumble of bright dots and dark spaces.

Jake nudged a large magnifying glass around the box as we looked on, illuminating a fourth of the bottom at a time. He paused in the bottom left corner, where a definite pattern emerged, taking up about a sixth of the new base. It resembled a triangle sitting on a cliff above a body of water, with three towers rising from the points of the triangle. The craftsmanship was remarkable; the stones had been arranged in tiny wave-like patterns to signify water below the cliff.

Asha's and Jake's eyes were wide, and I could only gape.

Lou put his palms on the table as he hovered over the letterbox. "I might actually know this place," he said slowly. "I think this is a representation of a castle outside Naples called Castello di Selva."

"I've never seen a castle like that," I said.

"It's more of a large fortified manor," Lou said, "built during Roman times."

"Wait," Jake said. He went to his bookshelf and selected a dusty oversize tome, checked the index, then opened the book for us to see. Lou swept a hand across the page. The three-sided fortification depicted on the page bore a remarkable resemblance to the pattern created by the letterbox stones.

"It does look like it," Asha murmured.

Jake stroked his chin. "Commie, what do you know about this site?"

"Not much, except it's *old*. I remembered it from a textbook in college."

"He doesn't forget very much," I said.

"What do the Celts have to do with the letterbox or this castle?" Asha asked. "Why do only a portion of the stones reveal a picture?"

"All good questions," Jake said, shaking his head, "and I don't have any answers. But at least we found something. I was beginning to think this box came from Kmart."

He started moving the magnifying glass around again. "I'm trying to see a pattern in the other parts, but it's just not there."

"Jake," I said, "move the magnifier back into the upper right portion, will you? No, not there—in the section with the castle. A little bit more . . . There, do you see it?"

The magnifier illuminated two curved lines, spaced barely apart and leading into the jumbled area above the representation of Castello di Selva.

"It looks like a trail or something," Asha said. "Leading to that other section."

"I think you're right," Jake said. "I guess that makes sense."

"Why does it make sen—" Asha began. "Oh, I almost forgot." She put a fist to her mouth. "Oh my."

Lou and I exchanged a glance, and I felt gooseflesh prickling the back of my neck as I remembered the words inscribed in Ogham.

Words that, as I stared at the letterbox, had assumed a new and eerily literal significance.

The God Path.

-10-

We made the unanimous decision to leave for Naples in the morning and investigate Castello di Selva. When we called to update Mr. Sofistere, he seemed extraordinarily pleased by the discovery and insisted on paying everyone's travel expenses. Though troubled by the strange encounter with the thieves outside St. Blaise Cathedral, he didn't have any insight as to their motivations.

While I honored Asha's request not to tell Lucius about the robed figures in the woods, I resolved to tell Jake and Lou about them the next chance I got.

Asha still hadn't said a word.

I was glad Jake had decided to hold onto the letterbox. It helped rationalize the decision to continue, because I had to assume—and the thought chilled me—that our mysterious robed figures would try to follow us to Naples.

Maybe it was foolish, but I was far from ready to go home.

Lou retired with a bottle of rum. Asha and I stood on our balcony, the night breeze ruffling our hair. Try as I might to relax, I couldn't stop thinking about the cowled figures and the cryptic words on the letterbox.

"I'm not in the least bit tired," I said. "Want to try out that casino?"

"Let's."

We changed clothes, then strolled through an upscale common area with sharply dressed guests lounging on divans and wicker lounge chairs. Outside the lobby, a flagstone walkway led through a series of pools to the hotel's private casino and disco.

We tried the blackjack table, where the drinks flowed and Asha had a few lucky turns with the cards. As she looked in delight at her growing pile of chips, I marveled at how every emotion and thought registered on her face, lighting it up with wonder, creasing it with worry, shadowing it with sadness, sparkling it with laughter. It was like reading a book and watching the movie at the same time.

Later we moved to the dance floor, sauntering straight to the center and dancing with the abandon of insobriety. Eventually we collapsed onto a sofa, commenting on the ridiculous things people do when surrounded by strangers.

I looked at her and grinned, feeling loose. "I think I'm danced out. Want to go night swimming?"

"You know what?" She stretched like a cat and ran a finger across my cheek. Her jasmine perfume was like a drug. "I think I do."

We followed the path to a secluded portion of the beach, the moonlit sea a postcard by our side. She began to undress, stopping at her underwear. I did the same, then grabbed her hand and splashed through the surf.

We floated further out, the inky depths a secret realm beneath us. The opaque surface seemed one-dimensional, as if it could slide off the darkened edge of the horizon. I moved my arms through the water to sparkle the plankton, specks of silvery starlight appearing and disappearing with the passage of my limbs.

"It's lovely," Asha murmured.

The water was cold, and Asha stepped out first, glistening in her lace underwear. I sat on the beach and wrapped my arms around her. I felt her shivering in the cool night air, and I rubbed her arms until the chill bumps receded.

She reached back and ran her fingers through my hair, then tilted her head back until our cheeks were touching. I caressed her stomach, her body writhing in tune to my touch, our lips moving ever closer.

We kissed hungrily, greedily. I ran my hands over her body, the small but firm thrust of her breasts, her narrow thighs, the soft flesh just below her stomach.

She stroked my face. "Let's go up," she said, her voice husky.

As soon as we entered the room, she pulled off her wet clothes, all of them this time. We climbed into the sheets.

Her skin was caramel porcelain, immaculately smooth. When I finally entered her, she whimpered softly and grabbed my hair, wrapping her limbs around me and rolling her eyes to the ceiling. She felt like no one ever had, impossibly good, the kind of sensory overload that only happens in a dream. We made love without reservation, intertwined as vines, robbing each other's essence like thieves.

I awoke dreamily the next morning, her scent enveloping the pillow. "Asha?"

"Out here," she responded from the balcony.

I took my time shuffling out of bed, enwrapped in the memory of the night before. I could still taste the warm insistence of her tongue, the creaminess of her skin.

She was sitting in one of the chairs facing the ocean. I came up behind her and massaged her shoulders. She felt stiff.

My hands stopped moving. "Is everything okay?"

She rose and leaned over the balcony. When she turned, I could tell by the guilt shadowing her eyes that things were far from okay. "Sure," she said, averting her eyes.

Awareness returned like the crack of a whip. "Do we need to talk?"

"No," she whispered, then leaned in for a quick kiss. "I'm going for a jog on the beach, okay? I need some exercise. I made coffee for you."

After she left, I stood on the balcony and watched the waves roll onto shore.

My coffee was cold by the time I went inside.

* * *

Our ferry was scheduled to disembark at five p.m. and arrive on the eastern coast of Italy the following morning. I spent most of the day restlessly pacing the beach.

I returned to the room and packed beside Asha in silence. Lou joined us downstairs, and we met Jake at the ferry port. After a few minutes, an announcement sounded from a loudspeaker.

"What'd they say?" Lou asked Jake. "My Croatian's not quite up to par."

"How should I know?"

"How long have you lived here?"

"Seven years," Jake said.

"And you don't speak the language?"

"I'm American, not Croatian."

"That's unbelievable."

Jake shrugged. "I get by on common sense. If you had any, you'd realize what the announcement said by the way everyone's rushin' to board the ferry."

The tri-level ferry wasn't crowded. We found a comfortable row of chairs across from the duty-free shop. Jake looked like he had been up all night again, and as soon as we put our gear down, he pulled his hat over his face. Asha announced she was going to look for some juice and walked off.

I watched her walk away, feeling queasy, then turned to Jake and Lou. "Let me pose a hypothetical to you: you're in the forest with your . . . companion . . . relaxing in a clearing. No one's around. Suddenly you see a person in front of you, twenty yards away. You look around and there are three more, forming a square around you. What would you do?"

Jake grinned. "I'd introduce them to Saint George."

Lou snorted. "A lot of good religion would do you there."

Jake pulled out a long knife from the inside of his boot. "You know, the saint who slew the dragon."

I looked at the weapon with raised eyebrows.

"You named your knife?" Lou said.

I folded my arms. "I'm being serious."

"So am I, Counselor," Jake said.

There was a pause when most people would have changed their expression or said something else. Jake did neither.

"Well, I didn't have a sword with me," I said. "And it was damned unnerving."

Lou sat up straighter. "This actually happened?"

"Yesterday, in the woods in the middle of the island. Asha and I stopped to rest, and these four figures surrounded us."

They both stared at me.

"They were wearing white robes with cowls, so I couldn't see their faces. Some tourists wandered in and the figures disappeared."

Jake placed his knife across his knee, keeping his hand on the hilt.

"I'd write it off as a prank," I said, "except I've seen one of them before. Outside Lafitte's, the night before we left New Orleans. Wearing the same outfit and staring at us through a window. He had a burn scar on the back of his hand. And when I got home that night, I saw one of them standing in the cemetery across the street. It freaked me out but I sort of pushed it away—you know New Orleans."

"Jesus," Lou said.

I thought back to the solitary forest encounter, shuddering as I remembered the way the figures had all advanced at the same time. "They look like they're in a cult or something."

"I don't know what to tell you, Counselor," Jake said, his face grim as he slid the knife back in his boot, "except to make sure we stick together. Maybe it has something to do with that gypsy who tried to steal the box, maybe not. Either way, there won't be any of those stunts if I'm around."

I tried my best to believe him.

Later that night, I wandered onto the deck, gazing at the ripples in the sea. I found a secluded spot to lie down, using my pack as a pillow. The soft breeze was a lover's caress, a canopy of stars twinkled in the velvet sky.

Earlier, the group had discussed the letterbox, but we knew we were only speculating. Everyone was anxious to see what wc would find at Castello di Selva.

I noticed movement to my left. On edge after the forest, I whipped around, but it was only Asha. She walked over and sat beside me, hugging her knees. I turned back to the sea, and after a time she stretched out next to me, laying her head on my chest. The familiar thrill went through me.

Darkness shrouded the deck as the remaining lights on the ship winked out. She nodded off to the gentle rocking of the ocean, but I remained awake much longer, my mind troubled by thoughts of the letterbox, the enigmatic figures shadowing us, and the even greater enigma lying beside me.

NAPLES

-11-

The ferry docked at Bari, a small town on Italy's Adriatic coastline, resigned to its role as a pit stop for travelers. We had time for an impossibly strong espresso before our train departed.

The four-hour train ride to Naples lulled me into a half-sleep. Through half-closed eyes I noticed Lou sleeping, and I could hear Asha and Jake conversing softly across the aisle.

"Mr. Sofistere said you moved to Croatia a number of years ago to classify objects at an ancient Roman temple near Split," Asha said. "I'm curious as to why you stayed. Is it the shop?"

"If I wanted to be in America," Jake said, "that's where I'd be."

"I didn't mean to pry." After a pause, Asha said, "It's just funny where life takes us. I like to think things happen for a reason, though I admit I'll never understand the purpose for some things." I felt her eyes glance my way, and I feigned sleep. "Aidan doesn't agree with me."

"What's our attorney say about it? Or will it cost me to find out?"

She laughed lightly. "He thinks there's a reason only in the sense of cause and effect, but not destiny or some cosmic force." The familiar sadness crept into her voice. "Somehow it's more disheartening to think there's no rhyme or reason to life, even for the tragedies. What do you think?"

He didn't answer for a long moment. When he did, his lighthearted tone had disappeared. "I don't think too much these days. My world's real simple. I have my wits, my work, and my faith, and I rely on them in that order."

I drifted back to sleep. I thought Jake one of those men without need to ponder their existence, passing through life in a satisfied linear motion.

I also thought him one of those men with whom all is never as simple as it appears.

After arriving in Naples, we took a taxi through the crowded city center. Layers of grime cloaked the historic edifices, and a web of serpentine streets curved around the town in no apparent order. The city felt like a movie set for Dante's *Inferno*.

We settled into a five-story hotel, tired and peeling, wedged into the middle of a crescent-moon side street. According to Lou, it was a short drive to Castello di Selva.

Despite the rough exterior, the inside of the hotel was pleasant and clean. Asha and I shared a room again, this time with two beds. After a shower, I found her writing in a small notebook.

"You keep a diary?" I asked.

"Not regular or anything."

She closed the notebook. I didn't inquire further.

"Rested?" she said. "You slept a lot on the train."

I gave her a pointed look. "I think I had some catching up to do from Dubrovnik."

She met my gaze, bit her lip, and looked out the window.

A knock interrupted us. I opened the door for Jake and Lou.

"We've got ancient maps to follow," Lou said.

Jake leaned on the door. "And I've gotta get out of this cracker box. I can't stand up in my shower."

I stood. "We're going now? To the castle?"

Jake was already walking away. "No better time than the present."

-12-

We grabbed a taxi and instructed the driver to take us to Castello di Selva. He shot us a funny look, muttered something in rapid-fire Italian, and sped into the polluted maze of the inner city. As he drove, the buildings seemed to lean over the streets, leaving the town in near-perpetual gloom.

We wound through the city and past the sprawl of the poverty-stricken outskirts, then climbed the hills to the north, until the Bay of Naples was a shimmer on the horizon. The taxi turned onto a pitted dirt road surrounded by a forest of oak, and I wondered if this was how all the tourists reached the castle. The place was remote.

Finally the taxi slowed, and the trees broke to reveal a clearing. On the far side, a worn path led to a small castle slumbering on the crown of a hill.

Or what was left of it. The castle was in ruins: holes in the outer wall gaped like empty eye sockets, pieces of cracked stone lay strewn about the grounds, crows covered the jagged tops of the towers.

Lou conversed in Italian with the driver. The driver smirked, and Lou grimaced as he translated. "He said the castle's been in ruins for the last hundred years. He thought we knew."

Wondering if it was a good idea to wander the ruins alone, I glanced at Asha, but she and Jake left the car and started walking down the path.

Lou and I exchanged a look. Lou shrugged, paid the driver and asked him to return when it got dark, and we caught up with Jake and Asha as the driver sped away.

Although the outer wall had largely been reduced to rubble, we could still make out the triangular shape of the fortification.After passing through an archway set into the more intact ruins of the inner wall, we found ourselves in a square courtyard covered in rocks and weeds, buttressed by a circular tower.

"What are we looking for?" I asked.

Jake put a hand on his hip as he surveyed the scene. "Anything that might be connected to the piece. A map, a drawing on a tapestry, an object of similar construction. Judging by the state of this rock pile, I don't have high hopes."

Lou chuckled as he ashed his cigarette. "You spend all night working out that plan?"

"Why spend time on research before we investigate the obvious?"

Three passages led into the castle proper. We started with the middle one, a long corridor which spilled into a series of tiny rooms, probably the servant's quarters. Jake and Lou checked the rooms on the left, while Asha and I kept to the right.

We wound our way down ancient walkways and in and out of rooms, sometimes having to clamber over stones blocking the passage. The place had been stripped long ago, and we didn't find anything that looked remotely connected to the letterbox.

One of the chambers had a hole in the ceiling. The failing evening light backlit the exposed sky like a giant movie screen.

"This place is eerie," Asha said. "And too quiet."

"I don't disagree," I said.

"If there was something here it was looted a long time ago, don't you think?"

"For sure," I said.

We met up with Jake and Lou in the central courtyard, their dulled faces reflecting our lack of success.

"I should have told the taxi to return sooner," Lou said.

Night was falling as if someone were closing a lid. Jake pulled a flask out of his back pocket and took a long pull. "Might as well make good use of the time."

As I sat cross-legged beside him, Asha pointed into the courtyard. "Is that a child over there? Near the center?"

Straining to peer into the darkened enclosure, I saw a shape that could have been a small boy sitting by himself, though I couldn't tell for sure. Asha was already moving closer. I followed her, Jake and Lou right behind me.

She was right. Sitting alone in the twilight of the courtyard, head bowed, was a dark-skinned, curly-headed boy. He was hugging his knees and rocking back and forth.

None of us seemed sure what to do.

"Hey," I called out. "Are you lost?"

No response.

"Son?" Jake said.

"He's Italian, morons," Lou whispered. "*Ciao, ragazzo,*" he said, louder.

Still no answer.

The boy continued rocking. When we moved closer, he stood with his head still bowed, his features too deep in shadow for us to get a good look. He turned and started walking away. From his size, I estimated he was nine or ten years old.

Asha called out to him. "What are you doing out here? Where're your parents?"

He kept walking.

"He's going towards the tower," Lou said. "That's strange—now there's a *light* on up there."

I turned and saw a soft glow emanating from a window close to the top of the fortification. "I think it's just moonlight filtering through," I said. "There must be another opening."

Asha looked around. "Where'd the boy go?"

Lou craned his neck. "Over there, I think. At the base of the tower. It's so dark it's hard to tell."

We moved closer. As we approached the tower, we saw no sign of the boy.

"Must have run off," Jake said. "The local kids probably come up here and pester tourists all the time."

"I don't know," she said. "There was something odd about him. And his clothes . . . ."

"What?" I said.

"Never mind."

There was a wooden door set into the base of the tower. Lou tugged on the handle, and the door swung open to reveal an iron staircase spiraling upwards.

I put a foot on the bottom step to test it. "It feels okay."

"Step up or step aside," Jake said.

I began to climb, testing every step. At the top of the staircase, a ladder extended into a narrow opening. I climbed through and found myself in a small round chamber, barren except for two windows.

One of the windows faced the courtyard we had just left. On the other side, overlooking a different courtyard, was a latticed opening the size of a shoebox, a chessboard pattern of weathered stone and open air. Moonlight streamed through the odd window, illuminating the chamber.

Jake climbed up behind me, followed by Asha. Lou came last, wiping his brow as he sucked in huge draughts of air.

Asha approached the checkered window. "That's an odd design."

"It was probably made for archers," Lou said, still catching his breath.

Jake walked over. "Do y'all see how there's a rectangular depression where the window is set into the stone? Anyone else thinkin' what I'm thinking?"

Lou snapped his fingers. "It's the same size as the letterbox."

Jake was already in motion. He pulled out the letterbox from his backpack and placed it into the shallow cavity formed by the chessboard-patterned window.

It fit perfectly.

-13-

We all peered at the letterbox. Nothing seemed to happen.

"Try turning it around and fitting the bottom into the opening," I suggested.

"I see what you mean," Jake said. "The arrow slits might change the pattern."

I nodded. "But it's still facing outward. We won't be able to see it."

"Just hold the box up in front of the window," Asha said. "So we can tell if the light forms a new pattern."

"That won't work," Lou said.

Asha tried anyway. As she held the letterbox up a few inches from the window, Jake set down his backpack and pulled out a magnifier and an expensive-looking camera. He positioned himself underneath the letterbox, scanning up and down.

"Commie's right. The map doesn't look any different."

"Of course I'm right. If we want to see if there's a new pattern," Lou said, pointing imperiously at the window, "we're going to have to place the bottom flush against the window and look at the box from the other side."

"In the middle of the air?" Asha said. "Maybe this isn't the right place."

Jake was shaking his head. "This isn't random."

I glanced up and saw something I hadn't noticed earlier: a rusty iron ring set into the ceiling. I tugged on it a few times before a trap door swung down to reveal a narrow opening. I rubbed my fingers; no one had pulled on that ring in a very long while.

"Access to the top for defenders," Lou murmured.

I jumped to grab the lip of the opening, and Jake helped push me through to the roof. I assumed a ladder existed at one time.

Gazing over the lip of the tower, I saw the ruins spread out before me, silent and imposing beneath a sliver of moon. After helping pull Jake up, we leaned over the side of the tower where the chessboard window faced.

"It's reachable," Jake said. "Someone can hold the letterbox against the window and I'll lean over with the camera. You can hold my feet."

I didn't like the idea of holding a two hundred-pound man over the edge of a tower, but Jake cut off my protest. "We're doing it," he said.

In the room below, Asha held the letterbox against the depression, and Jake slipped between two of the crenellated blocks on the lip of the tower and leaned over the edge. I held onto his legs, bracing myself by pushing my knees against the wall. His body was halfway off the tower, camera in one hand and magnifier in the other.

The shutter started clicking. "There's something there?" I asked.

"Hold on, just a few more. I'm almost—"

One of the stones bracing my knees broke free without warning and fell to the ground, just missing Jake's head. I scrambled to find another stone to brace with, but Jake's weight caused us to lurch forward.

"Aidan!" Jake yelled.

His knees were already over the ledge, and I gripped his calves in desperation, hugging them to my chest. I managed to slow our descent by pressing my body against the side of the tower, but he was too heavy, and the reprieve wasn't going to last. If another stone broke free, we were both going over.

"Lou," I shouted. "Get up here!"

"I can't pull myself up! I'm trying!"

Jake slipped another few inches. I clutched his jeans, my muscles aching from the weight of the grip. "Hold onto the window," I shouted.

He grunted. "I've got it with one hand, but I can't lose the camera."

I heard something shatter below; it must have been the magnifier. "Drop the damn camera!"

He slipped further. My torso was straddling the edge. I clutched Jake's ankles, fingers quivering from the strain.

"Not," he grunted, "gonna happen."

I watched, helpless, as he twisted his body around to toss the camera onto the roof. It landed beside me with a thud. My arms had numbed from the weight, and I had the sickening realization that he was about to slip out of my grasp.

I put every ounce of strength I had into holding him, but I was losing my grip. Just before he slipped away, I heard a noise behind me, and glanced back to see Asha climbing through the trap door. She rushed over to grasp my legs.

The reprieve gave me leverage and a burst of energy. I took a few quick breaths and pulled Jake closer. As my grip started to slip again, the pull on my arms lessened.

"I've got the window," Jake called up, "but I'm hangin' like a bat!"

I'd never felt so relieved. Blood flowed back into my arms, and I reeled him in by clutching on to his limbs and clothing. Jake finally put his hands on the edge of the tower and pulled himself up.

We lay on our backs, breathing heavily. I was too angry to speak.

Jake picked up the camera, a thin smile creasing his lips. "Got it."

-14-

Asha hugged me. "Are you ok?"

"I'm fine," I said, eying Jake as I caught my breath. "I wasn't the one hanging upside down over the courtyard."

He winked at me and clicked the side of his mouth. "'Preciate you, Counselor."

"Yeah."

We climbed back down. Lou looked embarrassed that he hadn't been able to help. After returning to the courtyard, we hovered around Jake, eager to hear what he had seen.

"Most of it's still gibberish, and I couldn't make out the first pattern because of the new distortion. But," Jake paused to light a cigarette, the corners of his mouth curling upward, "a new pattern appeared. In the section of the box above the representation of the castle."

"The portion of the box where the path leads," I said, my excitement flushing away my anger. "My God, it really is a map."

Jake nodded. "Looks that way."

"Did you recognize the pattern?" Lou asked.

"I was paying more attention to snapping photos and not dying. We can develop and enlarge the photos. I've got a macro lens."

I gritted my teeth as the adrenaline seeped out of my veins. "What I'd like to know is why whoever made this map constructed it so you have to be on the outside of the tower to see the pattern."

"I'd like to know that myself," Jake said, his voice tight.

I turned to Lou. "How'd you know it wouldn't work from the inside?"

"Something to do with quantum physics. I just know that if you shine light through an irregularly patterned object, and the light is reflected on another object in the distance, the light doesn't retain the shape or pattern of the object it shines through."

"Makes sense," I said. "When you shine a flashlight around, the beam doesn't take on the pattern of the objects."

"Exactly," Lou said.

"How old is this thing?" I marveled, turning over the letterbox in my hands. "Asha, what do you think Mr. Sofistere will say—" I stopped speaking, realizing she wasn't with the group.

"Guys," Asha called from somewhere in the courtyard, her voice oddly subdued. "Come over here."

She sounded close, but I couldn't make her out in the dim light.

"Where are you?" I asked. "What's going on?"

"Just come to the middle of the courtyard."

I headed towards the center, Jake and Lou right behind me. Asha's figure adumbrated in the darkness, and as we drew closer, I saw the little boy from earlier, sitting in the same position. Head down, hands hugging his knees, rocking back and forth.

"I thought I caught a glimpse of something," Asha said as we caught up to her. "He was like this when I got here. Same as before."

I shifted uncomfortably. The boy was wearing brown corduroy pants and a white, collared polo shirt. Dark curls fell to his collar, and his spindly arms wrapped his knees.

Asha moved closer. "Hi there," she said gently.

Right before she reached him, he stopped rocking and turned to look at her. Asha gasped and stumbled backwards.

"Asha?" I said.

She didn't respond. I went to her. She was looking at the boy with an intense stew of joy and horror and disbelief. I touched her shoulder. "What's wrong? Do you know him?"

For a wild moment I thought this was the same boy who had appeared on the wall our last night in New Orleans. Then he stood, and I saw his face.

It was light brown and, as his frame suggested, very young. He had a slightly crooked nose, similar to Asha's, and he extended a shy hand towards her, his lips parted with longing.

"Asha?" I asked again.

The boy moved closer and offered his other hand, as if asking her to accept his presence, pleading with her to communicate. She took a hesitant step forward. Her mouth opened and she made a sound, but her voice cracked and I couldn't understand her.

Asha was oblivious to everything but the boy, as if in a trance. He took another step forward, his hands still extended.

The two of them drew closer together, shadows merging in the gloom. Arms outstretched, Asha reached for the boy's hands.

Her fingers passed right through him.

-15-

I blinked, unsure if I had seen what I thought I had.

The boy's face turned from inquisitive to confused to distressed. Eyes wide, he dropped his arms and scampered backwards.

Asha stumbled towards him. "*No,*" she moaned.

My mouth opened, but I couldn't find my voice. The boy was vanishing into the darkness. Asha ran after him. I followed her out of the courtyard, to the edge of the forest. She had stopped and was whipping her head back and forth.

There was no sign of the boy.

I touched her shoulder. She shrugged me off, ran a few steps inside the forest, and then stopped, uncertain where to go. "Dev!" she screamed. "Deva!"

Jake, Lou, and I peered into the trees, but it was obvious searching the woods in the darkness would be fruitless.

"Asha?" I said gently. "Who was that?"

She looked up at me as if just realizing I was standing there, and then slumped against me, shaking so hard I worried she was having a seizure. Her words came in soft gasps. "It, it can't be. He wasn't . . . ."

I held her tight and didn't press her. I knew only that something was terribly, terribly wrong.

She wouldn't move from the forest's edge until we heard the rumble of an approaching car. I half-carried Asha to the edge of the ruins, where the headlights of our taxi illuminated the clearing below.

She stared straight ahead with glazed eyes as the taxi drove off. Lou looked at me with raised eyebrows, and Jake was gripping the seat rest.

No one uttered a word on the ride home.

We arrived at the hotel and agreed to reconvene in the morning. I paced the room while Asha was in the bathroom. I could hear light sobbing.

When she emerged, eyes red, she slid in bed beside me. Her movements were jerky and disjointed, as if her emotions had disassociated from her body.

I stroked her hair. She stared at the wall with an expression so despondent it frightened me. I took her hands in mine and waited for her to speak.

"That boy," she said finally, swallowing a few times to compose herself, "was my brother."

My eyes flared. "Your *brother?* I didn't even know you had a sibling."

"I did. He died when he was ten."

My hands went limp, and she let them slide away. I was too stunned to speak.

"It was nine years ago. I was sixteen. A drunk driver hit us on my brother's side of the car."

Sympathy for Asha vied for my top emotion, along with the visceral punch of hearing that I had just seen a dead child roaming the castle ruins.

"I was in the backseat and saw it happen," she continued, in the same wooden voice. "I watched him die." She put her hand on the silver bangle she always wore on her right wrist. "He gave this to me on my last birthday before he died. My mother was shopping for jewelry, and he told her she needed to buy it for me. I never take it off."

She broke down and had to compose herself again. "I haven't cried for him in years. With something like that . . . we cry and cry and after a time there's nothing left, you know? The pain doesn't lessen but there just aren't any more tears. But tonight . . . ." She closed her eyes and kept them shut for long moments. "He was reaching out for us in that courtyard. For *me*."

"I don't mean to be insensitive . . . but are you absolutely sure it was your brother? It was so dark and—"

"Do you think I don't know my brother's face? Those were his *clothes*. He was wearing them the day he died. It was him, Aidan. Oh, God, it was him."

I pulled her to me. It was like holding a mannequin, stiff and unfeeling. "I'm so sorry."

"I tried to hold his hands and it was like they weren't even there. My hands went *right through his*."

I had no idea how to comfort her. Had it been me in her position, I didn't think words would have sufficed. But I had to try.

"Remember what you made me promise?" I said gently. "In Dubrovnik?"

"Of course."

"Doesn't it give you some comfort to know he's out there?"

Her face whipped towards mine. "Comfort? Did you see him, huddled all by himself in the courtyard? He couldn't even talk. Like he's a . . . a . . . *thing*."

I looked away.

She put her head in my lap, and I stroked her back, her hair, her cheek. Eventually she fell asleep curled into me.

I lay with my hands behind my head, staring at the ceiling. I had asked her about her family before. She had always deflected my questions. Perhaps the memory was too painful to discuss.

The thought passed through my mind that she could be lying, but the pain and shock on her face when she had seen that little boy up close, the sheer emotion: that had been real.

I had the nagging sense that there was more to the story, but it was a different worry that kept me awake deep into the night, plaguing my mind with a single question that denied me the solace of sleep.

What had we seen in that courtyard?

-16-

When I woke, Asha was curled against my side. I flipped through some channels in Italian until she yawned and sat up.

"*Ciao, principessa,*" I said.

She managed a wan smile and squeezed my hand. "Thanks for last night."

"For what?"

"For being there."

"Yeah. Of course. How are you?"

She pressed her lips together. "Trying to . . . I don't know. Listen, will you do me a favor? I know Jake and Lou will have questions—can you tell them?"

"Sure."

I took a shower and made my way to the lobby while she cleaned up. Jake and Lou were having coffee at a table. Jake noticed the somber expression on my face and set his coffee down. I relayed what Asha had told me, and their faces drained.

"She's sure?" Jake asked.

I nodded. Lou mumbled something unintelligible and returned to his coffee.

A few minutes later Asha came down. Lou patted her shoulder as she sat beside me.

"I need to develop the photos and look into some things," Jake said. "Maybe you and the Commie could meet me around five at the coffee shop across the street here. Then let's all meet up for dinner." He looked at Asha. "I figured you could use some time to yourself."

"I still want to be in on everything," she said, "but thanks."

"Haven't you heard of digital cameras?" Lou asked.

"When mine breaks," Jake said, "maybe I'll look them up."

Lou rolled his eyes.

After Asha returned upstairs, Jake said, "If y'all will excuse me, I've got some research to do. Five o'clock?"

"We'll be there," I said, turning to Lou. "You know where we're going, don't you?"

"I strongly hope we're going to make another visit to our *haunted* castle."

"Glad we're on the same page."

"What for?" Jake said. "We have the photos."

"What do you mean *what for*?" Lou asked. "To find out what really happened last night."

Jake shrugged. "Suit yourself."

Lou hailed a taxi and instructed the driver to take us back to Castello di Selva. We wound our way through the city and he dropped us off in the same spot as before.

"Since it's Sofistere's dime," Lou said, "I told the driver to wait for us this time.""Good thinking." I glanced around. "This place looks a little friendlier in the daytime."

"Harder to play mind games in full sunlight."

"It looked pretty convincing to me."

He snorted. "Sorry, and I feel terrible for Asha, but do you know how easy it is to pull off a parlor trick like that? The question to ask is why."

We walked to the section of the courtyard where we had first seen the boy. After scouring the grounds and the base of the tower, I squatted and put my elbows on my knees. "All I see is a bunch of wine bottles and cigarette butts."

"There're too many footprints to tell whose is whose," Lou muttered.

We combed the rest of the courtyard and explored the three entrances to the castle. After an hour of searching we returned to the center of the courtyard, frustrated.

"Let's check the other side of the wall," Lou proposed. "Opposite the tower. Maybe someone set something up over there."

We backtracked to the outer wall, following it to where another opening led into the courtyard behind the tower. We peered around. It was a smaller version of the inner courtyard, vacant and uninteresting. The tower we had climbed the night before loomed above us, punctuated by the chessboard window.

I started to head back, then noticed Lou bent over the ground.

"Check this out," he said.

The section of grass near Lou was darker than the surrounding area, and stretched away in a straight line in either direction. Odd. I leaned down further and realized the inch-wide strip of grass was deadened, as if something had come along and caused a portion of the undergrowth to decay.

We followed the line until it intersected with another strip of deadened grass. This line ran along the ground in a curvy pattern that stretched almost the length of the courtyard. We noticed more lines branching off of the wavy one.

"That's just weird," I said, and Lou nodded. Then he looked up and began walking, cocking his head for me to follow.

"What're you thinking?" I said.

"It's probably nothing."

I followed him back to the inner courtyard and then to the foot of the tower before realizing what he wanted to do. Retracing our steps from the night before, we climbed to where the chessboard window provided a clear view of the courtyard through which we had just walked. I caught my breath as a chill coursed through me.

When viewed from above, the thin strips of blackened grass took on a whole new aspect, forming a pattern that spanned the entire courtyard. I could see, quite distinctly, four straight lines of dead undergrowth, each parallel to the other, running from the top to the bottom of the quad. A single wavy line connected the tops of the four straight lines, forming a pattern that, as we stared down at it, was instantly recognizable.

It was the same marking that was on the letterbox.

-17-

"Do you see that?" I whispered.

"Of course," Lou hissed.

I looked out the other window and scanned the inner courtyard, but saw only a bed of weeds littered with rocks. In the distance, the Bay of Naples was visible off the tip of the peninsula. The chills began again, and I felt exposed.

"What the hell is going on?" Lou said.

"I don't know. Should we check around some more?"

"I think we should get out of here."

"I'm not opposed to that."

The taxi driver sped away at Lou's urging. I turned to stare at the castle as we drove off, holding my gaze long after the castle ruins had disappeared from sight.

Needing to walk off our tension, we had the taxi drop us in the city center. We grabbed two *panini* and started towards our hotel. Touches of color dotted the city, a park here or a scenic fountain there, but for the most part Naples maintained its gloomy demeanor. Fleets of mopeds and miniature cars sped by as we navigated the absurdly narrow streets.

Lou stepped onto the curb as a horde of teenagers on Vespas almost ran us down. "I never thought I'd say this about an Italian city, but I don't care much for Naples."

"Depressing, isn't it?" I said. "It's a shame—if it was restored it'd be beautiful."

"It's like no one cares. So much culture and history covered by the worst layers of civilization."

I shrugged. "Food's good, though."

"Food is good."

"Women aren't bad, either."

"*É vero.*"

I stopped in front of a grimy cathedral sandwiched between a bank and a pizzeria. "So who do you think did that to the grass?"

"I've got no idea. Again, I don't think for one second there isn't a reasonable explanation. But I have to admit I'm curious to know what it is."

"The curiosities are beginning to pile up," I said.

We found our way back to the hotel and ducked into the coffee shop across the street. Again, a pleasant interior belied the chaos of the city outside. The café was small and rustic, flush with the aromatic scent of pastries and fresh coffee. We spotted Jake at a table in the back.

"You're late," he said.

A slim waitress with calloused hands and a throaty voice took our order. When she left, I told Jake what we had seen.

"It was formed out of dead grass?" he said.

We nodded.

"That can't be good." He pursed his lips and tugged on the brim of his hat. "Third time this marking has shown up. Perrott's bottle, the letterbox, and now here. I wish we had an idea what it was. I haven't had any luck on that front."

"So what now?" I said.

"We follow the map. It's all we have to go on. You ready to see what the next section looks like?" He rummaged through a backpack on the floor beside him. "I had images enlarged and copied."

We crowded in. "So it really revealed another location?" Lou said. "Do you recognize it?"

"I don't know where it is, but I know *what* it is." He set a folder down on the table. "A cemetery."

-18-

Jake pulled out a pair of enlarged photographs, passing one to Lou and one to me. "Take a look."

The center of the photograph depicted a plain shape: two rectangles standing upright and topped by another rectangle lying across them. Surrounding the central shape was a collection of squares capped by semicircles, with longer rectangles extending from the base of the squares.

Classic representations of graves and headstones.

"The problem is figuring out which one of the world's hundred million boneyards this one is." Jake grunted. "We should've asked the specter."

"I don't believe in ghosts," I said slowly, "but last night was . . . I'd be more likely to brush it aside if Asha wasn't so disturbed. She's convinced she saw her brother."

"I can't believe you're entertaining this conversation," Lou said.

Jake took a sip of coffee. "I suppose you think we ran into a little Italian boy who happens to look exactly like Asha's dead brother, wearing the same clothes he had on when he died, and who has this little problem with being incorporeal?"

"Or," Lou said, "Asha could be lying."

I remembered the shock in her eyes when she saw the boy's face. "I don't think she's lying," I said quietly.

Lou shrugged. "It was dark, anything could've happened." He flicked a wrist at Jake. "How come you're so pro-ghost, anyway? How does that fit with your papal worldview?"

Jake set his coffee down. I thought he was going to blow up, but his voice possessed an uncharacteristic evenness. "You think my beliefs are backwards, but what's more ignorant—subscribing to a two thousand-year-old belief system I've studied and experienced, or forming your own uneducated opinion on the matter? *Enlightened* doesn't mean devoid of faith or beliefs. It means having an open mind and dealing with the facts you've been given, even if what you discover differs from what you personally believe."

"Jake," Lou said carefully, as if talking to a three-year-old, "I went to church three times a week for sixteen years. And right now I'm doing exactly what I've been doing all my life, including when I used to get spanked for making my Sunday School teachers cry: I'm dealing with the facts. And the fact is, we're talking about ghosts. There's no evidence they exist."

"How about what you saw with your own two eyes last night? And where's the evidence they don't?"

Lou pounded on the table. "That's circular and you know it. Why believe in something you can't prove by science, by rational experience? If God exists, why not create some evidence we can see, or create us so we can all believe? He's God, isn't He?"

I kept waiting for Jake to reach across the table and throttle Lou, but the angrier Lou became, the calmer Jake seemed to grow. "The evidence is all around us," Jake said. "And God's logic isn't your logic."

"Apparently not. And for the record, I hate that argument." Lou waved a hand in disgust. "God is a crutch. A way to explain away pain and sadness and human frailty, when it's just the cruel natural order."

Jake lit a cigarette, his face as calm as fallen snow, and offered one to Lou. "I hear you, Commie. There's an almost unbearable amount of pain in the world, and I sure don't have all the answers."

Jake took a deep drag and turned to stare out the window, his face unreadable. I was jealous of both their worldviews; at least they had convictions one way or the other. Too often in life I was unable to take a stance, cursed with a mind that saw all the facets in every gem, never able to join a group or a cause or even a political party because I couldn't relate to the categorical thinking it required. My father called it wisdom, but the world called it social ostracism.

I broke the standoff. "Jake, any new thoughts on the letterbox?"

His eyes remained far away for a moment. "I still don't have a clue what it is. But I discovered a few interesting pieces of information."

"Such as?"

He looked down at the letterbox. "What do you know about the Druids?"

"I've heard of them, of course," I said. "Weren't they some sort of ancient priests from the British Isles? Lived in forests?"

"Rites of summer solstice, oak groves, mistletoe, all that jazz," Lou added.

Jake nodded. "The Druids helped the Celts conquer vast territories, but they were also the intellectuals of their day: scholars, religious mystics, philosophers, astronomers, and physicians. Like all organizations, there was a Druid food chain—and at the top of it were the high priests."

Jake signaled for another espresso. "These cats had a nasty reputation, and their area of specialization was the occult. The ancient world was terrified of them."

"So you think the Druids may have had something to do with the letterbox," Lou said, "because of the Ogham inscription, the dates, and the location."

"I thought of them the first time I saw the Ogham, but as I said, the Celtic priests—Druids—were very, very strict about not committing their knowledge to written form.'"

"Why the prohibition?" I asked.

"Mainly so their knowledge wouldn't fall into the wrong hands. They thought their occult secrets were too powerful for regular people to handle. Also, they thought memorization made for sharp Druids. It took more than twenty years to complete the Druidic studies. More to become a high priest."

I whistled. "They sound intense."

"You bet. And you want to know what their priests were infamous for in the ancient world?"

I wasn't sure that I did.

"Making shoeboxes with hidden maps?" Lou said.

"Human sacrifice. Among other things, they searched for auguries in the entrails of their victims."

I gave my coffee cup a nervous half-turn. "But you haven't connected them to the letterbox?"

"I can't find any mention of it. But remember, the only written records we have of the Druids are from outside sources."

"If the Druids are long gone and no written records survived," Lou said, "and we can't find any mention of the letterbox, then why are we concerned with them?"

"Two things," Jake said. "One, I learned long ago not to overlook coincidence. Too many things about the letterbox are connected to the Druids to dismiss them out of hand. Second, the Druid high priests had a distinguishing characteristic, verified by all of the cultures they came into contact with." He looked at Lou and me in turn, his face grim. "They always wore white robes."

-19-

Even after Lou and I saw the blackened symbol in the courtyard, the whole affair seemed unreal, an elaborate game that, like my growing feelings for Asha, made me feel alive and engaged. But now, as I thought about the times I had been alone or vulnerable with the figures in the white robes, I had the sensation of an insect crawling down my spine.

"The island forest outside Dubrovnik," I said. "That clearing was ringed by oak trees."

"Oak groves were Druid places of worship," Jake said.

I paled. "So we're being followed by a dangerous sect of Druids supposed to have been eradicated almost two thousand years ago?"

Jake pinched the butt of his cigarette. "We don't know for sure who they are."

"But we have a good idea," Lou said.

"So what do you propose? Tell the police that dead wizards in white robes are playing peek-a-boo in the woods and killing grass, and you're upset about it? Go ahead. I hear Italian sanitariums are real nice, up in the Alps."

"All we're saying," my voice rising, "is that maybe, just maybe, we need to watch our backs."

"I always do," Jake said softly.

I shook my head, disgusted. Jake ordered another espresso, his third since Lou and I had arrived, then downed it like a shot of whiskey. "Let's recap what we know about the letterbox," he said, stroking his whiskered chin as if the previous conversation had never happened. "The box was found in the Devonshire moors, which in Celtic times was one of the traditional strongholds of the Druids. It exhibits some type of obscure carving style unknown to the British Isles at the time. The Ogham inscription reads "Path of God," which is an oddity for two reasons: one because the Celts were polytheistic at the time, and two, that phrase clearly speaks to religion, the sole territory of the Druids—yet none of them were allowed to commit anything to written form."

Jake crossed his feet on the chair across from him. "So we've got ourselves quite a conundrum. Either Druids didn't inscribe the Ogham, or they made an exception for the letterbox. There's also a mysterious map expertly crafted out of tiny stones on the bottom of the box, unlike anything I've ever seen. So far the map has led us to a haunted castle in Italy, the next stop is a cemetery, and I haven't had a drink in far too long. That, at least, I can fix right now." Jake reached into his backpack, uncapped a flask, and took a long pull. "That about sum it up?"

"Don't forget the marking in the courtyard," I added.

He gave a dismissive wave. "I'll look into that when I get some time. What intrigues me most is the inscription."

Lou nodded. "The God Path. Maybe it's some type of code, or a clue to the map."

"Maybe it means what it says," Jake answered. "Follow the path and you'll find God."

Lou snorted. "Once again, back to reality."

"All right, people," I said, before they started arguing again. "We need to talk with Asha and Lucius."

"We'll call him tonight," Jake said. "And in the morning, we're finding that cemetery."

Asha met us for a late dinner at a restaurant adjacent to the coffee shop, the dark circles under her eyes betraying her state of mind. Jake showed her the pictures and we filled her in on what Lou and I had seen in the courtyard, as well as Jake's suspicions about a Druid connection. She swallowed and looked away.

After dinner we piled into the cramped but serviceable *stanza di affari* on the hotel's main floor. Asha dialed, pressed the speaker button, and Mr. Sofistere's voice crackled through the ether. I imagined him sitting in his parlor, the secrets of his mansion settled in the walls around him.

Jake leaned in. "Lucius? Can you hear us?"

"Perfectly. Have you discovered something new?"

Jake filled him in on the discovery of the second portion of the map, leaving out the boy at the castle.

Though composed as always, Mr. Sofistere's voice betrayed traces of eagerness. "Remarkable," he murmured. "I admit I had my doubts about the validity of the map."

"Looks like it's the real deal," Jake said.

"Have you reached any conclusions as to the origin of the piece?"

Jake paused. "I'm looking into the Celtic connection, including the Druids."

"I suppose that makes sense. I'll be conducting research from here as well. Please leave no avenue unexplored." No one spoke for a moment, and he said, "Is there anything else we need to discuss?"

I stared at my hands, wondering if Mr. Sofistere would have any insight into the strange occurrences, and why I was so hesitant to ask him. My eyes roved the table. Asha looked sad and lost in thought. I noticed Jake's eyes on her, detecting a glimmer of sympathy in his hardened gaze. Lou was half-listening and half-reading a copy of William Hjortsberg's *Falling Angel.*

"Nothing else," Jake said.

Like Asha, I knew he was keeping quiet so as not to risk being pulled from the search. Still, his words invoked a false sense of relief. Sitting in that bland conference room in a Western European hotel, surrounded by guidebooks and coffee stains, the eerie encounter at the castle and threats from white-robed figures seemed absurd.

"Whoever is willing," Mr. Sofistere said, "I'd like to continue. Lou, I'll extend the daily wage we discussed."

Jake and Asha quickly agreed. Lou and I glanced at each other for confirmation, then voiced our assent.

"I'm impressed with the progress. Everyone have a *buona sera* and remember to keep me updated." He relayed his parting words with quiet but distracted resolve, as if speaking to himself in his parlor. "I want to know what the letterbox is."

-20-

After our chat with Mr. Sofistere, Asha crawled into bed next to me. I watched her sleep and couldn't stop thinking about her brother.

We reconvened the next morning in the conference room. Jake drummed his fingers on the table. "I'll keep the letterbox with me and make some phone calls. I know some people who might be able to help narrow the search—an expert in ancient burial practices, and a Celtic historian at Oxford." He turned to Lou. "Since we have an Ogham inscription, one place to start lookin' will be the tombs of prominent Celts. Why don't you check out the Internet café down the street?"

"Sure," Lou said between mouthfuls.

"What about Asha and me?" I asked.

"I'm sending you two to the library for some research. Find the section on cemeteries—what's the word for that?"

"*Cimitero,*" Lou said.

"Come again?"

Lou rolled his eyes. "It's a cognate. Ce-me-te-ry. *Ci-mi-te-ro.*"

"You're both clever, I'm sure you'll manage. Look for something connected to the Celts or the Druids, maybe a picture similar to the one on the map. I know it's a long shot. Oh, and Commie—try to look more presentable. Italians are particular about their fashion."

Lou looked down at his green shorts and Princeton intramural soccer T-shirt, then back up at Jake's worn jeans and flannel shirt. "Me?" he said in disbelief. "You look like you just got pulled out of Hardees."

Asha stifled a laugh.

Jake stood. "This should be a good start. If nothing turns up, we'll reassess. Everybody straight?"

We all nodded.

The public library in Naples looked like a library should look. A marbled foyer branched into soothing side rooms filled with ornate bookshelves, and a broad staircase spiraled upward from the center of the room.

As we entered, an elderly librarian put down the book he was reading and peered at us between lowered reading glasses and jungle-thick eyebrows. "*Posso aiutarti*?"

"*Non parliamo Italiano, signore,*" I said, repeating Lou's coaching. *We don't speak Italian.*

"*Non c'e problema.*" He spoke in a friendly but vacuous manner. "I speaka little bit of *Inglese*. You are *Americani?*"

"Yes, *signore.*"

"We no have'a many books in *Inglese.*"

"Actually," I said, trying to speak slowly, "we would like to see pictures. Of cemeteries. *Cimitero.*"

"*Cimitero?*"

"*Si,*" I said.

He pointed at the door. "You go out, you do a left, and walka ten streets. Very nice *cimitero.*"

Asha stepped closer. "*Signore?*"

"Yes?"

"We want books. On cemeteries. *Cimiteri.*"

"Books? *Di cimiteri?*"

"Yes. With pictures."

"Aah. *Si*. Come."

He led us to the second floor, where narrow corridors wove in and out of the overburdened shelves, most of the dusty tomes looking as if they had been printed during the Roman Empire. It was the bibliophilic version of Naples' city streets.

We wound our way through the shelves until the librarian stopped in the middle of an aisle. He moved his hand in a semicircle, pointing out two long rows of shelves. There were far too many books for Asha and me to look through in a day.

"*Signore?*" Asha said. "Pictures?"

"Aah! *Solo* pictures."

He moved to the far left of the area he was showing us and pointed out three shelves with oversized books.

"*Mille gracie, signore.*" Asha said, smiling hugely at the librarian.

"No, itsa *mi* pleasure, *bella.*" He ambled off and we studied the three shelves. They looked manageable.

We pored through the tomes, searching the indexes for Italian keywords Lou had written down, perusing pictures of cemeteries, crypts, and tombs of all imaginable shapes and sizes. After an hour of searching, we found nothing other than vague references to Celtic burial mounds scattered across Europe. Next we sought out prominent Celts buried in Europe's cemeteries, combing the indexes for references to *Celtic* and *Druid.*

Hours later, we had nothing to show for our efforts. "This is disappointing," Asha said.

"I think Jake gave us the 'let's keep them occupied' task."

We finished with the last few books, finding nothing of interest. Asha sprawled on her back and released a deep, pensive sigh.

"Your brother?" I asked.

She squeezed her eyes shut. "I've got this nauseous feeling that won't go away. I may seem calmer on the outside, but I'm trying not to go insane."

"I understand. I don't know how I'd react." I took her hand. "I think you could use a dinner at a cozy trattoria tonight. Take your mind off it."

"That'd be nice." She squeezed my hand and then sat. "Let's put these books back and grab something at the café outside."

As we began to re-shelve the books, I heard a shuffling sound. I had a moment of panic, remembering the footsteps dragging through the French Quarter, then turned to find the librarian ambling up the aisle.

"Dida you find something?"

"No, *signore*," Asha said.

"What you looka for?"

"This." Asha pulled out an enlarged photo of the map. He adjusted his glasses and puzzled over the picture. "I no knowa this *cimitero.*"

Asha smiled at him. "We don't either. We're a little lost."

He pointed at the shape in the center of the photo, the two upright rectangles topped by another rectangle. "But I know what this looka like."

The shape was so simple I hadn't paid much attention to it. He pointed a bent finger at the photograph. "It looka like—I no know this word in *Inglese.*" He was quiet for a minute, trying to come up with the word. "Forgive me," he said. "I bring *dizionario.*"

He puttered off again, returning with a large English-Italian dictionary. He thumbed through it, then moved a shaky finger down the page. "*Dolmen.*"

Asha and I looked at each other in confusion. *Dolmen?*

Had he mispronounced the word? I checked the dictionary, Asha peering over my shoulder, but the English translation was the same: 'dolmen.' The definition was in Italian, so we were still lost.

We tried to get the librarian to explain what a dolmen was, but the language barrier was too great. We thanked him and he wandered off. Not wanting to pay fifty dollars to search on our smartphones, we stepped outside to find an Internet café and saw Lou's rotund body sauntering towards the entrance, whistling as he went.

I flagged him down. He said neither he nor Jake had found anything useful, nor had Jake's experts been useful. Jake sent him to see if we needed help with translation.

"We do," I said with an embarrassed frown, "with a word in English."

I filled him in, gave him the piece of paper, and he translated aloud. "Dolmen—a prehistoric stone structure typically having two upright stones and a capstone." He looked up. "Oh. Like a megalith, or menhir." A look of comprehension spread across his face. "Of course," he murmured. "It's so simple I can't believe I missed it."

"I'm still missing it," I said. Asha's face was also scrunched in confusion.

"Dolmen, menhir, megalith: they're all names for ancient stones, typically gathered together and arranged in a circle or another configuration. There're a number of them in England and other parts of Europe."

I snapped my fingers. "Like Stonehenge."

"Exactly."

"So?" I said.

"Don't you see? Stonehenge is the most famous, but the British Isles are littered with these megaliths. No one is sure who built them, but we know who later made use of them, for religious and astrological purposes."

"Let me guess," Asha said. "Celts."

"More specific."

"Druids," I said grimly, garnering a nod.

-21-

We hurried back to the library, planning to cross-reference *cemetery* with the various words for ancient stone structures, though none of us had any idea why a cemetery might be connected to a dolmen.

We again enlisted the help of the old librarian. He was grateful when Lou spoke with him in Italian.

"He says it'll be hard to cross-reference something like that with the library's outdated catalogue system," Lou said. "There's an employee computer in the basement we can use."

We followed the librarian down a set of stone steps to a drab employee area containing restrooms, a coffee maker, and a dinosaur of a computer hooked up to a gray monitor. The librarian signed on, and Asha and I crowded around Lou.

"What is this," Lou muttered, "a Commodore 64?" After a few moments, he leaned back in his chair. "We got a hit."

Halfway down the first page, one of the summaries below the search terms contained the words *cemetery* and *dolmen* right next to each other. Lou clicked on it.

The link was a news article from a San Francisco paper entitled "Spiritism in North America." Lou began reading from the article. "The famous French medium Allen Kardec . . . known for popularizing mediumship, reincarnation, mesmerism, and other spiritualistic practices into a uniform quasi-religion dubbed 'spiritism' . . . obtained a large following in Latin America, particularly Brazil, and then spread into North America . . . died suddenly in

1869 and was buried in Pere Lachaise Cemetery . . . the tomb is recognizable by the large dolmen that marks the entrance."

I whistled. "It's promising."

"Except what could this Kardec person and his tomb have to do with any of this?" Asha said.

Lou turned back to the computer. "No idea." He typed in Kardec's name and hundreds of search results were revealed. "Too many," he muttered. He combined Kardec with Pere Lachaise, and a slew of pages similar to the San Francisco article popped up. Nothing new or useful.

"Try Druid," Asha suggested. "Kardec and Druid."

"Doubtful. But I'll try."

We looked on in surprise as the search revealed a website containing both search terms. The site was a two-page biography of Kardec, and the interesting paragraph was halfway through the article, where *Druid* appeared in bold.

Lou read aloud. "Kardec was interested in numerous spiritual practices outside the sphere of accepted Western religious beliefs, including a strong interest in reincarnation . . . dabbled in Celtic mysticism . . . Kardec believed that in one of his former lives he had lived as a Druid priest."

My eyes widened. "That's our connection."

Lou leaned back and folded his arms. "There's one large problem here. Kardec died in 1869. If the letterbox is over fifteen hundred years old, then his tomb in Pere Lachaise can't possibly be the right place."

"Keep reading," I murmured. My eyes had already scanned the article, and I read aloud this time. "'The dolmen that serves as the entrance to the tomb of Mr. Kardec was supplied by an unnamed and wealthy follower of the late spiritist. The follower purchased the dolmen, along with another, smaller dolmen, from the British government. The dolmens were originally appropriated from an ancient Celtic necropolis for the construction of a highway, and the smaller dolmen is the oldest known megalith found at a burial ground. Reputedly at the bequest of Kardec,'" I emphasized the words, "'*the dolmen was placed at the entrance to his tomb to symbolize his past life as a Druid and his affinity in life and in death with the ancient Celtic religion.*'"

I looked up, a slow grin spreading across my face. "I think we might have found our cemetery."

Asha squeezed my arm. "An ancient Celtic burial ground with a dolmen—that's got to be it! Wait—shouldn't we be going to the original cemetery instead? That's the one that would be depicted on the map."

"I don't think so," I said. "I think the dolmen that was moved to Pere Lachaise is the key. It's the centerpiece of the map section, remember. The original cemetery was destroyed by the British government and anything that was there is lost anyway."

"Good point."

"Can someone buy something like a dolmen?" I asked her. "Wouldn't it be put in a museum or protected?"

"Not necessarily," Asha said. "The government frequently sells off lesser pieces to the highest bidder if it needs the revenue and no public interest groups protest too much. I've no doubt a dolmen in the path of government expansion could've been bought by a private collector."

We lingered over the screen, half of the tingling running down my spine stemming from satisfaction at our discovery, half deriving from the chilling realization that we had stumbled onto yet another connection between the letterbox and the Druid high priests.

-22-

We returned to the hotel to find Jake sitting in the lobby, hunched over a book. Asha related everything we discovered in the library, and Jake leaned back in his chair. The corners of his lips were upturned, but his eyes were cold. "Get packed for Paris."

We called Mr. Sofistere later that evening to update him. He expressed his excitement with our find, reiterated that he would fund our search, and urged us on to France. Again, I found nothing to be overtly suspicious about, except for my gut instinct that something about Lucius Sofistere wasn't right.

After the call, Jake said, "The next available train for Paris leaves the day after tomorrow."

"Why don't we just fly?" Lou asked.

"I don't fly unless I have to. I don't trust boxes with wings."

"Of course you don't."

Although eager to see where the map would lead, no one minded taking a day to recuperate, and I carried through on my promise to take Asha to dinner. I hadn't forgotten about Dubrovnik, but was willing to take a cautious step forward.

After consulting the concierge, she took my hand and made me promise we wouldn't talk about the letterbox, her brother, or anything else connected to the events of the past few weeks. We walked a block away to a quiet little *trattoria*, the kind where the family lived upstairs and picked their vegetables and herbs from a garden in the back.

After two glasses of Brunello di Montalcino and an order of bruschetta fresher than the first day of spring, the waiter arrived with a huge plate of *linguine con le vongole*.

I kept glancing at Asha as we ate. Her hair was drawn up, and her strapless dress was the same plum color as the wine. I had on jeans and a thin black shirt, enjoying the lingering balmy weather.

"Naples is growing on me," I said. "The food makes up for everything."

"Food is important in a relationship, don't you think? You probably spend more time eating together than anything else."

"Mm. I suppose so."

She took a sip of wine. "I like that we always share entrees."

"Me, too. I eat faster than you, so I get more food out of the deal."

She gave a mock gasp. "You wouldn't."

I eyed the empty plates. "I just did."

She traced a finger along my arm. "I thought I could trust you."

"Trust is relative. You can trust me in other situations, just not around food."

"What do you mean, trust is relative? That's ridiculous."

"Are you trying to tell me you always tell the truth?" I said.

"I like to think so."

"You never tell little white lies?"

She considered her answer. "Not really."

"*Everyone* tells little white lies. Or at least omissions."

"Omissions are different. Of course I don't go around telling everyone exactly what I think without being asked."

There was an awkward silence, and I knew she was thinking the same thing I was: there were a few things she hadn't said in Dubrovnik, on The Morning After.

I also knew there were things she hadn't told me about her past. I said, playfully but with an edge to my tone, "So what does it take to get you to confess?"

She stood and leaned down next to me, her dulcet eyes boring into mine.

"Wouldn't you like to know," she whispered, tracing my lips with her finger before turning and swaying to the restroom.

"You're the Devil," I muttered after she left. My mouth had gone dry, my skin prickling from her touch. I took a gulp of wine and realized I was wrong.

The Devil had nothing on her.

When we returned to our room, we found a bottle of champagne on the bed, along with a note from Mr. Sofistere. "'Your hard work is much appreciated,'" Asha quoted.

I opened the bottle, a Krug Clos du Mesnil. Prentice was right: Mr. Sofistere did have good taste. We sat on the bed and drank straight from the bottle. She ran her fingers through my hair and said, "I had a great time tonight."

After we finished the bottle, she lay beside me and stroked my chest with her fingernails. I loved her scent, even combined with the lingering garlic from dinner.

She crawled on top of me, hair falling into my face, the contours of her body melding into mine. The tips of our tongues touched, and then her lips found mine, warm and insistent.

Our kiss turned into more, and we sank into the sheets.

Since we had a day to spare, Jake decided to shake up his research and visit the ruined city of Pompeii. The time period was right—less than a century after Christ—and given the proximity to Castello di Selva and the frozen-in-time state of the architecture, he thought there was a sliver of a chance of seeing a fresco or a temple wall that might relate to the letterbox or its strange markings. I also thought he couldn't bear the thought of sitting around the hotel.

We left after breakfast. The journey took less than an hour. Except for the roofs, which had collapsed or burned, Pompeii's near-instantaneous destruction by Mt. Vesuvius had left the city disturbingly intact. It looked more deserted than ruined, as if the inhabitants had gathered up their roofs and left the city to its fate.

Intricate, sometimes erotic frescoes dotted the remains of the wealthier residences. Bodies were entombed in gray pumice, locked for eternity in the fetal position, screaming in anguish as hands covered faces in a desperate attempt to escape the horror raining down on them. I thought of Pompeii as a testament to the frailty of human life, preserved for all to see.

Jake found nothing of interest. As the sun began its descent, we made our way to our last stop, the Roman amphitheater on the far northeastern side. It was almost closing time, and we were the only visitors left to admire the imposing stone wall encircling the arena. Jake and Lou started debating an obscure point of Roman architecture as Asha and I stepped through the gated entrance, navigating a short tunnel that emerged into a grassy arena.

"I can't believe how well preserved it is," Asha said.

My eyes swept the ruins. When I turned towards the raised stone rows behind us, my breath caught in my throat and I clutched Asha's arm. Sitting above the entrance tunnel, a group of men in hooded white robes peered down on us like judges, as silent and unmoving as if they had been there for centuries.

-23-

I heard a loud scraping sound. Asha gasped, and Jake started yelling our names. "*Run*," I said, grabbing Asha's hand and fleeing back the way we had come.

When we reached the entrance to the tunnel, a huge iron portcullis had been lowered to block the exit. Jake and Lou were on the other side, trying to force it open. I joined them, but it wouldn't budge. I slammed my fist against the wall.

Jake swore. "I'll go for help. Commie, stay with them."

As Jake sprinted off, I looked at Asha's purse. "Where's the letterbox?"

"Jake has it in his backpack," she said, her voice shaky.

I turned and started walking back into the amphitheater. "I'm seeing what they want."

"Aidan!" Lou called out. "What are you doing?!"

I knew it wasn't the smartest play, but I was sick of their games. And were they really going to cause trouble on government property, with guards on the way and nowhere to go? Still, I felt coiled fear wrapped around my insides.

Asha caught up with me and took my hand. We emerged into the amphitheater, staying right by the tunnel mouth so we could dash inside.

A dozen men were sitting in a line on one of the rows above us. A thirteenth man stood in the middle, holding a wooden staff. Seeing the implacable figures looming above us brought Jake's history lesson on the practices of the ancient Druids, and their connections to the letterbox, crashing into the present.

Asha gripped my hand. "Do you see him?"

My eyes roved across the line of white robes, unsure what she was talking about until I saw the lone figure standing in the center. As my gaze took him in, moving from his cowled face down the length of his robe, I noticed the same burn scar on the back of his left hand that I had seen outside Lafitte's in New Orleans.

I also noticed that he wasn't standing at all. He was hovering a foot above the stone row below him, the bottom of his robe drifting in midair.

My mouth fell open. I couldn't take my eyes off the empty space between the stone and the man's robe.

"We have tried to warn you," the levitating figure said.

"Tried to warn us?" I replied, forcing pent-up anger into my words. "Staring at us through windows and cornering us in the woods?"

"You have something that belongs to us. We wish it returned."

"We don't have anything of yours," I said, trying to buy time for Jake. Asha gripped my hand tighter.

"You carry the Vessel of the God Path."

I swallowed. Hearing those words spoken by a man floating impossibly in midair, face shadowed by a cowl, caused a wave of gooseflesh to rise on my arms.

"We don't have it with us," I said. "And it's not yours to claim."

"It is not for you to possess."

"You're Druids, aren't you?" Asha said.

No response.

"What is it?" she said, taking a step forward. I tried to hold her back but she shook me off. "What's the God Path?"

The levitating man raised his staff above his head. As one, the Druids began to chant. It was a harsh, guttural collection of sounds, its resonance low and weighty. I didn't recognize any of the words or even the language; I didn't think it to be a language at all. It sounded like an incantation, a dark and secret tongue, full of sounds I wanted to block from my mind.

As the chanting gained in volume, the lead priest began to rise. Asha stopped advancing, and I stood next to her, both of us encased in a dumb silence. The incantation and its apparent connection to the levitation, the sheer *unnaturalness* of the whole scene, made me want to cover my ears, grab Asha, and run as fast and as far as we could.

But there was nowhere to go. The walls of the amphitheater surrounded us, our only exit was sealed. I looked back to see if Jake had brought help, but Lou was still standing by himself, hands gripping the bars.

The chanting ceased. The lead priest stopped rising. He hovered menacingly above the others, though I still couldn't see his face.

"Leave the Vessel in your quarters when you depart in the morning," he intoned. "Leave it and do not look back."

I was too stunned to respond. He tipped his staff in our direction. "This is your final warning. Do not be foolish. Depart from the God Path."

Asha's nails dug into my hand, and it took every ounce of willpower I possessed to walk, and not run, back through the tunnel. Finally we saw Jake sprinting towards us with two guards. After they unlocked the portcullis, we followed behind as the guards rushed into the amphitheater, necks craning to scan the circular stone rows.

There was no one in sight.

I recounted the bizarre scene for Jake, Lou, and the guards on our way to the exit. The guards took down our information and promised to investigate, but I could tell by their expressions they weren't taking me seriously.

As soon as they left and we boarded the train to Naples, Jake yanked off his hat and threw it on the seat, his auburn hair framing his face. "I don't know who these people are, but if they think they're gonna scare us into handing over the letterbox, they can think again."

Lou and I exchanged a troubled glance.

"Do you think they're really Druids?" Asha said.

"Who knows what they think they are," he said. "There're people these days who dress up like vampires and drink pig's blood."

"That man back there—he was *levitating*," Asha said. She covered her mouth with the back of her hand. "My God. The window in the tower—that must have been how they reached it."

"The box stays with me from now on," Jake said grimly, patting his backpack. "At all times."

I let out a deep breath, expelling tension. "We can have the hotel notify the police, but even if they believe us, we still have no idea who these people are."

Lou's voice was nervous. "So what now? The letterbox is interesting and all, and I'm sure that was a hoax, but I don't like being followed."

Jake was staring out the window, in the direction of Pompeii. "Neither do I. No more side trips, and we stay together."

As we returned in silence to Naples, I studied the faces of the others and saw the same mixture of apprehension and feverish curiosity that I knew defined my own. Despite the growing threat, the allure of the unknown had spun a tantalizing web around us all, and I felt trapped by the unseen strands, transfixed by my growing desire for answers.

Jake folded his arms and tipped his seat back, still facing away from us. "Get a good night's sleep. Our train leaves early."

-24-

When we returned to the hotel, Asha and I headed upstairs to pack. She closed her suitcase and sat beside me, a faraway expression on her face. "You know what I have to do."

I knew.

With rare exception, thoughts of her brother, though unvoiced, had shadowed her every glance since that night at the ruins, clouded her every smile.

"I'm not ready," she said. "But I have to go. We're leaving tomorrow."

"You know we won't let you go alone."

She squeezed my hand. "Thanks."

"I'll grab Jake and Lou."

Her hand slid away. "What if the Druids are there?"

"They said we have until the morning, and we'll be long gone by then." I pulled her close. "You don't have to do this."

"I have to try," she whispered.

Jake and Lou agreed to accompany us to the castle ruins. We all understood. If it were my brother, I would have risked the danger and done the same.

We left the hotel and walked down the street to hail a taxi. "Castello di Selva," I said. The driver looked at me funny, and Lou had to pay him double to get him to wait for us below the ruins.

We arrived without incident and walked to the courtyard, enveloped in darkness, the skeletal remains of the castle brooding on every side. After a careful look around, we saw no sign of anything amiss.

Asha cast a nervous glance into the courtyard. "I won't be long."

"You're going in alone?" I said, incredulous.

"Just a few feet. He might want to see me by myself, and I have to give him the chance."

I shook my head, and Jake nodded at me behind her back. "Promise me you won't leave the courtyard," I said.

"Don't worry."

I squeezed her hand, and she stepped into darkness.

After she left, the rest of us spaced out along the edge of the courtyard, on high alert for signs of the Druids. Nothing stirred but the breeze, and I sank into my thoughts.

I hadn't mentioned anything to anyone, mainly due to Asha's sensitivity to the subject and Lou's complete denial, but seeing the mysterious boy had made an indelible impression on me.

It had been a long time since I had reflected on my spirituality with more than a passing thought. But when one has a possible supernatural experience, one pauses.

Really pauses.

There were frequent news reports of people claiming to see ghosts and having various paranormal experiences. I had always scoffed them away, but now it had hit home.

Had I been confronted with direct and unambiguous evidence of life beyond the grave? If so, where did that leave me?

The encounter felt like a defining moment, an awareness of something beyond the mortal coil, and I didn't want the memory to slip away.

Yet I was afraid it would. I felt the nagging voice of reason increasing in tempo with every passing hour, the voice that says *you didn't see anything* or *there's no such thing as ghosts.*

Jake was right. We explain everything away. Far too often we have a moment of spiritual enlightenment, burning brightly with intention, until days or even hours later when we watch, helpless, as our newfound resolve fades to regret, and we return to our provincial worldview and our tunnel vision of reality. No wonder God, if He exists, has a hard time getting us to believe in Him. That which we cannot measure, store, or tag: we forget.

I had seen Asha's hands pass through the little boy with my own two eyes. I wanted—I needed—to delve into the marrow of that memory until it became a permanent fixture in my mind, a captured moment to explore.

Asha's scream pierced the darkness, shattering my ruminations.

The three of us sprinted into the courtyard. Halfway to the wall, Asha flew into my arms.

"What happened?" Jake asked. "Druids?"

She had to catch her breath before she could speak. "Just a cat. It jumped off the wall right next to me and I panicked."

"You're fine?"

She nodded, still breathing hard.

"Did you see anything?" I asked.

She averted her eyes. "No."

I swallowed my own disappointment.

"I had to try," she said, repeating her words from earlier. I noticed that neither sadness nor disappointment, while both were present, was the overriding emotion I heard in her voice.

It was guilt.

"I had to try," she said again.

Back in our room, she sat next to me on the bed, her voice soft as she touched her fingertips to her forehead. "I miss him so much, Aidan. He was my baby brother."

"I know." I held her tight, pushing away my unanswered questions. Now was not the time.

"What if he's lost out there? What do I do?"

Again I had no answers. She looked up at me, her chin petite and firm, and kissed me with an intensity I hadn't felt from her before. Her tongue probed my mouth, sensuous and greedy. I sank into the bed with her, both of us grasping at each other's clothes.

We seemed possessed by a supernatural passion deriving from our visit to the ruined courtyard, as if the hungry spirits of a bygone era had returned with us to the hotel. We clung to each other, our lovemaking intensified by fear of the unknown and by what we had witnessed at Pompeii, unable to get enough of each other's warm, tangible humanity.

We lay on our backs when we were finished, breathless, staring out the window at the mystery of the night sky.

PARIS

-25-

After a long and uneventful train ride, we arrived in Paris at dusk and took a taxi to a hotel Mr. Sofistere had arranged near the Bastille area. Since Pere Lachaise Cemetery was a stone's throw away, it seemed like a good idea to get a glimpse of our destination.

After a short walk, we found ourselves atop a low hill in the twentieth *arrondissement*, next to a sinuous cast-iron signpost heralding the entrance to the Pere Lachaise metro stop. Not far away, the cemetery's gray walls disappeared into darkness, enclosing entire city blocks within their eldritch grasp.

Asha craned her neck, trying to see how far the cemetery extended. "I didn't realize it was so big."

"What's with the castle-size wall?" Jake asked.

"I'm just glad we're going in the morning and not tonight," Asha said. "Wait—don't we need moonlight to see the next section of the map?"

"Jake and I discussed that on the train," I said. "We have some tools to create the effect of darkness during the daytime."

"Like what?"

"Towels," Jake said.

Lou chuckled. "Genius personified."

"Judging by that massive gate guarding the entrance," I said, "moonlight isn't an option."

* * *

On the way back to the hotel, we caught a glimpse of the Eiffel Tower. The famous spire climbed the night sky with a poet's eloquence, and I thought it the antithesis of Pere Lachaise, a shining monument to life.

I watched as Asha arched backwards for the view and interacted with the others, her animated smile and genuine laugh, the delicate movement of her hands when she spoke, the wisp of stray bang always floating about her chin.

A rush of emotion, powerful and sure, seized and then spun my senses like a rabbit shaken by the jaws of a tiger. When Asha and I entered our hotel room, she pulled me to bed. I could tell she was feeling the wine.

She kissed me but I eased away. I still hadn't forgotten the look of guilt in her eyes in Dubrovnik. "Maybe we should talk."

"I didn't really have talking in mind." She moved closer, until our lips brushed.

"You don't play fair," I said.

"Of course I do."

She continued kissing me. As my hands slid around her waist, my head spinning with desire, I made one last effort, concentrating all of my willpower on stopping the downward progress of my hands as they reached for the top of her silk underwear.

They didn't obey.

The next morning, the hotel phone rang like a fire alarm. Asha and I rolled out of bed and met Jake and Lou in the lounge. The place was a few clicks above the lodging in Naples.

"What a morning," Lou said. "The soap operas here would make Caligula blush. So what's the plan? Pere Lachaise after breakfast?"

"Yep," Jake said.

"What if we run into the Druids?" Asha said.

"It's daytime, there'll be plenty of people around." He shrugged. "You're free to stay here."

I didn't look up as I chewed my croissant. I knew no one would choose that option.

We lingered a while longer and then took to the tree-lined streets. Pere Lachaise's signature walls soon appeared alongside Boulevard de Menilmontant, and I felt a tingle of excitement that another portion of the map might be revealed.

As we paused at the gargantuan stone entrance to the cemetery, I wondered when I would become a permanent resident inside such a place and what I would accomplish before I arrived. I also couldn't help shivering at the thought of whatever it was we had seen in that courtyard. Glancing at Asha's troubled eyes and narrowed mouth, I knew she was thinking the same.

As my glance turned into a gaze, I realized that another emotion had invaded my psyche, a companion to my growing feelings.

Fear.

Fear of not being able to have her, fear of losing her, fear of being *with* her. Perhaps, I thought, fear was integral to desire: wanting someone so much that you trembled.

Standing before those walls guarding a city of finished lives, I found feeling for Asha the most terrifying proposition of my life.

I grimaced and willed it to go away. It was a horrible thing to have to live with.

But, my God, the possibilities.

We entered the gates.

-26-

I had seen impressive cemeteries before, but the spectacle spread before us was the Plato's cave of graveyards, all others mere shadows of the kingly Pere Lachaise. It was a necropolis of necropoli, an unending symphony of tombs, sarcophagi, mausoleums, vaults, and sepulchers.

Asha surveyed the sea of tombs with raised eyebrows. "I can't even see the other side."

Some of the crypts were the size of small houses, their secrets guarded for eternity by mythological creatures frozen in stone. "It's like the Taj Majal of graveyards," I said.

"The Taj Majal *is* a graveyard," Lou corrected. "Built for the wife of Shah Jehan, the fifth Mughal emperor."

"Shut up, Lou."

A wide cobblestone lane ran towards the middle, with smaller paths branching off it. The main thoroughfare even had a signpost: Avenue Transversale. As we strolled down the avenue with the other tourists, I felt as if we were on a supernatural safari, observing the natural habitat of the dead.

"It's scenic and all," Jake said, "but I'm itching to stomp around on Kardec's grave."

I noticed a pair of tourists bent over a map, and they informed us that brochures were available at the northern entrance. We made the trek and purchased one for ourselves. It didn't provide a complete listing of tombs, but it did include the gravesite of our famous spiritist.

At the center of Pere Lachaise, the two main thoroughfares, Avenue Transversale and Avenue des Etrangers Morts, intersected. We turned right and walked until we reached a small path branching to the right, close to where Kardec's tomb appeared on the map.

We dispersed and began searching for the tomb and the telltale dolmen. As I wandered further off the main road, the path narrowed and the tombs grew smaller and closer together. I smiled to myself: location counts, even in a cemetery.

I heard voices up ahead and saw a group of people standing in a loose circle. I drew closer and noticed a guard on the outside, watching the scruffy crowd with distaste.

Obnoxious laughter punctuated the conversation. I edged my way in. Everyone had gathered around a slab of granite set into the earth, easily the most nondescript gravesite I had seen.

I approached a white guy with long hair and an oversize Grateful Dead T-shirt. "What's going on?" I said.

I caught an odd glance and a whiff of bourbon. His accent was British. "You don't know who's buried here? Mr. Mojo Risin?'"

"Who?"

"Jim bloody Morrison. He died in Paris and they stuck him in here. You know, the Doors?"

I knew. "Is this some kind of ceremony? Why is there a guard?"

Again an odd look, as if the entire free world but me was clued in. "Someone's always here, mate. Got to keep the vigil. Fans got too rowdy a few years back, started leaving bottles and graffiti around, so the city keeps a guard posted."

I walked around the circle of worshippers, who didn't seem too bereaved, and my suspicion was confirmed as I approached the opposite side. Not meters away from Morrison's gravesite, within clear sight of a dozen people and a security guard, sat the dolmen marking the entrance to the tomb of Allan Kardec.

The guard glanced my way, and I dazzled him with a smile.

* * *

I gathered the others and we took stock of the situation. The ancient dolmen consisted of two large, upright rectangular stone blocks capped by another slab. It was positioned such that one had to walk underneath the top slab to reach the door of the tomb.

The crypt itself was a sizeable stone edifice. I couldn't tell if the iron door was locked, but even if not, we could hardly sneak inside with a *gendarme* standing meters away.

As the guard looked on with officious boredom, we conducted a fruitless inspection of the dolmen and the outside of the tomb. Asha frowned. "I thought the dolmen itself was the key."

"Whatever we're looking for might've been carried inside," I said. "And remember, there were two dolmens."

Jake glanced at the gendarme. "The baguette's already giving us the eye."

"So what now?" Asha said. "We can't get inside during the day and it's locked up at night."

"I don't reckon there're a lot of options. Who's up for a little midnight breaking and entering?"

"That's your plan?" Lou asked. "Break in at night, after what happened at Pompeii?"

"You got a better one?" Jake said.

"No, but—"

"Me either. If you think of one before dark, let me know. But I'm gettin' inside that tomb."

Midnight was the appointed hour. We wanted to ensure the streets would be dark and quiet, yet leave sufficient time to explore the crypt.

After lunch, Jake said he would take care of logistics and disappeared into the city. Lou settled into a chair in the lobby, watching a soccer game on TV with his feet propped up, arms waving at the referees, chatting in a variety of languages with the other guests.

Lou hadn't said whether he was going to the cemetery, but Asha didn't take any convincing. I knew it was reckless, but it had been reckless to come to Paris in the first place. The sooner we accomplished our task, the less chance anyone had to find us.

I wished Asha and I felt safe enough to enjoy the splendors of Paris. I would have taken her to gaze upon the city from Sacré-Coeur, stroll down the Champs-Elysees, dine in a bistro with chalkboard menus and then drift down the Seine at dusk.

Instead we strayed to the hotel's enclosed brick courtyard, which wasn't a bad consolation prize. A few wrought-iron tables surrounded a chestnut tree resplendent with the reds and golds of early fall. Ribbons of ivy accented the courtyard walls, and couples sipped drinks at the tables or canoodled on stone benches.

We let the sun warm us by the fountain. After chatting for a while, Asha quieted and leaned her head against my shoulder. Despite the looming visit to the cemetery, the intensity of my desire was a balloon of pressure expanding inside me. I moved to kiss her but she put a finger to my lips, smiled, and replaced her head on my shoulder.

"Paris is so beautiful," she murmured. "Don't you think it's the most beautiful city in the world?"

I fell silent, eying a couple kissing across the courtyard as if no one else was watching.

Beauty was a relative thing.

After dinner in the hotel, we met Jake and Lou in the lobby just before midnight.

"Fun day in the City of Love?" Lou said under his breath.

I gave him a bitter smile. "You coming with us?"

"I'm dying to see Jake's plan."

"Did you figure out how to get us in?" Asha asked Jake.

"Does a cat have climbing gear?"

We followed Jake to the entrance to Pere Lachaise, canvassing the streets for signs of the Druids. I couldn't see Jake greasing the palms of French officials or schmoozing a cemetery guard, so I didn't know what to expect as our entrance plan.

We continued along the street that paralleled the huge wall until we reached a series of homes backing on to the cemetery. Jake cut into a dark lot with houses on either side.

"Where're you going?" Asha asked, but he was already walking towards a copse of trees.

When Jake re-emerged, Lou snorted, and I chuckled. Jake was carrying a rusty aluminum ladder.

"I found an unlocked shed today. Owner's probably on vacation."

Jake leaned the ladder against the fifteen-foot wall and climbed atop the wall. We all followed. "Want to go first?" he asked me. "I'll stay behind for the ladder."

I tried to mask my unease. "Sure."

After shuffling along the wall until I was positioned over some soft-looking bushes, I lowered myself with my hands and dropped the remaining distance. I stood and brushed off the dirt, glanced at my surroundings, and drew a sharp breath.

I had landed in another world.

-27-

Crypts, vaults, and sarcophagi stuffed the fog-enshrouded grounds like a sinister sculpture garden. The fog was a mystery, since it was not present outside the walls. It seemed clichéd, as if put there for effect. But something about the cemetery must have been conducive to moisture, because the ghostly tendrils snaked around the trees and tombs to create a surreal, haunting landscape.

In the darkness, I couldn't discern the paths I knew wound in and around the crypts, so from my vantage point the tombs seemed to float chaotically within the fog. I shuddered and found myself wishing the others would hurry up and join me.

Asha dropped down and took in the scene, her eyes betraying similar thoughts to mine. "Look at this place," she murmured.

Jake and Lou started arguing atop the wall. After a few moments they lifted the ladder down. I started to position it to help Lou, but he went ahead and dropped. He landed awkwardly, crumpling to the ground and cursing.

I rushed over. "Are you okay?"

He stood and limped. "I'm fine, just a little sprain."

"You sure?" I said. "We can get you back to the other side."

"Not a chance. I'll ice it when I get back."

Jake dropped down lightly and seemed not to notice the scenery, but Lou's eyes had widened. "Who put up the horror movie set?"

"A little unnerving, isn't it?" I said. "Whoever made this map has done an excellent job of providing us with frightening places to explore."

"Does anyone know where we are?" Asha said. "Jake, did you bring the map?"

"Yeah, but it's not gonna do us much good until we find one of the main roads to use as a reference. I didn't realize it'd be so foggy in here."

I exchanged a glance with Asha. We could barely see ten feet ahead.

Jake switched on a flashlight. "Let's head towards the center."

The crunch of our footsteps was the only sound penetrating the solitude. Though Jake's confidence helped put me at ease, I couldn't shake a sense of foreboding as we followed the sinuous paths of earth and stone that wound through the maze of tombstones. Talking felt inappropriate, as if the place should not be disturbed, and I felt the kind of irrational dread one feels when alone in the dark, even though the others were right beside me.

"I can't believe we're in the middle of Paris," Asha said, with a shudder. "This place is its own little world."

"Jake, you're a little quiet," Lou said. "Are you communing with the French spirits? Trying to absorb a little culture?"

"I'm respecting the dead," he said, "and taking in the scenery. Some powerful symbols in here."

"Symbols?" Asha asked.

"Most of these crypts are Catholic. Catholic burials, Catholic guardians, Catholic symbols."

"So that's good, right? It's like being in church."

"More like being in war," he said quietly.

We passed a crypt the size of a small garage. I noticed the door was ajar. Stone gargoyles flanked the entrance, and the darkened interior of the tomb exerted a hypnotic attraction, a morbid temptation to uncover its secrets.

"I think we may be getting somewhere," Jake called out.

I couldn't see him through the fog. "Where are you?"

He emerged on the path ahead of us. "A little ways ahead it runs smack into one of the main drags."

We followed Jake to the larger byway, which ran perpendicular to the path we had been traversing. I was completely turned around. "Anyone have any idea which way the center is?"

We looked around and saw the same scene we had seen throughout our walk: fog, trees, and a jumble of crypts.

Asha shivered and drew her arms across her chest. “Someone pick a direction.”

Jake shrugged and headed down the road to the left. I kept glancing behind us. Nothing looked out of the ordinary, and it appeared we had made the right choice: ten minutes later we arrived at the center. The signposted intersection had seemed gimmicky during the day, but it felt appropriate at night, guiding the way into the city of the dead.

Jake inspected a headstone just off the road. He waved us over and pointed out a carving of a stylized flower with an arrow-shaped head, underneath a stone lion. “Do you remember this?”

“That fleur-de-lys?” I said. “I think so.”

“Me too,” Jake said. He pointed to the left, down Avenue des Etrangers Morts. “Our tomb is this way.”

Before we had taken five steps, a long, keening howl broke the silence, sounding as if it had come from inside the walls. Asha’s eyes widened in the halo of light from Jake’s flashlight.

Lou chuckled. “A little clichéd, don’t you think? A howl in the cemetery? It’s probably a night watchdog.”

“Guarding what?” Asha said, her voice shrill. “Corpses?”

I swallowed and told myself it was impossible to judge the distance of sound.

“Not to add fuel to the fire,” I said, “but let me also point out that we don’t know our way out of here.”

Jake waved impatiently in the general direction from which we had come. “It’s over there somewhere. It’s not like we’re in the Sahara.”

Asha shuffled her feet and looked away. I knew the strange howl wasn’t the only thing on her mind.

Our pace quickened as Jake led us down Avenue des Etrangers Morts. Soon after, we arrived at the stone menhir guarding the entrance to the tomb of Allan Kardec.

“I’ve never been so happy to see a crypt,” I muttered.

As we stood in front of the dolmen, a sense of accomplishment washed over me, my elation combating the sense of unease I had felt since entering Pere Lachaise.

Jake stepped to the iron door and pulled on the ornate bronze handle. The door swung open without a sound. We crowded inside and drew a collective breath, unprepared for what the moonlight revealed.

-28-

A large table, covered in finely embroidered green cloth, dominated the center of the crypt. The embroidery portrayed religious scenes from Africa or perhaps Brazil, with dozens of colorfully garbed worshippers dancing in abandon on a moonlit beach. Five plush, velvet-covered chairs lined each side of the table, and golden chalices waited to be quaffed. Next to an enormous silver bowl was a tome entitled *Le Livre des Esprits.*

Lou translated the title. "The Book of the Spirits."

Jake fingered a silver cross necklace he had pulled out from beneath his shirt. Asha ran a finger along the edge of the embroidery as I glanced around the room. Artwork and silken tapestries covered the walls, the tapestries depicting scenes from the East: maharajahs gesturing atop elephants, monks seated in various stages of meditation, beehive towers rising out of a jungle. The artwork was dark and occultist: books bursting into flame, black-robed figures holding steaming potions, satyrs preaching to crowds of animals.

Against the far wall, a silver throne squatted on a raised dais, complete with a wooden staff. Two portraits adorned the wall above the throne: a painting of a stocky woman with a powerful gaze, and a gold-framed likeness of Allan Kardec.

"Who's the hag?" Jake said.

"If I'm not mistaken," Lou said, favoring his hurt ankle as he leaned against the table, "that's H.P. Blavatsky."

"Who?" I asked.

"The founder of Theosophy, a nineteenth-century occult quasi-religion. She traveled the globe searching for insight into ancient magical practices.

According to her, the world is full of mystical wisdom and adepts in exotic places who can do miraculous things. She still has a large following. A complete kook, of course."

"Any ties to the Druids?"

"Dunno. I wouldn't be surprised if she studied them."

Asha drew her arms tight against her chest. "It looks like Kardec took a page out of Egyptian religion and wanted to be buried with his belongings."

"Pagans do pagan things," Jake said.

Lou's eyes narrowed as he stared at the entrance. "Who else here has noticed the two most interesting items in the room?"

No one replied, unsure if Lou was being serious or sarcastic.

"Number two is the lit candelabra by the entrance," Lou continued. "Judging by the lack of cobwebs and dust, it's apparent someone visits this place at least occasionally. But a lit candle means someone was here today."

"What's number one?" Asha said.

"Take a good long look at the table."

I did, and failed to notice anything out of the ordinary.

"Look under the embroidery," Lou said.

I moved a piece of the cloth aside, revealing a stone table. "I don't—" I began, then cut myself off as I moved aside more of the fabric. "Oh. I see. Very clever, Lou."

Lifting aside more of the embroidery revealed a thick, rectangular slab of stone supported by two smaller stones acting as legs.

"The second dolmen," Asha murmured.

I bent down and saw an oblong wooden container resting beneath the top piece of the dolmen, tucked between the two side slabs. "Novel place for a coffin."

Lou paced the room. "This has to be the correct location, since both dolmens are here. But how do we find the next portion of the map? Where do we put the letterbox?"

After taking a long look at the table, I put a hand on the silver bowl. "Jake, give me a hand with this."

The bowl was quite heavy, but we managed to set it on the floor. I removed the book and then the rest of the embroidery, revealing a small, familiar-size depression indenting the surface of the dolmen.

"I knew lawyers were good for something,'" Jake crowed. He set the letterbox top-down into the depression, such that the wooden bottom was exposed, crystals sparkling in the dim light.

Another perfect fit.

Jake rubbed his chin. "So where's the rest of it? We need to change the pattern."

"What if it's been lost or stolen?" I said.

A feverish light brightened Asha's eyes. "It's here somewhere," she said. "It has to be."

We searched the chamber beneath the unnerving gazes of H.P. Blavatsky and Allan Kardec, each second increasing my fear that we were overextending our stay. We looked behind every piece of fabric and art, turned over every movable object, but we found nothing to fit over the letterbox.

Lou climbed on the throne at the end of the room. He picked up the wooden staff and pointed it at Jake. "I hereby banish your twin demons of misguided beliefs and poor grammar."

"You're gettin' a big head, fat boy. Why don't you—" Jake stopped midsentence as Lou smirked and cupped the square head of the staff, which looked like a flat piece of ornate silver latticework. Jake's mouth broke into a slow grin.

"Of course," I said softly. "Druids and their staffs."

Lou carried the staff to the table and positioned the flattened head over the letterbox, moving it around until it fit snugly over a section of the stones. Asha and I hurried to snuff the candles, casting the room into semi-darkness. Once again a pattern of light and dark spread across the bottom of the letterbox. I felt a familiar, addictive thrill as a new portion of the map was revealed.

Jake fit his magnifier over the letterbox. I went to close the outside door to darken the room. As I approached the entrance, I noticed something that everyone, including myself, had overlooked.

Something that made my skin crawl.

"I just found interesting item number three," I called out in a tight voice. "Although I don't know if interesting is the word I'd use for this one. More like disturbing."

I pointed out a large iron padlock hanging on the wall next to the door. "There's a deadbolt for this door, as well as this padlock. Neither were in place. Why would a crypt with valuable jewelry and other items be left unsecured?"

Another howl from outside, louder and closer than the first.

Jake stopped snapping photos and banged a fist on the table. "Because they knew we were coming. They knew it and they let us in."

"Then why let us see the map?" Asha said.

Lou backed away from the table, his face pale. "Because they aren't expecting us to leave."

Jake swore, picked up the letterbox, and herded everyone outside. The tingling I had felt at our discovery turned into a cold splash of fear.

"We'll follow the main road to the nearest wall," Jake said. "Maybe there'll be a tree or a tomb we can use to climb out. If not, we follow the wall until we reach the ladder."

We again entered the nocturnal world of Pere Lachaise, my mind swimming with images from the occult artwork in the crypt. As Jake led us down the narrow path that would take us back to Avenue des Etrangers Morts, the howling resumed, closer than ever, and the trees seemed to close in, the fog hiding every imaginable and unimaginable thing. My nostrils flared with heightened adrenaline, inhaling the loamy smell of the cemetery.

When we stumbled onto Avenue des Etrangers Morts, the broad and familiar byway felt like a godsend. Jake's knife appeared in his hand as we hurried towards the center. The howling continued behind us, and my head felt strangely clear despite the rubbery feeling in my limbs.

"I can see the crossroads," Lou said.

Even though reaching the center would put us at the furthest point from an exit, we would have a choice of four directions to reach the wall, and we wouldn't have to wade through the morass of tombs and fog.

By the time we reached the landscaped area where the two avenues met, the howling had ceased. The fog wasn't quite as thick, and the moonlight provided enough illumination to see a good distance down the thoroughfares.

Asha cocked her head. "It's somehow worse when we can't hear anything."

"I tend to agree," Lou said, casting furtive looks around the cemetery.

We started down Avenue Transversale, back the way we had come, then stopped as if jerked by a rope. At the edge of our line of vision, in confirmation of our worst fears, the darkness came to life.

-29-

Two figures clothed in black, bent over as if very old and moving with an oddly jerky gait, strode out of the gloom. Just behind them were two Druids in white robes, cowls shielding their faces.

The source of the howling was also revealed. Each of the Druids grasped a leash with two enormous canines straining against the tethers. They looked like wolves, except they were solid black.

"Jesus Christ," Lou said, backing away.

I stood as if mired in quicksand, unable to tear my eyes from the unnatural procession. Part of me wanted to laugh, run over, pat them on the back, and congratulate them on the charade.

The rest of me wanted to scream.

One of the beasts tilted its head and let out a chilling howl. Asha dug her nails into my arm, and fear tumbled through me like an out-of-control acrobat.

"Look around," Jake said, his voice rigid. I spun, and my fear morphed into desperation.

Down the remaining three roads stood a group identical to the first: two white-robed Druids holding a canine by a leash, fronted by a pair of hunched-over figures in black. As in the woods outside Dubrovnik, all four groups moved forward in unison, the wolves baying and snarling.

Jake waved his knife. "Into the cemetery. They can't see us as well off the main paths." He pulled a second knife from his other boot and tossed it to me. "It's time to grow up, Counselor."

I caught the weapon and held it in front of me as we fled, all too cognizant of its unfamiliar weight. We dove into the thick of the cemetery, reason trampled by fear, forgetting about avenues and paths and cautious steps forward, hoping to somehow weave our way through the labyrinth of tombstones and reach the wall.

The canines bayed at full volume, and the fog seemed denser off the road. Time seemed to both stop and accelerate. We slipped between the crypts as fast as we could, unable to sprint because of the darkness and Lou's ankle. He was puffing gamely behind me, and I wasn't sure if his ankle or his physical condition was the greater barrier.

Just when I thought we were moving in circles, we emerged onto a path I thought I recognized. I stopped, breathing hard. "I'm pretty sure this is the path from earlier. I remember that obelisk."

"I think you're right," Lou said. He was facing a gray, slender tower rising primly out of the darkness.

"They're closing in," Jake said. "No time to rest."

We continued down the path, eyes straining for a glimpse of the wall. For the first time since we had seen the Druids coming down the avenues, I started to believe we had a chance of escaping the cemetery. I could taste the freedom waiting just outside.

Asha pointed. "There it is!"

As the gray bulk of the wall materialized, two of the stooped figures in black coalesced out of the darkness on the path ahead.

They shuffled and jerked forward, moving as if controlled by some unseen force. Their torn clothing hung like rags off their bodies, and black hoods covered their heads. I was transfixed, stunned by a horrible curiosity.

"What are they?" Asha whispered, hysteria creeping into her voice.

I grabbed her hand and backed away from the figures. Jake brandished his knife, and Asha screamed as two Druids and their wolves stepped out of the fog behind the things in black.

Jake led the retreat. My adrenaline was fading, tempered by exhaustion and loss of hope. My legs throbbed, Asha looked ready to collapse, and Jake was pulling Lou along behind him.

We reached a crossroads of small paths that I remembered from earlier.

An idea reached through my panic, and I herded everyone down the smaller trail to the left, into the heart of the cemetery.

Lou spoke between gasps, hands clutching his sides. "Are you crazy? This leads back to the center."

"I've got an idea. And they're not going to let us reach the wall."

The fact that the Druids weren't worried enough to run was an ominous sign. They had us surrounded and knew we couldn't last much longer.

"There," I said, pointing to the right. Just off the path, its mouth yawning darkness, was the open tomb we had passed earlier.

"That's your plan?" Asha said. "Hide in there? I think I'd rather stay outside."

Jake pointed behind us. "You sure about that?"

Two Druids emerged out of the fog. I looked to my right and saw another flash of white.

We tumbled into the crypt. Lou entered first, then stopped and threw his arms wide. "Careful."

A set of wide stone steps descended into darkness. The wide stairwell comprised almost the entire upper level.

Jake spat his words. "Down the stairs so I can shut the door."

As we groped our way down, I heard a heavy thud and the clank of an iron bar. Jake followed behind us, his flashlight illuminating a large rectangular room with stone walls stretching away from the bottom of the stairs.

The room was empty except for a granite coffin set against the far wall, flanked by candelabra. Neither the coffin nor the candelabra revealed signs of recent use.

Jake lit the candles with his lighter, then switched off the flashlight. "Saving my batteries," he muttered, as the candelabras twitched and sputtered behind him.

"How's the door going to hold up?" I asked.

"It's about the heaviest door I've ever seen, and there's a foot-thick iron bar across it. They're not getting in here without dynamite."

"Let's hope you're right."

"What about air?" Asha asked.

"We'll be fine until morning," Lou said. "This is a large space and the door's been open."

We heard howling outside, as well as banging on the door. I slid to the floor with my back against the wall, my body exhausted and my mind mired in disbelief.

What had we been running from?

Jake was pacing the room. "Even if they get in, only one thing at a time can fit down those stairs."

"They've got wolves, Jake!" Asha said. "Not to mention whatever those . . . things . . . were. What if they have some kind of magical way to open the door?"

"They're just men," Lou said, his voice weary. "Twisted, perhaps criminally insane men, but just men."

"Then what were those black things?"

"Costumes," Lou said. "Tricks. Effective and frightening, especially at night in a cemetery."

"Commie," Jake said, "I'm not even going to take the time to argue with you. Because this time I hope you're right. And . . ." he trailed off.

"And what?" Lou said.

"And nothing."

"Don't you hold back on us," Asha said.

Jake continued pacing in the small space, lips compressed. "When the Romans invaded the British Isles, there was mention of the high priests leading the way for the Druids, dressed in white robes and entering into battle with large wolves on leashes."

Asha swallowed. "And?"

Jake ran a hand through his hair, as if he didn't want to answer. "The high priests were rumored to have the power to raise and command the dead."

Asha slumped to the floor, her face ashen. "Those things out there—"

Jake held a hand up. "Quiet. I think the howling stopped."

He was right. The pounding on the door had also ceased, and a heavy silence filled the tomb.

"They've left or they can't get in," Lou said. "Either way, we can wait it out until morning."

As soon as Lou finished speaking, we heard a soft noise from above, a series of low thumps that grew steadily louder. Hands clenched, I backed towards the sarcophagus with the others.

The sound that we heard was footsteps.

Coming down the stairs.

-30-

The methodical footsteps drew closer to the bottom of the staircase. I moved beside Jake, the knife an alien thing in my clammy grasp. "Why didn't we hear the door open?"

"We would've heard it," Jake said.

Asha gasped when a dark shape appeared at the bottom of the stairwell, melding with the shadows created by the flickering candelabra. The figure was tall and swathed in black linens that covered it like a shroud. Folds of material concealed the face.

At first I recoiled, thinking one of the black-garbed figures had somehow gotten inside. Then the figure stood upright in a fluid motion, exhibiting none of the sporadic, jerky movements of the things outside.

"Who are you?" Jake asked.

The figure remained in the shadows, unmoving.

Lou snorted, then surprised me with the strength of his voice. "Are we on candid camera? Really, whoever-you-are, we're sick of these games. We're tired of being tricked and followed in forests and chased around in cemeteries. So why don't you tell us who you are, what's really going on, and how the hell you got in here?"

It shifted towards Lou, its face a silhouette in the darkness. "Louis Reginald Delfim."

It was a man's voice. He spoke in monotone, with the smoothness of an elevator door. A chill coursed through me when he called my friend by name.

"Congratulations on learning how to use the Internet," Lou said. A waver had crept into his voice. "Why don't you go ahead and tell us all our names?"

"That is not my interest."

Jake was watching the man closely. Lou's confidence returned when the figure didn't challenge his accusation. "Then what is? Early Halloween?"

"That which allows me to be here."

"You *must* be referring to the mysterious letterbox."

The man shifted to look at the backpack on the floor behind Jake, then took a step towards him.

"Whoa there, partner," Jake said.

"Did you get bored hanging out on street corners in Romania?" Lou pressed. "And for the love of God, how *did* you get in here?"

The man's head made a slow turn to face Lou. "How strange that one with no faith would mention God."

"Excuse me?"

"You have no faith," he said, as if stating a well-known fact. "Your mother saw to that."

Lou's mother had been in a car accident when Lou was fourteen, leaving her brain-injured. She suffered terribly, and remained mentally and physically handicapped. Although Lou had never been religious, the event transformed his budding atheism into a lifelong crusade.

Lou pointed his finger at the man. "Don't you *ever* speak of her. Do you hear me?"

"Doubting Louis," he mocked, the inflection slicing through the smoothness in his voice. "He has nothing to believe in."

I heard a faint clanging sound. I whipped my head around, but couldn't find the source of the noise.

Lou sneered. "That's because there *is* nothing to believe in."

"Your lack of faith poisons you." He turned back to Jake and took another step forward.

Jake put his other hand out. "That's far enough."

"Why don't you take off your funeral costume, you freak," Lou said.

Although cloaked in shadow, the man had moved far enough into the candlelight that I should have been able to discern his facial features. But as

I peered inside the cowl, I saw only shadows where a face should be. It had to be a trick of the light, or some sort of mask.

The man addressed Lou again. "Is that really what you wish? Perhaps you should consult with Kika. She might counsel otherwise. Shall I call her for you?"

I didn't know who Kika was or what he was talking about. But Lou did. His mouth caved, and he put a hand on the coffin to steady himself.

"This has gone far enough," Jake said. "Who are you, what do you know about the box, and how the *hell* did you get in here?"

The man took another step forward. He was ten feet away from Jake.

"I said that's *far enough.*"

Another step. "Give it to me," he whispered.

I gripped the handle of my knife.

"Not one more step," Jake said.

I looked from Jake to the man, and he seemed to flicker.

"Did you see that?" Asha said.

He flickered again and started walking faster. "*Give it to me,*" he said, but his voice wavered, as if the volume was coming in and out.

Jake stepped forward to meet him, knife clutched tight, stance low and threatening. The man's arms were outstretched, his sleeves hanging loose beneath his arms as he reached for Jake.

Just before they met, the man disappeared.

-31-

Jake canvassed the floor and walls where the man had been. "He's gone," he muttered, and bounded up the stairs.

I waited for Lou to snicker, but he leaned against the tomb and stared at the floor.

When Jake returned, his voice was grim. "The door to the outside's still locked."

"Maybe there's a secret door," I said. "Or it was some kind of projected image."

Asha seemed to snap out of a trance. She walked to where the man had been standing and ran her hands along the wall.

"Don't bother," Jake said. "He was here."

"How do you know? I think Aidan might be onto something."

Jake bent to grab something off the floor. "Because I thought of that. I had a few rocks in my pocket I picked up outside, and while we were talking I tossed one at him." He opened his hand to reveal a thumb-size rock. "I saw this hit his clothes and fall to the ground. I saw it and I heard it."

I remembered the faint clanking sound I had heard: Jake's rock falling to the stone floor after making contact with the man standing ten feet in front of us.

The same man who had disappeared into thin air from a locked and empty crypt, in full view of four witnesses.

"Then maybe he was hiding near the stairwell," I said slowly, though I knew there wasn't enough space for a man to hide, and it still didn't explain the disappearing act.

Jake looked at his watch. "Five-fifty a.m. Sun's almost up, and the gates open at six."

Asha sat and put her hands to her temples. I sat beside her, stunned and exhausted, until Jake went up the stairs ten minutes later and opened the tomb, letting in a flood of sunlight. I had begun to question whether we would ever see that particular sight again.

Lou put his weight on my shoulders as I helped him climb the stairs, and we emerged squinting into the light like newborn babes. There was no sign of wolves, Druids, or black-robed figures.

Pere Lachaise had returned to its innocuous daytime state.

It took me a long time to figure out the loud noise I was hearing was our hotel phone and not something chasing me in a dream. It didn't seem to want to stop, so I roused myself and picked up the receiver.

"It's noon," Lou said.

"Meet you downstairs."

I padded to the shower and let steaming water pour over me. The events of the night were dreamlike, a blur of nightmarish imagery. I waited on Asha to shower, and then we made our way to the lobby. Jake and Lou were sitting in a corner drinking coffee.

"You should all go home," Jake said, after Asha and I grabbed coffees and joined them. "There's some bad business going down, and I'd sleep better if you did."

Lou slumped in his chair. "They tried to hunt us down like animals."

Every synapse in my brain told me to get on the next plane to New Orleans. As curious as I was about the letterbox, the balance had tipped in favor of personal safety. I looked at Asha, but she wouldn't meet my eyes.

"I'm not going home," she said quietly.

I was stunned. I knew she'd been close to her brother, extremely close, but I didn't think that alone warranted this sort of recklessness. Then again, I didn't have a sibling.

Her eyes slipped towards mine, asking a wordless question.

Regardless of the danger, I knew I couldn't leave her. I'd have to try to talk some sense into her later. I nodded slowly, and her hand slipped over mine. Lou looked at the two of us as if we had just declared a suicide pact. Maybe we had.

I cradled my coffee cup. "There's no reason for you to stay, Lou."

He lit a cigarette and took two long drags, then waved the cigarette in the air. "I know I'm a coward, but I don't leave my friends. I'll stay in the hotel from now on."

Jake put a hand up, as if to say *you're all free to do what you want.* "Commie, who's Kika?"

"Just an old friend," Lou mumbled. Jake pressed his lips together and watched him, but Lou was staring at his feet.

"What were those things in black?" Asha said. "And that man in the tomb—did anyone else notice he didn't seem to have a face?"

"I did," I said. "It must've been a mask."

"The fact of the matter," Lou said, finally looking up, "is that once again we don't really know what we saw. It was dark and chaotic, and we were frightened and out of sorts. It was the perfect scenario to pull a few tricks of the mind."

Asha curled tighter into her chair. "It looked real enough to me. And the way those things in black moved, like they were being jerked around or controlled by someone . . . ." She turned to Jake. "You said the Druids had the power to raise the dead. Do you think my brother—" Her voice cracked, and she looked away. "That man in the crypt asked Jake to give him something. He could only have meant the letterbox." She looked around the room, her eyes wild. "Like it's somehow calling out to them."

Jake folded his arms. "We'll find out what's going on, I promise you. But we need to keep moving. The longer we sit around, the more time they have to find us."

"There's something that's been bothering me," I said. "Why didn't they just loose the wolves on us?"

"Maybe they aren't prepared to go that far," Lou said. "It was still the middle of Paris. Or maybe they think we have information they need."

"It felt like they were prepared to go pretty far," I muttered.

Asha's eyes found the window. "So what now?"

"We follow the map," Jake said.

Lou frowned. "And what, stick around here like sitting ducks until we figure out the next location?"

Jake leaned back in his chair. "I know where it is."

-32-

"Why didn't you say anything?" I said.

Jake shrugged. "Last night was a little hectic."

Asha clutched my knee. "So where is it?"

He lit a cigarette and slid the ashtray closer, taking a few drags before speaking. "Anyone heard of Kostel Utes?"

"Kos what?" I asked.

Even Lou looked stumped.

"It's a very old church close to Prague," Jake said. "To commemorate the founding, the church stuck a minor Catholic relic inside, which is why I know of the place. Never visited it, but I recognized it."

"What's the relic?" I asked.

"Doubt it has anything to do with our box. It's a reliquary for Saint . . . I forget which one."

"But how'd you recognize it?" Lou pressed.

"It's a rotunda with a steeple, sitting on a cliff outside Prague, above the Vltava River. Two things got me: the dogleg in the river below the church, and most of all, the cliff face covered in rock triangles."

"What?" Lou said.

Jake shook his head. "It's a geological formation caused by exfoliation or something, I can't remember. But it's very distinct. The map depicted the exact scene: rotunda, steeple, J-shaped bend in the river, and cliff covered in triangles. It's got to be it."

"What time period are we talking?" Asha asked.

"Ninth century."

Lou spoke from the side of his mouth as he lit up. "My guess? Whoever's following us doesn't know where the next location is." He blew a smoke ring and pointed with the tip of his cigarette. "I think they're after the map."

"I agree," I said. "And we have to stop helping them follow it. If we're smart, we can stay a step ahead. And if it gets too dangerous, if for one second we think we might have to go someplace that might not be safe, we *back off*."

"What about informing the authorities?" Asha said. "Can't they do something about these people?"

"And tell them how we broke into Pere Lachaise and a private crypt," Lou said, "and got chased by a group of occultists and wolves?"

"I hate to say it," I said, "but Lou's right. They're smart, and only show themselves when we're alone and vulnerable."

Jake wagged his finger in the air, as if he hadn't been paying attention. "I think the places on the map are supposed to be obvious to certain people."

"I've thought about that," I said. "Once you know the stones are a map, the locations aren't that difficult to figure out, if you're familiar with the sites—which I'm assuming the ancient Druids were."

"A church, a castle, and a cemetery," Jake mused. "There must be some connection."

I stood. "Back to Lou's point about the Druids not knowing where the map leads. If we're smart, we can send them on a wild goose chase, then give them the slip and be in Prague before they know we're gone. Let them play catch-up for a change."

Jake's lips compressed. "Let's run all this by Lucius and figure out a strategy. How's eight p.m. sound?"

"Lunchtime in the States," Asha said. "It's a good time to catch him."

Asha headed to the restroom. I followed Lou up the stairs. "You didn't say much in there," I said. "Has the font of useless knowledge run dry?"

"I'm still a little tired," he said, pulling away. "I'm going to grab a nap."

"Lou," I said as he reached the middle of the staircase, "who's Kika?"

Lou stopped moving and put a hand on the railing. "I told you. Just an old friend."

"I know all your old friends."

He muttered something I couldn't understand.

"I saw the effect it had on you," I said. "Why haven't I heard of her?"

Lou slumped against the wall, his back still to me. "It's impossible."

I climbed to face him. He looked as serious as I had ever seen him. "What is?"

He let out a slow breath. "During my comparison of syntax among dialects of Romance languages, I went to Brazil for two weeks. While I was there, I jumped in a taxi and visited a *favela*."

"The slum cities."

"You wouldn't believe how sad they are. While I was there, a little girl approached me begging for dollars. There were hundreds of beggars, but she really touched me. Eight years old at best and so filthy it broke my heart. Yet after all she'd been through, she was still so sweet and animated, and had a childlike look in her eyes. Her name was Kika. I gave her some money and came back every day for a week."

"So what happened? And why've you never told me any of this?"

I saw a tear form in Lou's eye. He turned away. I had never seen him cry.

"She acquired HIV from a blood transfusion when she was a baby, and developed AIDS. I went to the clinic with her. A nurse told me she had a few months to live. No family. Slept on the streets. I helped her as much as I could, gave her all the money I had, but it was a pitiful amount. I've never felt so helpless. I came back to the States and left her to die."

"You made her life a little brighter in the end. It was more than anyone else had ever done."

He bowed his head. "It wasn't enough."

"Is that why you were so upset in the tomb? The memory of her?"

He looked up at me. "Don't you get it? Kika is my burden and my memory. I've never told anyone that story, and she didn't even know my last name. *No one could possibly know about her.*"

-33-

I let Lou go and caught up with Asha in the lobby, unsure how to process what my friend had just told me. I stored it with the rest of the mounting impossibilities.

"There you are," she said. "Want to go to Notre Dame with me?"

Her voice didn't possess the thrill of discovery, so I knew there was something on her mind besides tourism. I looked down and noticed the bulge of the letterbox in her handbag.

"Go out with that? After last night?"

"There's something we haven't tried," she said.

"What's that?"

Her eyes flicked to the sun streaming in through the window, and she rested her hand on the contours of the letterbox. "Bringing the God Path to God."

I could tell by the set of her mouth she was going with or without me. "A taxi straight there and back," I said grimly.

She nodded, her gaze slipping to the side.

Jake was smoking outside the door and grabbed my arm as we walked past. I filled him in, and he said, "Be careful, Counselor. And be back before dark."

When we arrived at the huge plaza fronting the Gothic spectacle of Notre Dame, we took a moment to absorb the cathedral's majestic colonettes and entrance arches. The imposing façade dwarfed the tourists swarming before it.

I followed Asha as she strode through the throngs of people and into the dimly lit cathedral, our pupils dilating as they adjusted. The nave stretched out before us, and we walked between slender columns to the vaulted transept, then past the main altar to the choir hall, a more intimate area of worship and meditation.

Asha took an aisle seat on the far left side of the choir. We were alone. A tiny chapel was recessed into the wall beside us, lit by candles from the faithful.

I sat next to her. "What now?"

"I don't know. I just wanted to . . . see if anything happens."

We both quieted, and I couldn't help but feel a sense of awe as I contemplated the grandeur of the cathedral. It was quixotic, I had always thought, to attempt to evoke the majesty of God through human endeavors. Tilting against a windmill beyond our comprehension.

Yet I had to admit, whether due to the Great Architect in the Sky or simply the architect of Notre Dame, the cathedral exuded a powerful aura.

"I didn't think anything would happen," Asha said after a time, her voice small and sheepish.

"I understand."

"I feel foolish."

"With all that's going on," I said, "it was worth a shot." She started to stand, but there was something I had to get off my mind. "Asha, why'd you pull away when I tried to kiss you in the courtyard?"

She looked down at her hands.

"People who are into each other are generally interested in kissing after a night of intimacy, especially in a courtyard in the most romantic city on earth."

"You're right," she said softly.

I felt as if someone had slipped a knife under my ribcage. After a long moment she took my hand and said, "Sometimes I . . . shut down."

"I see."

Her hand moved to my cheek, and she ran her fingers through my hair. I stood still and wordless, the current from her touch as electric as ever. I still wanted to kiss her like we were on a goddamned movie set.

"It's not what you think," she whispered.

"Then what is it?"

"I just need some time. I—"

She cut off as a woman sat in the chair beside me. Her oval face possessed a timeless quality, and I could make no better guess as to her age than somewhere between thirty and forty-five. Luxurious pale curls reached halfway down her back, and anxious green eyes stared back at me. A necklace with an emerald teardrop pendant rested just below her neckline, and she wore a long-sleeved white dress that looked too formal for a weekday afternoon.

"My time is short," she said with a sense of urgency, and I started.

Asha and I exchanged a glance. I could tell she was just as confused. "Do I know you?" I asked the woman.

"I came to warn you."

"About what?"

Her gaze slipped downward, coming to rest on the side of Asha's handbag bulging from the letterbox.

Asha's eyes widened, and I rushed to get my words out. If this woman knew something, anything at all . . . "Do you know what the inscription means, where the map leads?"

Now the woman looked confused. "Inscription? Map?"

I pulled back as the obvious conclusion hit me. "You're with the Druids."

Her mouth curled downward, in a frown that still managed to be beautiful. "Don't you understand what you have?"

Asha took the letterbox out of her handbag. The woman stared at it, a mixture of fear and desire twisting her features. She started to reach for it, then drew back. "Leave it," she said. "Leave it and forget you ever saw it." Her eyes roved the cathedral. "There are others who aren't like me. Others you don't want to meet."

"What're you talking about?" I said in frustration.

She stood and backed away. "My time is gone. Please leave."

Asha stood. "Wait! I have to ask you something."

The woman had already started walking away.

Asha called out, "Do you know anything about my brother?"

The woman hesitated, then turned towards Asha with a sad, knowing expression.

Asha gave a spontaneous sob. "*Please.* If you know something, anything—where is he? Does he need me? Is he hurt, lost? Why—"

"I'm sorry. I have to go." The woman spun and walked rapidly away.

Asha jumped up and went after her, weaving through the startled worshippers and tourists. I hurried to keep up. We followed the woman past the chapel and into the plaza. We tried to run, but the crowds were too thick.

Asha pointed across the open space. "Over there!"

We raced to the far side of the entrance plaza, to a set of stairs leading underground. The entrance to the crypt. At the bottom of the long staircase, a turnstile was set into the roughhewn stone wall, blocking the entrance.

There was no sign of the woman. An older man sitting in a chair behind the turnstile put a hand up, pointing to a sign with admission prices.

"A woman!" I gushed. "She just came down here. Did you see her? Did she go into the crypt?"

His face wrinkled and his English was good, so I knew he understood me. "There was no woman here, *monsieur*. The last visitor left twenty minutes ago."

"*She just came down these stairs.*"

He held his palms up and gave me one of those condescending expressions the French have perfected.

Besides the staircase, the turnstile offered the only other exit. There were no tourists, nowhere else she could have gone.

Was the man part of the deception? I took another look at him, at the tired face and faded brown uniform. If he wasn't an hourly museum worker, then he was a damn good actor.

Asha started for the turnstile, and I grabbed her arm. "I know it's a museum, but we're not going down there by ourselves."

She clutched the turnstile. "She knows something about my brother."

I pulled her away, and Asha fell into my arms, a whimper of pure emotion escaping her lips that I knew encompassed all of her hopes and fears about her long-dead brother.

-34-

I led Asha up the stairs and back into the sunlight.

"She had to have gone into the crypt," she said. "But why would that man have lied?"

I had no response. Yet another mystery.

"Her reaction to the letterbox was strange," she continued. "As if she was afraid of it."

"It was all strange. My guess is the Druids sent her. Either to get us to leave the letterbox behind or to rattle us even more."

"But why be so evasive? And how could the Druids have known where we were going, or that I had the letterbox with me?"

"That I don't know." I stepped to the curb to flag a taxi. "Asha, let's go home."

She sighed and tried to look wistful, but failed to hide the obsessive look in her eyes. "We can't leave the others," she said.

I took her hand. "Jake's fine by himself, and Lou won't take convincing."

She shook her head, her next words a suit of armor encasing her with conviction. "He's my baby brother, Aidan, and he's out there somewhere. He's out there and he needs my help."

That evening we all met in the hotel's conference room. Jake and Lou had no insight as to our strange encounter.

Jake put his phone on speaker and we gathered around. I had done some thinking on the ride back from Notre Dame, and had an idea.

"Before we call Mr. Sofistere," I said, "I want to make a quick call."

"What're you thinking?" Jake said.

"I was trying to come up with ways to find out more information about the Druids, and I thought of Kardec's crypt. I think we can find out who owns it."

"Wouldn't the cemetery own it?" Asha asked.

"Cemeteries sell plots of lands to individuals, and those transactions are recorded." I grimaced. "I'm going to call someone. He's a pain to work with but he's good."

I dialed and we heard the jangle of a ringing phone. "Prentice Meyer's office." The voice belonged to Linda Gladstone, Prentice's secretary.

"Linda," I said, "tell Prentice to stop looking for mansions on the French Riviera he can't afford and get on the phone with Aidan."

Linda sounded flustered, as usual. "Yes, sir. I'll get him right away. Good to hear from you."

"You, too."

I heard muffled conversation and then the double click of a phone transfer.

"Aidy!" Prentice cried. "Where are you? And just so you know, I was shopping online at Saks. They have a new Helmut Lang line which my personal shopper failed to mention, the negligent bastard."

Jake looked at the phone like there was an alien on the other end.

"Paris," I said.

"I was picturing you someplace more like Karachi or Detroit, or some other third-world hellhole. You were always bringing some filly to firm functions who could barely speak English. People talk, you know. So how's unemployment?"

"Liberating," I said. "And terrifying. Listen, I need a small favor. I'd do it myself if I was stateside, but I need an answer while I'm here and you're the best I know."

"Of course," he preened. Flattery got one everywhere with Prentice. "What is it?"

"You have access to international property records, right? I understand that for the kind of construction deals you do, you conduct extensive title searches on property you purchase, sites you develop, et cetera."

"Correct," he said. "Excepting dictatorships and theocracies, property titles are a matter of public record. Though the extent we're able to search for and verify property owners differs by country."

"Understood. Listen, I need to trace ownership of a piece of property in France. I'll of course pay for your services."

"Don't be ridiculous. France has excellent public records. Better than here. It shouldn't be a problem, though it might take a few days to get a response. What's the address?"

I hesitated. "It's a plot of land in a cemetery. A crypt."

"Excuse me?"

"People buy plots of land in cemeteries just like anyplace else. You should be able to research it."

"That wasn't what alarmed me."

I forced a laugh. "I'm tracing my family history, and I've hit a snag. I think one of my relatives is buried in Pere Lachaise. Name of Allan Kardec." I spelled it for him. "I need the surname of the person who purchased the plot, so I can continue my records search."

"Pere Lachaise, eh? A fine place to be interred. I have serious doubts as to this Kardec person's relation to you, but I'll put a first-year on it. Shouldn't take long."

"It'd be a huge favor."

I hung up with Prentice, and we prepared to dial Mr. Sofistere. Jake spread his hands. "Take the lead, Counselor. You've got the slick tongue."

Asha dialed, and Mr. Sofistere's familiar baritone answered. I leaned in. "Mr. Sofistere? It's Aidan and the others."

"I was hoping to hear from you," he said. "How's Paris?"

"It's very French. We haven't had much time to enjoy the city, but the accommodations are superb."

"How's the search progressing? Were you able to locate Kardec's tomb?"

"We were," I said, the memories from the night before rushing at me like approaching headlights on a one-way road. "Although it turned into somewhat of an . . . event."

Mr. Sofistere didn't respond.

"We haven't said anything before now," I said, "and I apologize. We didn't think it was serious. To make a long story short, we believe we're being followed by a sect of modern-day Druids. Though to be honest, we're not sure who they are."

There was a prolonged period of silence. Somehow, despite the distance between us, I felt uncomfortable in his presence.

"Tell me more," he said finally, his voice low and even.

"We've seen them on a few occasions, always dressed in white robes. They seem to think they have a claim to the letterbox. They chased us through the cemetery, and we hid in a crypt until morning. It was not a pleasant experience."

The four of us shared a glance, an unspoken acknowledgment not to discuss the encounter with the shadowy figure in the tomb. Not when we weren't even sure if what we had seen was real.

When Mr. Sofistere spoke, there was an edge to his voice, the subtle but dangerous tone of a businessman whose interests are threatened. "Following is one thing, pursuit another. Was anyone injured? Perhaps we should cancel—"

Asha cut in. "Aidan's an attorney. It's his job to worry. No one was injured and we're fine."

I stared at her. Lou also looked shocked, but he didn't comment.

"Jake?" Mr. Sofistere said. "What's this about?"

"It's probably just a bunch of rejects from the Freemasons. I don't know how they found us, but I'll handle it."

"Aidan?"

I looked at the worry and sadness etched into Asha's eyes, and hoped I wouldn't regret my next words. I let out a breath before I spoke. "I don't think there's any real danger. At least not yet."

Asha squeezed my leg in thanks.

"How could they possibly know about the letterbox? And chasing you through a cemetery? Asha, are you sure you don't want to return—"

"Everything is fine," she said, with a light laugh. "I promise we'll be careful going forward. You said you wanted to know everything, so we thought you should know."

The tension in the room was like grime coating a window. Part of me regretted mentioning our pursuers at all, and part of me wanted Mr. Sofistere to order us off the search.

"If Jake wasn't there," he said at last, "I wouldn't even think about letting the rest of you continue." He hesitated long enough to make me wonder if he already knew something about the Druids—perhaps even why they were interested in the letterbox. I resolved in that instant to find out everything I could about Lucius Sofistere.

"History says the Druids vanished," Mr. Sofistere continued, "but elite sects have a way of surviving in the shadows. Who can say? But if the situation deteriorates, I *will* suspend the search."

We all shared another glance. It had already deteriorated.

"On the other hand, it means the letterbox is causing quite a stir. I'll continue investigating from over here. Did you manage to locate the next section of the map?"

Jake related what we had found. Mr. Sofistere was animated by the discovery. "I'll make the arrangements. When would you like to leave?"

"Tomorrow," Jake said.

I drummed my fingers on the table. "Perhaps you could make reservations for us on an airline to, say, Ireland. We'll purchase tickets to Prague at the train station just before we leave."

Mr. Sofistere rumbled his approval. "A good choice, especially with the Celtic connection. Is there anything else?"

Asha glanced around nervously, as if her secret fears were on display.

No one spoke.

* * *

Except for Jake, everyone seemed exhausted from the night before. Jake mentioned something about studying the letterbox while we slept. I think he had terminal insomnia.

I sat in bed with my back against the headboard, still trying to process the events of the last twenty-four hours. Asha slid under the covers. She always claimed a chill except on the warmest of days. It was the middle of October, and a finger of cold had wormed its way into the marrow of Paris.

I could feel her shivering next to me. "How can you be so cold?" I asked.

"I guess I was made for warmer climes. This bed is cozy, though." She snuggled in tight against me.

I stroked her hair, and she said, "I'm afraid."

"I can't say that I'm feeling relaxed."

"What's happening?"

"I don't know," I said.

I flipped off the reading light and slid down next to her. She settled into the crook of my arm. I kept thinking about her words at Notre Dame, but the longer we lay awake in silence, her body close against mine, the more the incident in the courtyard became the anomaly she had suggested it was.

I slept terribly and woke much too early. When I stumbled downstairs for coffee, I found Jake reading a paper and smoking. "What's the plan?" I asked.

"I have someplace I want to go before the train station."

"I thought Mr. Sofistere was buying plane tickets."

"I don't think it's very likely someone's checking flight reservations. I think it's more likely we're being followed. Let them do their spying and we'll put 'em on a train to Dublin, then take a night bus to Prague."

I nodded, thinking it was a good idea if Mr. Sofistere didn't know our route, either. "We can't be too careful," I said. "Do you mind if we tag along today? It's probably better if we stay together."

"Suit yourself," he said.

"Where're you going?"

His grin was enigmatic. "You'll see."

-35-

Later in the day, Jake handed a taxi driver a piece of paper with an address, and the four of us stepped out of the white Peugeot taxi in front of a plain-looking storefront with a sign that read JOIALLERIE.

"Jewelry shop," Lou translated. "What do you want with—ah. You want to analyze the stones on the bottom of the letterbox. Good idea."

"I heard some expats in the hotel discussing importing emeralds. This guy's supposed to be good."

We stepped inside. A huge bearded man stood behind a counter laden with an array of gemstones. I couldn't shake the notion he was a trained bear offering up the wares of a wealthy sheik.

"May I help you?" he said.

Jake never seemed surprised that foreigners spoke English, as if it was what they should be doing. "We need a little expert analyzin'."

"*Monsieur?*" the man said, confused by Jake's accent.

"We need an analysis of some gemstones," Lou said.

"What is it that you have?"

Jake pulled out the letterbox, turned it over, and showed him the bottom. "We need an opinion on these. It's hard to see right now, but—"

"Quartz crystals," the man said.

Jake's eyes widened.

"They are not hard to re-cog-nize," he said, his voice rising on the last syllable. "If I may be permitted to take to the back for a quick look see?"

"Sure," Jake said. "Be careful. It's an important family heirloom."

"*Oui oui.* But of course."

The man cupped the box in his paws and sidled through a rear door. After a while, he emerged with a thoughtful expression.

"Zee craftsmanship is amazing. The stones have been cut into extremely small pieces and . . . affixed . . . to the bottom of the box. And they form some kind of patt-ern in the bottom left corner."

"Yes, we're aware of that," Lou said. "Family tradition."

"And where is your family from?"

"England."

The man looked at Lou and then back at the letterbox. He shrugged, as if it wasn't his concern.

"How long do the crystals last?" Jake asked.

"They are mi-ne-rals, of course. Zhey last forever."

"I didn't realize crystals could illuminate so strongly," Asha said.

"*Oui.*" He ran his hands over the stones. "Your crystals are of a varietal especially conducive to illumination. Moreover, they are phosphorescent."

"What's the difference?" I asked.

"To fluoresce you need light source. Phosphorescent crystals can absorb the light slowly, and still illuminate after the light source is removed. They are rare, these stones. I cannot tell you where they were cut or put on the box, but I can tell you where they were most likely . . . where they were . . . what is zhe word . . . ." He snapped his fingers. "Har-vested."

"Where they're from," Lou stated.

"*Oui.*"

"And?" Jake asked, his voice sharp with eagerness.

"*Lituanie.* What is it you call this country?"

"Lithuania," Lou said.

The jeweler refused to take our francs, insisting it was no trouble. We thanked him and left. Jake told him he would make a good Southerner.

"Lithuania," I said as we left the shop. I knew it was one of the oldest countries in Europe, somewhere north of Poland on the Baltic Sea. "That's congruent with what Mr. Sofistere told us about the carving on the edges of the box. Remember? He said it was a style used in Southern Russia and the

Baltic States. And that it was odd that the box turned up in England when it did."

"But even if the stylized wood and stones are from or inspired by the Baltic region," Asha said, "the map and the Ogham inscription could have been added at any time and at any place. The more important question is what the Druids were using it for."

"I suppose you're right," Lou said, thoughtful. "When did the Druids die out?"

"It's hard to say," Jake said. "Unlike most indigenous religions they encountered, the Romans feared the Druids and went to great lengths to wipe them out. No one really knows how deep in Europe they pushed or how long they survived."

"Or whether they died out at all," Asha said quietly.

We talked it over for a few more minutes, not reaching any conclusions, and then made the long trek back to the hotel. Once again, we only seemed to encounter more questions.

Lou discovered that two buses left for Prague that night, at seven and at ten, from a bus station on the northern outskirts of Paris. We decided on the later bus, since it would be dark and we could make a show of going to bed before sneaking away.

Asha took a quick nap before we left, but I couldn't sleep. I hit an Internet café near our hotel and started my research on Lucius Sofistere. I found almost nothing on the Internet other than a thirty-year-old article in the *Times Picayune*, when Lucius had opened Antiques and Objets d'Art. Before that he was a blank.

Scratching my chin, I decided to play outside the sandbox. I logged onto LexisNexis, one of the world's two premier legal research sites, and used Toureau Dagmon's general default password to log on to the horribly expensive database. LexisNexis contained not just case law, but records of all types, including arrest and civil suit proceedings, mortgage history—just about anything an aggressive attorney might grab onto.

Mr. Sofistere was clean. Too clean. He didn't even have a residence or vehicle purchase history, which meant he must have bought his house through a corporation.

Who does that, I wondered?

Also, I'd never known someone from the New Orleans upper crust to be so low-key on the social scene. Someone as wealthy as Mr. Sofistere should have a socialite paper trail, unless he was going to great lengths to stay out of the limelight. The old *Times Picayune* article mentioned that he had just arrived in New Orleans, but, oddly, it hadn't noted from where.

My resources overseas were limited, so I called Bobby Gravois, a private investigator whom I had used on a few cases. Bobby was a hard-boiled Cajun on retainer with Toureau Dagmon, but he did plenty of work on the side. I trusted him and he was good.

First up: producing a birth record for one Lucius Sofistere.

-36-

A few hours remained before we were to slink into the night, fleeing pursuers we could not even name. I climbed to the rooftop terrace of our hotel, trying to organize the thoughts flooding my mind. Thoughts I had been storing until I had time to try to make sense of them.

When I caught a glimpse of the walls of Pere Lachaise in the distance, I wondered if my subconscious had guided me to the roof, perhaps to unite with the more overt half of my psyche, which dwelled on that terrible night in the cemetery every minute of every hour. Pere Lachaise had become a symbol of all that was dark and secret in life, all that lurks beneath the shallow veneer of that which we call normal.

Not in my wildest dreams, aloft in my ivory tower of law, could I have imagined an experience like this. We were trekking across Europe, searching for a map that might lead to nowhere or to something that had been lost to time or thieves, pursued by unknown and terrifying entities. There was no reward, no monetary gain, no promise of fame or fortune.

So why go on?

Asha was the easiest to figure out. She was convinced her little brother's spirit was lost and reaching out to her, and she believed the letterbox had somehow facilitated this encounter from the beyond.

I could see it in her eyes. She was past rationality. Asha was desperate to help her brother and she wasn't going to stop.

I also knew there was more to the story, some important detail or past event which she had yet to reveal. I was afraid that if pressed, Asha might tell me something I didn't want to hear.

But I knew it was time to ask.

Jake was, well, Jake. The danger, the search, the uncertainty: none of these things seemed to faze him. Jake's profession was the pursuit and study of religious relics, so I understood the determination to discover the letterbox's secrets. Yet he was an anomaly to me, a religious man who lived as if he had nothing to lose.

I had looked into Jake's eyes, as well. The man did not fear death—and not in an *I-will-be-in-heaven-someday* kind of way. The sentiment was more *I-have-nothing-to-live-for-and-death-can-kiss-my-ass*.

Whether or not the rest of us continued, for whatever reasons he had buried in his stoic heart, I knew Jake would pursue the secrets of the letterbox to the bitter end.

And Lou: my closest friend was most comfortable on his couch or reclining at his favorite table in Maison. He did not like change, shied away from danger, and alleged that he did not care about the spiritual connotations of the search.

So why was Lou still around? My guess was because his life was a tribute to half-finished pursuits. Lou had always aimed not for the stars, but for the light switch next to the television. Though he had a number of advanced degrees, those came easy to him; being a student and obtaining degrees was the path of least resistance.

I thought this quest was an opportunity for Lou to make a mark, to finish something. He wanted to prove to us—and more importantly to himself—that he could do it.

Moreover, Lou had not been himself since the man in the crypt had asked about Kika. I didn't know how the man had found out about her, but it had shaken Lou. Shaken him hard. I doubted he was about to become a believer, but what atheist didn't long, in a deep dark corner of his self-proclaimed nonexistent soul, for meaning and purpose and creation, rather than cosmic dice?

And me? The more obvious reason was the soft-spoken, enigmatic, dark-eyed girl I was falling in love with. Because of her brother, Asha was seeing this quest through, and the only thing I knew for certain was that she wouldn't be alone.

But there was another reason.

I didn't know where the ancient path of the letterbox might lead us. I had no answers for the things we had seen. But the possibility existed that we had witnessed occurrences without rational explanation—supernatural occurrences—and that the map we were following was exactly what the letterbox claimed it to be, in its dead and forgotten language.

The God Path.

What a brazen, ludicrous, irresistible claim.

I realized how much I wanted it to be real. Like the secret heart of the atheist, I too yearned for purpose, a reason for love and suffering and simple human existence.

How could I live the rest of my life knowing I might have uncovered even the tiniest, most obfuscated part of *the* answer?

It was unthinkable.

I returned to the hotel just before dark and found Asha waiting in our room, her face strained.

"Where were you?" she said. "I was worried."

I gave her a quick kiss. "I just needed to try and clear my head."

"Is it clear?"

"Not at all."

I threw my pack together and we left the hotel. We met Jake and Lou two blocks down the street, outside a kiosk. The streets were quiet as we waited for a cab. After switching taxis at the Gare de l'Est bus station, we directed the driver to a station in the Montpellier district. Lou asked him to take a circuitous route, and we saw no sign of pursuit.

I was surprised at how barren the station was. We bought our tickets and headed to terminal number two; the ten p.m. bus to Prague was the only scheduled departure.

As we waited in uneasy anticipation for the driver, keeping an eye out for the Druids, I kept expecting the shifty men lolling about the bus station to shuck off their rags and reveal those gleaming white robes.

At last a short, balding man with a worn gray uniform and an insipid face walked over to platform two. In a listless voice, he called out for all passengers to board. No one stirred except us. We loaded our luggage under the bus and shrugged off the driver's halfhearted attempts to help us. We chose seats in the rear as the bus warmed up.

"I hope they get on a plane to Ireland," Lou said. "Serve the bastards right."

Jake maintained his hawkish stare out the window. "We might be in the clear for now, but we need to move fast in Prague."

He turned to his side, leaned against the window, and pulled his hat over his face. I hadn't planned to sleep, but the darkness and soft hum of the bus lulled me. I began to drift, comforted by the weight of Asha's head against my shoulder.

We passed the German and Czech borders. Passengers got on and off. Sometime deep in the night, the bus slowed and then ground to a halt. I stretched and lifted my head, looking for lights signaling our arrival at a station, but I saw nothing except darkness and a sliver of asphalt.

"Where are we?" Asha murmured.

"I don't know," I said, realizing uneasily that we were the only passengers left.

"Maybe the driver needs to take a leak," Lou said.

I poked my head up and saw the driver sitting up front, doing nothing.

"Hey," Jake said. "*Bonjour hombre! Ciao!*"

The driver didn't move. Out of the corner of my eye I saw a flash of light. I looked out the window and gave a strangled cry.

Asha screamed. "Oh my God!"

In a barren field to the left of the bus, fifty yards away, the night sky had brightened, lit by a huge tripod stand that had burst into flame. Hanging from the apex of the tripod was a round wooden cage, swinging slowly back and forth in the fire.

Suspended inside the cage, limbs attached to the bars in a spread-eagle position, was a man pumping out jagged, soul-scraping screams.

-37-

I stared in frozen dread at the spectacle, nauseated by the stench of charred flesh drifting to the bus. Seeing a line of white-robed Druids walking steadily towards us snapped me back to reality. Behind them, a group of figures in black rags shuffled and jerked around the base of the tripod stand.

"*Drive!*" Jake yelled at the conductor, who was staring open-mouthed at the sinister parade.

"What is that?" the driver asked in a frightened voice.

Jake took out his knife and sprinted to the front of the bus. "I'm not here to hurt you, but if you don't start this bus right this second I'm gonna give you a smiley face where it don't belong."

The driver didn't need a translation. He fumbled for the keys and shoved them into the ignition. The bus rumbled to life.

"Jake!" Lou yelled. "They're almost here!"

I turned and saw the Druids steps away from the windows, some of them going for the rear door and some approaching the front.

"Aidan, watch the rear door. Cut anyone that makes it in. Lou and Asha, watch the windows."

I pulled the knife Jake had given me and stood in front of the emergency exit. The bus lurched forward, and I cursed the fact we weren't in a more mobile vehicle.

I heard a loud *crack* and glanced back. A Druid had broken through the glass on the front door. Jake kicked him twice in the chest from the top of the steps. The Druid doubled over and fell off the bus. Another approached, and Jake did the same. Lou and Asha were racing around the bus, trying to lock all the windows. When I turned back, I saw a Druid with an axe ready to swing at the emergency exit.

I held my knife up, trying to keep my hand steady, adrenaline as much as fear affecting my reflexes. I ducked behind a seat as the Druid's axe struck the exit window, spraying glass across the back of the bus. I heard a scream from behind as I stood to face the man, but I couldn't turn around. The back entrance was wide open.

The Druid dropped his axe and grabbed onto the bus. I stomped on his fingers until he let go, but two more rushed the opening. One of them pulled himself halfway up, and I followed Jake's lead and kicked him in the face. He fell off, and I kicked at the other one. I missed and the momentum of the kick spun me around—and then I slipped.

It might have been blood or sweat or loose glass, but I ended up on my side in the aisle, looking straight at the Druid who had almost pulled himself inside. All I could see was shadowy features under the white cowl, and panic overtook me. I kicked at him from my back as hard and as fast as I could, thinking only of the man suspended inside the cage, burning alive on the side of the highway.

The Druid fell off at the same time two more grabbed onto the back of the bus. I scrambled for the knife and yelled for help. Finally the bus began to pick up steam, and Jake sprinted back to help me. He kicked off another Druid, and as the bus sped up, the remaining assailant dropped away.

I stood panting in front of the broken rear window, peering through the darkness to see if they were still pursuing us, smoke from the swinging cage polluting the night sky. I kept swallowing to avoid vomiting from the smell.

Then I turned and saw Lou kneeling in the aisle, holding Asha's head in his lap as blood poured down her face.

-38-

A soft *no* escaped my lips. I rushed to take off my outer shirt and gently lifted the back of Asha's head. My hands trembled as I pulled up the armrest and helped Lou ease her into a prone position.

"I think I'm okay," she groaned, and I felt relief on a scale I hadn't known existed. Her eyes shifted to look at me, and she managed a faint smile.

I checked her pulse, forcing myself to keep a clear head. Lou handed me his water bottle. I started cleaning blood off her face.

"She must have been hit by flying glass when they broke through the window," Jake said. "These buses are so old their glass shatters like a plate."

We cleaned up enough blood to uncover the wound: a long cut just above her hairline.

"Somebody give me a clean shirt," Jake said, "and I'll make a bandage."

She looked down at her hands and shirt. "There's so much blood."

"You've got quite a gash," Jake said as he wrapped the wound. "You're gonna be fine, but you gave us a scare." He turned to me and said, his voice low, "Don't let her sleep with that head injury."

She eased against the seat rest. Jake and I looked at each other, and I followed him to the front of the bus.

Jake grabbed the back of the driver's neck. The bus slowed, and Jake leaned over. "Don't slow down. Just keep doing what you're doing."

The bus resumed its acceleration.

"Looks like you speak a little English," Jake said, his voice calm but with an unmistakable edge. "Is that right?"

"Yes. Little."

"But you un-der-stand me?"

"Yes. Please speak slow."

"Oh, I will. Now answer my questions, or I'm gonna throw you out the door and drive this bus myself. Do you have any doubt I'll do that?"

The driver looked back at Jake, eyes wide. "No."

"Good. Now, where's the closest hospital?"

"*Plzeň*. Pilsen."

The driver's seedy little voice fit his appearance. His hands shook on the wheel as he answered Jake's questions, and it was clear that self-preservation was his number one priority in life.

"First off, you're gonna drive us straight to the closest hospital in Pilsen."

The driver nodded and tried to look back, but Jake tightened his grip. "I sorry about—" the driver began.

"I don't want your sorry. Just answer my questions. Why'd you stop the bus?"

"Last night, in Paris. I vas drinking at bar and two men approach. One man say, 'Do you vant to make easy money?' I say of course. He say, 'Very simple. Tomorrow night, on route to *Praha*, you do one simple thing. Very simple.'

"He say me, 'You know train bridge after Czech border? Ten kilometers after bridge, you stop bus for five minutes. No more. Stay in seat. Then you start bus and go to *Praha*. Very simple. Three hundred euros.' I say yes, and he give me money."

"Which bar?" I asked.

"I no know. In Montmarte."

"Didn't you think what the man asked was a little strange?"

"Of course," he said. "But it vas simple thing, and for three hundred euros . . . five minutes, he say. Vhy not?"

"I guess you got your why not," Jake said. "Who were they? What'd they look like?"

"Two men. I no see faces. They have . . . have . . . ."

I made a motion of pulling a cowl over my face. "Hoods?"

"Yes, yes. Cover faces. And bar is dark. Please, I know nothing more. I swear it."

"Did one of these men have a burn scar on the back of his hand?"

He thought for a moment, then swallowed and nodded. Jake tightened his grip, then leaned down next to the driver's ear. "Those men who gave you the money, the ones responsible for that shenanigan outside the bus? They're like Santa Claus compared to me. If you don't take us straight to the nearest hospital, you're gonna wish you were back in that cage with the burning man."

Jake eased his grip, and the driver whipped his head up and down in agreement.

We returned to the others. I sat next to Asha and she grabbed my hand.

"I could smell it," she said. "I could smell the flesh."

"Me, too."

"They couldn't have," she whispered, fear and shock smothering her face.

Jake went to his backpack and pulled out an old, thin, leather-bound book. The title was *History of the Druids.* He flipped through the book until he came to an earmarked page. When I saw what it was, my stomach bottomed out, and I gripped the seat in front of me.

In the center of the page loomed a replica of the scene we had just witnessed: a man, suspended spread-eagled inside a human birdcage, screaming as his body writhed in flames.

"Jesus," Lou said.

His face grim, Jake read a passage from the book. "'The penchant of the Druid high priests for human sacrifices shocked even the Romans, who were accustomed to such sights in the brutal world of the arena. Celtic prisoners of war were routinely given to the high priests, who made sacrifices to their gods of these unfortunate captives. Caesar reports how captives were burned alive in giant wicker cages.'"

CZECH REPUBLIC

-39-

True to his word, the driver took us to an urgent-care center on the outskirts of Plzeň, the birthplace of Pilsner beer. Asha's wound required stitches. After her discharge, we splurged on a taxi for the final hour into Prague.

So much for sneaking into the Czech Republic. Instead we limped, tired and frightened and angry, discretion a forgotten ambition, into a secure Western hotel in a quiet neighborhood near the old town.

That night we gathered in Lou's room. My old friend was smoking next to a cracked window, and Asha sat next to me on the bed, staring into space. Jake paced the room like a caged animal.

"I know what we think we saw outside the bus," Lou said, "but what did we really see? I refuse to believe that was real."

"I don't care if it was real," Asha said. "It was *sick*."

Jake kept pacing the room. Lou folded his arms and grimaced. "I won't disagree with that."

Asha kneaded her hands together, then spoke with bravado I could tell was forced. "The next portion of the map is in a church. We'll go there during the day, figure out where to go next, and move on. They've yet to approach us in a crowd."

I felt madness cavorting about the room. I realized I had underestimated the impact of seeing her brother. Asha wasn't thinking straight when it came to the letterbox. She wasn't thinking at all.

But once again, she had taken the choice away from me.

"You know it won't be that easy," Lou muttered.

Jake took the letterbox out of his backpack and set it on the bed, face-down. We crowded around. "Each map section takes up roughly the same amount of space, and the map is running in a snake-like pattern from the bottom left to the upper right corner. There appear to be six sections, and we're here, at the third, right now."

I stated the obvious. "Halfway."

As we all stared at the map, I knew the others were thinking the same thing I was: after what we had been through on the first half of the journey, I didn't even want to think about what might happen on the second.

Later that night, as I lay in bed with Asha still and quiet in my arms, trying to find solace in sleep, I again felt as if I were under some sort of spell. I tried to tell myself we would be more careful, that justice would be served and secrets revealed. Instead I could think only of Asha's hands passing through those of her brother, of running headlong through Pere Lachaise cemetery, of the shrouded figure in the tomb, and of the man in the wicker cage, screaming as the flames consumed him.

Per the doctor's orders, we holed up inside the hotel for two days while Asha convalesced, putting off Mr. Sofistere's questions by claiming she had a nasty flu. Lou and I scoured the news for reports of a man burned to death near the Czech border—surely there would be something—but no word came through. We filed a police report that turned into an interrogation. After admitting we never saw a corpse and could not ID anyone involved, the Czech police asked us if we had been taking drugs and all but shoved us out the door. If the bus driver was still around, we knew he would lie to save his job.

Fear was a miserable manner of existence. Asha walked around the hotel in a trance, eyes red-rimmed and haunted, gazing out of windows with listless eyes. I began looking over my shoulder with every step, imagining a flash of white around a corner or down a darkened hallway.

When Asha removed her bandage on the morning of the third day, the wound was still red around the stitches. Keeping a furtive lookout for the Druids, we passed through Prague's Old Town on the way to the train terminal for Kostel Utes. The morning sun illuminated the fairytale architecture hovering with ethereal splendor above the maze of cobblestone streets. Despite the threat we knew awaited, the beauty of Prague still took my breath away. We walked past the magnificent Charles Bridge on our way to the terminal, and soon we were paralleling the Vltava for the thirty-minute ride to Jake's church.

Fall had arrived in earnest. Prague was on a geographic par with southern Canada, and a distinct chill permeated the air when we stepped off the train at Kostel Utes. At once we saw the rotunda sitting proudly on a cliff face marked by hundreds of small, triangular rock formations jutting out as if in bas-relief. Jake was right—it was a distinct geological feature.

Once again, the scene depicted on the letterbox map had come to life.

"Where's the steeple?" Asha asked. A white cross atop the roof gave the only indication that the edifice was a church.

Jake frowned. "Good question."

A paved road ran through a cluster of provincial homes and shops set along the bank, crossing the river via a narrow bridge. There was no taxi in sight, so we nervously crossed the bridge on foot, then followed the road up the hill.

"I hate climbing," Lou said, as we hiked up the cliff. "We need an Internet quest."

"Shut your pie-hole," Jake said.

"You need to learn to appreciate the finer things in life," Lou wheezed. "Like complaining. It's liberating."

"I never wanted a sister," Jake muttered.

Although short, the climb was steep, and Lou still favored his injured ankle. The road led to an empty church parking lot.

After scouring the grounds and the road below for signs of the Druids, we stepped into a plain gray narthex. Open double doors led to a sanctuary of equal thrift. The only two items in view were a chest-high wooden table to the left of the chapel doors, and a lower table to the right. A padlocked glass case dominated the higher table, an array of church literature was spread out on the lower.

Jake crossed himself and stepped to the glass case. Beneath a plaque engraved in Czech, the case housed a Bible, rosary beads, a crucifix, a clay bowl, and a strip of tattered white cloth blotted with dark stains.

Lou peered down at the reliquary. "Ridiculous."

Jake cut off his retort as a tall, middle-aged priest with an angular forehead emerged from a side corridor.

"Can I help you?" he asked, in perfect English. "I'm Father Novak."

Silver hairs graced his temples, and his face possessed a magnetic calm.

"Father, I'm Jake Fleniken, a Catholic scholar. We were traveling in the area, and I thought I'd drop in for a look."

"A scholar?" he said brightly. "What a privilege. Sadly, our church used to be much more interesting. During the Occupation, the Soviets turned the church into a military outpost. Many of our historic items were spirited away to other churches. We've been pushing to have these returned, but so far we've only managed to bring back this reliquary."

I exchanged a glance with Jake.

"I'm sure this church with its rich history," I said, "once contained some fascinating Catholic relics."

The priest smiled, wistful. "I've only seen pictures. In fact, I have a book memorializing that very subject. Would you care to take a look?"

"If you have the time," Jake said.

"It's been a slow day." He gave a rueful grin. "Actually, it's been a slow year. And I've neglected my priestly duties. Would any of you like to give confession before we begin?"

Asha and Lou and I declined. Jake shuffled his feet and looked down. "Father, I . . . no, not today."

I wondered how long it had been since Jake's last confession.

Father Novak left the room and returned with a thin hardback tome. It was difficult to stay focused as he flipped through the book and translated the tedious story of Kostel Utes. Lou's eyes glossed over, Asha maintained a distracted smile, and even Jake was losing patience.

The priest droned on. "This ancient cross is one of two objects found at the original site which, curiously enough, are Celtic in origin." He flipped the page. "The next item—"

"Father," I said. From Jake's raised eyebrows, I noticed he had caught the same thing. "Sorry to interrupt, but can we go back to that page?"

Father Novak looked surprised at our interest. "Of course." He flipped the page, and we took a good look at the picture. It depicted a solid iron cross with a circle surrounding the intersection of the two halves of the crucifix.

"How interesting," Asha said sweetly, catching on. "I didn't realize the Celts were in Bohemia."

"Oh, yes, for quite some time."

"What about the other Celtic object that was mentioned?" Jake asked. "I'm curious about that."

The priest ran his eyes down the page. "Let me check the index." He flipped to the back of the book. "Celtic Cross and . . . Celtic Triquetra. Or triad. Page one hundred and twelve. Let's see."

The priest flipped through the book again, stopping at an illustration of a large bronze medallion with an unusual shape: a tripartite symbol composed of three interlocking compressed circles. The intertwined circles, each of which reminded me of the Christian fish symbol without the tail, created a space in the middle that looked like the bottom half of a heart.

Unlike the rest of the solid medallion, bronze bars ran both horizontally and vertically across the open space in the center, creating a design remarkably similar to the chessboard window at Castello di Selva.

-40-

Father Novak continued to read, oblivious to our barely restrained elation. "Although originally pagan icons, both the Celtic Cross and the Triquetra evolved into symbols of Christianity."

"Father, does the text state where these two relics were taken?" Jake asked. "We wouldn't mind checking them out if we get the chance."

The priest turned to a previous page. "The cross was sent to a museum in Cesky Krumlov, and the triad was sent to Kostnice Chapel. Kostnice is in Kutna Hora, a small town less than an hour from Prague by train."

He closed the book and gave us directions. We thanked him for his time and hurried down the cliff.

By the time we returned to Prague, the sun had started to descend. To avoid traveling at night, we packed up the next morning and took the first train out.

Kutna Hora was a typical Bavarian town: sloping red-tiled roofs, constricted cobblestoned streets, spires rising above the town like gigantic black needles. I had only visited this part of Europe in the crowded summer months, and the lack of tourists lent the town an isolated feel. The quiet Gothic center was unsettling, as if the buildings themselves lorded over the town.

We found a decent hotel tucked safely into the center of town, dropped our bags, and asked for directions to the chapel. We found Kostnice standing off by itself, atop a low hill littered with weathered tombstones. The cemetery was unkempt, full of weeds and moss-covered grave markers.

"There aren't a lot of people around," Asha said nervously. "What if—"

"It's the middle of the day in a town," Jake said. "Not to mention it's a chapel."

"I don't know what that's got to do with anything," Lou said, "but at least there's a guard at the door."

The chapel's massive stone center tapered to a severe arch at the entrance, reminding me of the neck of a dragon. When Jake opened the imposing wooden door, I took a step back, and Asha inhaled sharply beside me.

Just past the entrance, a flight of steps led downward, and a large cross hung on the cracked stone wall of the stairwell. What shocked me was not the crucifix, but the architect's choice of materials.

The cross was fashioned out of human bones.

Femurs, ulnas, and tibias had been strung together to form the two sections of the cross, and human skulls capped the four ends. We descended to find ourselves in a low-ceilinged antechamber that opened into a much larger room. Candles placed throughout the chapel illuminated walls with the same rough, pitted surface as the stairwell.

There were bones everywhere: draping the walls, framing the archways, hanging from the ceiling, adorning the furnishings, *comprising* the furnishings. Statues of bones, candelabras of bones, portraits of bone, Catholic accoutrements carved from bone.

"Oh my," Asha murmured.

Lou arched his eyebrows, and even Jake looked taken aback. I could only stare in macabre fascination.

"I've heard of ossuaries being made into functional structures before," Lou said, "but never a *church*."

Jake nodded. "I've seen plenty, but nothing like this."

"Ossuary?" I asked.

"A place for storing human bones."

"Who would want to do that?" Asha said, peering upward at the centerpiece of the room, an enormous chandelier dripping strands of bones.

We split up and searched for the Triquetra. The staircase was the only exit, and a vaulted ceiling capped the large room. Four archways signaled alcoves in each corner, and when I drew closer to one, I saw that the alcove concealed a fat, dusty pyramid of bones that rose high above my head. The bone tower interlocked without any discernible support or pattern, and a man-size opening led into the darkened center. I peered nervously inside. It was empty.

Asha walked over. "Any luck?"

"Not yet," I said.

She shuddered. "This place creeps me out. At least in Pere Lachaise the bones weren't visible."

We kept searching. Fronting an alcove near the rear of the chapel was a wooden Christ figure hanging on a cross. Human skulls, situated at the foot of the effigy and tilted upwards in silent regard, mocked the figure as they mocked everything else in the church, screaming with throatless voices: *Believe in what you will, but you will be as us one day.*

An old woman knelt in front of the Christ figure. It was hard to believe this was a functioning place of worship, and even harder to believe someone would choose to utilize it.

I walked behind the Christ figure. Set into the rear wall of the alcove, behind a waist-high rope, was a two-tiered glass case with an array of objects inside. I didn't recognize any of the other pieces, but sitting on the upper shelf was a three-pointed bronze medallion with a curiously patterned center.

The Triquetra.

Asha squeezed my arm, and I waved the others over. Jake and Lou joined us behind the rope. "That's it, all right," Jake said. "Locked up tight."

"What does it represent?" I asked, gazing at the wizened relic.

"It's a little unclear," Jake said, "but the Celts believed in the power of threes, including the three personifications of the mother goddess. At some point, it became a symbol of the Holy Trinity."

Lou threw his hands up. "How do you know all of this and still believe in Christianity?"

"The Holy Trinity is just an adaptive theological doctrine, Commie. Part of the early Church's attempt to understand God and the Resurrection, with the language that they knew. Once you figure out a better way, be sure to let me know. I'll give the Pope a call."

Lou snorted and shook his head.

"So what do we do?" Asha asked.

"Right now, nothing," Jake said. "I need to think, and I've had about enough of this dungeon."

"I second that," Asha said.

As we left the chapel, a man loitering on the street sidled up in threadbare brown overalls. He had the worn look of someone aged prematurely by hard labor, and he wheezed like a lifelong smoker. "Vould you like tour of city?"

We tried to walk away, but he followed us, regaling us with the magnificent places in Kutna Hora only he could show us. Finally Asha stopped, handed him a few bills with a kind smile, and pointed at the ossuary. "Tell us about this place."

The man straightened, pleased to have an audience.

"You stand in front Kostnice Ossuary," he said in tourist English marked by the Slavic lack of articles. "Built in fourteenth century after Abbot of Sedlec bring back dirt," he reached down to grab a handful of earth, "from Golgotha. Where Christ vas crucified. Abbot sprinkle dirt on ground, and Kostnice become holy ground."

"But why all the bones?" Asha asked.

"Plague bring too many dead bodies to cemetery. There vas half-blind monk looking after chapel. He vas mad." He cackled as he said this, as if conjuring an image of the disturbed architect of Kostnice.

"Monk take bones from cemetery and carry them inside, make room for new corpses. Everyone too concerned with plague to notice. Monk make things inside, all from human bones. Forty thousand bones inside Kostnice."

Asha forced a smile. "You know your church."

"I am night vatchman. I give tours during day, in church and in town."

Jake gave me a sly glance. "I'm a photographer. I don't want a tour, but I'll tell you what I do want. And I'll pay you for it."

The man leaned forward at the mention of payment.

"That church would make a great addition to my work," Jake continued. "I took some photos, but I want one of the Christ figure in candlelight. Artistic touch and all that. Being the caretaker, I'm sure you have the keys to the place. Let me inside one night, just for a few minutes, and I'll make it worth your while."

The man looked around. "I no think I can—"

Jake pulled out a hundred-note euro, and the man's eyes widened. Jake started to slide the bill back into his wallet.

"Vait—" the man said. "How much time you need?"

"Fifteen minutes."

"For one hundred euro?"

"That's right," Jake said, keeping the bill exposed.

The caretaker flexed his hands. "No one can see you."

"Don't you worry," Jake said. "When do we meet?"

"Saturday night is best, ten o'clock. Ve meet here. Fifteen minutes, no more. I vill light candles."

"What's your name?" Jake asked.

"Josef."

"Joe, you made a wise decision."

Asha exploded as soon as the man walked off. "We promised we weren't going anywhere else at night!"

"We're not," Lou said. "Or at least I'm not."

I didn't say anything. I knew Jake was going in with or without us.

Jake shrugged. "The opportunity was too good to pass up. It's Saturday night, there'll be plenty of people out and about. Especially as early as ten. Don't worry, I plan on going by myself. I just need a few minutes."

Asha shook her head, and I knew what she was going to say before she said it.

"I don't like this *at all*," she said, "but we stay together. And if there aren't lots of people out, or there's a sign that something isn't right, we find another way."

Jake just grinned.

-41-

Two days of isolation in the hotel, waiting for the next piece of the puzzle while our fears metastasized into tangible things: shadows that slinked around corners, nameless things lurking behind closed doors, a dead current of air drifting into a courtyard.

After dinner in the hotel on the first night, I got a call from Bobby Gravois, my private investigator. I slipped into the lobby to take it.

"You found something?" I asked.

"It's what I didn't find that interests me." His rich Cajun twang sounded incongruous in the middle of Central Europe. "And what I didn't find was a birth certificate."

"Sorry?" I said. "Everyone has a birth certificate."

"I hear ya, podna. But our guy's been scrubbed."

"How do you know?"

"It's got that feel. CIA or witness protection or something. Lucius Sofistere—at least the one living in New Orleans—shouldn't exist. But he does, so that means a false identity. Not sure how far you want to go with this, but—"

"Far."

"You want him, huh?"

"Can you do it? Find out who he is?"

"Probably not," he said slowly, "but I know a guy."

The next afternoon we huddled on wooden benches in front of the hotel, sipping coffee across the street from a sprawling Gothic cathedral with a statue-lined terrace. The day was chilly but tolerable in the sun.

Asha looped an arm through mine. "What do you think we'll find?" she said. "If we reach the end of the map?"

Lou took a puff on his cigarette. "The secret recipe to Italian pizza. Or a gigantic television that spans the universe, with porn from nine dimensions."

"I'm serious," Asha said.

"When it comes to God," Jake said, "you never get what you're looking for. We'll find what we find."

Lou rolled his eyes. When I didn't respond, she nudged me. "Well?"

I hesitated. "I . . . don't know what to think anymore."

"Why are you all so afraid to talk about it?" she said, sitting up. "Don't pretend you haven't thought about what's happened. You've seen the same things I've seen."

"We're being tricked," Lou said. "I don't know how yet, and some of . . . I don't know how they're doing it. And I don't know why. But there *is* an explanation for all of this."

Jake shook his head. "I thought you might've learned something by now. All of you. Open your eyes. Things are *happening* because of this box."

I couldn't help but let my eyes roam upwards, to the sky above and the infinite blackness beyond.

Oh, how I longed for a taste of Jake's faith.

Lou snorted. "We'll start making progress when we stop looking for fairytale answers."

"Let's talk about something we can put a name to," I said. "What's to stop the Druids from showing up at Kostnice tonight?"

"Publicity," Jake replied. "They haven't approached us in a crowd and they won't start tonight. We'll slip in, do our business, and slip back out."

Asha touched her scar and swallowed.

That night, I had left our window cracked to freshen the air, and the breeze rippled through the curtains like the tips of tiny waves. Though we were on the third floor, I closed and locked the window before Asha and I crawled into bed, remembering the levitating Druid at Pompeii.

Two candles flickered at the end of the bed, feathering the room with a hint of gold. Asha stretched languidly under the covers and ran a finger across my chest. Things had seemed more natural between us the last few days.

"I have thought about it, you know," I said. "Where this whole thing is going."

"It's impossible not to."

"I don't know what I believe anymore. I want to believe in something, but . . . I'm sick of saying I don't know."

"We'll get through it," she said. "Whatever it is."

"You don't know that."

That night I felt an edge to our lovemaking. We simply couldn't shake our sense of dread, the tense feeling that something was about to happen, that her dead brother or a Druid or worse was about to come floating through the window.

I dreamt that night of dark things. Things I couldn't talk about in the morning because I couldn't name them to begin with.

Things I begged to forget.

Saturday night arrived at last. Gargoyles peered down from rooftops as we trekked through town, mouths agape, their reptilian eyes seeming to follow us on our way to the "Bone Church," as Jake had dubbed the ossuary.

Similar to Dubrovnik, though in a less sophisticated fashion, the town came alive on the weekend. People of all ages packed the streets, enjoying the last few days of tolerable weather. There was no sign of danger, and we had kept a constant vigil since our arrival in Kutna Hora, scanning relentlessly for a telltale flash of white.

Our guide emerged from a narrow walkway that ran behind the chapel. I turned to Lou, who had proclaimed all week that he was going to wait at the hotel while we went inside.

"Meet you later?" I said.

Lou muttered something to himself, then glanced down the street and at the chapel. "I suppose there're enough people around. Let's get this over with."

The caretaker gave the street a furtive glance, led us to the entrance, and inserted a skeleton key. One by one, we slipped through the doorway.

Just before the caretaker sealed us inside, Jake stuck a hand out, stopping the door. "Now, Joe, we've kept this little deal a secret, haven't we?"

"Of course. If someone know I lose job."

"No one's approached you askin' about us? I've got some . . . competition . . . that has a nasty way of popping up."

Josef looked at Jake in genuine confusion. "No one know."

Jake gave him a long stare. Finally he nodded, then slid a hundred-euro bill into the caretaker's hands. "Just making sure."

Josef closed the door behind us. There were no other entrances and we felt comfortable knowing we had an easy means of egress.

True to his word, Josef had kept a number of candles lit. We had no trouble seeing inside the chapel, but as we looked around to ensure we were alone, I thought I might have preferred the Bone Church to remain in darkness.

Like Pere Lachaise, the ossuary took naturally to the gloom. Bones gleamed eerily in the soft candlelight, dominating the visual interior of the church. I experienced a strange compulsion to stop and run my hands over their smooth surfaces, but we kept to the task and hurried to the alcove housing the Triquetra.

Jake had claimed he could open the locked case. I didn't doubt his abilities, but worried more about a security system. We hadn't seen anything of the sort on our visit, but that didn't mean there wasn't security in place at night, or that the case wasn't rigged.

Again our fears were unrealized. Jake took a hooked metal filing out of his pocket and, after a few minutes, opened the case without an alarm breaking the silence. The chapel itself was secure, and I reasoned that the objects in the case possessed no great value to thieves.

Lou and I set the heavy glass case on the floor. Jake took out the letterbox, and we held our breath as he turned it upside down and placed the patterned center of the Triquetra atop the portion of the stones where the map should continue. After a few moments of gently moving the Triquetra around, it settled into place.

Asha gripped my arm. "Another fit."

"Cut the light," Jake said.

Lou and I made our way around the ossuary extinguishing the candles. When I passed the huge pyramid of bone in the corner, my eyes slid inside the darkened opening to make sure nothing was concealed within, as if I were a child peering into a closet.

We left two candles at the bottom of the staircase, emitting just enough light to guide us back. "Is that good?" I called out.

"The crystals are shining like cat's eyes."

As Lou and I made our way back to the group, I heard the rapid click of Jake's camera. I supposed we had told the caretaker the truth: we were taking nighttime photos of a sort.

Jake stopped shooting as we walked up. "Mission accomplished."

We replaced the glass case, anxious to study the next portion of the map.

"I feel tired or something," Lou said. "Kind of off."

I realized I felt the same as Lou. It had been a long week and a stressful evening.

"You complainin' again?"

"We're all drained," Asha said, "but let's take it outside. I just want to leave."

As we turned to exit, the room was cast into darkness.

-42-

My next breath stuck in my throat. I couldn't see my hand in front of my face, and I felt horribly exposed.

"Nobody panic," Jake said. "It was a probably a draft by the door. My flashlight's in the bag somewhere—lemme see if I can find it. Can't see a blooming thing in here."

I swallowed. What kind of draft traveled all the way down a staircase?

Trying to stay calm, I called Asha's name and reached for her hand. "Over here," she whispered, off to my left. I took a step in her direction with my hands extended.

She called my name again, a few steps away, and I moved towards the sound of her voice. She must be looking for a light switch. Where was that flashlight?

"Asha?" I asked.

"Over here," she whispered again. "By the wall."

My legs grew heavy, and I wanted to lie down and sleep. Something wasn't right. I was about to call out to Jake when Asha said, "Are you close?"

"Stop moving," I said in exasperation. "I'm coming to you."

I bumped into something knobby and dry. *Bone.* I flinched but kept my hands in front of me, moving a few feet over and then shuffling forward. My hands grazed a larger, solid surface, and I realized I must have reached one of the walls.

"I'm right over here," Asha said.

Her voice seemed to be coming from directly ahead. I followed the sound and kept one hand on the wall. The chapel wasn't that big. She *had* to be moving. That, or we both had been walking in circles. I was becoming more and more annoyed at her for not staying in place.

"Jake, where the hell is that flashlight?" I called out. "Lou?"

No answer. I felt a cold sweat breaking out.

I forced myself to keep calm, and took out a switchblade Jake had lent me. I popped the blade. "Asha, can you *stop moving*? It's too dark to wander around."

I heard a muffled sound from up ahead, then a voice cry out in pain.

"Did you trip?" I asked, moving forward as fast as I could in the darkness. I heard another noise, a sound like something being dragged along the floor.

A soft glow of light emanated from up ahead. I started to breathe a sigh of relief—Jake or Lou must have found a candle. "Where is everyone?"

Still no answer.

My hands shook as I crept towards the light. After feeling my way around a corner, I stared in shock at the illuminated scene. Somehow I had entered a dusty stone passageway with a low ceiling, dimly lit by candles in iron sconces. The corridor stretched as far as I could see.

A series of chills swept through me. Where was I, and how had I gotten there?

I checked my phone. No signal. I tried not to panic, but I was losing that battle. My mind screamed at me to turn and race for the exit, but I had to find Asha.

The scraping sound resumed.

"Asha?" I said again, then decided to keep quiet and increase my pace. I could vaguely make out someone ahead of me, further along the tunnel. I couldn't tell who it was, but he or she was moving away. I pressed forward as silently as I could.

As I drew closer, at the edge of my field of vision, I saw a white, hooded shape dragging something through the tunnel that looked like a sack.

I could barely think through the blood rushing to my brain. I couldn't risk calling out, so I crept forward, straining to see while staying well behind the Druid.

A few feet later, I stepped in something sticky. I glanced down and noticed a trail of red liquid on the floor behind the Druid, glistening in the dim light.

I bent to touch it. It was wet. Fresh.

My hands started to shake. I hurried forward and saw the Druid pulling a burlap sack along the floor of the tunnel, with someone struggling inside it.

Someone with wavy black hair trailing from the sack, and a wound leaking blood onto the floor.

OhmyGod.

"Help me," Asha's muffled voice cried out.

Without stopping, the Druid swung his leg in a low arc and kicked Asha through the sack. She shrieked in pain, and he continued dragging her into the depths of the tunnel.

I gripped the handle of the switchblade and sprinted forward, my odd lethargy drowned in pure emotion.

She struggled, and the Druid kicked her again. Harder.

I thought I might implode from the rush of horrified adrenaline. I barreled forward as Asha made a feeble attempt to crawl out of the sack.

This time the Druid stopped, grabbed her head with both hands, and shoved the sack against the wall. Blood flew in every direction, and Asha's scream rattled through the corridor.

Right before I reached them, the Druid made another final, terrible thrust, and I heard a thud as Asha's head met the wall. She went limp and her head lolled out of the sack.

"Asha!" I roared, with the primal fury of the animal trapped inside us all.

I caught up to them and, without the slightest hesitation, plunged the knife as deep into the back of the Druid as it would go.

-43-

I grabbed the Druid's robe with one hand and drove the knife in again and again, unable to think through my grief and rage. The ease with which my knife slid into him surprised me. Too easy, like slicing ripe tomatoes.

Too easy.

I stopped in shock, realizing my knife was sliding so effortlessly through the white robe because there was nothing inside. I let go of both. The knife clanged to the floor, along with the slashed robe.

A burlap sack lay on the floor beside the robes, and I tore into it. Feathery, weightless grains poured out.

Sawdust.

There was no sign of anyone or anything else. No Druid, no Asha, no blood on the floor.

What was happening?

I called out for Asha, but I could barely gather the strength to use my voice. The lethargy I had been feeling returned in force. The room started moving in slow circles, as if I were intoxicated. I fell to my knees and searched in vain for a sign of her.

Then I saw it.

A shadow, walking towards me from the opposite end of the tunnel. I could describe it no other way. It looked like a shadow had coalesced into human form and was striding slowly, purposefully, in my direction.

I tried to get up but failed. My vision blurred as I slumped to my knees again, and the shadow stopped a foot away from me. I recoiled; I could *feel* its presence.

Fear of the unknown, of the supernatural, is not like other fears; it is not a fear of what a thing will do, as one fears a wild animal, but fear in the mere fact that the thing exists. It is not really even fear at all, but dread. A debilitating horror that the thing you are confronted with is not natural, is not of this world.

It pointed at the discarded robe. I looked at the slash marks from my knife, then back up at the shadow.

"I don't understand," I said weakly. "Asha—"

"Dust," it said, in a harsh, intelligent whisper. "You killed for dust."

This was all wrong. I had *seen* what the Druid was doing. Hadn't I?

It stepped aside, revealing an image that burned into my mind.

Ten feet ahead on the tunnel floor, a man lay naked and face-down. He wasn't moving and his back was covered in red slashes. Fresh blood pooled on the ground beside him. I didn't know how I had missed seeing the body, or how his robes had ended up in a separate place.

I gasped. "What is this? Where's Asha!"

I stared at the corpse sprawled on the floor. I didn't know . . . I couldn't think . . . *what had I done?*

The thing swept his hand across the body. "Look on that of which you are capable."

I tried to stand but sank lower, to my elbows. I knew I had to find a way to escape and help the others. Yet I couldn't seem to focus, and dark thoughts sprang unbidden into my mind.

I had wanted to put that knife so deep into the Druid's back that it would never come out. I laughed at myself, slightly hysterical. I didn't care one bit about the morality of that act. I didn't care if it damned me forever. All I could think about was Asha's head being driven—

Please, God, let it not have been her.

The thing still hovered above me. I could see the shadows that formed its feet and legs pooling on the stone floor. My hands gripped the pitted surface and pushed, but I collapsed on my stomach.

"Now you have seen," it said, in its sibilant whisper. "Now you know."

I lay on the floor as the thing watched in silence. It seemed to shrink and enlarge at the same time, amorphous, never coming to rest. I couldn't tell if the effect was real or inside my head.

It drew closer, almost touching me. Words sprang unbidden to my lips, a half-remembered childhood prayer.

"You come to this place bearing *that*," it said, "without faith, without knowledge of yourself? What is it you think awaits you?"

"Asha," I moaned. "Where is she?"

"I suggest you meet yourself before you continue," it said. "Look into the recesses of your soul, to the places you fear to name, to the dark below the dark—"

As my consciousness slipped away, the last thing I remembered was wondering whether this vile thing would enter my dreams and continue poisoning my mind.

I closed my eyes and felt no more.

-44-

I groaned.

It was so dark I couldn't see a thing, and my head felt like someone was pounding a nail into it. Where was I? And why was no one—I remembered.

It all came back in a rush, though everything seemed foggy. Surreal. I cast a fearful glance into the darkness, searching for dead bodies and walking shadows, then managed to call out for Asha.

"Aidan? Is that you?"

Lou's voice. It sounded shaky.

"Lou! Thank God. Where are you?"

"Over here," he said.

I started towards him, then cringed as a light erupted in my face.

"Sorry about that," Jake's familiar drawl called out. He looked a little pale, but his voice was firm. He swung the flashlight around, illuminating Lou, who looked unhurt.

"Asha!" I cried out again, when I didn't see her.

She stepped into the light, off to my left. Except for a disturbed look on her face, she seemed fine. No bloodstains, no torn clothes, no crushed back of the—I shuddered away that mental image and went to her, shivery with relief.

"I thought I'd never see you again," I whispered.

"What? I'm a bit groggy, but fine. I'm . . ." she trailed off. "I saw some things."

"So did I. Terrible things."

"Why don't we get out of this place before we start yapping?" Jake said. "Everyone all right? No broken bones or twisted ankles?"

We all nodded.

He picked up his backpack. "Good. Then let's—" he broke off midsentence as he pawed through the backpack, turning it upside down and then letting it fall out of his hands.

It was empty.

Asha looked even more stricken than Jake. She started a feverish search of the floor. "You must have dropped it. We have to find it."

Jake lit the candles with his lighter. We combed the chapel but found no sign of the letterbox.

"It's not here," Jake said in disbelief. "They snatched it while we were out."

Asha slumped against the wall, and Lou put his hands to his temples. "My head feels like it's been hit with a baseball bat."

"I felt odd soon after we walked in here," I said.

"They must have drugged us."

Jake slammed a fist into the wall. "Cowards!"

Before we left, we searched the chapel a final time for a trapdoor, a hidden passage, anything we might have missed.

There was nothing but bones and dust.

Jake and Asha looked numb as we filed outside. The horizon gleamed with first light, and in the semi-darkness we noticed a shape slumped in the bushes beside the steps. We hurried to Josef and turned him over. The caretaker's head sagged in Jake's grasp.

Jake checked his pulse. "He's fine. Although *he* might've been hit by a baseball bat. There's a huge knot on top." He reached into his backpack and took out a bottle of water, then poured some on Josef's face and massaged his temples.

The caretaker stirred. "Vhat happened?"

"You don't remember?"

Josef squinted in confusion, trying to think through the fog of his newly awakened state. I knew the feeling.

"Here," Jake said, moving Josef's hand to the bump on his head. "You must have tripped and fell."

"Yes," he murmured.

We offered to take him to a hospital, but he shrugged us off and wandered away, holding his head and muttering to himself.

We trudged back to our hotel through the early-morning calm of Kutna Hora's cobblestone streets, stunned by the loss of the letterbox. We went our separate ways as soon as we reached the hotel, the events of the night careening through my mind like a derailed locomotive.

Exhausted, I stumbled into bed and held Asha tight. I thought I might never let her go.

Asha and I pulled ourselves out of bed at noon. We found Jake and Lou smoking in silence in the common room. Everyone had the same haunted look I knew was in my own eyes, and Jake looked like he hadn't slept.

"You saw something, too?" Asha asked them. "Both of you?"

Lou stared out the window. Jake took a long drag on his cigarette.

"Jake?" Asha repeated.

He began pacing the room. "It's not important."

"Maybe it would help if we all shared what we saw," Asha said.

"I said it's not important."

Asha and I exchanged a glance. "Did they take the camera?" she asked.

"Nope," Jake said. "And I've got the photos.

Lou voiced the obvious, still staring out the window. "They won't do us much good now."

As I looked at the agonized faces of my friends, I realized something had happened to me in that tunnel. An anger had bubbled over, one born of pain and fear and frustration, one which had started to emerge the first time the Druids had appeared in the woods and made me feel weak and helpless. An anger which had reached a crescendo when Asha had been injured on the bus, and which had gone beyond the breaking point in Kostnice.

What they had done to me in the chapel had been terrible beyond words, unforgivable. I didn't even care how they had done it.

I just knew someone had to pay.

I pounded the wall with my fist. "*Damn them.*"

Asha looked at me in surprise.

"I want to do something," I said, fists clenched. "I just don't know what."

"That's good, Counselor," Jake said softly. "Now you're getting in the game." He took another long drag and blew the smoke out. "And I do know what to do. I'm gonna figure out where the next location is, I'm gonna go there, and somewhere along the way I'm gonna get the letterbox back and settle a little score with the people following us. You might call it my new mission in life."

Asha was chewing on her lip and looking at her hands. Lou turned back to the window as Jake stood to leave.

"As soon as I figure out the next location," he said, his voice low and menacing, "I'm leaving."

-45-

Jake disappeared for the afternoon. The rest of us lingered in the common room, afraid to venture off alone, hovering over our coffees like monks who had taken a vow of silence.

After dinner at the hotel, Asha and I drifted to the patio. Leaves sprinkled the ground, a smattering of stars hovered overhead.

I sat on a wide stone bench with my back against a tree. Asha sat in front of me, encircled in my arms. Although I wanted to forget what I had seen and done, I felt the nearly insatiable urge to communicate one feels after a traumatic event.

"I killed someone, Asha."

She whipped around to face me.

"At least I tried to. Last night in the chapel or . . . an underground tunnel . . . I really don't know where I was. But I was following you and it happened so fast and—"

"Wait," she said. "Slow down. Start from the beginning."

My words poured forth in a cacophony of purged guilt and memories. I worried she would judge me for what I had done, but the thought of not telling her the truth seemed more abhorrent than any consequences my words might have.

Asha's face had gone white by the time I finished.

"Do you despise me?" I asked.

She traced a finger down my cheek. "You thought you were protecting me."

I looked away. I knew the end was justified; it was the means that bothered me.

She crossed her legs and rested her chin in her hands. "I was never in a sack, and I never called out to you inside the chapel."

"Then who—it sounded just like you. And the head in the sack, except there was only sawdust . . . ." I put my head in my hands. "Didn't you hear me calling? What were you doing?"

"Let's finish your story first. Someone obviously led you away from us so they could . . . ." Her face twisted into a furious expression. "I would have died if it had been you and I was watching. I'm glad you did what you did."

She looked down at my clenched fists. "It's over," she whispered.

"I thought you were dead. Before I killed him, I thought you were dead. I'll never forget the feeling."

She stroked my arm and drew me close. "You didn't kill anyone," she said gently. "You do realize that? You were tricked and drugged and nothing you thought you saw really happened."

"But why? To get me out of the chapel? Why not just drug me or hit me? Why put me through that?"

"I don't know. They're evil."

"I know I was drugged, but that shadow thing . . . something was there, Asha."

"Okay," she soothed. "Okay."

"You believe in spirits. Do you think it was an evil spirit?"

Her left hand twitched and moved to her knee. "I don't want to think that way. I don't want you to think you saw an evil spirit."

"But you think it's possible."

This time her hands moved to her brow, steepling against her forehead. She kept her face covered for long moments before meeting my gaze again, her eyes a whirlpool of emotion. "There's something you need to know. About my past."

My own fears receded, replaced by a dormant queasiness.

She let out a long breath. "I was a child prodigy."

I looked up, unsure what I had expected to hear but sure it wasn't that. "What kind of prodigy?"

"I could talk to people," she said softly, her voice drifting away from the present. "That is, people who had passed away. Spirits."

I blinked. That was most definitely not what I had expected to hear.

"You were a medium?" I couldn't hide the relief in my voice. I had worried she was married or a fugitive or involved in something shady with Mr. Sofistere. "What's wrong with that? And why do you no longer . . . ." I remembered her constant searching, her obsession with all things spiritual. "Something happened, didn't it?"

She nodded, eyes and voice lowered. "I spoke to my first spirit when I was twelve. For five years I helped people speak to their loved ones, and I was even on talk shows. It felt like a circus. And then," she swallowed, "my brother died. He died and it all went away."

"I don't understand."

"I never heard another voice, never communicated with another spirit. It's like I was cut off from that world at the moment I needed it most. I wanted to hear from him so badly, Aidan. Just one little word, an impression . . . but there was *nothing*. As if it had all been in my mind. And that's what everyone thought, the doctors and even my parents. That it was all in my mind. That's even . . . that's even what I've come to believe."

"That's why you've been searching so hard for evidence of the supernatural. To find your brother, but also searching for proof that . . . ."

"You can say it. Searching for proof I wasn't crazy. That I never heard anything but the voices inside my own head."

I took her hand, and she looked down. "There's something else," she said. "Ever since my brother died, I haven't really felt with my heart. I know things in my head, but it's as if there's a black hole inside me, sucking my emotions away."

"Did you . . . have you tried to get professional help with this?" I asked gently.

"My parents made me go to a shrink for a year. You can imagine how that went. Either I was crazy or a liar, because how could their little prodigy fail to talk to the one person everyone needed to hear from most? We never recovered. I went to school overseas, my mom died a few years later, and my dad and I barely talk. He still doesn't believe me."

"And now?" I asked, afraid of the answer.

"I'm sorry I didn't tell you. I mean if I might be crazy, if I can't feel and love like I should . . . being alone has been the far easier route."

I swallowed and looked away.

She smiled and draped her hands on my shoulders. "Then I met you."

Her smile was laden with a deep sadness, though I detected a tinge of hope pulling at the corners.

But maybe that was my own projection.

"I was afraid I'd never be able to love, and didn't want to hurt you. And yes, I wasn't sure of my feelings after we made love. But ever since I saw my brother at the castle, I've started to feel again. *Really* feel. I can't promise I'm back to normal, but there's something there—and not just in my head."

It was enough for me. Maybe someone else would have required more than a glimmer of hope from the person he loved, but after the story I had heard, after everything we had been through, it was enough for me right then.

I squeezed her hand, and the light in her eyes dimmed. "The chapel," she said, as if to herself.

I gathered her into my arms as the chill of the night crept over us.

"When the candles went out," she began, "I reached for your hand and whispered your name. You didn't respond. I figured you were looking for a candle. I started to call out, but then I saw a light. It was soft and white, brighter than the glow of candlelight, and I remember thinking that it gave me a peaceful feeling. I walked towards it, caught up in the moment but in the back of my mind wondering where everyone was."

Her face creased at the memory, and she took a moment to continue. "I walked for too long to still be in the chapel. The light moved with me, and I kept following it. I felt funny, like my head was spinning, but as I said, I was in the moment. When the light finally stopped moving, I realized I was at the end of a tunnel. A tunnel just like yours. Low ceiling, stone floor. When I turned around, I saw my brother."

"My God, Asha. Why didn't you say anything earlier?"

"I've seen your face all day. I knew you'd seen something horrible. I wanted to wait until the right time."

"What happened?"

"I cried out to him, and he moved towards me. I couldn't tell if he was walking or floating. It was almost as if he was . . . doing both. He reached out to me, just like he did at the castle. I opened my arms and then—"

She choked up and looked away. "He started to float backwards, against his will. It was as if something was pulling him back. He kept reaching out to me, opening his mouth but with no words coming out. Oh, Aidan!" she cried, burying her face into me.

I stroked her hair and she looked up through moistened eyes. "I started running but I couldn't reach him. He kept floating backwards down the tunnel. I ran and I ran and then—he was gone. The light went out and I was alone in the darkness. I felt tired and disoriented. I drifted asleep and when I woke up, I was back in the chapel."

"I'm sorry," I whispered. I wished I had something better to say.

"He's so lost, Aidan. I have to figure out how to help him."

I held her under the stars. She clung to me and shivered. Eventually I led her to the room, where she lay on the bed like an automaton, staring at the ceiling. I flipped the lights and slid in beside her.

"I've always wanted so much to believe in God," she said. "But if there's a God, why wouldn't my brother be in heaven? He was *ten*. He wouldn't be some thing drifting through a void. His expression—he needs my help, Aidan. I know it as surely as I've known anything."

She took a deep, quivering breath. "If there is someplace else, maybe he needs me to lead him there. I used to get that from some of the spirits: that they were lost and needed help finding their way. Lots of mediums do. I was just too young to understand any of it, and too afraid to ask. I was always afraid, you know. You see these movies and television shows where the mediums are always at peace with the spirit world. I never was. It *terrified* me, talking to people who weren't alive."

I slipped an arm around her. She was quiet for so long I thought she was asleep, and then her voice startled me. "Why haven't I seen him before? Why now? There must be something about the letterbox that calls to him or lets him appear. Is the letterbox some sort of bridge to lost souls?"

"I don't know," I said. "I wish I did."

She murmured her last words that night to me dreamily, yet with perfect clarity, like a final revelation on a deathbed. "I can't believe in a God who would take my brother away and let this happen to him. I just can't."

-46-

I slept fitfully, rising out of bed as the last tendrils of darkness slithered out of sight. After tracing a finger down Asha's cheek, I made my way downstairs. To my surprise, I found Lou, not Jake, sitting in a chair in the Spartan lobby, drinking coffee out of a plastic cup.

"What're you doing up?" I said.

"Couldn't sleep. You?"

"Same." I poured a cup of coffee, sat beside Lou, and told him what had happened in the chapel.

His eyes got wider and wider. When I finished, his head bobbed slowly up and down. "It's amazing the places you can smoke in Eastern Europe. The movies, the mall, airplanes. It's a national pastime. I've seen people ashing on *no smoking* signs."

"Thanks for listening."

Lou frowned and tilted his head back. "I'm thinking. Genius requires time."

I groaned. Lou never stopped.

"Did you try to touch the shadow thing?" he asked.

"I was too weak at that point. And I didn't particularly want to touch it."

"So you don't know if it was corporeal?"

"It was there, Lou."

"I'm sure *something* was there. We were just drugged and don't know what it was. Did it have horns and a pitchfork? A little red cape?"

"It's not funny."

His laughter sounded forced. "Did Asha see anything similar?"

"No."

Lou waited for me to elaborate, then spread his hands. "That's quite a story she's got there. Her brother again?"

I gave a short nod.

"I understand you two are connected and all that, and have your little secrets. Whereas I, your best friend for a decade, have been relegated to the role of secondhand acquaintance."

I couldn't help but give a short laugh, though I had the feeling he was trying to divert attention from his own story. "So what happened to you in the chapel? Did you see something?"

Lou shrugged. "It was ridiculous. Hilarious. If I hadn't been drugged, I'd have laughed out loud."

I didn't respond. He sighed and lit a cigarette. "Why should I care, anyway? I saw a light, same as you. I went to check it out. It seemed further away than it should've been, but it's hard to judge distance in the dark. I didn't think too much about it, until I realized that—"

"You were in a tunnel-like passageway just like mine."

"Yeah," he said. "Asha, too?"

I nodded.

"The passage stretched in either direction and I couldn't see the light source. When I started back the way I came, I heard the voice."

"Voice?"

He laughed again. It came off hollow and affected. "It was coming from the opposite end of the passage. A little girl's voice, speaking a particular urban dialect of Brazilian Portuguese."

Goose flesh started to prickle my arms.

"A remarkable resemblance to Kika's speech pattern. Kudos to whoever engineered it."

I already knew Lou was bothered by the strange occurrence much more than he was letting on. Lou would never admit that the things happening to us might be supernatural in origin, and his defense mechanism, as it had been ever since I had known him, was to make light of whatever confused or frightened him. I didn't fault him; it was just his way of dealing with the world.

"What'd she say?" I asked.

"She asked me to come closer. I walked towards the voice, trying to figure out where they had the hidden recorder. Soon I came to the end of the tunnel."

"Was she there?"

"No one was. By this time I felt strange and realized something was happening. I also remember smelling something odd, like almonds tinged with gasoline."

"Maybe the drugged state had nothing to do with what we saw in the tunnels," I said. "Maybe the Druids drugged us so they could steal the letterbox and then—"

"And then what? Something lured us out of the chapel and into these tunnels where it could play with our minds? Who was it, Aidan? God, Satan, the Easter Bunny? It was the Druids."

I cradled my coffee cup. "I understand drugging us and taking the letterbox. But why bother with the rest?"

"They're sadistic. Maybe they wanted to make sure we were too frightened to follow them."

"I hadn't considered that."

We were quiet for a moment, lost in our thoughts.

"Lou?"

"Yeah?"

"Finish your story. What happened with Kika?"

"Nothing. The voice said something and I fell unconscious."

"What'd it say?"

He attempted a wry grin, but it turned into a bitter, lopsided smile. "She told me she's waiting for me, and I told her it'd be nice to see her again. Then her voice changed."

"Changed?"

His mouth twisted. He seemed to be debating keeping up his pretense of jocularity. "She sounded sad, and told me I'm not going to get to go where she is. Because when I die, I'm going to that *other* place."

I averted my eyes.

"I'm going to see if Jake's around," Lou muttered. "Help him research."

I headed upstairs to find Asha curled in a chair, writing in her small, leather-bound journal. She set it aside and we headed downstairs to grab a late lunch. Near the end of our meal, Jake and Lou burst into the hotel's tiny cafe.

They rushed over to us. Jake pounded his fist on the table. "We found it!"

"The next location?" Asha asked, gripping her glass.

Lou plopped into his seat with a thoughtful expression. "It makes sense."

Jake spread a few photos on the table. "These are from the Bone Church. I had them developed."

Asha and I leaned in. The photo of the glowing stones on the bottom of the letterbox depicted a familiar image: a series of standing stones of varying heights—dolmens—arranged in a rough circle.

"Stonehenge," Asha said, before I could get it out.

"That's what we thought, too," Lou said. "It looks similar, but the relative size of the stones is different, the spacing isn't right."

Jake cut in. "There are plenty of ancient dolmen sites scattered throughout the British Isles. Stonehenge just happens to be the most famous. I called a colleague of mine this morning, an archaeologist at Oxford, and faxed him the photos. He got back to me and said this circle of rocks is an archaeological site called Avon Tor."

"Where's it located?" I asked.

"In the Devonshire moors." Jake folded his arms. "A few kilometers from Cranmere Pool."

I leaned back in my chair and whistled.

"That's where the letterbox was found," Asha murmured. "Back to the beginning."

Jake's lips compressed. "Looks that way."

Lou shifted from foot to foot, his excitement dimming. "I want to find out what's going on as much as anyone, but we can't do anything without the map. And I'm not about to go chasing after these people."

I hesitated, glancing at Asha. "Of course not," I muttered.

She caught my glance and took a deep breath. "I saw my brother again inside the chapel."

"I thought that might be the case," Jake said quietly.

"I think the letterbox is somehow allowing him to come to me. If there's the slightest chance I can help him—" She cut herself off and touched her ankh choker. "I'm going to the moors."

"The Druids are probably already at Avon Tor," Jake said. "It's time to call Lucius and get on with it."

Lou shook his head and looked down at his hands. My only consolation, and the only fact that lent our decision any sanity, was that perhaps, after the Druids' theft of the letterbox, we were no longer on their radar.

But we were about to walk right back onto it.

-47-

I felt the need to exorcise some of my stress with physical exertion. Not feeling safe enough for a walk, I settled for pacing the courtyard. The innocence of the sunny day grated on me, the smiling hotel guests an affront to my wounded psyche.

I reflected on the events in the chapel. Whether I had killed that Druid was unimportant, I realized. What mattered was that I *thought* I had. My capacity for violence had been laid bare, in all its sinister glory.

I was searching for meaning, but my search had previously been conducted through the rose-colored glasses of a peaceful childhood and an innate sense of self-worth. I didn't kill people. I didn't get put in situations in which I even had the chance.

I wondered if that was how normal people forced into a theater of war felt: as if they had just discovered a monster living inside them, coexisting alongside their humanity.

So why didn't we give our bestial nature free rein more often? A God-instilled moral compass, Jake would answer. Darwinist socialization, Lou would say. Cosmic goodwill, Asha would reply.

As always, I saw all sides to the argument, and the experience made my lingering questions even more urgent. I needed to know why someone had put me through that. I needed to know why I had been capable of doing what I had done. I needed to know what it meant that I had done it. More than ever, I needed to know what *it* was all about: the search for answers in darkened crypts, killing each other in the name of God—life, love, beauty, tragedy, good, evil, laughter, tears.

I needed answers—and I sensed that the letterbox was hiding them.

* * *

Jake talked the manager into letting us use his office phone to call Mr. Sofistere. We crowded into the cramped space and put the phone on speaker.

"While we're here," I said, "we might as well call Prentice and see if he's found anything."

After a spell of static, Prentice's voice cut through. "Aidy, I'm glad it's you. I have some news. Oh, and you should know they've put a new associate in your office. Kevin McLemore—isn't that a lovely name? He's only twenty-six. Delicious skin, and fresh as a spring morning. Linda!"

I heard a voice in the background. "Yes, Mr. Meyer?"

"Could you please call Mr. McLemore and tell him to come in here and take his pants off?"

"Prentice!" Linda yelled. "You're going to get us both fired!"

"No one can take a joke anymore," Prentice muttered.

I rolled my eyes. It was nothing I hadn't heard before. "You said you found something?"

"I'm afraid to report that the plot of land in Pere Lachaise no longer belongs to your family, unless you're related to a corporation. Which is an interesting thought. The tax benefits could be formidable."

"Which corporation?" I said, and Jake leaned forward.

"I had to jump through some hoops to find what you wanted, since the corporation that owns the plot has fronts in place to misdirect the casual seeker. But we both know I'm far from the casual seeker. I actually ended up meeting a charming Frenchman who works in the Parisian judicial records department. But I digress. The plot where Allan Kardec is buried was originally purchased by an individual from California, a wealthy businessman by the name of Ryan Lenard. He held the deed until five years ago, when he sold the plot to a corporation."

I made a note to check for a connection between Mr. Sofistere and this corporation as soon as I had the chance. "Why would someone sell a cemetery plot to a corporation?" I asked.

"For money, of course. The question is why would a corporation *purchase* a cemetery plot?"

"True," I mused. "What's the name of the corp?"

"Donn Enterprises, Inc."

"Doesn't ring a bell. And it doesn't sound French."

"The plot's registered under a French name, but the corporation that owns the plot is British. Now, why would a British corporation buy a French cemetery plot? Shady, Aidy, very shady. By the way, are you sure you're related to this Kardec person? I looked him up. He was a complete nutcase who started some kind of cult in Brazil. Lenard was one of his followers."

"It's an unfortunate legacy."

"There is one more thing, which may or may not interest you."

"I'm interested," I said.

"Out of curiosity, I checked out Donn Enterprises, Inc. on Westlaw. Pretty disappointing. Donn is a REIT with a tiny market cap and no corporate scandals, as far as I could tell. Even its place of incorporation is drab, some town in the middle of South West England."

"Do you remember the name?"

"One sec, I jotted it down . . . there it is. Grimspound."

I thanked him and slowly hung up the phone.

"The Druids just made their first mistake," Jake crowed. "Lettin' an attorney into their crypt."

I pursed my lips. "Everything's pointing to the moors. And I want to know who owns this corporation."

"I think I can help with that," Lou said, with a tight-lipped smile. "Prentice should've tried searching for *Donn* on Google instead of Westlaw. Donn is the Celtic god of the dead."

There was an uneasy silence, and Jake rubbed at his stubble. "Let's call Lucius."

Asha pulled out Mr. Sofistere's number and dialed. Her employer's voice resonated in the small room. "Superb timing. I just closed the shop. How's the search coming? I trust there have been no more encounters with our mysterious white-robed men?"

At first no one moved, then Jake and I leaned in at the same time. I let him speak. "They haven't shown up since we left Paris," he said.

I nodded. Nice word choice. I knew Jake wasn't telling Mr. Sofistere everything because he didn't want him to call off the search. I was on the same page, for a different reason: I didn't trust the man.

"That's good news."

Jake threw a lopsided smirk at the phone. "Unfortunately, that's not all the news, and I'll cut to it. Someone came in while we were asleep and stole the letterbox."

A long silence. "I see."

Asha leaned in, her face stricken. "We're so sorry. I just can't believe . . . we were being so careful."

"I believe we can assume who did this."

"What're you going to do?" Asha said.

His voice had a flinty edge. "I'm going to find these people and retrieve my possession."

"Then we're on the same page," Jake said. "We think we know where they are. You remember Kardec's tomb in Pere Lachaise? Aidan did some research, and turns out it's owned by a corporation called Donn Enterprises. Donn is also—"

"The Celtic god of the dead," Mr. Sofistere said quietly.

"You got it. The corporation is headquartered in the moors, someplace called Grimspound."

"I know the place. It's the only town within proximity of Cranmere Pool, which I'm sure is no coincidence."

"There's more," Jake said. "We found the key to the next portion of the map, and it's also in the moors. A ring of dolmens like Stonehenge, name of Avon Tor."

"Excellent news." Lucius fell silent for a moment. "I think its best if I met you myself in Grimspound. I'd like to hear the entire story when I arrive."

That took me aback. I would have to ramp up my background search.

"Be careful," Asha said. "I know we don't have the letterbox, but these people . . . ." she trailed off.

Are capable of anything, I finished for her in my head.

-48-

Asha tumbled into sleep. I couldn't seem to grow tired, so I gave up and headed to the lobby, where guests sometimes left books in English lying around. As I came down the stairs, I noticed Jake sitting in a chair, reading a worn textbook.

He looked up. "Couldn't sleep?"

I flopped in the chair across from him. "I seem to sleep less and less these days."

"Welcome to the club. Worrying about your girl?"

"I have a lot on my mind. But yes, I'm worried about her."

His eyes bored into mine, as if looking right through me. He returned to his book, but I noticed after a few minutes that he hadn't turned a page.

"What'd you see in that church, Jake?"

He didn't answer.

"I didn't mean to intrude," I said. "I just thought it might be useful information."

"It's not."

After another minute of uncomfortable silence, I said, "How long do you plan to stay in Croatia?"

"You ask a lot of questions, don't you?"

"If you want to be alone, I respect that." I stood to leave, but he flicked a wrist, motioning me back to my chair.

"One reason I stayed in Croatia is because people don't ask questions there. And I don't speak Croatian, so anyone who asks a question I can't talk to anyway." He closed the textbook and lit a cigarette, taking a few puffs before he spoke again. "It's been a long time since anyone's asked me any questions."

"Gives you plenty of time to think about your answers."

He gave a short, forced laugh. "I guess that's right."

He continued smoking, and I saw a paperback lying on the table next to me. A political thriller, judging from the cover image of a bloody dagger superimposed on the White House. I started to flip through it.

"I was married once," Jake said softly.

I slid the book back onto the table.

"I met her at Mass when I was at Harvard. She was Northern, pedigreed, sophisticated, beautiful. Everything I wasn't. I never got why she loved me, but she did. You and the girl remind me of the way we used to be. We could never be apart, and we just saw life in the same way, despite our different backgrounds. I don't know what else to call it, except for fate. God's plan, true love, all that crap."

He focused on his cigarette. I kept quiet, my body language assuring him of my complete attention.

"God I loved her. Loved her more than I've loved anything. I grew up Catholic near Memphis, Tennessee. One grandfather was an O'Sircy, the other was Cherokee. That's one hell of a heritage: drinkers and fighters on both sides. I guess the one thing they had in common was a dumb blind faith in God, which trickled down to me, because if you're an Irish-American-Indian you better believe in something.

"But I was no altar boy, and I was hardly from Brentwood. There're parts around Memphis that, well, they aren't nice places. Anyway, I ended up at Catholic school and, for all my other flaws, I had a knack for the books. School was a way out. I discovered I even had a genuine interest in Catholic history and religious objects. I suppose you could say God and the Church have been assumed all my life." He held the dying tip of the cigarette an inch from his face. "*She* was not assumed. I never dreamed I'd find anyone like her, could have someone that good in my life. I knew I didn't deserve her, but there she was."

"What happened?" I said quietly, as sure as I'd ever been of anything that something had.

"We had ten incredible years together. Happiest time of my life, and it ain't even close. She taught theology, I worked off grants. One time I was off to Cairo to trace the history of a Coptic manuscript. While I was away, I got a phone call from a hospital in Boston."

He swallowed, his mouth narrow.

"My wife had been raped. Someone caught her in the parking lot outside our church. Beat her up pretty bad. It was a terrible time. After a while the pain became bearable for her—until she began to show."

I ran a hand through my hair and left it cupping the back of my neck.

"We had just decided to have kids. She couldn't deal with the fact that she had her rapist's child inside her instead of mine."

He was talking to himself now, the way people do when remembering something tragic.

"My wife was a very religious woman, even through the rape. But the baby inside her became an unbearable dilemma. She hated the fact that it was there, but abortion is a sin in Catholicism. Not just any sin. A mortal sin."

"I thought suicide was the only mortal sin."

"A common misperception. Abortion, murder, there's a few more. The reason suicide is different, and infamous, is because mortal sins are just that, sins of mortality—not eternity. But when you commit suicide, there's no chance to confess. You die while in a state of mortal sin, which means there's no redemption. You go to Hell and you ain't getting out."

"Ah."

"My wife knew she could confess after the abortion, but devout people don't willingly commit any sin. The stress damn near killed her. I supported her, told her to do whatever she thought was right. I could never have stopped loving her, and I would've been fine with the kid."

His words poured forth, and I had the feeling I was the only person who had heard this story in a very long time. If ever.

"Twenty-six weeks into the pregnancy I had to leave town again, a day trip to Cambridge. While I was gone I got a call from our priest. He'd received a call from my wife earlier in the day, from an abortion clinic. She went in by herself, couldn't bear to have me watch. Doctors aren't supposed to abort at such a late stage, but they will in certain cases, even though the procedure can be dangerous to the mother."

He looked down at his hands. "The baby was so far advanced they decided to perform a hysterectomy. But something went wrong. They couldn't stop the bleeding. She had the doctor call both me and our priest. When the doctor tried to reach me I," Jake stopped, and got as close to being choked up as I had ever seen him, "wasn't available. By the time the priest arrived, she was dead."

I sat back in my chair, my shoulders slumping. "Jake, I'm so sorry. Sorry sounds hopelessly inadequate. I can tell how much you loved her."

"Her loss was unbearable to me. It still is. But that isn't the kicker."

I looked at him in confusion.

"She called *me* because I'm her husband. But she had the doc call the Father because she knew she was about to die, and had just committed a mortal sin. She wanted to confess before she died."

My comprehension arrived like a physical blow.

"She died in a state of mortal sin," he said, "just like a suicide. According to Catholic doctrine, my wife died and went to Hell."

Thinking of the impact of the tragic event on Jake left me numb. I imagined myself as a believer and a similar thing happening to Asha, and my soul shrank from the thought.

"God exists all right—I have no doubt about that. But if my wife is damned, then I don't know if I can love Him. And for that, I might be damned as well."

The hush of night filled the common room. I didn't move, sensing he wasn't quite finished.

"I'll spend the rest of my life lookin' for the relic, the hidden scripture, the buried scroll, something that questions the Church's doctrine on the issue. I'll gladly refute and even embarrass the Church if it means there's a chance my wife's in Heaven."

He stopped and lit another cigarette. His shaky thumb mirrored the grief in his eyes. "Or maybe I'll find something else that sets it straight. There's something out there, Counselor, I can feel it in my bones." He looked me in the eye, his hands steady once again. "I don't know what we'll find at the end of this path. But after the things we've seen . . . I'll see it through or die trying."

As powerful as his story was, I sensed there was a portion untold. And he still hadn't told me what he had seen in the Bone Church.

Jake gave a hollow laugh. "Got more than you bargained for, didn't you?"

I was still trying to find the right words, knowing my sympathy was the last thing Jake wanted. "So that's why you stayed in Croatia. Home was too painful."

"I didn't leave my house for a year after she died. When the Vatican called and offered me the project in Croatia, I knew it was time to start searching. It's easier there, somehow, with the shop and my research gigs."

"I understand."

He chuckled. "Those Sistine Chapel posters sell like hotcakes."

"I can only imagine."

I picked up the paperback, and he leaned back in his chair. "You know, Counselor, I haven't told a soul that story since I left the States."

"I appreciate your trust."

Jake pursed his lips and nodded. I opened the book, then looked up before I started reading. "Did they ever catch the man who did it?"

"The rapist?"

I nodded.

"The authorities never found the guy."

"Damn," I muttered.

Jake ground his cigarette into the ashtray and stood. Right before he reached the staircase, he looked back at me with predatory calm. "I said the *authorities* never found him."

-49-

We returned to Prague the next morning and bought tickets to London. A backup due to weather caused a delay, and we ended up languishing at Ruzyne Airport, in an alcove near our boarding gate.

One of those long airport benches with plastic seats ran along the rear wall of the alcove. Lou managed to turn it into a makeshift sofa. Jake stood at the entrance, scanning the crowd for danger.

Asha and I sat on the frayed green carpet, side by side with our backs against the wall. We were all lost in our thoughts until Asha broke the silence. "What if the letterbox wasn't supposed to be found?"

Both Lou and Jake shifted to look at her.

"What did the Druids find all those centuries ago, and why did they bury it?"

I saw Jake's face cloud over. Lou was staring at a fixed point to Jake's left.

"Jake, you're the expert," she said. "Give us some answers."

Jake stroked his chin as he watched the crowd. "There are some incongruities I'm trying to reconcile. The origin, the monotheism, and the construction of the box, for starters. That knowledge alone could be revelatory from a scholarly standpoint." He crossed his arms. "I've never heard of anything that claims to be a literal path to God, complete with map inside as special bonus feature. I don't know what we have on our hands, but I think this map is leading us someplace I haven't been before. Someplace maybe no one has been, at least for a very long time."

Despite all that had happened, I felt a shiver of excitement at his words.

"But if we finish what we started," Jake said, his face tightening, "we may not like what we find."

Asha's eyes turned troubled as she absorbed his words and stared into the crowd. I longed to stroke her cheek until the softness returned, though I knew my growing feelings might not be reciprocated. I knew she had reservations, I knew of her deep-seated issues with emotion.

Yet I didn't care. I couldn't stop. As I sat at Ruzyne Airport in the Czech Republic, embroiled in that insane quest, I felt gorged with desire, bloated, puffed up like a fat Roman emperor.

Loving Asha was the closest thing to meaning I had ever had.

As I crossed my legs on the worn carpet, I realized there was another, equally mysterious seed sprouting inside me: that of belief.

Was there, indeed, something to uncover? Something apart from mortal skin and decaying bone, something to give us hope that we were not just collections of subatomic particles glued together by chance, colliding with useless zeal inside a cold and unfeeling universe?

A mental image of the letterbox sprang to mind, followed by a memory of lying on the stone floor in the tunnels beneath Kostnice, at the mercy of the shadow thing.

The loudspeaker squawked, and I joined the others in the haphazard line forming by the counter. My mouth felt dry as we moved through the gate.

DARTMOOR, ENGLAND

-50-

We left Prague in the middle of the night. By the time we landed at Heathrow, took the tube into Charing Cross, and stepped outside, we were entrenched in our first dawn in the English-speaking world in weeks.

The day began overcast, but the brisk London air had always made me feel keen and invigorated. We took the Underground to Victoria Station, a cavernous sprawl of mass transit, and purchased tickets for the two o'clock train to Exeter, the last stop before the moors.

After grabbing lunch at one of the gritty tourist pubs hovering like flies around Victoria Station, we boarded a train to the boggy grave of the letterbox.

"When did Arthur Conan Doyle write *The Hound of the Baskervilles?*" Asha asked as the train chugged through the sculpted British countryside. "Didn't that take place in the moors?"

"Early nineteen hundreds," Lou said. "And yes, it did. Another, lesser known fact: the esteemed Sir Arthur was obsessed with the occult."

Asha turned towards Lou, the familiar intensity sparking her eyes. Lou continued, "He was a member of The Ghost Club—no joke—and even knew Madame Blavatsky. He sat in on a number of her séances."

"The woman whose portrait's hanging in Kardec's tomb?" Asha asked, giving a small shiver before looking out the window.

"Commie, tell us something useful or shut your trap."

Four hours after leaving London, the train pulled into Exeter, a middle-class university town with an enormous Anglican cathedral. We stood and examined the board with the bus schedules.

Lou yawned. "Why don't we just stay here for the night?"

"Or," Jake said, moving closer to the board, "we could take a little detour and stay someplace a little more interesting."

I eyed the name at which he was pointing: Chagstead.

The town nearest to the estate of James Perrott—the man who had drawn the mysterious letterbox symbol on his calling card and left it under a cairn at Cranmere Pool.

Jake crossed his arms. "A bus leaves in fifteen minutes."

No one argued.

Twenty minutes outside Exeter, the countryside took on a wilder feel, more overgrown and less populated by cottages and farms, the roads narrowing as they wound through denser vegetation.

Half an hour later we saw the brown and gray smudge of civilization on the horizon, and soon the bus was pulling into a car park on the edge of a tiny town. The driver announced our arrival at Chagstead.

Down the road from the bus station, two-story almshouses lined the pair of streets that essentially comprised the village, intersecting in a town square dominated by a pretty spired church.

We found a bed and breakfast with a blue roof and eaves, run by a silver-haired woman named Mrs. Leckie. Although stooped, she walked with a purposeful grace, and her rural English accent was a step back in time.

Asha's room and mine was a simple affair, white-paneled and rustic, with a window above the headboard affording a view of the village. When we returned downstairs to join Jake and Lou, Mrs. Leckie had set out a tea service and a plate of scones.

"What brings you to Chagstead?" she asked.

"We're doing some research in the area," I said.

"On the moors?"

I tried a scone. A little hard for my taste, but I ate it to be polite. "Have you heard of James Perrott?"

"Of course. You must be letterboxers."

I looked up, surprised.

"They come around every now and again, asking about Perrott. I suppose you know his old estate is outside of town. It's a bed and breakfast now. Twenty-minute drive, or you can walk it in an hour if you cut through the woods. It's just past Teign Gorge."

Jake leaned forward. "I'm a religious historian, and there's another topic that interests me at the moment."

The wrinkles on Mrs. Leckie's forehead lifted as she awaited the question.

"We're investigating rumors about a modern-day remnant of the Druids. You ever hear of anything like that?"

She paused mid-pour, glancing out a window into the darkened village. "Not around here," she said. After a curt goodnight, she disappeared up the stairs.

Asha and I collapsed into the soft bed. "I'm too tired to take off my clothes."

"I can help you with that," I said.

"What a gentleman."

"I do what I can."

I flicked the lights, fulfilled my promise, and slid in beside her. She purred as I massaged her. "You're too good to me," she said.

"Do you deserve it?"

"Probably not. Does anyone?"

"Probably not," I said.

"My parents always said they deserved each other," she said. "They had an arranged marriage."

"You never told me that."

"I suppose it's a bit embarrassing. They were never in love, but they were happy and made a good team. My dad doesn't believe in the fairytale of passionate soulmates, and calls it a Western ideal. I mean, of course people from all cultures fall in love, but he thinks Americans expect it too much and think they can't be happy without it."

"And what do you think?" I said, feeling a tightness in my chest as I asked the question.

"Of course I want it. Who doesn't?"

That wasn't what I was asking.

"How do you know what you have isn't fleeting," she continued, "or based on some temporary physical or even emotional connection that won't last a year of marriage?"

I rolled over, turning my back to her. She snaked her arms around me, stroking my chest and kissing my neck. I closed my eyes, knowing I would succumb to the drug of her naked body entwined in mine.

You just know, I thought to myself. *That's how you know for sure.*

You just know.

I woke earlier than everyone except Jake, and used the time to conduct research on Mrs. Leckie's computer. I found nothing else on Donn Enterprises, and not a hint of a connection to Mr. Sofistere. Frustrated, I checked my email, but still no word from my private investigator.

After a hearty English breakfast, we took a taxi to Perrott's estate. Despite my nervousness about traipsing through the Druids' backyard, I couldn't help but admire the beauty of the countryside as we passed alongside low green hills, the lush Teign Gorge, pastures, fields, and pockets of purple and gold heather that looked like overland beds of coral.

The manor was a sprawling country estate, replete with manicured grounds and stone walls. A middle-aged man emerged to greet us with an avuncular smile. His bald head and fair English skin were tinged pink by the sun. "Welcome to Teign Manor. You're looking for a room?"

"Not exactly," Jake said. "We're staying over in Chagstead and wanted to see the home of James Perrott."

"Ah, yes," he said. "Letterboxers?"

"Sure."

"I get that request a few times a year. Feel free to browse, but be careful not to disturb the rooms. We've tried to maintain the house close to its original condition."

"Are you related to the Perrotts?"

"The family sold off the estate a while back. It's been a bed and breakfast for some time now. You might find the library and the game room of particular interest. They still contain Perrott's personal effects and haven't been altered since he lived here." He pointed to his right. "They're down this corridor."

We tried the library first. Two side walls showcased floor-to-ceiling bookcases, and a massive stone fireplace dominated the far wall.

Jake frowned as he took in the mountain of books. "Why don't you two find the game room," he said to Asha and me. "I'll use the wayward scholar here to help skim the titles."

Asha and I continued down the hallway. An open door on the left revealed a room which, judging by the pool table and mounted heads and animal skins covering the walls, served as the game room.

I closed the door behind us. Dull light seeped through the burnt-orange drapes, and an antique painting the size of a quilt hung on the wall to our left. The painting portrayed a barren expanse of windswept hills and plateaus, devoid of all but the shabbiest of vegetation, surrounding a lifeless bog. The scene was beautiful in a stark and lonely way.

"Cranmere Pool," Asha said, reading from a bronze plaque beneath the painting. She met my eyes. "Where the letterbox was found."

We both gazed at the painting, willing it to tell its story. Asha's stare fell so intensely upon the desolate scene I assumed she was thinking of her brother. After a spell, she approached the painting, positioning both hands on one side of the frame. "Aidan—take the other side."

I grabbed hold. "Don't lift," she said, "just pull straight out. We might have to wiggle a little."

My eyes flicked to the closed door. "What're we doing?"

"You'll see. Just pull."

The heavy frame slid out of the wall and we eased it to the ground, exposing an empty space in the wall about the size of a small safe.

"How'd you know?" I asked.

"This framing style is typical of Perrott's era. See how deep the frame is? It was a common place for concealing valuables." She sighed. "There's nothing here."

I ran my finger along the inside of the wall; it came back coated with dust. She put her fist to her mouth in thought, then ran her fingers along the back edge of the canvas. "There's another place I've seen things hidden in paintings from old estates. Let's see . . . there! Do you see it?"

One of her fingernails had exposed a slit on the back of the painting, running six inches along the edge.

"Looks natural to me," I said. "Like the canvas separated from the frame over time."

"Let's find out. Help me hold it so this side is down."

We gave it a shake, and the corner of a faded blue envelope fell into the crack in the canvas. Asha carefully pulled it out.

A wax seal secured the aged flap of the envelope. Impressed into the wax was a now-familiar symbol: the same marking James Perrott had left under a cairn on the shore of Cranmere Pool in 1854, as well as the one Lou and I had seen scorched into the earth at the ruins of Castello di Selva.

The same symbol that was on the letterbox.

-51-

I looked nervously around the room, as if the Druids could somehow divine that we were prying into their affairs.

"This looks like it's been here since Perrott's day," Asha whispered.

The door creaked open. My pulse spiked as I whipped the envelope out of her hand and inside my windbreaker. Jake walked in, eyes widening when he saw the painting on the floor. I showed him the envelope, and his eyes lasered onto it. "Commie, watch the door."

Before anyone could protest, Jake broke the seal with his pocketknife, pulling out a letter the color of a tobacco stain. The pages seemed to creak as he unfolded them, and we crowded in to read the stilted handwriting.

Dear Reader,

I write to you, my unknown progeny of spirit, in a state of despair. My time grows short, and I am no closer to fulfilling what I once believed, with all of my heart and soul, to be my destiny. I cannot bring to words what it does to a man to know that he is about to die, while the object of his lifelong search yet eludes his grasp.

I surmise that the finder of this letter will be following in my footsteps, searching for the Vessel of the God Path. If you know naught of which I speak, then I beseech you to replace this letter and forget it ever graced your sight. If you hesitate, remember to respect the wishes of a dead man as you would one day wish your own respected. If you hesitate further, then heed my words: you want no part of this madness.

If, however, you are a fellow initiate of the Order, one who has heard the whispered secret of the God Path and has come seeking my knowledge, then you know the promise of the Vessel is irresistible. For who cannot yearn to possess such a thing?

As I write, I can sense your hope upon discovery of this missive. Sadly, I confess that I write out of commiseration rather than revelation. As the legends hint, I have searched and searched near Cranmere, I have followed the rituals of our grove and called upon the knowledge of the ancients. I left our symbol at the pool to simmer and reach for wisdom, but by most unfortunate fate, a wanderer ventured into this land of no return and disrupted the ritual. He has seen our mark, but did not, could not, comprehend its meaning. Now the others know what I have done, and I am watched. My forbidden search has ended.

I am an old man now, alone in my frustration. Man was not meant to carry his secrets to his grave, and so I confide in you alone, my nameless successor.

Know, Dear Reader, that I understand. If search you must, and search you shall, then take your search to Cranmere, for I know in the marrow of my bones that if the Vessel exists, then near to there it lies. And if you do manage to uncover the Vessel and walk upon the God Path, then perhaps, as a thing beyond the grave, I will be a step ahead of you, already in possession of the secrets of life and death. If instead I am adrift in whatever realm lies beyond this world, lost and lonely and without answers still, then I can only hope that I will be able to look upon your discoveries from afar, a satisfied wraith at last.

James Reginald Perrott, High Priest of the Druidae

Jake slid the letter back in the envelope and replaced it in the frame. After I helped him lift the painting, we searched the house in vain for further evidence Perrott might have left behind.

I felt that we had uncovered his last clue to the world.

After lunch at the bed and breakfast, we caught another taxi back to Chagstead. I was still unnerved by the letter, and kept an eye on the rearview the entire way.

"So that's what he was doing at Cranmere all those years ago," Asha mused beside me. "Searching for the letterbox, or the 'Vessel' as he called it."

Lou nodded. "Perrott was a Druid high priest, and the marking on the letterbox was their symbol. That explains some things."

Asha glanced at Jake's backpack and swallowed. "Why was the search for the Vessel forbidden? What did they think it was?"

"They told you what they thought it was right there on the box," Jake said.

"The letter presents an interesting dilemma," I said. "If even searching for the letterbox was banned by the high priests, then why are they chasing after it now?"

"Maybe they want to find it and bury it again," Asha said.

"Maybe," I said slowly. "Or maybe today's Druids aren't as principled as those of Perrott's day. Judging from the letter, the location of the letterbox was a mystery even to the high priests, and I'm guessing whoever was following us was just as surprised as everyone else when it was unearthed."

"Perrott's letter was so sad," Asha said. "I guess it doesn't help us much now."

As we crested a hill, the cluster of Chagstead's homes and shops appeared on the horizon, the late afternoon sun bathing the town in golden hues.

"Oh, it helps," Jake said. "The man dedicated his life to the search, and he was acting on inside information." He turned to stare out the window. "And I want to know where he got it."

We stayed in Chagstead for another night, to avoid crossing the moors in darkness. During dinner, Ms. Leckie stood on the perimeter as she had the night before, sipping her tea and arranging small details of the room to her satisfaction.

An elderly couple from Bristol joined us at the table. Their height, angular faces, and modest dress reminded me of a British Norman Rockwell.

"What brings you to Chagstead?" the husband asked. "It's a bit off the beaten path for Americans."

"Just seeing the sights," Jake said.

"I couldn't help but hear you discussing Grimspound."

Jake nodded.

"Excellent day hikes around there. You can walk for miles without seeing a soul."

"That's as desolate a place as lies on the moor," the wife said, with a shudder. "When the fog rolls in . . . things haven't changed much there, you know. Those are the old moors, bleak as bleak can be. They say there're still pagans in that part of the country."

I noticed Ms. Leckie staring at the woman out of the corner of her eye.

"Bloody hell, woman," the husband said. "Grimspound is just a little remote. You'll be fine as long as you don't wander off the road, as the open moor is quite treacherous up that way." He glared at his wife. "And not because of pagans. Every year someone loses their way in the fog and drowns in the peat bogs."

"I don't know," she said, trailing off. "I'd believe about anything that came out of that place."

"That's because you'd believe anything about anywhere."

"The moors don't look so desolate to me," Asha said. "We drove outside of town today, and it was quite lovely."

"We're not on the moor yet," the husband said. "Common mistake, though." He pointed out the window, and we followed his outstretched finger. "You see that ridgeline off in the distance? Just over the plateau, underneath those storm clouds—*that's* where the moors begin."

The next morning, the weekly bus to Grimspound rumbled out of town. The scenery underwent a gradual change as we approached the ridgeline, growing starker and more barren. The weather also changed, even though we had only traveled a few miles. A mist began to form, becoming denser as we elevated, until a gray sky swallowed the sun.

When we reached the top of the first ridgeline, the difference in scenery became dramatic, the vegetation morphing from lush forest to a stubble of coarse brown undergrowth. I recalled the description Mrs. Leckie had given of Dartmoor over breakfast: a three hundred-and-sixty-five-square-mile granite plateau, full of treacherous peat bogs, barren moorland, and ancient tors—rock formations left over from Neolithic times. Mysterious beacons of an older, more primal world.

The feeling of isolation was intense. Even when the fog did not obscure the scenery and I could see for miles, the expansive nature of the plateau only contributed to the remoteness. I thought of the moors as nature's version of being alone in a crowded city.

We rode up, down, and over the sloping plateaus, numbed by the endless brown vegetation. Finally a group of low, weathered stone buildings broke the spell, and we pulled into a village that looked nothing like Chagstead.

Narrow streets ran through the town in maze-like fashion, and the granite cottages and shops were clustered together so tightly they looked like a compound.

Bunched together, I thought, as if forming a circle of protection.

Wispy smoke poured out of thatched roof chimneys, merging with the mist covering the town. The place had a much older feel than Chagstead, and the townspeople had a grim and subdued air, stemming, I supposed, from the rigors of life on the moor. A granite church squatted in the center of the village, the elongated Celtic crosses in the graveyard a vivid reminder of the town's connection to the past.

As we exited the bus, I felt more like an intruder than in any place I had ever visited. We had already garnered a number of suspicious looks, and I couldn't shake the feeling that the Druids were watching us from some hidden vantage point on the moor, waiting for us to step outside the safety of the village.

I noticed a wooden sign swinging in the wind above the one-bus car park.

Grimspound.

-52-

Mr. Sofistere had arranged for us to stay at the Belstone Inn, a solid granite edifice that matched the rest of the buildings in Grimspound. The innkeeper, who knew Mr. Sofistere by name, led us into a common room containing a stone fireplace, wooden rafters, an assortment of chairs and sofas, and a view of the moors through a bay window.

We sat down to a lunch of homemade rabbit pie and blackcurrant crumble with clotted cream. We asked the innkeeper if he knew of a Donn Enterprises in town, and he wryly informed us we should try Grimspound's financial district. He then snapped his fingers and informed us that there was "a large chateau named Donn a mile outside of town, at the top of a ridgeline, just past Fogman's Wood."

After lunch, Asha yawned and retired to her room. Jake gave Lou and me a pointed look. "I could use a walk after that lunch."

"You're going to Chateau Donn, aren't you?" I said.

"Listen. Lucius will swoop in on his private jet and rent the most expensive suite in town. As soon as he arrives, they'll move the letterbox again, if they haven't already. Right now they have no idea we're coming, and I plan to use that to our advantage."

Lou started to protest, and Jake held his hand up. "The innkeeper told us it's right outside town. I'm just taking a quick look. Feel free to hit the pub."

"Can we at least drive? Rent a taxi?"

"No taxis or car rentals in town. I already checked."

Lou waved a hand in disgust, and I blew out a long breath as we stepped outside, into the chilly afternoon air. "Just keep to the road," I said, telling myself there was no danger in taking a short walk on a modern, two-lane highway in the middle of England. "How's your ankle, Lou?" I asked, trying to give him an out.

Lou waved a hand and stumped after Jake, who was already walking down the street.

As we left town and entered the moors on foot, the scenery felt even more visceral. Starker, vaster, more desolate. The road left the village and began a gradual climb, circling behind the rolling plateau that shadowed the west side of Grimspound. Once we crested the plateau, an enormous stone manor perched on a precipice came into view. Turreted towers supported both ends of the chateau, and a smaller one rose from the center.

Down the other side of the ridge a strange sight appeared: a dense green forest stretching alongside the road. As we grew closer, we noticed the trees were twisted and stunted, the undergrowth unkempt.

"That must be Fogman's Wood," Jake said.

Lou put his hands on his hips. "This is far enough for me. I'm not walking right up to the chateau, not even on a public road in broad daylight."

Jake was looking at Fogman's Wood, and I followed the outline of the forest as it ran beside the road to the chateau. "It appears, gentlemen, that nature has presented us with the perfect solution."

"It is convenient," I said.

Lou shot me an irritated look. "Have you forgotten Pere Lachaise? The bus? The chapel?"

"I haven't forgotten a thing," I murmured, crossing my arms and remembering the blood streaming down Asha's face, and what they had forced me to see beneath the Bone Church.

No, I had forgotten nothing at all.

"Do you see where we are?" Lou said, waving his arms. "I don't think the neighborhood watch comes up here."

"Chateau Donn is a corporation," Jake said. "They're not going to come after us during afternoon tea."

"A corporation named for the Celtic god of the dead," Lou muttered.

Jake pulled his backpack tighter. "I'm taking a quick look. Come if you want."

Jake started walking, and I followed. Lou cursed and caught up. As much as I wanted revenge on the Druids, I vowed to stay out of sight in the trees.

A path led into Fogman's Wood from the road. Our eyes widened as we took in the dwarfed and misshapen trees twisting out of the ground in fantastical shapes, their roots contorted in a desperate attempt to find nutrients. Mossy rocks and boulders peppered the path, and enough leaves remained on the low canopy of trees to leave the forest in perpetual gloom.

"The shape of this forest is too regular," Lou said. "It was planted by someone, and I don't think we need to guess at whom. These are oak trees."

The path stayed close to the edge of the wood. We passed a large clearing that reminded me of the island forest outside Dubrovnik, and I tried to push away my sense of dread, telling myself that a few feet to my right it was broad daylight on a paved road in Western Europe.

We glimpsed our destination getting closer, until at last we found ourselves just across the road from Château Donn. Jagged slopes of moorland stretched away behind the chateau. We crouched at the edge of the forest, behind a boulder.

Thick granite comprised the body of the chateau. The octagonal middle tower protruded from the front of the stone façade, and high hedges fronted everything except the main entrance, where a manicured path led to a door inlaid with iron grillwork and adorned with a granite raven's head.

Château Donn was an imposing sight, sitting on the edge of the ridge, lording over its domain. We gazed at the house for long minutes, seeing no signs of life.

True to his word, Jake declared he had seen enough and was ready to head back. It had grown late. The light inside the forest had dimmed, and we had to pick our way carefully along the root-and-boulder-strewn path. Soon after we passed the clearing, Lou stopped and cocked his head.

"What was that?" he said.

I peered into the silent trees. "What?"

"I heard something moving."

"It's a forest," Jake said. "Things move around."

We continued walking, and then I heard it, too. A rustling in the trees, coming from deeper inside the wood. "There's something in here with us," I whispered.

"Keep calm," Jake said. "It's just an animal."

"What if it's a wolf?" Lou said.

"It's not a wolf."

I heard the noise again, louder. I looked to my right and saw a shape darting through the trees. A shape clothed in white.

My stomach curled in fear, and I felt the now-familiar punch of adrenaline. "Jake—"

"I saw it," he said, knife already in hand. "Just keep walking. As soon as we hit the road, we'll be fine. It can't be far."

As we crept through the forest, I thought it the furthest distance I had ever walked. We kept catching glimpses of white flashing through the trees, and I waited for Druids or black-robed figures or worse to come lunging for us out of the bowels of the forest. At last we saw the main road up ahead, but my relief turned to terror when I saw the white shapes blocking the path at the edge of the trees.

I looked left, and saw more robed figures on the road. As one, they stepped into the forest, heading our way.

Jake cursed and herded us to the right, deeper into the wood. It was the only place left to go. "*Go*. The forest isn't that wide, and when we hit the moor, we can outrun them."

Fear clutched at my limbs. "What about the one we saw through the trees?"

"I've got something for him," Jake said, fingering his knife.

We moved as fast we could through the maze of gnarled roots, teetering on the edge of panic. Jake had to switch on his flashlight to see the forest floor, and we abandoned any pretense of stealth.

We heard rustling behind us and to our left, but a glimmer of evening light poked through the trees in front of us. I almost wept when I didn't see a phalanx of white robes lining that side of the forest.

"Hurry," Jake pressed. "They didn't count on us going deeper and they can't watch the whole forest."

As we reached the tree line, I couldn't believe our luck. There was no white robe in sight. The open moor loomed in front of us, and if we could just get across the next ridge, a quarter mile away, we'd be in sight of the village and no one would dare touch us.

"Run!" Jake said.

I sprinted into the moor, propelled by a burst of adrenaline. The mossy undergrowth was much spongier than it appeared from a distance, and on my third step I sank to my knees. With my next step, I plunged into a layer of peat as deep as my thigh, and out of the corner of my eye, I saw Lou disappear.

It happened so fast it took me a second to process. Then I yelled. "Lou!"

I lunged to my left and sank to my waist. I had the sudden realization as to why no Druids had been waiting for us on this side of the forest.

It was a deathtrap of peat bogs.

I half swam, half crawled through the watery hole. It was less dense than quicksand, easier to both sink and wade through, which caused a jolt of horror when I thought of Lou. How deep had he plunged?

Jake rushed over and helped pull me to solid ground. "Where's Commie?"

"He sank."

Without hesitation I jumped into the bog where I had last seen Lou, not caring what happened next. I didn't feel my feet hit bottom, and realized I could swim through the muck.

But I couldn't see. The bog was as dark as an ocean bottom, and I felt around frantically for my friend. It hadn't been more than a minute, but Lou was a pack-a-day smoker. I felt a surge of relief when I hit bottom, then a moment of panic when my foot got stuck in the peat. I grabbed the side of the bog with both hands, using a root for support while I yanked my foot out.

I swam in a circle, reaching blindly with all four limbs and avoiding the bottom, hoping to find Lou with my flailing. I was sure I had jumped in the bog close to where he had gone down, but inches could mean life or death.

Then there was a light in the darkness, an enfeebled glow penetrating the gloom. I realized it must be Jake's flashlight. I spun in every direction and saw Lou a few feet to my left, a watery shadow sunk to his thighs in the muck, struggling to free himself.

I darted over to him and motioned with my palms for him to stop moving. Then I took both his hands in mine, pulling with all my might.

He didn't budge.

My breath was failing. Lou couldn't have much air left, and I tried and failed to lift him out of the muck. I couldn't risk going for help and losing sight of him.

I dove towards Lou's legs, took his left thigh in both hands and tugged on it. It lifted a few inches, and I pulled until the leg sucked free.

Lou almost fell backwards into the bog, but I stabilized him and yanked the other leg out. We swam to the surface together. Jake pulled us to firmer ground, and we collapsed gasping on our backs.

-53-

The crisp air was the sweetest thing I had ever tasted. After Lou gathered his breath, we crept along the forest edge towards the road. We didn't see any more sign of the Druids; they had either left us for dead or made their point.

I walked in a daze back to the village, enraged and stunned and terrified. Even Jake looked cowed, though I think it was because he felt guilty. I was livid at him for putting us in danger, and no less angry at myself for letting him do it.

Strangely enough, Lou seemed the most unaffected. He complained bitterly about being wet and cold, but had yet to say a word about his near-drowning. I attributed it to shock, and a bit of perverse pride.

When we reached the outskirts of the village, three white-robed, hooded shapes raced towards us. I had my knife in hand before realizing the shapes were half as tall as we were, laughing as they broke apart and skipped around us.

"Happy Samhain!" one called out.

"Kids," Jake said in disbelief. "Dressing up as Druids."

"Happy Samhain?" I asked.

"I've been doing some research on our neighborhood god of the dead. Donn presided over a certain festival celebrated by the Celts, a festival that culminated in one night in particular: a night which the ancient pagans believed stood as a bridge between the world of the living and the world of the dead. I didn't realize anyone still celebrated it by its ancient name, but apparently they do. In the Christian world, the day took on another name, which you both should've figured out by now."

Of course—I had almost forgotten that it was October 30.

"Halloween," Lou wheezed, holding his sides from exertion.

As the darkness matured, Jake pulled out a cigarette and settled into his storytelling demeanor. "The Celts believed the year was divided into two halves, the light and the dark, and that for a brief time, the borders between the two dissolved. They called this time Samhain, and believed it fell on All Hallow's Eve. October 31."

"What did the Druids have to do with Samhain?" I asked. Lou and I were shivering in the cool air, walking quickly to keep warm.

"Everything. The Celts believed that during Samhain, mortals could pass more easily to the spirit world, and vice versa. Due to the dangerous flux of power, the Druids offered up plenty of sacrifices and gifts." He paused. "Since the high priests were involved, I think you know what kind of sacrifices we're discussing."

I shot a nervous glance into the darkness.

"Why the costumes?" Lou asked. "Or was that a later addition?"

"The Celts believed that on Samhain, disembodied spirits would come in search of living bodies to possess. Naturally, the living didn't want to play ball. The villagers extinguished the fires in their homes to make them cold and undesirable, then dressed up in ghoulish costumes and paraded around the neighborhood to frighten away the spirits."

"How did something like that carry over?" I said.

"The Christian church was unable to get the pagans to stop observing the holiday, since pagans do pagan things, so Rome decided to sprinkle holy water on it and give it a new name. New on top of old."

We digested the information as we walked through the village, until Jake stopped and put a hand on his hip. "It's perfect," he said. "Beautiful."

"I already dislike your train of thought," Lou said.

"Every high priest worth his pagan salt will be celebrating Samhain, especially on All Hallow's Eve. And when Druids celebrate Samhain, they do it *outside.*"

Lou pulled at his wet clothes. "*Look* at this, Jake. Why don't you just wait for Mr. Sofistere?"

"Because Chateau Donn will be wide open on All Hallow's Eve. I know it. I feel it." He flicked his cigarette into the darkness. "It might be our only shot, and it'll be risky, but I'm getting our letterbox back. I'm getting it back tomorrow night."

I was too tired and cold to deal with Jake and his reckless plans. When we reached Belstone I changed out of my wet clothes and found Asha warming herself by the hearth in the common room, tucked under a quilt.

"Enjoying the fire?" I asked.

"Immensely."

"What's on your mind?"

"I don't know," she said. "Nothing. Everything."

I detailed what had happened and said, "Jake wants to break into Chateau Donn on Friday night." I didn't feel like sidestepping the issue.

She squeezed my hand and murmured all the right words of sympathy, then turned back to the fire.

I didn't like where this was going. "Let Jake go by himself," I said. "He doesn't need us."

She lowered her eyes and whispered, "Maybe not, but someone else does."

Lou's attempts to dissuade Jake from his scheme failed before they began. Jake had an infectious way of convincing us his plans were safe and viable, and no one wanted to be left behind. He even had the gall to suggest we would be safer *inside* the chateau on Samhain.

More importantly, I had begun, like Asha, to stop caring about risks that should be cared about. I wanted the letterbox back, I wanted answers, I wanted revenge. The issue of safety became insidiously moot. I felt as if we were members of a cult and Jake was our charismatic leader, conditioning us for danger, guiding us bit by bit into risks we never would have undertaken in the beginning.

We of course did not plan to plunge forth blindly, ignorant and unprepared. Jake had made a number of scouting visits to Fogman's Wood and constructed a working map of the chateau. Our plan centered around Jake's map, his lock-picking skills, and a hidden means of entry and egress to the chateau of which he claimed knowledge. It looked solid on paper, but I didn't fear the plan. I feared the twin surprise attacks of chance and chaos, the forces that lay outside of every plan, crouching inside a veil of unpredictability.

The innkeeper confirmed that not all of the region's inhabitants had abandoned their pagan roots. It was whispered that in secret places on the moor, in the silence of the scattered groves and tors, the ancient rituals were still practiced. "Or," he said with a smirk, "perhaps it's the spirits of the Druids still roaming the earth, attempting to return on the day when the veil between worlds is lifted."

No one seemed to know much about Chateau Donn, except it was the home of a very old and rich family who kept to themselves. More rumors existed concerning mysterious activity in and around the chateau, but no one seemed able or willing to provide any information of substance.

From the safety of the inn, we observed the preparations transforming the town into a vessel for Samhain. The townspeople covered every house and building with sinister-looking decorations, children ran through the streets dressed as an array of haunts and ghouls. Samhain in Grimspound felt like a grander and darker version of the holiday I knew as Halloween.

The older, more primal version.

The real version.

-54-

The night of Samhain arrived. We dressed warmly, for the days had grown cold and the nights colder. As we stepped outside under a gibbous moon, we looked upon a Grimspound that had completely altered its identity, transformed by the madness of Samhain. Every last home and shop had cobwebs and black sheets covering its doorways, goblins and gargoyles leered from rooftop perches, skeletal wardens presided over entrance gates.

Revelers packed the streets of the village, every single one wearing a frightening disguise. I appreciated Jake's latest addition to the plan, which we had procured the day before: costumes. We would have instantly stuck out without them. Asha and I chose a witch and warlock tandem, Lou decided on a grotesque troll, and Jake of course opted for a white robe and hood.

I had to admit the costumes increased our chances of making it to the chateau unseen, though as we walked the streets of Grimspound, surrounded on all sides by every imaginable creature of the night, I couldn't shake the feeling that the Druids and ghouls roaming the town could sense our alien presence.

And that some of the people behind the white-robed costumes were real Druids, watching us walk right into their hands.

We were bumped and jostled on our way out, the party spilling indiscriminately into every corner of the town. People screamed and shouted, everyone run amok in an effort to frighten away the spirits.

Truly, madness had settled on Grimspound.

* * *

The moon hung heavy in the sky by the time we passed the last building and stepped onto the moor. I was relieved to leave the chaos of the town behind, though bonfires and costumed merrymakers still lined the roads.

The further we walked, the more the party dwindled. No one paid us the slightest attention, and we felt confident we had slipped by unnoticed.

"So this is the night when the Celts believed spirits could pass to this side," Asha said quietly.

"Yup," Jake said.

I knew what Asha was thinking before she whispered it.

"I wonder if my brother is here."

We continued towards the chateau, this time keeping to the road. We saw no more revelers and spent the journey huddled together, casting wary glances into the thick fog that had settled on the moor.

At last the walls of Chateau Donn poked through the gloom, covered in Samhain decorations. The black sheets and cobwebs made the brooding chateau, standing on its isolated aerie in the moors, look like a genuine haunted castle.

Jake claimed he had found a way to enter the chateau unseen. We followed him as he slipped off the road and onto the moor just before the grounds. He led us through a series of hedges and past an unlocked gate, then to a small door in the rear of the manor, a gardener's or servant's entrance. The chateau appeared deserted.

Jake took a small set of tools out of his backpack. Within minutes he was tugging on the iron handle. The door swung outward and we peered inside, seeing no signs of life.

Enough light seeped in from outside to illuminate the storage room in which we found ourselves. Wooden boxes and an assortment of garden tools were piled along the walls.

We closed the door and stood motionless, straining to hear sounds of activity.

"Where to now?" I asked.

"I've been able to map most of the chateau by spying from various angles, and I should know where we are soon after we get inside. The main entrance and the rooms off it are where I've seen the most activity. We'll start there and work our way back. There's one room in particular everyone seems interested in."

"It's probably the kitchen," Lou muttered.

"Let's find what we came for and get out," Asha said.

My breath caught in my throat as Jake opened the door at the far end of the room, revealing a foyer with pitted stone walls and hallways branching perpendicularly to the left and right. An image of the tunnels beneath Kostnice floated towards me, but I pushed it away. I couldn't let myself dwell on how terrified I was.

Jake chose the hallway to the left. Sconces spaced along the wall provided dim illumination. After a few dozen yards, he frowned. "We must be in an older section. The rest of the chateau is more modern."

"I thought you had the place mapped," Lou said. "Surely we'd be in the front wing by now?"

"This must be one of the areas I couldn't see. Let's keep going and see where it leads. We can always double back."

Something felt amiss, but we had seen no other route options. I kept waiting for the lightheadedness I felt in Kostnice to return.

We passed a closed and locked door on our right. After walking a good bit more, the corridor ended at a wall. Stone passageways, also lit by sconces, branched off to either side.

Jake grunted. "We entered on the rear-left side of the chateau. There can't be a passageway to the left, unless somehow we're bearing to the right."

"I don't think we've been bearing to the right," Lou said, studying the passageway ahead and behind us.

I peered back into the shadows, noticing the sconces had a slight uphill slant. "We've been going down."

"We must be underground by now," Asha said.

Jake swore. "There's got to be a way to reach the upper level. Once we're there, I'll know where we are. And look on the bright side. It's much less likely there'll be anyone down here."

"Number one," Lou began, "that's not very comforting. Number two, they're not keeping these candles lit for the cockroaches."

"Let's stop talking and move," I said, having already come to the same conclusion about the lit candles. "Going right makes sense, since the left passage has to lead away from the chateau."

We passed another locked door on our right, in the middle of the corridor, and at the end of that passage we encountered another pair of corridors branching to either side. We kept right, traveled what seemed like an equal distance, saw another door, and came to the end of that passageway. We repeated the process one more time and ended up back where we started.

"These must be escape tunnels," Lou said. "They were fairly common back in the day, in case of an invasion or a peasant revolt."

"So why the lit sconces?" Jake said, then answered his own question. "They use the tunnels to sneak out."

We glanced down the corridors, no one enjoying that train of thought.

"We're going to have to try one of the doors," Asha said. "It's the only place the stairs to the upper level could be. They've got to get down here somehow."

I knew we had overextended our stay, but I didn't want to be the first to crack. We retraced our steps to the door in the middle of the first passageway. Jake took out his tools and went to work as the rest of us shuffled in silence. When the lock clicked, he pulled the door open, revealing another sconce-lit corridor.

We saw nothing of interest until we came to a round chamber at the intersection of four passageways. A narrow iron staircase led both up and down. Above our heads, the stairs led to the pull-handle of a trapdoor set into the ceiling. We couldn't make out what lay at the bottom of the stairs.

"The chateau must be right above us," Jake said. He started up the stairs, then stopped, turned, and rushed a finger to his lips.

I could hear, quite distinctly, footsteps and voices on the level above. The four of us stilled in the corridor like mimes pausing for effect. While I couldn't make out the words, the voices were growing louder, approaching the top of the stairs.

Jake swore under his breath and bounded down the staircase, to the lower level. Not knowing what else to do, we followed behind, terrified of making a noise. When we reached the stone floor at the base of the stairs, we huddled together.

"There was no time to head down one of the tunnels," Jake whispered in the darkness.

"So now we're stuck down here like rats?" Lou said, hysteria creeping into his voice.

"We wait for them to go away, and proceed as planned."

"You said no risks," I hissed. "Someone's up there. We're going back."

Jake didn't respond at first, then let loose a string of curses in a low voice. I heard him rummaging through his backpack. "Might as well see where we are," he whispered.

"We should stay quiet and then *go,*" Lou said.

I cringed when Jake flicked on the flashlight and waved it around the room. Wine bottles were set into the walls in high stacks, small holes having been cut into the stone to accommodate the wine.

"Not much down here," he said, disappointed. "I suppose we can—"

Jake stopped midsentence as the footsteps returned, this time numerous pairs of feet that stopped just above the trapdoor.

Lou moved for the stairs as Jake flicked off the light. Jake grabbed him.

"Let me go!" Lou said in a hoarse whisper.

"*Think,* man. We won't make it down those long corridors in time. Chances are they're coming down the stairs to slip outside, not because they're thirsty."

I grabbed both their arms. "Shut up and move away from the stairs."

We heard the creak of a hinge. Light flooded the stairwell. We were tucked into a corner of the cellar, hidden from view but trapped like fish in a net if anyone found us. The footsteps descending the iron staircase rang in my ears like a thousand church bells. Heart pounding, I pressed against the wine bottles.

I heard at least three sets of footsteps coming down the stairs, but it seemed Jake was right: the footfalls receded down one of the corridors rather than continuing to descend. A sigh of relief shuddered through me. I didn't want to contemplate what might have happened had the Druids decided to enter their cellar.

We waited a few eternal minutes before daring to stir. I had pulled out a wine bottle in case I needed something to swing. Jake turned on his flashlight as I started to replace the bottle, and I noticed something odd.

"Hey," I said quietly. "This bottle isn't dusty."

Lou shrugged. "So someone didn't like the vintage."

As Jake walked over, I checked the bottles above and below the one I had pulled out. Neither were dusty, but the ones on either side had a thick layer of grime. Jake shone his light into the chest-high hole in the corner where I had grabbed the first bottle. We crowded in and saw a rope cord dangling inside a shaft cut into the stone.

I gripped the bottle I was holding, and Jake whistled. Then he reached inside and pulled on the rope.

The entire section of the wall began to slide silently to the left. It stopped to reveal an iron door, padlocked and imposing. Asha gripped my hand. After a glance up the stairs, Jake set his pack down, pulled out a few tools, and bent over the lock. Although it took longer than usual, we soon heard the familiar click, and Jake stood with the padlock dangling from his fingers, grinning like a cat in the cupboard.

The door opened to reveal a cavernous darkness. We took a tentative step forward as Jake shone the flashlight inside, then reared back in shock.

Four of the black-clothed figures we had seen in the cemetery and outside the bus loomed in the center of the room, reaching for us with outstretched arms. This time their hoods were thrown back, revealing four grayish-white skulls resting grotesquely inside the hoods, leering at us with fleshless grins.

-55-

Asha screamed. I couldn't make a sound, because a surge of panicked adrenaline had left my mouth dry and my muscles full of slush. I was paralyzed, unable to think through the onslaught of fear.

Asha stumbled towards the door. Lou stood staring dumbly at the creatures. I recovered my senses enough to move, wishing to God we had never descended into that hole of horrors. At least the Druids were flesh and blood. These abominations—*oh, God.*

My only thought was that we had to get out of that room. I grabbed Lou, turned to see where Asha was—and then noticed what Jake was doing.

He was walking right towards the things.

"Jake!" Asha cried.

As I watched in shock, he whipped his knife out of his boot in one smooth motion, walked right up to the black thing in the center, and made a swift slicing motion into the air above it. I heard a loud snap, and the thing collapsed in a heap.

I stared at the scene for a long, uncomprehending moment. Then I looked at the other black things and realized what was wrong. Although their outstretched arms gave the appearance of movement, they weren't coming any closer.

Jake turned to us, lips compressed, and shone his flashlight above the black thing to the left of center. We crowded in to get a look, still afraid they might spring to life, and saw a thin wire attached to the top of its hood. Jake moved his flashlight upwards, following the wire to where it attached to the rafters.

"Puppets," he said.

I opened the tattered black robe as Jake provided light. Underneath the rags, a wire frame supported the mid-section, ran throughout the "body" of the figure into the arms and legs, then passed through the back of the hood. I pushed the thing, and it started to bob and jerk, an unnatural-looking spasm.

"I told you they weren't real," Lou muttered.

Asha stared at the contraptions with a look of relief tinged with disappointment, like someone who had discovered the family ghost was a stray branch scratching against a window pane.

Someone who on some level wished it wasn't just a branch.

"How'd you know?" I asked Jake. My hands were still shaking.

"I noticed they weren't moving forward, waved the light around, and saw the wires. Commie, get the door. Except for the evil puppets, I think it's safe to say we're alone down here."

Jake found a pair of sconces and lit the candles with his lighter, casting the room in a soft glow. The stone vault was half as big as the common room at Belstone. Bookcases and shelves lined the walls. We saw signs of recent use: no dust covered the shelves, the secret door hadn't squeaked, and fresh wax pooled beneath the candles.

The books were a mixed bag, ranging from a collection of literature on the Celts to tomes on black magic. Some looked brand-new, some had turned brittle with age. In addition to the books, occult items filled the shelves: animal skulls, goblets and talismans, tarot cards, pentagrams, insects preserved in glass jars.

Lou stood over a large wooden box. He opened it and pulled out a long white robe, then another.

I grimaced, turned to the shelf I had been perusing, and picked up a pair of flute-like whistles. "Dog whistles."

Jake was flipping through a large, leather-bound tome titled *Advanced Magic and Sleight of Hand*. "There're some pages marked. Levitation, voice-throwing, techniques for concealing movement. Sound familiar?"

"It's starting to be revoltingly clear," I said.

I heard a gasp and turned to see Asha kneeling above an open chest. When I saw what she was holding, my heart bottomed out, followed by a surge of rage.

It was a photo of her and her brother. In the photo he was wearing the same white-collared shirt and brown pants he had been wearing the night he appeared to us at the castle.

"This was taken the day he died. I kept a copy in my nightstand. How did they—it doesn't matter. It's all a trick," she said in disbelief. "How could they?"

She let the photo drop and slumped to the floor. Jake knelt beside a locked chest, larger than the others. With Lou perched over his shoulder, he took out his tools and soon had the lid popped open.

Jake gave a satisfied grunt, reached into the chest, and pulled out the letterbox.

We replaced everything as best we could, stuffed the severed black-robed puppet into a chest, doused the candles, climbed the staircase, and left Chateau Donn without incident. I think we all shared similar feelings: excitement at finding the letterbox, outrage at being tricked, fear that we were still a target, and relief that the Druids were mortal after all.

But I felt something else.

I felt as if the seed of belief the quest had nurtured in me, a seed which I had just begun to cultivate, had evaporated into the night, leaving me a hollow shell.

I glanced at Asha, but she looked right through me, an oily disappointment smeared across her face.

Parlor tricks notwithstanding, the Druids' attacks had been all too real, and the darkness felt alive on the walk back to Grimspound. I couldn't stop glancing over my shoulder.

Lou broke the silence first. There was a trace of smugness in his voice. "Mission accomplished. Though it seems a little anticlimactic, after all we've been through."

"Did you forget the map?" Jake said. "Perrott's journal?"

"I'm sure the map leads somewhere," Asha said. "Just not to . . . ." She bowed her head, her voice quiet. "I still don't understand how they managed to—I guess it doesn't matter anymore."

I slipped an arm around her. She felt stiff.

We arrived at Grimspound without incident. A few Samhain parties still thrived on the streets, but the inn was quiet except for the crackling of the fire. I mumbled goodnight to Jake and Lou, and followed Asha upstairs.

She lay on her back on the bed, staring at the ceiling.

I leaned on an elbow. "Do you want to talk about it?"

"What's left to say?"

I didn't know, but I had to try to plug the hole in her heart. "I'm sorry about your brother. I know you thought things would be different."

Her lips barely seemed to move when she spoke. "I buried him ten years ago, and what I've been through since then almost . . . but I was learning to cope. To have this shoved back on me, to think there might be a chance—those *bastards*."

"It's unforgivable," I said.

"I don't understand, Aidan. That was his face. It wasn't some Italian urchin."

"It was dark at the castle," I said gently. "And at Kutna Hora, you were drugged."

She turned on her side, facing away from me as she fought back tears. My love for her made her pain my own.

The Druids had played the worst trick imaginable on Asha.

Asha remained aloof the next morning, tucked inside her shell. I knew the loss went deeper than her brother. Like me, Asha had begun to caress a glimmer of hope that the letterbox would lead to something ineffable, to something which she had once grasped herself, or thought she had.

Something which had left her questioning her sanity ever since.

I tried to massage her to relieve some of her tension, but she gave me a halfhearted smile, said she needed time to think, and pulled away. She ran a hot bath instead.

When we made our way downstairs, Lou and Jake were engaged in conversation in the common room with someone in a dark wool suit. He turned as we entered.

"Mr. Sofistere!" Asha said. "You're early."

He smiled and embraced her. Despite my suspicions, I was glad to see her animated.

"When did you arrive?" she asked.

"I've had time to drop my bags and chat briefly with these two gentlemen." His face darkened. "They informed me of last night's events."

I glanced beside Jake and noticed the bulge in his backpack. How long would it be, I wondered, before the Druids made a visit to their cellar?

Mr. Sofistere poured a cup of coffee and sat by the fire. "Why don't we take it from the beginning? I've waited a long time to hear the full story."

As we recounted the strange and now shameful events that had befallen us, the heaviness of soul that had descended after our discoveries in the chateau returned in force. We told Lucius everything except for our individual experiences in the tunnels beneath the Bone Church. I felt that the questions raised within me, regardless of the veracity of the events, were my own cross to bear.

"When I visited Cranmere Pool," Mr. Sofistere said, looking to the side as if recalling a lost memory, "the geologist who unearthed the letterbox mentioned strange visions he had experienced during the extraction. He had been working all night, so to be honest, I paid him no mind."

Jake's eyes whipped towards Mr. Sofistere.

"The Druids must have known about the dig," Asha said bitterly, "and started their tricks from the beginning."

"Indeed," Mr. Sofistere murmured.

Lou shrugged. "We were deceived. End of story."

"Not exactly," Jake said.

-56-

Jake pulled the letterbox out of his backpack. "I went to Avon Tor this morning. I've seen the rest of the map."

Mr. Sofistere leaned forward. "Go on."

"I found a dolmen at the site that narrows to a thin rectangular slab. I climbed up and found a depression with a bunch of tiny little holes. It's cleverly done, and looks like weathered granite. But when I attached the letterbox and examined the slab from the other side—" He paused, his eyes flicking to the bay window "—there was a new pattern."

"Just one?" Lou said. "There should be two map sections left."

"This one took up twice as much space as the others."

"And did you recognize the location?" Mr. Sofistere asked.

"No," Jake said slowly. "But it was very peculiar. Here, I'll show you."

He pulled a series of photos from his backpack and laid them on the table. We crowded in. The photos revealed a pyramid terraced with step-like sections, as if one could walk to the top. A number of pointed lines resembling spires surrounded the pyramid.

"It's a ziggurat," Lou said. "A type of temple prevalent in ancient Mesopotamia."

Jake clicked his tongue. "That's right." He pointed at the spired shapes, which rose around the pyramid at uneven heights and in seemingly haphazard fashion. "I've got no idea what those are."

"I may be able to shed some light on this," Mr. Sofistere said, turning the letterbox over in his hands. "What do you know about the places you've visited? The locations on the map."

"That if there's a connection, we're not seein' it."

"On the surface they appear to be a random collection of sites," Mr. Sofistere agreed. "However, I've been researching the locations as you've uncovered them, and each of the places you've visited, as well as Avon Tor, possesses something in common. Something of which you're already aware for two of the locations. Namely, Kostel Utes and Avon Tor."

Jake stood and started to pace. "One is a church . . . one is a collection of dolmens."

"The key is in their past," Mr. Sofistere said. "What they once were."

"I suppose those two were both—of course," Jake said, snapping his fingers. "And I bet—that has to be it."

"They were both pagan temples," Lou said softly.

Jake groaned and pressed his fingers to his forehead. "Why didn't I think of this? The depiction I thought was Kostel Utes might even have been pagan imagery. The cliff face and river wouldn't change over time, and both the rotunda and the steeple—an obelisk pointing to the heavens—were typical pagan structures."

"We know for sure Kostel Utes was built on an ancient pagan site," Mr. Sofistere said. "And Avon Tor and the stone circles were built thousands of years ago."

"A huge number of early Christian churches were erected on top of pagan sites, or utilized the existing structure." Jake said. "It was easier to convert people if they were allowed to pray in their own temples."

"But Pere Lachaise?" Asha said. "Castello di Selva? Wait—it wouldn't be Pere Lachaise. It would be the old burial ground in England."

"That's right," Mr. Sofistere murmured. "Though numerous cemeteries were also built on top of pagan sites."

"The theory gives us a common thread," Lou said, "but what's the bigger picture? Why these five? What's the map for?"

"Those are the right questions. I'm sorry to say I don't have the answers."

"Where do the Druids fit in?" Jake said.

Mr. Sofistere opened his palms. "I still haven't found any reference to the box or the map in Celtic lore. But at one point or another, the Celts were prevalent in Gaul, Bohemia, an area near Naples, and of course the British Isles."

"Whatever the map leads to," I said, "the Druids must think it's pretty valuable to go to these extremes."

Sofistere wagged a finger. "I have another theory about that. As you know, we have no known written records from the Druids and thus no real knowledge of their practices. However, I found a few oblique references, ignored because they've never been sustained, postulating a theory that when the Druids were forced into hiding across Europe by the persecution of the Roman Empire, the high priests secreted away their most sacred items. I think our modern-day Druids might believe the map was made to conceal a repository of Druid wisdom. A treasure trove of lost spells, rites, lore, and other knowledge. The value of such a find would be astronomical."

I turned to the fire. His theory did not interest me in the slightest. The thought of a worldly treasure somehow made it even more disappointing that the letterbox was, after all, only a box.

"Or perhaps the locations on the map had spiritual significance to the Druids," Mr. Sofistere continued. "Jake's going to help me research the answer to those questions." He put his hands on his knees. "Regardless, I thank all of you for your efforts. You've been an enormous help. I'm sorry beyond words for the trouble you've experienced, and I'll be speaking to the authorities about these people."

"It's over," Asha said, her voice listless once again.

Mr. Sofistere regarded her with sympathetic eyes, while Jake and Lou began arguing about nothing in particular.

I stared at the ashes in the bottom of the hearth.

Lou spent the afternoon watching television in the common room, taking breaks to smoke and to remind me he had been right all along. Business as usual, though I sensed a quiet regret underlying his demeanor.

I sat with him for a while, unable to concentrate on either the television or the inn's literary offerings. Finally I headed upstairs to ask Asha if she wanted to make a stop before we returned to New Orleans. Somewhere sunny and beautiful, someplace that might help us forget.

She wasn't in the room. When I glanced out the window, at the sweep of moors in the distance, I noticed her journal on the bedside table, poking out from beneath her sweater.

I gave it a guilty glance, as one does an intimate object not meant to be disturbed. My glance turned into a prolonged gaze, and I picked it up, my insecurities whispering to me from the back of my mind.

She doesn't love you, the voice said. *You know it but you can't admit it. She may like you, she may enjoy your company, she may enjoy dining and talking and traveling the world and exploring your connection and even making love to you—but she doesn't really love you.*

I opened the journal to the bookmarked page, then closed it.

This wasn't me.

Yet as I was closing the journal, my eye, in the subconscious yet willful roving that eyes do, picked up a word in the middle of the page.

Not just a word—a name.

My name.

-57-

I let out a long, shuddering breath. I still couldn't do it. Moving as if in a fog, I closed the journal and started to place it back on the table. Asha walked in while it was still in my hands.

"What are you doing?" she said. "Is that my journal?"

I told her I didn't read it, but I could tell she didn't believe me. She looked at the journal and then backed out of the room. I could also tell, by her shocked and guilty expression, that there was something in the journal she didn't want me to see.

I replaced the journal and followed her to the cobblestone street outside the inn. When she turned, her smile looked forced. "I'm going for a short walk. I'll stay close."

I could see in her eyes what I knew in my heart. It might not be the best timing, but I could no longer pretend, to myself or to her. I knew what I had to do and what the outcome would be.

A slow drizzle had begun, a crystallization of my sentiment. I felt jittery, as if I had been up for three days straight. "We need to talk."

Her eyes wouldn't meet mine. "About what?"

"I didn't read your journal. But if I did, I wouldn't have been very pleased, would I?"

Her stare dropped to the ground. I waited for her to say something, anything to dispute what I had said. Her silence was a thunderclap.

"I'm in love with you, Asha."

The weight of those words had pressed upon me for so many days that I felt as if Quasimodo's hump had just been sliced off my back. I had to voice it and give her that chance. I never would have forgiven myself if I hadn't.

She took a deep breath and finally looked up. Again the guilty eyes.

She approached and cupped my face in her hands. "Thank you for saying that. Oh, Aidan—do we have to do this right now, with all that's happened? I thought we were going to take it as it comes."

"If it was just a matter of mood . . . I can take it as it comes as long as we're on the same page, or somewhere in the same chapter. I don't think you're even reading the same book."

A tear dropped like mercury from her eye. "I'm sorry," she said. "I thought I was getting better. Does it have to be all or nothing? Why can't we give it more time?"

"Because the wait is destroying me." She moved to touch my face again, and I gently caught her wrists. "And because love *is* all or nothing, Asha. This isn't our first date. It's either there or it's not by now, and you know that."

"I want so much to make this work," she said, a trembling hand shadowing her eyes. "More than anything I've ever wanted."

"I believe you," I whispered. "But it's not good enough. I wish it was."

Huge brown eyes peered up at me, long lashes glistening with moisture. As I looked in those eyes, reflective of a soul I felt I knew better than any in this world, I couldn't believe what I was going to lose.

I gave her one last chance to capitulate. Those three words came easy the second time, a broken dam that could never be repaired.

She remained silent. No little white lies for her. She stepped closer, and I pressed my lips against the top of her forehead. She lifted her face to me. I walked away and didn't look back.

-58-

Our split happened so fast it felt like a rip in the fabric of reality.

Heedless of danger, I walked to the edge of town and gazed on the moors, shaking as if I had drunk a gallon of coffee.

Meaning? I had found it, all right. It was in a beautiful world on the other side of the mirror, a world I could see but not step into.

I found a pub and warmed myself by the fire. After a few too many pints and progressively darker thoughts, I grew restless and walked to the edge of town. Night had settled, and I stared at the cold and lonely moors. Never had I been in a place where civilization ended so abruptly, swallowed by the vastness of nature. I shivered despite my warm coat.

I was not quite desperate enough to walk alone on the moors at night, but neither was I able to bear the thought of running into the others. I decided to return to the inn and sleep in the common room, then leave in the morning for home.

As I turned to leave, I heard a noise behind me, on the moor. I whipped around. A tall man in a dark overcoat was striding towards me out of the gloom, his collar upturned.

I chose to stand and face him. Despair is a wonderful creator of courage.

He had a hawkish nose, a dark brow, and thin lips fixed with a somber expression. "Aidan," he said. "We need to talk."

I took a step back. "How do you know my name?"

His eyes flicked to the side, into the moor. "I'm a Druid."

My mouth opened but I couldn't find my voice. I stared at him with a mixture of shock, fear, and rage.

"Wrong answer," said a different voice, and Jake materialized out of the darkness behind the man, holding a knife sideways across his throat.

The Druid put his hands out, palms up. "I only wish to talk."

"Any of your friends around?" Jake said. "Because if they are, and this is a setup, then you get cut first."

"There is only me, and I came only to talk."

I gave the man this: his voice never wavered.

Which made me nervous.

Jake stepped in front of him, keeping the knife in place. "In the middle of the night on the moor? Interestin' place for a conversation."

"Due to our past . . . interactions . . . certain precautions had to be taken. Judging by the knife against my neck, I'm sure you understand my desire for discretion."

"How'd you know I was out here?" I asked Jake.

"Everyone's lookin' for you. We thought one of our friends here," he inclined his head towards the Druid, "might have snatched you."

"I needed some fresh air," I mumbled.

Jake looked at me oddly. "Some bartender said you were talking nonsense about walking around the moors all night. I started circling the edge of town, and saw you with Tall and Black here. You all right?"

"Sure."

Jake turned back to the Druid. "So? What do you want? It better be good, or I might start remembering a number of incidents that reflect very poorly on you and your friends."

The man finally swallowed. "First of all, I never approved of the measures taken by my Order. Most of us didn't."

"You damn well better not have," Jake said.

"Who are you?" I asked.

"You know who we are."

"We know you're Druids. But are you the descendants of the high priests or did you just go out and buy some white robes?"

"Suffice to say we are followers of our Order."

"You're fruitcakes, is what you are," Jake said. "And I'll decide what's important. What're you looking for? Where does the map lead?"

The man spoke slowly, as if deciding what to reveal. "We have reason to believe that when the Elders were persecuted, they hid a trove of forbidden knowledge, despite the prohibition."

Jake and I exchanged a glance at the acknowledgment of Mr. Sofistere's hypothesis.

"The legend of the Vessel has been passed down orally for generations. When it was uncovered, and found empty, we were sure the map would lead to our forgotten legacy."

"And it didn't," I said, my voice flat.

"We've reached a dead end. If the last location on the map was once known, or if the Vessel contained something of importance, the knowledge has been lost."

"You came out here just to tell us that?" I said, incredulous.

The Druid glanced uneasily into the moors. "I wanted to apologize. Our intention was never to harm you. We're not a malevolent Order." His eyes moved downward. "At least, not most of us."

"I don't think an apology's quite gonna do it," Jake said.

I felt a coldness settling in as I remembered the deception played on Asha, the events at Kutna Hora, Lou almost drowning in the peat bog, and everything else that had happened. "You caused some of us terrible pain," I said. "You put our lives in danger."

"We were only trying to frighten you. Asha's injury was an unfortunate accident."

"Unfortunate?" I said, my voice tight. "And Lou? He almost *died* in that peat bog."

The man looked shocked. "I was assured by . . . I was told there weren't any bogs that deep near the woods."

"Well, there were," Jake said, pressing the knife tighter.

"I'm truly sorry."

It wasn't enough. Not nearly enough. All the rage and frustration I felt from the quest came bubbling to the surface, stoked by the breakup with Asha. I shoved Jake aside and grabbed the man by the collar, yanking him towards me.

"Have you no soul? Causing me to think I killed someone? Causing Asha to think her dead brother is haunting her, causing her to live with this day after day? How could that possibly have helped your damnable cause?"

I was shaking him. He didn't resist and I backhanded him across the face. I stopped my second blow because I saw him cringe, and because he was looking at me with a strange expression.

"What're you talking about?" he said. "Killed someone? Haunting?"

I shoved him away in disgust.

"Lose it, brother," Jake said. "You hired some local boy in Naples to pretend to be Asha's dead brother."

"I admit that was the plan," he said slowly. "And I agree, a particularly heartless trick. For the record, I voted against it."

Jake snorted, and it took all of my willpower to refrain from striking him again.

"But it never happened," he said.

This time Jake grabbed him by the collar.

He spoke quickly and put his palms up. "We hired a street child in Naples, a boy who looked like the one in the picture we took from Asha's apartment. To be honest, there wasn't a remarkable resemblance. We were counting on the effects of shock and darkness and planned to distort his voice through a speaker, telling her to return the letterbox. We paid half the money beforehand, which was a mistake. The boy never showed and we had to abandon the plan. We never sent anyone to the castle."

-59-

I looked at Jake, who appeared just as confused.

"Then who was the boy?" I asked the Druid. "We all saw him. He led us to the tower."

"The first and only time we approached the castle was the day before you arrived. We explored the ruins and blackened our symbol into the courtyard."

"Why in the world should we believe you?"

He spread his hands. "Why would we point out the next location to you?"

It was a good point, one I had wondered about before.

Jake pressed the knife across his throat again. The Druid seemed shaken for the first time. "I swear I'm telling you the truth. *There was no boy.*"

Jake slowly let his hand drop.

"Why don't you tell us what measures you took to retrieve the box," I said, not sure what to think. "After Naples."

He took a deep breath and nodded. "We thought Pompeii would have a more pronounced effect. When you continued to Paris, we followed, planning to trap you in the cemetery. As you know, we were already using Kardec's tomb as a meeting place. Very clever, by the way, figuring out the dolmens. We were impressed."

"How'd you get inside the cemetery with the dogs?" Jake asked.

"Paris has catacombs crisscrossing the city. Many years ago, we built an entrance from the catacombs right into Kardec's tomb."

"Go on."

"Our goal that night was to frighten you into leaving the Vessel. We planned to corner you and demand its return, and I suspect we would have been successful."

Neither Jake nor I contradicted him.

"But you barricaded yourself in that tomb, and we were forced to leave before the cemetery opened."

Jake and I again exchanged a glance. "What about the man in the black shroud?" I asked.

He frowned. "We were outside the tomb the entire time. No one entered that tomb unless he was in there to begin with."

Jake raised the knife again. "I told you what I'd do if you're lying—"

"I assure you again I have no idea what you're talking about," he said hurriedly, eying the knife.

"Did you send a young woman to Notre Dame in Paris?" I asked. "Blond and very pretty?"

"Absolutely not."

I crossed my arms. I had no reason to trust him, but what could he gain by lying? Was this some ploy to retrieve the letterbox? "The scene outside the bus?" I asked.

"We set a dead pig and the wicker cage on fire. The man was wearing flame-retardant material and we took him down as soon as you were out of sight."

"Breaking onto the bus?"

He raised his palms. "Again, we were trying to frighten you into leaving the Vessel. We didn't expect you to resist as you did. You gave a few of our people quite a scare."

"They're lucky I didn't kill them," Jake muttered.

"After that, we decided the situation was escalating to a point to which we were not prepared to go. So we devised the plan at Kutna Hora."

"You drugged us," I said.

"I apologize if you had a headache afterwards, but the drug was harmless. A general anesthetic."

"I figured as much," Jake said. "I also figure you're goin' to tell us you had nothing to do with what happened inside the ossuary."

"We pumped the drug into the chapel and waited for the fumes to dissipate, walked in when you were fast asleep, retrieved the Vessel, and left."

Jake gave a short, hysterical laugh. "Right."

"I guess we can never prove if you're lying," I said.

"Lying? About what?"

"Things happened inside Kostnice," I said. "Involving one of your people in the tunnels beneath the ossuary."

"I assure you that's quite impossible. You were unconscious before and after any of us encountered you. And I don't know of any tunnels underneath Kostnice."

"Neither do we."

We stood in the darkness, facing each other with uneasy stares. The man looked as if he were about to say something else, then gave the moors another nervous glance.

"What?" Jake asked. "If you're holding something back . . . ."

"There's another reason I came tonight," the man said. "I wasn't sure how to tell you, because I don't know if I believe it myself." His voice dropped and he looked shaken. "But after what you've told me . . . ."

"Spit it out," Jake said.

He expelled a breath. "I'm the most knowledgeable historian of our Order. After we recovered the Vessel, I was chosen to carry it to Avon Tor to decipher the last site on the map."

"And you went."

"Yes. But something happened at Avon Tor, similar to the things you're telling me."

He paused, and Jake ran his thumb along the flat of his blade.

The Druid pressed his lips together. "It was dusk, and I was alone on the moor. It was all rather dreamlike, but I saw some things . . . people from my life . . . who couldn't have been there."

"Why not?" I said.

"Because they were already dead."

My skin started to prickle.

"I ran away and looked back only once, but it's the one thing in my life I would take back if I could. I saw . . . a thing. A walking shadow. I don't know how else to describe it. It was dark, and I was scared and confused. Perhaps it wasn't really there. Perhaps *they* weren't really there. I got to my car and left as fast as I could."

He stopped, visibly upset. All of my experience as an attorney screamed that this man was telling the truth.

I saw Jake looking at him with narrowed eyes and a tight mouth. I wondered what Jake had seen at Avon Tor.

"Why don't you tell us what you know about this 'Vessel,'" Jake said.

"Our oral tradition speaks of a wooden container buried on the moor that houses something important. Powerful. The legend is vague and, as you can imagine, distorted through centuries of oral transference. Some believe the Vessel is connected to the spirit world and possesses occult secrets. Most of us simply believe it will lead to historical insights or lost knowledge. Yet we've exhausted all avenues and found neither a hidden repository nor the last site on the map."

"That's all you know about the box?" Jake said. "That the Druid high priests made it? Isn't there some sort of record?"

He gave us a sideways glance. "Druids didn't make the box."

"Huh?" Jake said. "But the dates, the Ogham—"

"Let me clarify. Druids constructed the sides and the map on the bottom. But the oral traditions reveal that the Elders constructed the Vessel and the Pathway around a Sacred Tablet."

"The lid," Jake murmured.

"Nothing about the design on the lid comports with what we know of the Elders. We don't know why this particular piece of wood was chosen, and the histories don't say. Those of us who believe in the more . . . spiritual . . . nature of the Vessel believe the lid to be a relic from a forgotten age, a relic which the Elders knew possessed special significance. To be honest, I never subscribed to any of that." His lips compressed, and his eyes slid to the moors once again.

"So who made the Sacred Tablet?" I asked, following his gaze into the gloom.

"No one knows."

-60-

"There's a final thing you should be aware of," the Druid said. "There's a difference of opinion among our Order concerning the Vessel. Or shall I say a schism."

"Let me guess," Jake said. "The rogue faction is the one who told you those bogs were two feet deep."

He didn't deny it. "A few of us believe more strongly in the . . . mystical . . . abilities of the Vessel. And I fear these members are prepared to go to great lengths to see it returned."

"My turn to take a guess," I said grimly. "Their leader has a burn scar on the back of his left hand."

He gave a curt nod.

"What do you mean, *a few of us believe?*" Jake asked. "Spell it out."

"The man you've described was given an ultimatum to suspend the search. In response, he fled the Order, vowing to recover the Vessel at any cost. We have no idea where he's gone. But we felt it right you should know."

Jake snarled and raised the knife again. "His name? And don't even try to wiggle out of telling me."

"Nyles. Nyles Kempthorne. But the name means nothing. We all join the Order under assumed identities."

A line of white-robed Druids emerged from the darkness behind him. They didn't advance, but the message was clear, and Jake and I were forced to back away and let the man slip into the night.

We returned to Belstone, wary of the threat that still existed, chewing on the answers we had received. Answers that had, yet again, only raised more questions.

The others were waiting for us in the common room. Lou looked as relieved as I had ever seen him, and Asha's eyes were red. I let her hug me, though I felt drained of emotion.

As the fire popped and crackled, Jake and I told the others what had happened. I was reluctant to bring Asha's emotions for her brother back into the fold, but her eyes looked dull when we finished, as if our story had only deepened her mistrust.

She put her fingers to her temples and shut her eyes. "More lies," she said bitterly. "It's just more lies."

He looked pretty damn serious to me, I thought, but said nothing. It was better if she didn't have her hopes raised. Not by someone we had no reason to trust.

Mr. Sofistere looked furious and then thoughtful. He admitted he had only date-tested the false bottom of the letterbox, and not the lid, which gave some weight to the Druid's story.

Lou scoffed and muttered something about agreeing with Asha.

When I woke the next morning, Asha was gone, and I didn't see any of her things. I dressed and hurried downstairs. Asha and Mr. Sofistere were eating breakfast in the dining room, their suitcases on the floor beside them.

"We're taking a private car to London this morning," Asha said, "and then flying home. I was hoping you'd come with us."

"What about Jake and Lou?"

"Given the new information," Mr. Sofistere said, "Jake requested a few more days with the letterbox. Lou has decided to join him. I should get back to the shop. Asha and I can support them better from home, if anything new is uncovered."

"Please come," Asha said. "What if the man with the scar returns?"

"That wouldn't be good for his health," Jake said, strolling in carrying the letterbox.

I glanced at Asha, then down at the letterbox. I wasn't finished with the quest, and I wasn't about to suffer through a long trip home with Asha. "I'll stick it out with Jake and Lou."

Breakfast was awkward. When Asha and Mr. Sofistere rose to leave, I mumbled a rote goodbye. Asha hugged me tightly.

"Please be careful," she whispered.

"Travel safe."

After Asha and Mr. Sofistere left, I spent the afternoon by the fire. Her absence felt like a carousel without children, wooden animals traveling in an endless loop.

Jake came down for dinner. We ate in silence until Lou entered the dining area with the letterbox in hand, staring at it with a fascinated expression.

"Commie?" Jake asked.

Lou set the letterbox down. "You know the decorative markings on the lid? The one we've all seen a thousand times?"

"Yep."

"They're not decorative."

"They're not?" I said, peering at the lines of flowery etchings we'd assumed were merely ornamental. "Then what are they?"

"A language," Lou said. "Very cleverly disguised."

Jake gripped the table. "So what's it say?"

"Let me try to explain." Lou kicked his feet up. "Written language began, as far as we know, around 3200 B.C.E., in the city of Uruk in Mesopotamia. The language was called Sumerian and the writing system was dubbed Mesopotamian cuneiform. A derivative of Sumerian, a language called Akkadian, soon evolved. Akkadian is more complicated than Sumerian, because any given Akkadian cuneiform sign had various sound values based on both Akkadian and Sumerian meanings. It was a logosyllabic writing system with isolated instances of purely logographic writing."

"Commie?"

"Yes?"

"We're not linguists."

Lou sighed as if carrying the weight of the world. "I'm trying to bring it down—fine. I'll simplify even further. I began noticing patterns in the 'decorations' on the letterbox; patterns that I know signify grammatical structure and syntax and a host of other things indicative of the presence of a language. As I began trying to break down the symbols and find a pattern, I finally realized what I was looking at—it was Akkadian!"

Lou began talking faster. "Akkadian was based on a peculiar wedge-shaped cuneiform style that, when elongated and distorted, can look flowery. Imagine a very early form of cursive. I think the decoration on the letterbox is Akkadian, mixed in with some purely frivolous markings. I haven't heard of this being done before with Akkadian, but writing is a communicative art, and stylistic liberties have always been taken."

Lou's new information, coupled with the tale we had heard from the Druid, caused a tingling to spread throughout my body. I clapped him on the shoulder. "Great work."

"I'll call Lucius in the morning," Jake said, "but what's the bottom line? What do the runes mean?"

"Since we're in the middle of the moors," Lou said, "and my resources are limited to pub menus, I can't decode it yet. I've already sent faxes to a few specialists in the time period."

Jake sank into his seat. "Not bad, Commie," he said grudgingly. "And it fits with what we know."

"How's that—" Lou began, then cut himself off and snapped his fingers. "Ziggurats were common in Mesopotamia."

Jake tipped his hat.

"Why the odd step-like shape?" I asked.

"Ziggurats can be thought of as ancient religious escalators," Jake said, "built to bring man closer to God. Unfortunately, ziggurats were prolific in that time period and in that part of the world, so it's impossible to tell which one the map is supposed to represent. The pointy symbols are another story. I've got no idea what those signify, but we should be looking for an ancient ziggurat surrounded by spires or slender pillars."

A silence descended, and I knew we were all wondering the same thing: what could long-dead Druid priests, the letterbox, and our disturbing experiences possibly have to do with ziggurats and an ancient Mesopotamian language?

-61-

After dinner, Lou asked me why I hadn't left with Asha. I told them what had happened. Lou's face wrinkled, and Jake squeezed my shoulder and fell silent, going to that place he went when I knew he was thinking about his wife.

When I returned to my room, I found a letter folded under my pillow. I got a surge of nervous adrenaline as I opened it.

Dearest Aidan,

Whether or not you read my journal—and I believe you that you didn't—my state of mind since our discovery at the chateau does not even begin to encompass how I feel about you. I never understood the concept of a soulmate until I met you, and I can't really comprehend that it might be over.

But I know that, at least in your eyes, it is. And I can't blame you.

I saw a face last night, haunting my sleep. He came to me as my brother and when I went to embrace him, he stripped away his mask and an evil, grinning Druid was in his place. I screamed until I woke. Oh, how I hate them for what they did.

To have to deal with the loss of my brother as well as my ability to see into the beyond, or whatever accursed trick of fate was played on my young mind, was hard enough, but to have those losses affect my relationship with my parents and my sanity and my ability to feel, and to now ruin my relationship with you, is more than I can bear.

By the time you read this, I'll be on my way to New Orleans to try to make sense of the things that have happened, if any can be made. I know you don't want to hear this, but I can't accept that everything can end like it did.

I know that's a selfish thing to say.

Love always,

Asha

I stared numbly at the letter, and turned out the light.

Not used to sleeping without Asha, I slept in fits and starts. Every time I woke, I imagined someone staring at me outside the window.

Someone with a burn scar on the back of his hand, the bottom of his white robes floating in midair.

A ringing phone jolted me awake the next morning. It was Bobby Gravois, my private investigator.

"You sitting down, Bubba?" he said.

"Should I be?"

"Took me a while, but I found your guy. I've got a buddy in D.C., an old partner from N.O.P.D. who moved to the Feds a while back."

I pressed the phone tighter. "How'd he find him?"

"I sent him a photo of Sofistere, and he cross-referenced a couple of international crime databases. Pegged him on Interpol's facial recognition scanner."

My face felt flushed. "He's a criminal?"

"Not exactly. Your guy's real name is Jurgen Krassnig."

"He's German?" I asked, with a hollow feeling at being deceived.

"Austrian. Born in Linz in 1950, degree in accounting, upper middle class. Mother was French, maiden name of Sofistere. His pop was the criminal: a high-ranking Nazi suspected of a major looting in Belarus, though he was never prosecuted. Guess what he stole?"

I realized I was holding my breath. "What?"

"Jewish religious artifacts. Things like scrolls and thousand-year-old Torahs. Priceless relics. Jurgen's mother died of cancer in '81, and Pop kicked the bucket in '82—the same year Jurgen Krassnig ceased to appear on the public record. Lucius Sofistere showed up in New Orleans a few months later, an independently wealthy man."

"He got rich off his father's Nazi loot," I murmured. "His father must have sat on the money and willed it to him. So he's not a wanted man?"

"Both Jurgen and Lucius have squeaky-clean records. We did find business connections to half of the shadiest tomb raiders and treasure hunters on the globe, but that's no crime. Your guy scours the globe for his trinkets, and he's good at it. Sticks to the countries where he won't run afoul of the law."

I ran a hand through my hair. I told him to research the name Nyles Kempthorne, warned him it could be a pseudonym, and said, "Did you find anything on Donn Enterprises?"

"Not a thing. If there's a connection to your guy, it's lost on me. Oh, and he has a good track record with charity. Gives away quite a lot of pieces to museums, foundations, churches."

"Probably tax write-offs," I muttered.

I hung up, wondering how much Asha knew.

Not that it would matter. I knew now that she had taken the job at Antiques and Objets d'Art because it afforded her exposure to a steady stream of religious objects from all over the world.

In her mind, the best way to try to recapture her lost ability.

The best way to reach her brother.

Jake spent the day puzzling over the last location on the map, while Lou worked to decipher the Akkadian text. I restlessly paced the inn, unable to stop thinking about the Druid's story, wondering if we could trust him, checking the hands of everyone I saw for a burn scar.

I joined Jake for a quick dinner at the village's lone cafe. We picked up sandwiches and sat on a bench behind the granite church that dominated the center of town, next to a cemetery built around a collection of standing stones. The circular arrangement of the dolmens reminded me of a much smaller Stonehenge, except the stones were rougher cut.

The ruggedly beautiful day, clear and bright, was a rarity. When Jake went back for more mustard, I tried to work the new information about Mr. Sofistere into the puzzle.

Try as I might, I couldn't see how his secret impacted the search. It was frustrating, since I had harbored suspicions about his involvement.

If not him, then who?

I also thought about Asha, as I had for almost every waking moment. Knowing that nothing I could do would make her look at me in the way I wanted was the bitterest pill I had ever swallowed. To move on, I felt I would have to kill the best part of myself: the part of me that had loved her and that loved her still.

"Aidan," a female voice said.

I jumped up, spun, and did a double-take. The blond woman Asha and I had seen at Notre Dame was walking towards me out of the cemetery, wearing the same white dress as Paris, despite the cold.

At first I wasn't positive it was the same woman, but her smile of recognition and flashing green pendant erased any doubt. She walked right up to me, handsome and poised, blond curls spilling onto her chest. I was wary of a Druid trick, but saw no one else with her.

"What're you doing here?" My question sounded ridiculous, even to myself.

"You still don't know, do you?"

"What?"

"I have even less time than in Paris," she said. "This place isn't as strong, but you have to be warned."

"Sorry? Warned about what?"

"What I told you about the last time," she said, her attractive mouth curling in frustration. "Please get rid of it."

"We're not doing this again," I said. "Especially if you can't tell me who you are, what the letterbox is, or what the threat's about."

Her voice grew urgent. "If you insist on continuing, you should know there will be a choice. A final test. And you must—"

"Now that's what I call gettin' back on that horse, Counselor," Jake said, walking up behind the woman.

At the sound of his voice, the woman stilled and looked ready to bolt, a doe caught in her hunter's sights. Her eyes shifted left to right, but she wouldn't turn to face him.

Jake stepped around to meet her. She tried to spin away, but he caught a glimpse of her face, and her reaction to his voice paled in comparison to his. Jake gave a strangled cry and sank to his knees, a single word reaching his lips.

"Vivian," he whispered.

He reached his arms out to her in supplication, unrecognizable as the Jake I knew. He was a man resurrected, transformed in that very instant.

I didn't need to ask how he knew her name. This was not some casual acquaintance or long-lost friend. This was, or Jake believed her to be, his wife. His dead wife. I knew it as certainly as I had known anything.

Jake was still on his knees. She moved to cup his face in her hands, but just before she touched him, a look of such anguish and regret crossed her face that I didn't doubt my guess for a second.

Her whole body started to shimmer, and she backed away. Her lips formed words but she was unable to evoke a sound.

Jake stood, reaching for her as if underwater. She turned and ran into the cemetery. Before Jake could follow, or even take a step, she disappeared midstride, into thin air.

"No!" Jake cried. He ran to the spot where she had disappeared, his eyes sweeping across the tombstones. "Vivian! *Vivian!*"

He took a step in one direction, and then another, and then another. I could only watch in helpless frustration. I didn't help him look because there was nowhere she could have gone.

Jake dropped to his knees and moaned. I put a hand on his shoulder, and he clutched it with an iron grip. "It was her," he said. "I heard her voice in the ossuary but thought it was a dream. She started to warn me about a choice, and then I saw something black in the tunnel. A shadow. Then she was gone. Someone took her away from me again, Aidan."

His voice shook and he paused to collect himself. "She's still here, somehow. She must be trapped and needs my help—my God, Aidan, *that was her.*"

He stood and regained his composure, purpose replacing pain. "This is the girl you saw at Notre Dame?"

"Yes."

"Was she wearing that emerald pendant?"

I nodded. "You recognize it?"

"I gave it to her as a wedding gift. I *buried* her with it."

I could only stare at him in shock.

"Tell me about her," he said greedily. "Tell me everything she said, every movement she made."

Still unsure what to believe, I gave the drowning man his request, recounting everything I could about Vivian's brief visits.

"What's she warning us about?" he said. "Of what we'll find? I wonder why she never told you her name. She must not have wanted to upset me. Something must—"

A look of horror crossed his face. "She's in Hell," he whispered. "I don't know how she manages to appear sometimes, but that black thing drags her back." His eyes flared like Roman candles. "There's hope, Counselor. She knows something about this quest that someone doesn't want her to talk about. *The letterbox must be a way to help her!*"

I said nothing. I didn't want to point out that she had come to warn *us.*

"She's beautiful, isn't she?"

"Very," I said.

Jake stood up straight, taller than I had ever seen him. "Whatever it is," he said, "it involves that box. I swear to you, nothing on this earth or anywhere else, not the Devil himself, will stop me from discovering its secrets. Get ready to gear up, Counselor. We're finishing this."

-62-

We reached Belstone as the sun cast an amber glow over the horizon, dipping the little village in honey. Lou was on a conference phone in the common room when we returned. He waved us over and put the phone on speaker. "It's Sofistere and Asha," Lou said.

"Hi, guys," Asha said.

We returned her greeting. As I stared at the phone, I had the comforting feeling that she was in the room with me. I pushed it away, annoyed.

"What's going on?" Jake said roughly, talking over his emotions.

Lou held up a small stack of papers. "Two faxes. One from a professor at Princeton, one from a request Lucius made."

"Lou, why don't you begin with what you discovered?" Mr. Sofistere said.

"The good news," Lou said, "is that I've deciphered the individual characters of the Akkadian inscriptions."

Jake stepped forward, hands clenched.

"I'll show you as soon as you give me back the letterbox. Why'd you take it, anyway? You know I've been studying it."

Jake pulled the letterbox out of the backpack. "Because it doesn't leave my sight."

His eyes met mine. He had taken it with us to dinner, and left it with me when he ran back for mustard.

Lou took the letterbox. "As I was saying. There are two parts to this: first, the Akkadian script hidden within the decorative border. Unfortunately, it isn't straightforward. Worked into the characters are a collection of cuneiform numbers and . . . symbols . . . for lack of a better way to describe them. It almost looks like some sort of formula. I'm looking into the possibilities; it might be astronomical or mathematical calculations, a primitive form of longitudinal and latitudinal coordinates, I just don't know."

"That's not what I wanted to hear," Jake said. "And the second?"

"The second is the larger rune on the side of the letterbox, the same one on Perrott's card. Like the flowery writing, it confused me because it's not etched in typical cuneiform script. But I'm told it's definitely an artful collection of Akkadian characters—a word—perhaps adapted from an original writing."

Lou paused, and Jake's question was almost a grovel. "*And*?"

"The problem with this one," Lou said, "is that I have no idea, nor does my professor who specializes in ancient writing systems, what the word means. It could be a name or a location or a piece of chocolate cake, for all we know."

"I don't get it," Jake said. "You know the Akkadian alphabet, right? Can't you figure it out?"

"It's a problem of context," Lou said. "Imagine if you were studying English and you saw a name for the first time, like *Pennsylvania*. You might be able to figure out that the letters form a word, but unless you had a sentence to put it with, or had seen it before, you wouldn't know what it means. It could be any number of things that hasn't appeared in known Akkadian writings. Especially since stylistic liberties were taken."

"I need something I can work with."

"You're welcome," Lou said.

Jake turned to the speakerphone. "You got anythin' more concrete for me, Lucius?"

"After we realized the lid originated elsewhere, I widened the search to non-Celtic cultures. One of the people to whom I sent an inquiry was a colleague who specializes in Middle Eastern and Near-Asian pre-Christian religion and culture, Dr. Philip Clifton of the British Museum." I heard him shuffling papers. "From his initial response, it appears we've been searching for answers in the wrong place."

Despite what I had learned about Mr. Sofistere, I again found myself on the edge of my seat, craving knowledge of the letterbox like an addict growing closer and closer to the source of his ruination.

Jake flexed his fingers, as if he were going to reach into the phone and grab the papers. "So what does he have to say?"

"He hasn't found mention of this particular piece," Mr. Sofistere said, "but he's uncovered more information concerning the locations on the map. By the way, he's offered us access to the British Museum to continue our research. But before you decide whether to accept, let me relate his findings. How much do you know about pagan temples?"

"Apparently not enough," Jake said.

"Pagans—and I am using the term simply to designate pre-Christian peoples not associated with modern religious traditions—built their temples in very specific places, as randomly as they might appear on the ancient landscape. This occurred not just in Europe, but around the world."

Jake and Lou nodded along, as if this were no surprise.

"From Europe to Northern Africa to the Americas," Mr. Sofistere said, "thousands of dolmens, great and small, dotted the landscape. As you probably know, Stonehenge, Avon Tor, and other megalithic sites have proven to be highly accurate astronomical calculators. But that's just the surface effect. The *building sites* had a much greater importance. The Neolithic pagans who chose the locations were concerned with tellurian, or earthly, energy currents, and their relationship to cosmic forces. They believed that a collection of metaphysical energy lines dissected the planet in a discernible pattern, forming the boundary between the physical and spiritual worlds. Most ancient points of interest in Britain, for example, seem to be connected along straight lines on the map."

"They're called ley lines," Jake said. "A number of early religious structures were reputed to have been built on them."

"Good. Yes. It was quite a common belief—I daresay almost universal. The aborigines of Australia, for example, believed in similar lines of energy and thought they were 'activated' by walking along the pathways and singing tribal songs. There are *rock paintings* depicting what can only be viewed as ley lines."

Mr. Sofistere paused to let us digest his words. "It was also believed that these lines of energy crossed at certain places. And at these points of intersection, special religious structures were built—special because the ancients believed the spirit world drew much closer to the physical world at these sites, perhaps even touching."

"Like a temple version of Samhain," Jake said.

"Exactly. A place, rather than a time, where the two worlds draw together. The problem is, we can only speculate where the ancients built these structures. But my hypothesis is that each location on the letterbox map represents an intersection point of ley lines."

My eyes met Jake's. He opened his mouth to speak, swallowed, and then nodded at me. I told the others who we had seen near the ring of dolmens in the cemetery.

Lou blanched, and Asha gasped loud enough for us to hear. Because of the sensitive nature of the topic, no one knew what to say, and there was a long spell of silence.

Jake's mouth was set. It was clear he didn't want to field any questions.

"So where do the Druids and their map fit in?" Lou said finally.

"We know the Druids studied telluric currents and ley lines," Mr. Sofistere said. "Perhaps, fearing their days were numbered, they wanted to record the location of some of the more powerful intersections. Or perhaps, as we've surmised, the letterbox map leads to a hidden repository of knowledge. Or maybe it's a map of the places the Druids ended up settling after they were persecuted, a code for where followers could gather. I'm obviously speculating, and I've no idea why Akkadian is involved. Jake, what do you make of this information?"

Jake folded his arms. "What I make of it is that we're catching the next train to London."

-63-

Before we rang off, I said, "Lucius, do you have a minute?"

Jake disappeared with Lou, deep in conversation about the letterbox. I took the phone off speaker and asked Lucius to do the same.

"I'm hearing a strange tone to your voice," he said. "Does this have to do with Jake seeing his wife?"

"It has to do with Jurgen Krassnig."

Silence.

"I see," he said finally. "As an attorney, you should know that very few things in life are black and white."

"I'd say Nazi loot qualifies," I said.

His voice sounded like it had aged twenty years in the last thirty seconds. "Are you familiar with the Jewish concept of atonement?"

"No."

"I'm not Jewish or even religious, but I do believe that if one wrongs a certain people or culture, then the wrong should be addressed according to the corresponding custom."

I sensed him running a hand through his coiffed hair.

"The Jewish theory underlying atonement is restoration—righting wrongs, as well as returning man to his original state in the eyes of God. Free from sin and restored." He paused. "For some wrongs, perhaps restoration is unattainable. But it is possible to try."

"Let me get this straight," I said. "You're atoning for your father's sins by stealing artifacts using tomb robbers and mercenaries, and then giving a portion of the profits to charity?"

His voice became heated. "I don't consort with mercenaries or procurers—I *buy* from them. I take what they've stolen and give it back."

"What about the shop?"

"Most of the pieces are not for sale. I restore them and find the proper home. I gave up my life, everything I know, for this cause."

I was shocked he had admitted that much, though I supposed that even if the statute of limitations had not expired, any actual war crimes had been committed by his father. And I doubted there was any evidence.

Or maybe I was wrong, and the obsession I'd seen in his eyes hadn't involved the spiritual world or even money, but atonement for his father's sins. His family's conscience eating him from within.

I was betting on a combination of all three.

"You seem like a reasonable man, Aidan. What is the better choice, to return a fortune to squandering politicians, or to devote one's life to helping restore the cultural integrity of a people my father wronged, as well as others?"

I was no theologian, and it was his conscience, not mine. What mattered was how his decisions affected my friends and the search.

I let him stew, my eyes twin daggers pointed at the phone.

"Expose my identity if you will," he said wearily, recognizing the ace I'd been keeping, "but I'm not a monster."

"To be honest, I don't care about that. But if I find out you've lied to me or put any of us in danger, then get ready to see your true name plastered on a billboard on Canal Street."

"I've never lied to you, Aidan. And the last thing I would do is put any of you in danger."

"What about the letterbox?" I said.

"What do you mean?"

"Where did you get it?"

"It was entrusted to me by the owner, a private collector who discovered it during a dig and hired me to classify it."

"What aren't you telling us?"

His voice turned quizzical. "I'm just as in the dark as you, I assure you of that."

I asked a few more questions, but try as I might, I found no evidence of deception.

And so I packed my bags for London. Despite my mistrust of Lucius Sofistere, né Jurgen Krassnig, it appeared he was just as baffled as everyone else concerning the origin of the letterbox. I decided not to tell the others what I had found, including Asha. As long as it didn't affect our safety, I felt that was Lucius's decision.

A sane man in my position, I knew, would turn around and go home. There were too many unanswered questions and threats of danger hovering around us.

Yet I had seen, with my own two eyes, Jake's beloved disappear into thin air. My belief in the possibilities of the quest, once shattered, had been resurrected.

In spite of Vivian's warning, in spite of our disturbing experiences with the unknown and the Druid faction hunting the letterbox, I knew I would travel to the ends of the earth for the chance to discover what had made the first caveman gaze upon the night sky and tremble, inscribing his fear and wonder on the lonely cave wall.

LONDON

-64-

Though the half-day trip to London passed without incident, Lou and I stuck to Jake like a clump of wet grass, shrinking into our seats whenever a new passenger entered our compartment. The Druids were averse to crowds, but I knew this was the endgame, and our adversaries were desperate.

We stayed at a hotel near Russell Square, a short walk from the British Museum. Jake and Lou poured all of their energy into studying the Akkadian inscription and the map. I helped as best I could, providing research skills and logic, yet for the most part left the scholarly work to the scholars.

During breaks from the research, I paced the storied halls of the British Museum, trying to separate Asha herself from the emotions her memory evoked. Those feelings had nothing to do with her now. They were mine alone to remember, an electric current of life that would always stay with me.

Yet at times, in the still, secret parts of the day and in the dreamlike whispers of the night, the memory of her would return. I feared a shadow might always remain in a corner of my heart, but perhaps this shadow served a purpose: balancing a too-hopeful spirit, grounding starry-eyed infatuation with the wisdom of the past.

Two days passed. Still no progress on the letterbox, and still no sign of our pursuers.

After lunch I checked my email on my phone. No news from my P.I., but near the top of my inbox was a brief note from Prentice.

Aidy, I have news. Call me.

I glanced at the time: eight a.m. in the States. I decided to splurge on an international roaming call, and stepped into the hallway to ring Prentice.

"Aidy! A London number? I'm glad you've decided to slink back into the first world."

I wasn't in the mood for frivolous conversation. "What's up?"

"Testy these days, aren't we? I miss the times when I'd come into your office and you were forced to listen to me." He gave a tragic sigh. "Do you remember I told you I'd obtained the records for that French corporation, Donn Enterprises, from a contact in Paris?"

"Sure."

"Well," he said smugly, "a sordid *affaire de couer* is budding. Aiming to impress my Gallic Romeo, I decided to pursue the matter a little further. I didn't get far. Donn Enterprises' corporate purpose is so vague it's laughable. I do approve of whatever law afforded them such secrecy; shareholders don't need to be privy to the inner workings of corporations. This country is going down the tubes with its pseudo-democratic ideals."

I rolled my eyes. "What do you have, Prentice?"

I heard him gulping down coffee. "Donn isn't the end of the line. I discovered a parent company."

I gripped the phone. "Who owns it?"

"The web was tangled, but long story short: Donn was bought out earlier this year by a holding company named S.T., Inc."

"Never heard of it."

"Me, either. There's no record of activity of any sort, anywhere in the world, except for the fact that S.T., Inc. was incorporated in March of this year and its sole corporate act was to purchase Donn Enterprises. Oh, and I found the name of its principal, which is the only other thing it's required by law to disclose."

"Who is it?" I asked.

"M.A. Chenisdeaux."

I ended the conversation and stared at the names I had written down on a piece of paper, certain I'd never heard of either the corporation or its principal. After a few moments of pacing, I again dialed a New Orleans number and had a curt but necessary conversation with Mr. Sofistere.

When the call ended, I rushed back to the British Museum, completely unnerved by what he'd told me.

-65-

I skirted the imposing pillars heralding the entrance to the world's largest repository of pilfered goods, bypassing the marble entrance hall for a side door unavailable to the public. Mr. Sofistere's contact, Dr. Clifton, had arranged access to a private section of the British Museum reserved for staff, scientists, and scholars.

I traversed a narrow hallway, swept past labs and archives, and finally reached a reading room deep within the bowels of the museum. The room was a classic British medley of dark wood and leather furniture.

I found Lou and Jake sprawled in overstuffed chairs, surrounded by stacks of gilt-edged tomes. Paper coffee cups littered a coffee table. Both men looked frustrated and edgy.

"I just learned a couple of interesting things," I said, slumping into another of the large chairs. "Interesting and . . . disturbing."

Jake sat up, and I rehashed the conversation with Prentice.

"Corporations have parents all the time," Lou said.

"I'm not going to kill you with suspense. After I talked to Prentice, I called Mr. Sofistere to run the information by him. He'd never heard of S.T., Inc. But it turns out the individual who hired Mr. Sofistere to research the letterbox is none other than M.A. Chenisdeaux, the principal of S.T., Inc. and the new owner of Donn Enterprises."

Jake whistled. "So what's the story?"

"That's the thing," I said. "Mr. Sofistere was even more surprised than I was. He said he's never even met him. A few months back he got a call from Chenisdeaux, who sounded like a savvy collector. He told Lucius about a promising dig in Dartmoor, and said he'd already purchased the land and acquired the rights. He was eager to begin researching, and wanted someone to retrieve and study whatever was brought to the surface. Lucius was intrigued and agreed. You know the rest. Lucius tried to call a few times, but he hasn't heard from Chenisdeaux since before the letterbox was dug up. By the time he got suspicious, things had gotten out of hand."

"Why didn't he tell us?" Lou said.

"He didn't think it mattered, but it's also bad form. Given the course of events, he no longer cares about breaking confidence." I leaned forward, elbows on my knees, hands clasped. "Mr. Sofistere retrieved the letterbox in May. However, the dig began in March, the day after the geologists' sensors revealed something buried beneath Cranmere Pool. They started digging on March seventh, to be exact. Guess what else happened on March seventh?"

They looked at me with raised eyebrows.

"S.T., Inc. became a corporate entity."

"Weird," Lou said.

Jake frowned. "I don't get it. Why chase after their own damn box?"

I rose to pour a cup of coffee. "I think Chenisdeaux needed someone to find this treasure the Druids believe the letterbox once contained. What better place to send the letterbox than to Mr. Sofistere, who specializes in such things?"

"Okay," Lou said. "But why not just tell us?"

"The only thing I can think of is that he knows something about the things that have happened. Maybe something that would make anyone in his right mind turn around and forget he'd ever heard of the letterbox."

"But if Chenisdeaux owns Chateau Donn," Lou said, "that implies he's in league with the Druids—why not just give them the box instead of Lucius?"

"That I don't know," I said slowly. "All we do know is that Chenisdeaux is wealthy, secretive, and powerful—and that he's probably using us. Maybe he's discovering everything as we are. Maybe he's watching us. The bottom line is, we have no idea what we've gotten ourselves into."

Lou leaned forward. "You think Sofistere could be in league with Chenisdeaux?"

"I think he's been straight with us about the letterbox," I said, after a pause.

"I'd be surprised," Jake said. "I've known Lucius for years. I'd be very surprised."

Oh, I thought, *you'd be surprised about a few things.*

Jake flicked a wrist. "Besides, why tell us about Chenisdeaux if he's in league with him? He could've just kept it secret."

"Good point," Lou said.

Jake folded his arms. "You said Lucius told you two things. What's the other?"

I blew out a breath. "He's been researching the ancient temples that used to exist at the map locations. Nothing new on Castello di Selva or the British sites, but when he turned his attention to Kostel Utes . . . you remember Father Novak? The nice old priest who helped us out?"

"Yep."

"Lucius placed a call to Father Novak to see if he could shed some light on the site's history." I hesitated, a chill coursing through me as I remembered the end of our conversation. "Mr. Sofistere couldn't reach anyone at the church, so he called the local diocese in Prague to see if they could help. He was informed that the church at Kostel Utes was closed the morning we were there, and that there is no Father Novak. Or rather, there's no longer a Father Novak. He died twenty years ago."

-66-

Lou's hands slid off the book he was holding. Jake looked just as shocked.

"I had some time to think about this on the way over," I said. "That information led me to revisit another train of thought, one I've been pondering for a while."

My left foot began tapping. "Think about Father Novak leading us to Kostnice, think about Asha's brother walking right up to the tower, think about the conveniently open tomb in Pere Lachaise where we hid from the Druids. Maybe even think of the librarian in Naples pointing out *dolmen* in the dictionary." I leaned forward. "I think we've had help."

Lou nodded. "I've thought of that, too. But the idea is absurd; who would be helping us?"

"If you haven't noticed," Jake said, "then let me be the one to point out that most, if not all, of the help we've had has come from the deceased."

Lou and I stared at Jake as the truth of that statement sunk in.

"I don't believe in ghosts," Lou said finally, "but it's all moot right now." He crumpled his paper cup and tossed it onto the table. "We can't find the last place on the map. There were thousands of ziggurats built. I can't find any reference whatsoever to this Akkadian word or to the collection of numbers and symbols on the lid. As much as I hate to admit it, I have no idea what the letterbox is trying to tell us, if anything."

"That's because, lads," a booming, erudite voice called out, "you're still looking in the wrong place."

I whipped around, thinking of the Druids. Instead I saw a towering British man, taller even than Jake, striding into the room carrying the oldest book I had ever laid eyes on, a tome cracked and yellowed from age. He set it down with aplomb on the table. A slip of paper bookmarked a page in the middle.

He wore his traveler's clothes as well as he wore his age: khaki cargo pants and a bomber jacket, weathered boots, and a wide-brimmed hat. He reminded me of the British travelers from old movies, privileged and intrepid individuals who spent their fortunes in pursuit of the unknown.

He allowed us a slightly mocking smile, as if he possessed a secret he was withholding for effect. I wondered how long he had been listening in the doorway. "It appears I've forgotten my manners," he said. "Do forgive me. I'm Dr. Philip Clifton, and I presume you're the three gentlemen Mr. Sofistere warned me about? I highly doubt three other young Americans would be subjecting themselves to the confines of the British Museum on a Friday night, with the heart of London waiting just outside."

"You're early, I'm not young, and I sure as Christmas don't have time for that nonsense," Jake said, jerking his thumb towards the door. "You claim we're lookin' in the wrong place. Where should we be looking?"

"Dr. Fleniken, your reputation precedes you."

"It better," Jake said.

Dr. Clifton's lips retreated into a thin smile. "Mr. Sofistere suggested I impart the results of my research in person, but I've a limited window of time. How much do you know about Akkadian and the peoples who spoke it?"

Lou kicked his legs up and put his hands behind his head. "I'm a trained linguist, but Akkadian isn't my area of expertise. What I do know is that it's an extremely ancient language. Old Akkadian, which I believe this to be, flourished between 2500 and 1950 B.C.E. Nearly five thousand years ago."

Dr. Clifton spread his hands in approval, and Lou continued. "Akkadian is a Semitic language, spoken in ancient Mesopotamia, and can be traced back almost to the beginning of written history. The Semitic language family has two main sub branches, East Semitic and West Semitic. The East Semitic branch, the language of the Babylonian and Assyrian civilizations and from which Akkadian derives, is extinct. West Semitic is the precursor to Arabic and Hebrew and other Canaanite languages, including Aramaic and its language families. The West Semitic language family and its offspring are, so to speak, the lingua franca of the world's major monotheistic religions: Judaism, Christianity, and Islam."

"I'll help fill in the gaps on the cultural side," Dr. Clifton said. "Paganism is something of a misnomer, for it implies an alternative to standard religion, and pagans are commonly thought of as 'alternative religious practitioners.' In fact, pagan religions are not alternatives: they're the prototypes. Without speaking to the validity or non-validity of any religion, it is simply a fact that most, if not all, of the myths—historical events if you are one of faith—that comprise the backbone of the world's religions have their roots in one pagan legend or another. There is a flood, or an Eden, or a resurrection of life, as far back as religious history dates. Even the cross was a symbol common to early pagan religions."

Dr. Clifton's combination of scholarly bearing and rugged competence lent him an aura of authenticity that left even me, the suspicious attorney, at ease and in his confidence.

"Akkadian," Dr. Clifton continued, "was the language of the Babylonians, the most influential pagan civilization of its day. Perhaps ever. Akkadian, gentlemen, is the language of archetypal religion, of the origin of myth."

Jake threw his hands up. "Where you headed, doc?"

Dr. Clifton started to pace, one hand hanging at his side, the other coming up to gesture as he spoke. "I understand you have a rudimentary knowledge of the alleged ley lines, including the theory that their energy is much more intense at an intersection point—intense enough, under proper circumstances, to be channeled."

"Which was why the stone circles were built," Lou said, and got another affirmative nod. "But how? What are the dolmens and megaliths supposed to *do?*"

"No one is certain, besides the fact that they served various astrological purposes. However, the commonly held belief is that the stones acted as a sort of channeling device that allowed metaphysical energy to flow and coalesce. We think these ancient cultures believed that, through the use of megalithic structures, they were gathering, conducting, and stimulating the flow of this energy. Rather like spiritual acupuncture."

"Pagan poppycock," Jake said, though without his usual conviction.

"Perhaps," Dr. Clifton replied, then wagged a finger. "But let us connect the dots. The ancient Babylonians took their ley lines very seriously. More so than any other culture. They built enormous temples where they believed the points of intersection to lie, and performed lengthy and complex rituals to channel their power."

"How did anyone know where these ley lines were in the first place?" I asked.

"Great question. The Babylonians developed an entire class of priests, reputed to be psychics, who were devoted to the task of pinpointing and utilizing ley lines. They developed the concept of the dowsing rod and used mathematical calculations involving the position of the heavenly bodies, as well as other advanced methods, to determine where the ley lines ran." He smirked. "No one knows how good they were at it, because no one can prove that ley lines exist. But the Babylonians, and a multitude of other cultures, were absolutely convinced of their power. I would also mention that some of the places reputed to be ley lines possess a high level of geomagnetic energy, and that modern-day psychics claim they can feel heightened spiritual energy at sites such as Stonehenge."

"We've seen all of this in our research," Lou said.

Dr. Clifton smiled as if he had doled out the tip of the iceberg. "Apart from the megaliths, the Babylonian priests developed another way to channel the energy of the ley lines. A method they believed was much more effective, much more difficult to implement—and much more dangerous."

"*That* we haven't seen," Jake said.

"People who subscribe to ley lines believe you can harness their power by entering into a trance, opening yourself to the energies. However, these neo-pagans are clearly not versed in ancient Akkadian. If they were, they would realize they're missing a vital element."

Lou cracked his knuckles without looking down. "Which was?"

"The Babylonians believed that, through the proper use of astronomy, mathematics, language, and divination, combined with precise calculations of where the ley lines ran, one could greatly enhance the channeling of metaphysical energy. They developed a code—a formula, if you will—using complex rituals and calculations involving the above-mentioned spheres of knowledge."

Jake frowned. "A formula? For channeling spiritual energy?"

"The concept exists in some form or another in every religion on earth, including Christianity. What do you think prayer is? Rites, liturgies, monastic chants? Versions of the same thing. Efforts to call upon the spirit world, to reach God through the use of language. Mathematics, science, and pseudo-sciences often come into play as well. Think of the Kabbalah and the codes of the Torah; the hidden teachings of the Gnostics; Hindu and Buddhist mantras; Islamic rituals; the repetition of Christian prayers and liturgies; the precise semantics of an exorcism. All are calculated, ritualistic efforts to invoke the power of the divine. Dr. Fleniken, you're far more versed in religion than I. Tell me, am I wrong?"

Jake pursed his lips. "In theory, no."

"The Babylonians believed they had developed something that served the same purpose: a formula that facilitated contact with the spirit world, especially when brought into the presence of a heightened theater, such as an intersection of ley lines. I believe an appropriate analogy might be . . . let us say . . . performing a Catholic rite on holy ground."

Jake's face tightened. Lou and I exchanged a glance, and one phrase in particular had stood out to me. *Facilitated contact with the spirit world.*

"The Babylonians believed their 'formula' to be their greatest discovery, as well as their most sacred knowledge, known to only a handful of high-ranking priests. It was their holy grail, their ark of the covenant."

"What exactly did they think they'd discovered?" I asked.

"On its own, the formula was considered a way to commune with God. A type of mantra or prayer. However, the Babylonians believed that if the formula was inscribed upon an object and brought within proximity of a ley line, the formula would expand and magnify the energy channels to a much greater degree."

"My God," Lou said, in a near-whisper. "The Babylonians would have used Akkadian. The symbols on the letterbox—*is that the formula?*"

"I believe that is exactly what it is," Dr. Clifton said.

-67-

"There's no way to be certain," Dr. Clifton continued. "Due to its complexity and gravity, the formula was only inscribed on a handful of objects. I consulted a few colleagues and the only one who had even heard of it, a Sumerian scholar at Oxford, laughed and said that, if such a thing ever existed, it surely has been lost to time, and in any event would be impossible to verify."

"What's supposed to happen when this . . . formula . . . comes into proximity with a ley line?" I asked.

"A normal ley line wouldn't produce much of an effect, even when combined with the formula. However, the Babylonians believed that at an intersection point, with the help of the formula, it would be possible to communicate with entities from the spirit world."

My eyes slunk to the letterbox, poised on a low table next to Jake. "Think about the places we've had an encounter," I said. "At the castle, Kostel Utes . . . ."

"Places on the map," Jake said grimly. "Points of intersection."

"Yes, but also at the ossuary and Pere LaChaise and the two times your wife appeared, at Notre Dame and by the dolmen in Grimspound."

"Notre Dame was built on top of a Roman temple," Jake said. "I've a strong suspicion that's the case with the Bone Church and Pere Lachaise, as well."

I paused with the weight of my next words. "Every time we've visited an ancient religious site with the letterbox, we've had some sort of unexplainable encounter. With someone or something. And at no other time has this happened."

Despite the fact that we were tucked away within the confines of the British Museum, gooseflesh began running in waves along my arms. Jake looked stricken. While Lou was staring at the fire, I could tell he was listening intently.

"Note that the Babylonians believed even the points of intersection contained limited energy," Dr. Clifton said, "and that they varied in strength."

"Vivian kept saying she didn't have much time," I said. "And the way everyone kept disappearing . . . yet when Jake tossed the stone at the man in the crypt, it made contact. Pere Lachaise must be a more powerful site."

Lou turned back from the fire, sneering. "Or it was a trick. Let's keep our heads here."

"Shut up, Commie."

Dr. Clifton stopped pacing in front of the table with the letterbox. "There was another belief among the Babylonians—a belief that there existed a specific place on earth where more than two ley lines intersected. A place, in fact, where they *all* intersected. A power center, a nexus: a sacred site where the Babylonians believed the physical and spiritual worlds were so intertwined that even without the formula, ghosts and spirits could manifest at will. Unfortunately, as far as I can tell, the Babylonians never managed to pinpoint the location."

Jake's voice was thick. "What if the formula was brought to this place? Did they have a theory?"

"The two things they speculated would happen are clear. First, they thought the barrier between our world and the spiritual realm would dissolve, and that it might be possible to travel between the two."

I knew by Jake's rapt expression what he was thinking. His wife, mortal once again.

"And the second?" Jake said.

Dr. Clifton put his hands on the table. "The Babylonians believed that at this one place on earth, with the presence of the formula, one might encounter a divine being. A god."

-68-

"A theophany," Lou said, with a hollow chuckle. "A manifestation of a god to a human."

As if lured by a snake charmer, my gaze veered downward, to the ancient Babylonian artifact. The letterbox seemed to possess a new and puissant essence, the symbol of our hopes and fears, a manifestation of our dreams and nightmares.

Jake jumped up and began pacing. "Even if this is all true, the box is useless without the location of the nexus. You said the Babylonians themselves didn't know where it was."

Dr. Clifton moved his hands to the cover of the tome he had brought with him. "As I said, the Babylonians had a highly developed system of discovering and tracing tellurian energy. They believed the ley lines all curved slightly inward, meeting at one point in the middle, and they knew some of them curved across other ley lines to create intersection points. The 'straight-line' effect of ley lines on modern maps is not necessarily inaccurate, for the lines were thought to be extremely long and the curve gradual. Amazingly, the Babylonian theory makes sense if you consider that the world is round; their slightly curved ley lines and nexus point fit perfectly within a spherical surface. But I digress. The Babylonians took their knowledge and made a map of the ley lines they believed ran across the earth, superimposing the lines over the areas of the world they had mapped."

He opened the book and stepped aside. "I believe this should speak for itself."

I felt a heaviness in the air as I bent over the tome. Though I didn't recognize the specific geographical entities, there were universal representations of mountains, oceans, and deserts. I saw human figures dotting the landscape, warriors and priests and kings. Strange-looking boats hovered in seas without borders, and there was the unique addition that made this map unlike any I had ever seen: the presence of dozens of lines running across the earth, crossing each other at various points, all spiraling inward to meet at a pinprick in the upper left corner.

The meeting point of the lines was northwest of the area that had been mapped extensively and which represented the known regions of the world at the time. No cartographical markings existed near this meeting point. I racked my brain to try to remember what area of the world this might represent in relation to the Near East, but the map was too old and inaccurate for me to hazard a guess.

The map bore only one marking near the meeting point: a rune-like symbol, topped by a wavy line, that was neither ley line nor cartographical representation.

Lou put both stocky arms on the table and leaned over the map. "It's the same symbol," he said in awe, stating what I had already noticed, and which caused a tingling to flood my nerve endings. "Next to the meeting of the ley lines—that's the symbol on the letterbox."

"As you can see," Dr. Clifton said, "the Babylonians named the site, though they had yet to discover the actual location."

"The nexus," Jake whispered, gripping his chair and leaning forward.

"So what now?" Lou asked.

"I'm sorry to say I've exhausted the sources within my field. If there's an answer to this puzzle, I'm afraid you'll need to look elsewhere." He closed the book. "Gentlemen, I wish you the best. I have other engagements, and must pass the torch."

Jake slumped in his seat, and I felt a stab of despair. So close, yet so far.

"Perhaps it's an impossible task," Dr. Clifton said, noticing our dejection, "but you opened the door when you discovered the Akkadian inscription on the letterbox." His gaze rested on the map, and then on the symbol carved into the letterbox. "You have a name."

* * *

After Dr. Clifton left, Jake paced back and forth with an intense scowl. Lou drummed his fingers on the table as he stared at the letterbox. I was deep in thought, absorbing everything that had happened.

Lou stopped his finger movement. "We need a new strategy," he said.

Jake waved a hand. "Tell us something we don't know."

"If the nexus was really that important, there had to have been ancient search parties out looking for it. Scouring the globe. And if anyone found it, I'm guessing there was some kind of temple or monument built at the site."

"I like where you're going with this," Jake said. "You're thinking this theoretical place of worship might have been marked with the letterbox symbol."

Lou gave a slow nod. "It's a long shot. But it's the only shot I can think of."

We took Lou's idea and ran with it, scouring the museum's archives for books on ancient ziggurats, cathedrals, shrines, temples—anything that might fit the bill. We grabbed sandwiches from the cafeteria for dinner and settled in for the long haul. Midnight came and went, and when I finally looked up, it was three a.m.

I rubbed my eyes; they were starting to blur. "I'm getting diminishing returns."

Lou yawned and agreed. Jake didn't respond for a moment, then snarled and slammed shut the book he was reading.

Jake agreed to leave the museum, mainly because he didn't want us walking to the hotel by ourselves. Vowing to return at first light, we slipped out the side entrance and hurried down the street.

Lou and Jake lit up as we walked, then started comparing research notes. Halfway to the hotel, Jake said out of the side of his mouth, so low I could barely hear him, "We've got company. Keep walking and act normal."

Every muscle in my body tensed. I canvassed the street in front of us, seeing nothing but empty pavement and a corridor of ash-colored buildings. Heeding Jake's advice, I resisted the urge to look over my shoulder.

Lou and Jake kept discussing the search. I heard a flutter in the back of Lou's voice, but Jake's was clear and firm.

I braced for the worst, though I could detect no sign of pursuit. What had Jake heard? Why hadn't they ambushed us already? The streets were deserted.

The hotel was three blocks away. It was the longest ten minutes of my life, but we reached it without incident. I let out a huge breath, shivery with adrenaline. I started to speak but Jake cut me off with a glance.

We climbed the stairs to our hallway. Halfway to our room, Jake put a hand out, stopping us. He gathered us close and spoke in a whisper. "We had eyes on us. Two pairs."

"White robes?" I asked.

"Jackets with hoods."

"Maybe they were just thugs," Lou said weakly, and Jake withered him with a glance.

"Why didn't they go for us?" I asked.

Jake shrugged off his backpack, which contained the letterbox. "My guess? They want us to do their work for them. They'll see what we find and then move in."

Lou peered nervously down the hallway. "So what do we do?"

"Get some sleep. Act normal. Don't discuss anything in the room. When we go to the museum in the morning, put anything you can't leave behind in my backpack."

After a few hours of restless sleep, we stuffed our toiletries and a change of clothes into Jake's backpack, along with the letterbox. It was a smart move; we could leave at a moment's notice if we found anything.

We researched all day, guzzling coffee and eating cold sandwiches from the café in the atrium. Besides the cleaning lady, no one bothered us.

Late that night, craving a bit of fresh air, I followed Jake outside during one of his smoke breaks. We had our backs against the wall, watching the street. Right after Jake flicked away his butt, Lou burst out of the door, his eyes wide.

"Guys," he said, "I found something."

* * *

We rushed back inside, crowding around another impossibly old book. The title was in Latin.

Lou waved his hands as he spoke. "This is a Roman history book, circa 1100 A.D. Basically it's an accounting of the fringes of the Roman Empire at the time. The passage of interest concerns a forested area just south of Russia and controlled by barbaric tribes. A Roman explorer documented his journey to the region."

"Surely you weren't just reading ancient history books in Latin," I said. "What drew you to the passage?"

"I was flipping through books with references to ancient temples," Lou said, grinning like a kid who had just discovered a cabinet full of chocolate bars. He opened the tome to a bookmarked page. On the right half was a page of unbroken Latin script, and on the left was a single drawing that took up most of the page.

The symbol on the letterbox.

A shiver of excitement coursed through me. After taking a long look at the drawing, Jake sank into one of the chairs. "What's it say?" he croaked. "I'll read it for myself later, but give me the gist."

"The Roman explorer stumbled upon the ruins of an ancient temple complex. The ruins were deep inside the forest—a collection of megaliths, altars, and pagan symbols. And get this—the central structure was a ziggurat built around a hill, surrounded by hundreds of spears planted upright into the ground."

Jake flew out of his seat, his long hair flying. "A temple with spears—the pointed symbols on the map. That's got to be it!"

"No one from the local tribes knew who had made the ruins. They used the forest for worship, but were afraid of the temple and refused to go inside. The Roman speculated they had planted the spears themselves—probably as a superstitious method of protection from whatever the temple contained or represented."

"Not too unusual," Jake said. "Numerous civilizations left only their architecture as a legacy."

"The explorer found the letterbox symbol engraved all over the ruins. It was so strange he copied it down and reported his find to Rome. Luckily for us, an enterprising scholar included a drawing in this book."

"So correct me if I'm wrong," I said, "but don't we still have to find this place? Or is there more?"

"I don't know exactly what region it's in," Lou said, "but I've got a very good guess, as should you by now. A land of vast primeval forests south of Russia, with a rich pagan history that continues to this day. A land known for harvesting crystals especially conducive to illumination. A land with a history of woodworking, including a style distinctive to wood carvers in the Baltic area up until the end of the first millennium."

Jake was grinning with knowledge.

"Lithuania," I murmured.

Yet even if a Babylonian search party had found its way to the Baltic forests, I wondered, and built the temple depicted in Lou's book, why had the site been abandoned?

"Lithuania's a big country," I said. "Do we have a map of this temple's location to start with?"

"No," Lou said, "but I think we have a good chance of finding it. What do you think, Jake?"

"Oh yeah," he said, exchanging a knowing look with Lou.

"Am I missing something?" I asked.

"Just one of the rules of thumb of historical research," Lou said. "As we've seen, it can be incredibly hard to find something buried in the past. But what, our fearless leader, isn't nearly as difficult?"

Jake gave a grim smile and started unwrapping a pack of cigarettes. "Tracing it forward."

-69-

We returned to our hotel for another few hours of sleep, leaving the museum as if nothing unusual had happened. No one accosted us, but I wondered how much rope our enemies would give us before deciding to make a play for the letterbox. We badly needed the location of the nexus.

The next morning, after we set up camp in our reading room, I went to the main atrium to grab breakfast sandwiches for the group. As I entered the huge room, I locked eyes with a pair of people in wool overcoats. They looked away as soon as I saw them, and the dark-haired man, who was in the process of pulling off a pair of gloves, stopped what he was doing.

My heart skipped a beat. I entered the cafeteria line as nonchalantly as I could. I couldn't be certain, because I had never seen his face, but I felt sure it was the Druid with the burned hand. Why else would he look at me and then away, and more importantly, pull his gloves back on inside the building?

Yet it was more than that: it was something about his face, his predatory eyes and the arrogant set to his mouth, as if he possessed knowledge that others did not. Secret knowledge.

I made sure to imprint their appearances in my mind. The woman seemed vaguely familiar, a thin older lady with long gray hair and close-set eyes. I couldn't remember where, but I thought I might have seen her before. The man was tall and narrow-shouldered, roughly fifty years old, and his pale, craggy face looked as if it had once been handsome.

Safely ensconced in a line of people, I risked a glance over my shoulder, and then took a longer look around the atrium.

There was no sign of them.

I took a circuitous route back to our reading room and told Jake and Lou about the encounter.

"You think they realized you made them?" Jake asked, unwrapping his egg and bacon sandwich.

"I'm not sure. Probably."

He grunted. "They won't like being ID'd, and who knows how many more there are. We need to find what we're after and get the hell out of Dodge."

I couldn't have been more in agreement. As the morning wore on, I kept telling myself that things were getting too dicey, that I should get on a plane back to the States.

And then I made a discovery.

"Look at this," I said, pointing out a drawing in yet another history book about the Baltic region, this one from the early sixteenth century. It was an undeniable representation of a ruined ziggurat surrounded by spears, though there was no sign of the letterbox symbol.

Lou broke into a wide grin as he picked up the book. "How many of these do you think there were in the Baltics?"

Jake slapped me on the back and then cracked his knuckles, his mouth tight. "We're on the map."

It took the rest of the day and most of the night, but now that we had a more recent reference point, we were able to trace the history of the ziggurat site through settlement, wars, pestilence, the onset of Christianity, and the anti-religious travails of Communist rule. We learned that the people of the region had destroyed and rebuilt the ruins many times over, and in many different guises, eventually erasing all evidence of the Akkadian symbol. Though the site had gone by many different names, it remained a mysterious and feared place of worship, buried deep within the forest.

At six a.m., blurry-eyed after an entire night of research, Lou was flipping through a history of modern Lithuania. I poured my umpteenth cup of coffee as Lou looked up, an incredulous look on his face. "I can't believe it. It's right there, and it's not even a secret. The Lithuanians call it the Hill of Crosses, and it's a pilgrimage site near the town of Šiauliai."

"The Hill of Crosses," Jake repeated. He rose slowly to his feet, as if in a dream. "Commie, are you saying what I think you're saying?"

"Nexus or not, this is the location we've been researching. I'm sure of it."

The three of us could have been the subjects of a still-life painting. Then the adrenaline hit, and we whooped and danced around the room.

When the initial excitement wore off, Jake looked ready to bolt out the door. He started giving rapid-fire orders. "Commie, make sure you know exactly where we're going. Counselor, get us some grub for the road and look natural doing it. They'll think we're holed up for the day. I'll pack up and we'll hit the road in thirty minutes."

"Won't they just follow us?" I asked.

Jake winked at me. "Not from the exit we're gonna use."

Access card in hand, we entered a portion of the basement I'd never seen before, a warren of narrow corridors and rooms piled high with crates. As we wolfed down breakfast sandwiches, Jake led us through the maze as if he had mapped it, stopping only to retrieve a crowbar he had planted in a box in one of the rooms.

One of the hallways dead-ended at an old metal door secured with a rusty padlock. It looked like no one had been around for years. Jake took out his lock-pick set and, after much pulling and grunting, removed the padlock.

The door opened to reveal a round, brick-walled vestibule as cold and musty as a tomb. A dusty staircase descended into darkness.

"What is this place?" Lou said, peering nervously down.

"The old employee entrance to the British Museum tube station."

"The what?" I said. "There is no such thing."

Jake grinned. "There used to be. I figured we might need an escape route, and took a look at the building schematics. When I saw this old addition, the light bulb went on."

I ran a hand through my hair, not relishing the thought of trekking through an abandoned tube station with the Druids so near. As usual, Jake didn't give us time to debate. We replaced the padlock as best we could, used our cellphones to light the way, and then started down the staircase, our footsteps echoing in the stillness.

To keep my mind off the vulnerability of our position, I asked a question that had been bothering me. "How did the letterbox," I said, "if it truly is a Babylonian artifact, end up buried in the moors?"

"The Romans scattered the Druids across Europe," Jake said. "They must have found the ziggurat site and the Akkadian-inscribed tablet when they pushed into the Baltic forests."

"But why break with tradition and add the Ogham inscription?" Lou asked.

"Seems obvious, doesn't it? Something happened to them at the nexus. Something powerful enough to convince them to record it, and turn the tablet into a religious object of their own."

"And the map?" I said. "What do you think about Sofistere's guess, that it indicates sites throughout Europe where the Druids met under persecution, or leads to a treasure buried at the ziggurat site?"

"You want to know what I think, Counselor? I think the Druids saw the same things we did, and they made the map as a sort of spiritual testing ground. A way to prepare the traveler, at intersections of the ley lines, for the journey to the nexus."

The silence of the passage punctuated Jake's words, until Lou snorted. "You should have been born in the Middle Ages."

"That still doesn't explain the monotheism," I said to Jake. "Why name God in the singular on the letterbox?"

"Polytheism doesn't preclude belief in a supreme being," Jake said. "Most pagan cultures believed in a being or force similar to our concept of an omnipotent God, and the various spirits and deities they worshipped were viewed as lesser gods, or different facets of the same gem. This applies to

Hindus, Buddhists, Native Americans, and indigenous African religions, to name a few. The Druids didn't keep records, but maybe they referred to their concept of God in the singular, despite the fact that they worshipped various aspects of the spiritual and natural world. Maybe they thought God was the spiritual energy that ran along the ley lines. Or maybe," his voice turned grim, "they had a change of heart in Lithuania."

The bottom of the staircase materialized, ending at another door. I looked over my shoulder for the hundredth time, but there was no sign of pursuit.

"What we do know is this," Jake continued. "The Druids took the letterbox back to their homeland, all the way on the other side of the world, and they buried it as deep as they could."

Jake picked the lock again. The door squeaked open to reveal a cavernous room with tiled walls and a rounded ceiling. A rush of stale and even cooler air greeted us.

Detritus littered the floor. As I skirted a pile of bricks, I felt as if we were explorers in some dystopian future, poking through the ruins of a lost civilization.

Four hallways with arched entrances branched into darkness. The room wasn't big enough to be the main entrance to a station, and I guessed it was a connector hall.

"Where does this come out?" I said. "Won't the exits be locked from the other side?"

"Probably." He raised the crowbar. "That's what this is for."

"That's your plan?" Lou said, incredulous. "Find a random door and smash through?"

"Have some faith, Commie. I know it's hard for you."

He led us down the second corridor to our left. We walked as fast as we could, just short of a run. I kept expecting to hear rats, the plop of water, or worse—the sound of booted footsteps. But there was only deafening silence.

A hundred feet down the corridor, Jake stopped in front of a door with its seams set flush into the wall. I would have walked right by it.

Jake attacked the locking mechanism with his crowbar. It took a while, but it was old and he was able to rip through it. We opened the door and stepped into a smaller tunnel with a sleeker ceiling and walls.

"Engineering tunnel," Jake said. "It should lead straight to the surface."

The tunnel sloped gradually upward, eventually merging with a sewer tunnel, and we climbed out of the first grate we saw. Thankfully it exited on a side street with little traffic. A few pedestrians gawked at us as we climbed out, and we hurried around the corner.

I clapped Jake on the back, relieved beyond words to be above ground. Yet it somehow seemed too easy. I had almost begun to attribute the Druids' abilities to follow us to supernatural powers, and even after their deceptions were revealed, it was hard to shake the notion. Not to mention the creeping suspicion that someone was helping us from the shadows, herding us to our doom.

What machinations had been put in place when the letterbox was unearthed from its watery grave?

Lou stopped someone to ask directions to the nearest tube stop, and they pointed us towards Holborn.

"What about Covent Garden?" Jake asked, and I knew what he was thinking. The Druids might have someone watching the tube stops nearest the museum.

We got our bearings and rushed to the city center. As I entered Covent Garden alongside a crush of pedestrians, I kept imagining furtive glances from the corners of the station, cowled faces watching our every move.

-70-

Jake called Mr. Sofistere from a payphone at Heathrow, informing him of everything we had learned. Lucius was stunned by our discoveries, and gave us permission to take the letterbox to Lithuania to finish the quest. He also relayed that he had tried to contact the elusive Mr. Chenisdeaux again, to no avail.

I asked Jake if Asha had been on the phone, and he said she was. While I knew she'd want to be here, I was glad she was out of harm's way. Despite my efforts to heal, I missed her terribly.

The seats at our gate were all taken. As we hunkered down in a corner, I glanced at Jake, leaning against the wall and watching the crowd, and Lou, sitting cross-legged on the floor and staring at his lap.

The only thing on Jake's mind, I knew, was the logistical planning for our trip to the Hill of Crosses.

Lou, on the other hand, looked as pensive as I had ever seen him. Regardless of one's convictions, the events which we had witnessed, combined with what we had learned from Dr. Clifton, would have given the greatest skeptic pause.

And Lou was the greatest skeptic.

On the taxi ride to Heathrow, Lou reiterated his long-standing position that there was nothing supernatural about anything we had experienced. He prophesied that the explanations would be revealed in due course, in logical clarity, and that Jake and I would be laughing at our gullibility. Yet behind the bravado and the simmering fear, I saw a flicker of doubt in his eyes.

I didn't dispute the accuracy of the information imparted by Dr. Clifton, and I had to admit that incredible things had happened. But who, in the face of the impossible, does not harbor doubt? Even the stoutest of saints, the staunchest of believers: surely they have their reservations, somewhere in the depths of their souls. We are only human, after all, and can only speculate.

Or can we? Had we been presented with an opportunity to do more than guess? What awaited us at the enigmatic Hill of Crosses? Would we learn the truth behind the seemingly supernatural events we had experienced? Would something terrible be revealed, some horror from beyond? Or was the danger all too human, a group of religious fanatics who would stop at nothing to get what they wanted?

Why take the risk, I asked myself for the thousandth time? Why not get on a plane and go back to New Orleans?

But I knew the answer. The carrot in front of us now was the same one that had sprouted when I saw Asha's hands pass through those of her brother at Castello di Selva. The same carrot that sustained me after the incredible events at Pere Lachaise, and Kutna Hora, and in Grimspound.

It was the carrot of knowledge leading us on, dangling within our grasp. Another bite of the apple, impossible to resist.

Perhaps, in the end, Lou would be proven right, and everything would be revealed as a deception of obscene magnitude. But the possibility remained. It was right before us now.

Even if our presence at the Hill of Crosses with the letterbox meant that we would be placing our lives, and perhaps our very souls, in peril, the lure of forbidden knowledge hovered before us like the world's lushest piece of fruit, waiting to be plucked by our eager mortal hands.

LITHUANIA

-71-

The flight passed without incident, though I remained on edge. Despite the cleverness of Jake's exit strategy, I had a hard time believing we had given the remaining Druids the slip.

After an early afternoon arrival in Vilnius, the capital of Lithuania, we took a taxi to the central train station. Next up was a five-hour ride to Siauliai, the town nearest the Hill of Crosses. Lithuanian was a difficult language, even for Lou, and everything we had read suggested that it was very easy to get lost on the roads. It was a tough decision, but we decided public transport was the prudent choice. We couldn't afford a detour.

I absorbed Vilnius as the taxi drove in. The city boasts one of the largest old towns in Europe, a king's bounty of monuments and historic buildings spread throughout a jumble of cobblestone streets. Yet Vilnius possessed a dark and gritty edge that was lacking in other European capitals. Mindless Soviet high-rises ringed the city center; beggars and street urchins lounged on UNESCO world heritage sites; disaffected youth prowled wide frozen boulevards. A sense of chaos permeated the city, and as the taxi crawled through the center, I noticed a host of unmarked, dead-end streets and quaint medieval walkways that would turn, without warning, into cracked passages leading to abandoned ghettos.

I didn't have much time to put my finger on exactly what Lithuania evoked in me. But the architecture, the remote locale, the antiquated culture . . . if nothing else, Lithuania felt *old*. Connected to the earth as it once had been. Even the local wares and handicrafts, hawked by street vendors and showcasing the country's pagan roots, contributed to the feeling. Carvings of strange creatures stared back at us from streetside display tables: trees with human faces, rings of faeries dancing in the streams, fantastical forest dwellers trapped in amber.

Our train left at four p.m., and we holed up in an Internet café next to the station while we waited. Jake and I scanned the crowds while Lou did some research on the Hill of Crosses. Finally we took our seats on the rusty locomotive that would carry us to Siauliai.

It was almost dark when the train pulled out of Vilnius. We knew we were traveling through a vast, heavily forested landscape, but the premature nightfall of Lithuania's northern latitude obscured the scenery. During the long ride, Lou recounted some of the shrouded history of the Hill of Crosses.

Due to its isolated geography, Lithuania remained the last pagan stronghold of Europe, holding onto its roots long after other countries had turned to Rome and Byzantium for spiritual guidance. Until a hundred years ago, the ruins of the various temples that had once crowned the Hill of Crosses had still been present, and the site remained a sacred shrine to the peoples of the region who still worshipped in the ancient ways. A century ago, however, the Lithuanian arm of the Catholic Church sent emissaries to destroy the ruins, attempting to Christianize it by erecting three large crosses on the apex of the hill.

After this, an odd phenomenon occurred: the hill began to fill up with crosses of all sorts. The cross was an important symbol to numerous pagan cultures, and the archaic versions sprouted up alongside the Christian ones. Church officials were mystified as to who was planting the crosses and attempted to remove them, but they kept metastasizing.

The Church was in a quandary. The site was too inaccessible to be watched on a regular basis, and further, Lou reported in a cynical but subdued tone, reports of hauntings and strange visions poured forth from the officials who visited the hill. Fits of insanity and suicides also occurred.

The Church decided to solve the problem by giving the hill its present name and, due to the quantity of spiritual activity reported, declaring it a holy site. The Church then proceeded to ignore the place entirely. The visits and reports from the Vatican ceased, and Lou found only sporadic mention of the Hill of Crosses during the previous fifty years.

"Not to add fuel to the fire," I said uneasily, "but all of those accounts—they occurred *without* the letterbox.

"It all sounds like a huge bag of ignorant drivel to me," Lou said. He shifted in his seat. While he may not have accepted as true what he had just told us, I could tell it had affected him.

"You're welcome to run on home," Jake said.

"I've come this far. Besides, who'll be there to say I told you so when we don't find anything? And since when did you start believing in pagan legends?"

Jake folded his arms as he turned to stare into the darkened forest. "I've learned one thing for sure in my profession: whether or not the Christian record of God is an accurate one, and I do believe that it is, it's not the only one out there."

It was only nine p.m. when we arrived at Siauliai, though it felt like the middle of the night. As we stepped off the platform at the ramshackle train station, we saw a strip of cracked, weed-covered pavement marking the route into town.

There were no taxis. Soon after we started walking, the other passengers left the road for barely visible paths snaking into the forest. The three of us drew close together, a sense of foreboding already having descended. Minutes later, the road broadened to reveal a collection of houses and low buildings rising uneasily out of the darkness.

-72-

We lodged at the first place we encountered, a boarding house on the edge of town. Lou managed to fumble through enough Lithuanian to pay for our rooms, and we crawled onto the thin mattresses.

I slept fitfully, my rest troubled by sepulchral visions. I would awaken with a start and then wonder, as I lay in a cold sweat in the darkness after my nightmares, whether the Hill of Crosses was invading our dreams.

Early the next morning, sleep-deprived but ready to get on with the journey, I wandered into the breakfast nook and found Jake and Lou sitting at a table, drinking coffee and smoking in silence.

I sat next to Lou. "I had terrible dreams."

Lou looked up in surprise. "Me, too."

Jake set the letterbox on the table. "Today's the day. I just need to find out when the bus leaves, and pick up a few supplies in town."

Lou shrugged. "I suppose we might as well get this superstitious nonsense over with."

Jake started to reply when the door creaked open. We looked to see who was coming in, expecting another boarder or the landlord.

Instead, the last person I expected to see stepped into view, wrapped in a beige fur-lined coat and matching shawl, her dark hair spilling over her collar.

Asha.

She looked achingly beautiful, in the way a lover does after a prolonged absence, though we had parted less than a week before. Yet she also felt distant, a ghost from a life I once had led and a person I once had been. She looked at me, too, with new eyes: eyes that no longer expressed such openness to the world, eyes that had seen for themselves the terrible power of love and deception.

I rose to help her with her bag. She intercepted me with a hug. Though her embrace caused the familiar fluttering in my chest, it was no longer a sharp pang, but a dull ache somewhere deep inside.

"Good to see you," Jake said. "I figure you're itchin' for a walk in the woods?"

"After what you found in London," she said, looking straight at me, "I knew I had to be here. I jumped on a plane to Vilnius last night."

"How'd you know where we were staying?" Lou asked.

"I was worried I'd miss you, so Mr. Sofistere hired a driver to take me to Siauliai overnight. It's a tiny town, and someone at the first place I tried knew where the Americans were staying. I don't think they get many visitors."

"Good timing," Jake said. "We're leavin' in a few hours." He gave me a brief look, both commiseration and resolve reflected in his glance.

Lou told her about his research on the Hill of Crosses. She looked out the window, at the forest looming at the edge of town, and then at the letterbox resting on the table beside Jake. "Have you . . . experienced . . . anything yet?"

"Our dreams weren't too pleasant last night," I said.

"A subconscious reaction," Lou said. "Who wouldn't have nightmares after that kind of story?"

Asha turned to Lou, smiling for the first time. "Same old Lou."

Jake leaned in, an edge to his voice. "Commie, you're trembling in your boots right now. Admit it."

"I'll admit nothing, you gullible peasant. If we're lucky, we'll find something culturally significant."

Lou's words rang hollow. Jake's mouth was set in a thin line, his eyes faraway, and Asha was looking out the window again.

I tried and failed to relax as I finished my coffee. In addition to my shock at seeing Asha and my fear that the Druids would find us, I couldn't shake, as much as I tried, the feeling that someone—or some*thing*—was waiting for us at the Hill of Crosses.

-73-

The bus was scheduled to leave at two. Deciding not to separate for any reason, we followed Jake into town to gather a few last-minute supplies, in case we needed to stay at the hill for longer than a few hours. We had no idea what to expect or how long it would take to explore.

Sleepy and nondescript, Siauliai had a timeless quality to it. Perhaps it was the stoop of the Baltic townspeople huddled in their drab winter clothing, or the provincial nature of the shops, or the ageless forest surrounding the town. Whatever the origin, it felt as if Siauliai had always been a forgotten outpost, hovering on the edge of civilization since the dawn of man.

A dusting of fresh snow salted the ground. We made our final preparations, stuffing the overnight gear into two backpacks. Jake took the heavier one and fit the letterbox snugly inside. I took the other. We forced down a few bites of dense Lithuanian bread, none of us possessing much of an appetite, and made our way to the station.

The bus out of Siauliai was a rusty artifact that ran from Vilnius to Kaunus. Lou showed the driver written instructions he had prepared, asking to be let off at the foot of the path to the Hill of Crosses. The driver gave him a long look, then a sharp nod.

We traveled a narrow road that cut straight through the forest. The sun had already begun its descent, adding shades of gray to the bleached landscape. Icicles dripped and melted over the latticework of branches, blurring the scenery into an eerie impressionist painting of a winter land.

"At least we shook the Druids," Lou said.

Jake replied without averting his gaze from the window. "I hope you're right. But this ain't over yet."

Asha left her seat to slide in beside me. I was glad she was seeing the quest through, but hated to see her put herself in danger again—both physical and mental. I knew what it must have cost her to renew her hopes for her brother.

"I know this isn't really the time"—she gave the window a nervous glance—"but I don't know what's going to happen when we reach the hill, and I wanted to say a few things."

I waited for her to continue, unsure what I wanted to hear.

"I've done some thinking," she said, hesitant.

"So have I."

"You were right about the journal. About what was inside."

I turned my head to the side.

She took my hand. "But it was only a little part of what I was feeling. A snapshot, a single line of a poem."

"Don't gloss things over," I said quietly. "You weren't feeling what I was."

"I can't deny that. But I *was* feeling, even if it wasn't everything you wanted at the time. I admit, I probably would have reacted the same as you. But you were wrong about one thing—it's not all or nothing. I don't think love ever is. Would we even want to be with someone who doesn't keep a tiny little piece of themselves?"

I stared at the seat in front of me. I needed time to think, and right now, we had other things to worry about.

"Aidan, I think things have—"

"What the hell is that!"

I whipped around and saw Lou's face plastered to the window, peering into the gloom. He looked pale.

I looked outside and saw only trees, ice, and snow. "What?"

"I swear—I swear I just saw, right inside the forest, a body hanging from a tree."

My hands clenched.

Jake stood. "Commie, you sure—"

Asha shrieked. "There's another one!"

I spun, searching for where she was pointing, and saw it for myself. Just inside the edge of the woods, hanging from a noose strung from a low branch, was a body clothed in rags, its head lolling to the side. I gripped the back of the seat.

None of the other passengers seemed worried, and the driver gave a short, raspy chuckle. He rattled off something unintelligible in Lithuanian, swept his right arm at the forest, and then pointed up ahead, where another body hung from a branch.

"It's some sort of scarecrow," Jake said, and I realized he was right. Gray rags had been draped over a straw figure, such that from a distance it resembled a body hanging limply from the trees.

Asha shuddered. "I don't care if they're real or not. It feels like we're in a forest with dead people hanging all over it."

"Scarecrows are placed to scare things away," Jake said. "Usually animals. But I don't think these are here for the squirrels."

"Ridiculous," Lou huffed. "It's the twenty-first century."

"There's something in these woods," Jake said, fingering the silver cross necklace he had pulled out from beneath his shirt. "I can feel it."

Lou snorted. Asha continued staring out the window, fists balled in her lap.

I sank into my seat. It all seemed so vital and foolish at the same time, so real and unreal. I felt as if we were in a collective dream, a child's playground of the mind where fantasy and reality had at some point merged.

Yet I could not deny the things we had witnessed, the history of the dark place we were about to enter. An unnatural dread began to overtake me.

The bus ground to a halt.

-74-

The driver waved us out, and we stepped off the bus in the middle of a thick forest. No other passengers exited. A wooden sign loomed beside the road, stuck into the ground on a rusty metal pole. A red cross had been painted on the sign. Beneath it, a barely visible footpath snaked into the woods.

Before the bus pulled away, the driver pointed at his watch and held up six fingers. We assumed, from having read the bus schedule, that he was referring to the only bus scheduled to return this way—at six o'clock in the evening. It was at least an hour walk to the Hill of Crosses, and the thought of spending the night in these woods caused my chest to tighten.

Despite the barrenness of the season, the woods felt dense, stuffed with birch trees, snow, and icicles. Fingerlike branches filled the space between the trunks, spreading through the forest like a vast arboreal web. The sun had descended behind the tree line, and the icy forest shone in the near-darkness with a white glow, giving the twilight world we were about to step into a preternatural feel.

"Darkness again," Jake said in disgust. "If we'd left at nine in the morning, there would've been an eclipse."

"It's so quiet," Asha murmured.

Jake took the lead. After a few steps he drew back, reaching for the cross around his neck again.

I saw what had startled him. Just inside the forest, positioned behind two large trees such that one had to enter the woods to see them, hung two of the scarecrow figures. Only these two didn't look like the others. The heads of these guardians were horned and misshapen, much more grotesque than the figures we had seen from the bus. They hung ominously on each side of the path, an unmistakable warning to those who would venture forth.

Asha swallowed. "Someone's taking their guard duty more seriously."

We took cautious steps forward, between the two effigies. The woods smelled damp. The only sounds were our shoes crunching into the frozen forest floor and the occasional crack of a branch snapping under the ice.

Bizarre trapezoidal tombstones began to appear beside the path, their stone surfaces pockmarked with age. Jake surmised they were pagan burial markers from centuries past. As we passed a particularly thick cluster of the ancient graves, I thought I heard footsteps pattering in rapid succession behind me. I spun but saw nothing.

"Did anyone hear that?" I said, stopping to peer into the woods.

"It sounded like someone was running through the woods," Asha said, drawing her coat tighter. "Only it sounded too fast."

A few minutes later we encountered a wooden totem, six feet high and thick as a man's waist. Rune-like markings covered the pole, and a square-shaped cross had been carved into the top.

Jake grunted. "Pagan symbols, or at least that cross is. I don't recognize the markings. Commie?"

Lou bent to study the pole. "It's not a rune with which I'm familiar. I would say the markings are decorative, except they look too . . . deliberate."

More totems appeared, both on and off the path. Most bore carvings of animals, real and absurd, and all were covered in runes.

Jake put a hand out to stop the group. Up ahead, the largest totem so far blocked the path, easily reaching twelve feet high. Standing right in front of it, feet planted wide and arms folded, was a short and stocky Amerindian man in a gray tunic, silently watching us approach.

He had cropped silver hair and a flat face. His thin, Roman-style tunic reached to his knees. How could he stand the cold, I wondered?

"Stay behind me," Jake said, and started walking forward.

As soon as we moved towards him, the man stepped behind the totem.

"Hey," Jake called out, running up.

We caught up to Jake on the other side of the pole. There was no sign of the man.

I heard footsteps again in the woods, this time on both sides, as if two people were racing through the forest at an impossible speed. I scoured the woods but saw nothing.

The footsteps died. I paled, and Lou and Asha backed into the middle of the path.

"It's beginning," Jake said.

Asha had a slightly crazed look in her eyes. "What is?"

Jake took the letterbox out of his pack. "This."

We started forward again, this time huddled together. The unseen footsteps became frequent companions. We kept scanning the woods, but there was never anything to be seen. We pressed on, becoming more and more unnerved.

Lou pointed to our right, whispering hoarsely for us to look. Through a patchwork of branches, we saw the man in the gray tunic standing with his arms at his sides in the middle of the forest, watching us. He turned to face us as we passed. Jake took a step into the woods towards him, and the man disappeared.

Lou blanched. Asha caught her breath, and I clenched my fists.

Jake increased his pace. "We've got to reach the hill."

"And do what?" I said. "It could be worse there."

He didn't answer, and the rest of us hurried after him. The woods pressed all around, suffocating. The footsteps in the forest resumed, and I did my best to ignore them, concentrating on putting one foot in front of the other.

Shapes began to appear at the edges of our vision, dark things that fluttered in and out of the failing light too quickly for us to recognize. At times the shadows would seem to fly towards us, and we would duck our heads in fear, only to look up and see nothing.

The man in the gray tunic appeared more frequently, a specter whose existence even Lou, his head roving side to side in terror, could not deny. Most disturbing was the way he watched us, staring at us with a blank expression before disappearing.

The footsteps were all around us now. I didn't know how much more I could take. I was frightened almost beyond reason, trying to block out the sounds we shouldn't have been hearing and the things we shouldn't have seen. It wasn't real, I kept telling myself. It was a trick. It had to be.

We rounded a bend, and the path spilled into a large, open clearing. Within the treeless space rose a large hill, its heights unseen in the blackness above. As we poured into the clearing, gibbering with fear, no one needed to ask what we had stumbled upon, for the hill was covered, as a honeycomb swarming with bees, with crosses.

-75-

We stopped to catch our breath, realizing the footsteps and apparitions had ceased. Crosses of all shapes and sizes blanketed the surface of the hill, leaning crazily in every direction and giving the hill a deranged appearance. Some of the crosses rose more than ten feet high, and the shortest ones rested mere inches from the ground. I saw crosses made of wood, metal, bronze, copper, iron, and silver; crosses overlapping or nailed to other crosses; crosses with poles as thick as a man and as tiny as two fingers crossed together. Some were actual crucifixes, bearing carvings or figurines of Jesus, with incredibly worn rosary beads draped across them. Pagan symbols adorned others: runes, anthropomorphic animals, and other fantastical shapes.

We warily approached the hill. Two enormous totems stood on either side of a footpath leading upwards. Shrubby vegetation covered the hill; it would have been impossible to ascend off the path without cutting through the thicket of crosses and overgrowth.

A square stone cross topped each of the totems. We stood in silence before the pair of silent guardians, and I knew what everyone was thinking: the forest had been bad enough, and we had yet to step foot on the hill.

As we started up the path, a man holding a gun emerged from behind one of the totems. A man dressed in a white robe, with a burn scar on the back of his left hand.

His cowl was thrown back, revealing the same craggy face I had seen in the atrium of the British Museum. From his unbalanced expression, I knew without asking he had seen the same things we had.

"So this is how it is?" Jake said.

"Hand it over," the man rasped. "I won't ask twice."

Jake pressed his lips together but slowly took out the letterbox. The Druid edged forward, keeping the gun trained on Jake.

"How'd you find us, Nyles?" Jake said. "Magic?"

He smirked. "You should have paid more attention to the cleaning crew."

It took me a second, but then I put it together: the older lady with him in the museum, and the woman I had seen shuffling out of our reading room with her hair in a fishnet. I hadn't gotten a good look at the cleaning lady's face, but I realized the two of them were the same height and thin build.

"You bugged our reading room," I said. "You knew we were coming. I don't get it, though. Where's the woman? The rest of your faction?"

The man swung the gun towards me, causing my knees to feel watery. Anger coursed through me as well, both at the deadly piece of metal pointed in my direction, and the derailing of our quest.

We had been so close.

"Move," Nyles said, his voice quivering with eagerness. "Single file. If anyone steps out, I won't hesitate to shoot.

We had no choice but to obey. Asha fell in after Jake, and I stepped behind her and gripped her hand. Lou brought up the rear.

"I get it perfectly, Counselor," Jake said as we started forward, loud enough for the man to hear. "He's using us as guinea pigs, and he ditched his crew because he wants whatever he finds for himself."

"That, and I don't plan on coming back," the Druid said in a low voice behind us, as if speaking to himself.

The path wound around the hill. Despite the premature darkness, enough light shone forth from the three-quarter moon, reflecting off the sheen of snow, to enable us to see. Nyles wouldn't let us use a flashlight; I presumed he was wary of disturbing the hill.

The wall of crosses and totems on either side created a hedge-like passage. After a five-minute walk, the path spilled into a gently sloped clearing with five identical paths curving up the hill. A wooden signpost was stuck into the ground in front of each path.

Nyles stopped, his face slack. "None of this was here before," he said. "There were no signs, no paths."

"That's because you didn't have the box," Jake said.

"It's because he set it all up," Lou whispered in my ear.

Asha risked a glance back at me, and I could tell she was as confused and terrified as I was.

The hill possessed the stillness of an empty building. The Druid made us wait in the center of the clearing while he inspected the signs. He stopped for a long moment in front of the fifth one, then waved us forward. "Down this path. Now."

The signposts were set ten yards apart. As I approached, I read the wooden signpost to Nyles's left, and what I saw made my mouth go dry and my heart pound against my chest.

Carved in archaic, pointed font into the old signpost, appearing as if it had stood on the hill for centuries, was a single word.

I was looking at my own name.

-76-

The sign in front of the Druid read Nyles Kempthorne, and the sign next to that bore Asha's name. Jake risked a step towards the other signs, and then swore. "This one's mine. The other is the Commie's."

"Back in line!" Nyles barked.

The Druid forced us down the path beside the sign bearing his name. He followed from behind. After fifty feet, we came to an impenetrable wall of hedge and crosses blocking the path.

We returned to the clearing, and he made us try the path with the signpost bearing my name, and then the other three. All ended at a wall of hedge and crosses.

The Druid snarled. "What's this?"

Could he have set it all up, I wondered? If so, why? And when would he have had the time?

"The hill wants us to go alone," Asha said quietly.

Nyles considered her response, then pointed the gun at Lou. "You. Down your path. See if the barrier's there and come right back."

Lou hesitated. The Druid pointed the gun at him. "*Now*."

Lou started towards his path as if approaching his execution. "Be careful," I called out.

While the Druid was watching, Jake caught my attention and gave a single nod in the direction of the signposts. I didn't know what it meant, except to be ready.

No one so much as twitched when Lou disappeared from view. Long seconds passed, and just when Nyles snarled and took a step forward, Lou's voice rang through the clearing. It sounded hoarse. "It's gone!" he shouted. "The barrier's gone!"

The Druid's eyes lit up, and he shifted his attention for a split second, turning his head towards the sound of Lou's voice. Jake took advantage. As quick as a cobra, he sprang across the clearing, barreling into the Druid with his shoulder. Nyles went tumbling backwards. Both the gun and the letterbox flew out of his hands.

"Run!" I said to Asha. She didn't need any urging. The signposted pathways were the closest exits, and she raced towards hers. I moved to follow, glancing to the side as I did.

The letterbox had fallen next to Jake. He scooped it up. The gun landed close to the Druid, and Nyles lunged for it. I saw Jake hesitate, then dart for his signpost.

"Go, Counselor!" he shouted. "Down your path!"

I started to follow Asha, then veered towards mine at the last moment. It was closer, and what if Jake and Asha were right and the only path open to me was my own? What if, by following Asha, I botched her escape as well?

It was a damnable choice, but I decided that if my path was still blocked, I could double back and go to Asha. Nyles would likely try his own path or chase after Jake.

I sprinted past my sign and down the corridor of hedgerows and crosses. I ran for fifty feet and then one hundred. The wall of thorny hedge and crosses that had previously blocked my path, an impenetrable barrier I had seen with my own two eyes just minutes before, had vanished.

I risked a glance back. Fifty feet behind me, impossibly, the wall of hedge and crosses was in place again, blocking my return. I ran back and pressed against it, feeling and probing various parts of the wall, but succeeded only in pricking my hand on the thorns.

I swore. Now I couldn't help Asha.

What the hell was going on?

A terrible sense of isolation descended. My breath drifted away in frosty wisps, my inhalations the only interruption to the silence. The pathway curved up the hill in front of me, lit by the faint white glow of the Baltic twilight.

Should I stay where I was, or risk the path?

No matter the danger, if there was a chance I could help Asha and the others, I had to try. Yet it wasn't the earthly dangers that gave me pause. What would I find if I kept walking? I had no one haunting me, no one from my past to whisper my name in the darkness and urge me forward.

I had traveled all this way, through trial and tribulation and worse, risking my life to find meaning—all to discover the answers to life's questions.

What if I did find that . . . something else? What was it I was looking for? Did I want to shrink in horror from something ghastly, something beyond the limits of my imagination? Did I want to lie prostrate before a perfect being I could never hope to please? Did I want to be disappointed by an imperfect one? Was there something down that path, some version of God, I even *wanted* to find?

I laughed bitterly to myself. We are all too human.

I began to walk.

I would know.

-77-

When I rounded the first corner, the man in the gray tunic was standing ten feet away.

Fear whisked through me like the shock of an icy mountain stream. He stood motionless, looking through me as if staring at a point behind my back.

I called out to him in desperation. "Who are you?"

He disappeared.

I was beyond debating the reality of the things I was seeing. The journey through the woods, the signs, the disappearing walls, this . . . spirit. There was nothing left to ponder. I had to press on, dismally aware that my only means of return was lost to me.

A high hedge of crosses still bordered the path on either side, and I trekked upwards, into the highest reaches of the hill. I concentrated on putting one foot in front of the other, trying to block out the memory of the things I had seen, focused on reaching the end of the path.

And then I heard the voices.

They began as a murmur in the stillness of the night. Unintelligible wisps of sound, drifting on dead currents of air, whispering to me. I couldn't discern the words; I didn't want to. Were they the voices of lost souls, brought to this place by the presence of the letterbox? Were the others experiencing the same thing? I tried to block it out by covering my ears, but the sound managed to penetrate. I shuddered and walked faster, dread pulsating through me in electric waves.

The man in gray appeared again on the path ahead. I stopped, and he turned his back to me. I called out to him again, not expecting a response and not getting one. I stood for a moment longer and then, not knowing what else to do, I walked towards him. He began to walk as well. I stopped again, and he stopped. I walked towards him faster, and he did the same.

Was I following him, or was he somehow keeping pace with me? I couldn't tell. He became a permanent fixture on my walk, his bare legs maintaining a steady cadence beneath the tunic. I even tried running towards him, but he walked faster, somehow keeping the same distance between us.

I felt the solid edge of sanity slipping away. The voices continued murmuring, and I heard my name coalescing in the darkness. *Aidan*, they called. *Aidan* . . . .

I didn't know how much more I could take. "Asha! Jake! Lou!" I shouted, over and over. There was no response, no succor.

I put my head in my hands. The whispering grew louder, invasive, a cacophony of unnatural sound. I bent down, found a rock, and threw it at the man in the gray tunic. It passed right through him.

"Say something, damn you!"

I pressed forward, then sensed a presence behind me. I grew cold even before I turned, somehow knowing what I would find. It was the same feeling I had had on one other occasion, an experience I had tried to erase from my mind.

No, I whispered.

I turned and saw the creature that had tortured my mind at Kostnice, the shadow thing, its amorphous form heaving up and down on the path.

I careened up the path without reason, without purpose, as fast as my legs would carry me. I didn't bother looking back; I could sense it behind me. The man in the gray tunic had disappeared, but the voices maintained their whispered assault on my sanity.

I had to reach the summit. I couldn't be alone on this hill, with those voices, with that *thing*.

It began to talk as I ran, its voice a rough susurration. "You flee in vain."

I ran.

"You knew the dangers that awaited you in this place. What did you think you would find? Knowledge? Answers? Wisdom?"

I ran.

"*God?* Is that what you seek? Did you actually think He would leave His lofty perch and come to you? Why not ask for something else, something more reasonable? Something more like me?"

Oh, how I ran.

"I am not what you think, I am nothing you would ever have imagined. But you know me. I began to show you in the tunnels beneath Kostnice, when you took another man's life. That was just a hint of that which you are capable. A taste."

I sprinted until I could run no more, and then continued down the path half-walking, half-stumbling. Fear was a forgotten luxury: I had reached a point of despair I never imagined existed. I came for answers, and found this? A twisted shadow, a half-life, a miserable evil that lurks on after death?

I collapsed. My legs would go no further. I had lost all sense of time and place, the voices would not stop whispering in my ear, the shadow thing would not cease tormenting my mind.

Why had I come here? What had I done?

"You believe in nothing. You cannot even be true to yourself. Let me help you find the way." The voice turned mocking. "Do you know who I am?"

I thrust my hands over my ears and laid my head against the ground. "Oh, God," I cried, "save me from this creature!"

"*Do you know who I am?*"

"Who are you, then?" I screamed into the darkness, with the voices of the dead swirling around me. "Who are you, you damnable thing?"

"I am you," it whispered in my ear.

-78-

I felt someone or something pick me up by my waist. I tried to resist, but the grip was immensely strong, and something pressed upon the back of my neck such that I couldn't turn around. It carried me along the path at a frenzied pace, and I collapsed in its grip.

The path opened into a square clearing surrounded by a wall of crosses. I was deposited in a simple wooden chair. When I looked back, I saw no one else in the open space, nor did I see an opening by which I might have entered. The shadow creature had disappeared, the whispered voices silenced.

Facing me were two doorways set into the wall of crosses. One was a normal-sized doorway cut into the hedge. Beyond it, I saw a footpath similar to the one I had been following.

The other doorway was . . . unnatural. It was of a similar size to the other door, but it was completely—impossibly—opaque, such that I could not see the slightest bit inside of it. A rectangle of inky blackness living within the wall of crosses.

A man emerged out of the opaque doorway. His step was light, but he was elderly and reminded me of my paternal grandfather, a spry old man who had continued to run marathons at the age of seventy. Wisps of gray hair dotted the man's age-spotted head. He was bespectacled, of average height, and slightly stooped. A hooked nose protruded between sharp eyes and a thin mouth. A gray wool overcoat reached to the tops of his black shoes, and the edges of a white shirt poked through at the throat and sleeves.

My body was finished, my mind numb. I was relieved beyond words that the voices and the shadow creature no longer tormented me, but I did not trust that the old man was a change for the better.

I gathered the strength to talk. "Who are you?"

Hands folded in front of him, he regarded me with a grave expression. "Who do you think?"

"I don't know."

He said nothing.

"Where are my friends?"

"They have their own concerns."

I shuffled my feet. "What concerns?"

Again no response.

"Is this real?" I asked. "Any of it?"

I knew my words sounded trite. I didn't know what to say.

"Is it not happening?" he asked.

"Why am I here?"

"You came here."

I stood and looked around the strange room. "What is this place?"

"It has been called by many names. It is called the Hill of Crosses now."

"Is it the nexus of the ley lines?"

"It has been called that as well."

"But *is* it?"

"It is what it is."

I clenched my hands in frustration. "So what now? Do we stand here and talk in riddles? What do you want from me?"

"It is not about what I want from you. I know why you came, and what you seek is within your grasp."

"I don't understand."

"Answers. Knowledge. Purpose. Meaning. All these things are before you now."

He had neither moved nor changed his neutral expression.

I licked my lips. "What do you mean?"

He stepped aside from the opaque doorway. I edged forward, trying to see inside, but it was as if I were staring into a void darker than the darkest of nights, a black hole trapped within the wall.

He held out both hands to the doorway, palms up, showcasing it. "This is the doorway to that which you seek. You need only walk inside."

I gave a short, hysterical chuckle. "My answers are on the other side of that door? Behind the wall of crosses?"

"I'm afraid it's not that kind of doorway."

"What kind is it, then?"

"I think you know the purpose of this place," he said.

"The bridge between worlds," I replied, almost jokingly, not expecting a response.

He nodded, once.

I would have laughed at the whole absurd situation, at his ridiculous nod, had I not experienced all that I had on the journey, and especially on the Hill of Crosses.

"I just step through and find the answers," I said in disbelief.

"Yes."

"So what's the catch?"

"You know that as well, Aidan."

I shivered when he said my name. "I won't be able to return, will I?"

He again moved his head, this time side to side.

"Where does the other door lead? The normal one?"

"To the other side of the wall."

"What about my friends?"

"They have their own choices to make."

"Why is this happening?" I asked.

"You brought that which you carry to this place. You sought this choice."

"I don't remember asking for this."

"You don't always have to use words to ask."

I looked down at my feet, then back up. "Let's assume you're telling the truth. There's a spirit world and that doorway leads to it. Won't I be there one day, anyway? Won't I have the answers when I die?"

"Perhaps. Perhaps not."

"Why perhaps?"

"That depends on you."

"What do you mean?"

"There will be other choices in your life. There are always choices."

"What choices?"

He stood there impassively, saying nothing.

"You're not going to help me, are you?" I said. "Why has the letterbox only shown us evil things?"

"Is that all you've seen?" he asked.

I remembered Asha's brother, and Vivian. "Perhaps not," I said slowly, then had another flash of insight. "If the letterbox opens the doorway and spirits are able to pass through, then only those who are unhappy would come here. That's right, isn't it?"

"Not entirely."

"Or spirits who might want to appear for a particular reason, like Asha's brother and Vivian."

Another silence, which I had begun to take for acquiescence.

"What was that black thing? The shadow creature that was chasing me. He seemed . . . different."

"Another piece of knowledge you already possess."

"*Tell me,*" I said in desperation, needing at least one concrete answer in the midst of this madness.

He reached into his overcoat and pulled out a large, handheld mirror. "Look," he commanded.

I took a step closer. Behind my reflection in the mirror I saw—I spun, gasping in horror.

There was nothing behind me. But I had just seen . . . I turned back around, and hovering behind me in the mirror, *on* me, attached to my body like a parasite, was the shadow creature that had tormented me at Kostnice and on the hill just minutes before.

I shrank in fear, then looked behind me again and saw nothing. "What is it?"

"It is part of your essence. Because of what you brought here, it is able to separate itself. It is very strong here."

"What am I?" I whispered in horror. "If I step through the black doorway, will I become . . . *that* one day?"

"By entering the doorway in this place, you will have sidestepped certain choices."

I hadn't expected that answer. "So the black doorway is the better choice?"

"Better is a relative term."

"Relative to what? The other choices I might make in life? The ones you won't tell me about?"

I took his maddening silence for another acquiescence.

"Why is it uncertain, if I don't go through that doorway, what I'll become?"

"Because you have the freedom to make your own choices," he said.

"But there are questions to which I might never know the answers, according to you, unless I step through the black doorway. That's unfair."

He smiled again. Even his smiles were neutral, as if he was merely acknowledging a point by smiling.

"Will I be happy if I choose the black doorway?" I said.

"That depends on your definition of happiness."

"Is it heaven?" I whispered.

"You cannot possibly comprehend what lies beyond the doorway until you choose to step through it."

"Are you God?" I blurted out.

He chuckled.

The black doorway started to waver, as if becoming less substantial.

"What's happening?" I said.

"You must choose. The doorway will not last much longer."

I started to panic. Everything flashed through my mind. That place, the choice, my life. I didn't have time to ponder the ludicrous nature of what was happening; at the moment, it seemed as real as anything had in my entire life. I could see the doorway shimmering, wavering, like no earthly doorway could do.

Why should I not step through that doorway? Isn't that what I had come for? Answers?

Or perhaps I wouldn't want to return. Perhaps I would be someplace beautiful. Isn't that what he had intimated? A place where I would never become that . . . thing . . . I had seen in the mirror. Shouldn't I make sure that didn't happen? What if I made the wrong choices later in life?

My eyes flicked to the doorway. It looked even less substantial, fading away.

I had a failed career, no purpose in life. My beloved did not love me. I bowed my head, feeling more lost and alone than I ever had.

But still, to turn my back on everything . . . I clasped my hands to my head, unable to choose.

He held up the mirror. I gazed into it again and saw a rush of terrible images: war, murder, rape, incest. I drew back in horror, cringing, but I couldn't look away. The evils of the world came at me in a barrage, assaulting my humanity, bringing me to my knees. I saw beheadings broadcast online, chemical warfare on children, men and women torn apart by their neighbors in a frenzy of violence. The Holocaust, the slave ships, the slaughter of the Native Americans. Children sick and dying, emaciated from hunger, bathing in rivers of sewage, used as sex slaves and drug mules. I saw concentration camps and torture chambers and other depravities that had no place in human existence.

Yet they existed. Not only did they exist—they were *common*.

I don't know how long I sat there, staring at the unfathomable evil of the world. Were we human or were we devils? How could I possibly choose to live in such a place?

Choking back my bile, I watched as the images stopped and my reflection returned. Now the black shadow reached halfway inside my body, its appendages tucked into my reflected form.

He was right, I knew. He wasn't just showing me how polluted the world was, he was showing me my own place in the Freak Show.

And he was offering me a way out.

He passed his hand over the mirror. The images disappeared.

I wiped my mouth, numbed by what I had seen. At that moment I couldn't imagine *not* reaching out to whatever hope lay beyond that doorway.

I took a step forward, but he put out a gnarled hand. "There's one more image you should see, in order that you may choose fairly."

I didn't need to see any more horrors. I just wanted it to stop.

He passed his hand over the mirror again. As promised, a final image appeared. My eyes widened in surprise. I glanced at the wavering portal, then turned back and gazed for long moments upon that last image.

In the corner of my vision, the black doorway grew less and less substantial. I sensed I had seconds to decide.

I closed my eyes, a peculiar warmth washing over me.

And then I made my choice.

-79-

I strode down the path behind the normal, earthly doorway. I somehow knew that if I looked back, it would all be gone: the room surrounded by the wall of crosses, the mysterious old man, the impossible doorway. But I didn't turn around. I didn't look back. I knew, deep inside, that I had made the right choice, and I felt, for the first time in a very long while, a sense of peace.

I walked for a few minutes longer, until the corridor emptied into a tunnel of crosses and overgrowth. I navigated the tunnel and emerged into a large open space beneath a star-filled sky.

I had reached the summit.

Four other passageways, identical to mine, spilled into the top of the hill. I watched Lou, Jake, and Asha each emerge from a different passageway, almost simultaneously. They looked as world-weary as I felt.

There was one other person in the clearing, standing at the apex of the hill. I cringed, thinking it was Nyles, but it was someone I had never seen before. At first glance, I thought he looked like a middle-aged traveling salesman. His bland face was anchored by an almost square jaw and an almost clever mouth, and his hair was short and sandy. He was similar in height to Jake, though thicker around the middle.

I exchanged a quick glance with the others. We bunched together and warily approached him. "Are you . . ." Asha began, looking back down the hill.

He finished whatever thought she had started. "I'm afraid not."

His voice was cultured and devoid of an accent. He was dressed, with startling incongruity for the locale, in a black business suit with a gray shirt and a white handkerchief. He looked serious in the way of a banker poring over a credit history: slightly grim, no-nonsense, yet not entirely unpleasant. I had seen so many unbelievable things that I hardly cared to question what he was doing standing at the top of a hill in the middle of the Lithuanian woods in a business suit.

Jake had no such reservations. "Who the hell are you?"

"You can call me Mr. Chenisdeaux."

That got our attention. Jake's mouth hung open, and we all stared at the man.

"I believe a couple of things are in order. First of all, congratulations. You're all most resourceful and courageous. You completed the scenario surprisingly quickly and with great cleverness. You've done our business a great service, and we—"

Jake took a step forward. "Whoa, whoa. Scenario? Business? I swear I'll—"

Asha put a hand on his shoulder. "Jake."

"Thank you," the man said. "As I was saying, and I know this comes as a bit of a shock, but as the corporation's representative I'm here to see you on your way and reward you for your troubles. Now, if you'll please return the letterbox—"

"See us on our way?" Asha said. "What're you talking about? What corporation?"

"S.T., Inc.," I said softly.

He spread a palm. "Correct."

Asha paled. "Who was that gray-haired woman in front of the doorway? The one in the sari?"

"Part of the scenario, of course," he said.

I turned to Asha. "You saw a doorway also?"

"Two," she said. Lou and Jake nodded as well.

Lou folded his arms. "How'd you pull off the black doorway? Was it some kind of recorded image?"

"You're a bright one," Chenisdeaux said, rolling his eyes. "If you'd be quiet for a moment, I'll explain."

We looked at each other in uneasy confusion.

"Fine," I said. "Explain."

He resumed speaking in a rote monotone, as if reciting something from memory. "I'm the principal of a corporation named S.T., Inc. The initials stand for Spirit Tours, Incorporated."

He let the words sink in. I felt the blood drain from my face.

"Our slogan is 'Spirit Tours: The Heart and Soul of Adventure Travel.' Catchy, isn't it? Of course, we keep that to ourselves, for obvious reasons. The basic idea is nothing new, you realize. Psychics, palm readers, astronomers, charlatans, even the world's organized religions: they've all been doing the same thing for centuries. Millennia. We're just better organized and, if I do say so myself, better managed. You see, people always have, and always will, go to the greatest lengths imaginable to have a spiritual experience."

The others looked as stunned as I felt.

"Quite frankly," he continued, "people will do anything for evidence that even *hints* that God exists. They want to know that something is out there that makes them feel better about the harsh, finite reality of our world."

I felt as if my thoughts over the past few months were being repeated to me.

"Our market research indicates that most people will pay inordinate amounts of money for a personal and believable supernatural experience. After observing our live test model which you have so graciously completed, we now have quantifiable evidence."

Jake gave a hoarse laugh. "You're tryin' to tell me all of this has been a *setup?* Part of some corporate game?"

"But *why?*" Asha said. She looked dazed.

The man gave a thin smile. "For profit, of course. We plan to advertise our services to a select few individuals who can afford our exorbitant prices. In a clandestine manner, the word will be spread that an . . . organization . . . exists that can offer an otherworldly experience, staffed by the world's greatest psychics and paranormal researchers. Our jaded and wealthy clients will flock to us, seeking the ultimate fix from the tedium of their lives. And we will give them nothing less than a life-changing brush with the spirit world."

-80-

Jake waved a hand in a semicircle, showcasing the hill. "I suppose you're gonna tell me you've engineered everything that's happened to us?"

"Of course," the man said. "You don't actually—do you *still* think that it was real?"

"I'd like to hear your explanation of just how you managed to accomplish all of this."

"Where shall I begin?"

Jake took a step forward. "How about with the times we almost died?"

"You were never in any real danger," Chenisdeaux said, "except for losing your soul." He gave a low chuckle. "Excuse me. Industry joke." He regained his pristine composure. "Everything you've experienced has been carefully planned and executed by S.T., Inc. The only physical injury of which I'm aware was the unfortunate accident involving Ms. Rana. The perpetrator, of course, is no longer with our company."

Jake snorted. "The Druids are working for you, too?"

"We employ a number of the finest magicians and actors in the world, all paid extremely well and subject to strict confidentiality agreements."

"*Actors?*" Asha said shrilly. "*Magicians*? My brother—no. I *know* that was him."

"People believe what they wish to believe," Chenisdeaux said softly.

"So where's Nyles?" I asked. "I suppose the gun wasn't loaded?"

The man winked at me. "Perhaps he chose the other doorway."

Jake folded his arms. "Vivian?"

Chenisdeaux cocked his head and raised his eyebrows.

"Wrong," Jake said. "She and I had a little conversation before the two doorways, in front of You Know Who. I asked her questions only she could answer, and she passed with flying colors."

"Our research facilities are world-class, and our corporation utilizes the most advanced methods of illusion known to man. That said, it's simple to deceive the masses. Think of the famous hoaxes of the world, some of which lasted for centuries. The Shroud of Turin. The Cottingley photos. I won't even bother mentioning some of the fringe religious texts." He stifled a laugh. "Golden tablets and crystal glasses."

"Words are cheap," Jake said. "We just saw a man in a gray tunic disappear in front of our faces."

"Holographic images are only the beginning of the tools we use to ensure the most 'authentic' of supernatural experiences. Making someone disappear is quite simple; stage performers routinely make elephants disappear in front of hundreds of onlookers. Through the use of a complicated system of mirrors, the elephant is moved to a backstage area set up to appear as the real stage. The mirrors are positioned to allow the audience to think it is still looking at the animal on the front stage. Whenever the magician is ready to make the elephant disappear, he simply shuts down the mirrors." He grinned. "Voila. No more elephant."

"Hard to do in a locked crypt," Jake said.

"You'd be surprised how far a little misdirection will take you. Perhaps the man in the crypt in Pere Lachaise emerged and exited through a secret door, with the final image of him reaching for you projected into the crypt with mirrors. That's the tip of the iceberg, the barest of beginnings. You've no idea the advances science has made in the fields of holography and visual illusion. We can do things that you would—" he smiled, "not believe."

"And I suppose that's how you made someone disappear in Grimspound in full daylight?" Jake asked. "You couldn't possibly have had time to set that up."

"Simple illusions, actually. Our actors followed you everywhere and prepared long in advance for when the opportunity arose."

I looked back and forth between the two. My head was spinning.

"Kika?" Lou asked. "How'd you find out about her? That has nothing to do with illusion."

"Good old-fashioned research. You wrote about her in a journal you kept during college. It took a while, but our research team managed to locate it."

I looked at Lou. "Is that true?"

"I lost it years ago, but . . . yeah." He shrugged, thoughtful. "It's possible."

"We're *extremely* thorough," Mr. Chenisdeaux said.

"My brother?" Asha whispered.

"Clever disguises, dim lighting, old photographs, muffled voices. Tricks of the mind."

"But he said things to me, before the doorway. I was sure . . ." Asha bowed her head.

I wasn't nearly as ready to capitulate. "The shadow creature? The tunnels beneath Kostnice, the events of tonight?"

"It's quite easy to create a shadow creature, project a voice, utilize virtual reality to create the illusion of movement. Especially when drugged."

"The man in the gray tunic?" I asked.

"A projection, of course. Did you touch him?"

I grimaced. "What about the letterbox itself? We date-tested it."

Chenisdeaux turned to regard Jake, who I presumed had the letterbox in his backpack. "That's actually authentic. The map is real, the legend of the nexus is real, everything your scholar told you in London is true. The perfect backstory was already in place, and we had only to set the quest in motion. In fact, we couldn't have dreamed up a better scenario. And who knows. Maybe it *is* real. We didn't check into that."

He smirked, and I wanted to smash his cavalier face. "The black doorway?" I said. "The mirror?"

"Must you know all our secrets?" He sighed. "The 'mirror' was a tiny screen with pre-recorded images, including the 'creature' we superimposed over your reflection. As I said, we have the finest technology available, as well as very clever scientists in our employ. If we can send a man to the moon and destroy the world with atoms, I believe we can fake a few ghosts."

"What was the point of the doorway, if it didn't lead anywhere?" Lou asked.

"We needed a test group in order to evaluate our products, to see how far you were willing to go. We were quite surprised when none of you chose the other doorway, after all that had happened."

"My God," Asha said. "*How could you?*"

He wagged a finger in the air. "You must be asking yourself why we chose you in particular. After all, you didn't sign up for any of this."

"Go on and give us a few more lies," Jake said.

"We needed normal, rational people to sample our scenarios. We've been observing your reactions to the planned occurrences the entire way. We knew Lucius would include Asha and Jake in the search, but the addition of Aidan and Lou was highly fortuitous. Your varying degrees of faith, and varying willingness to accept spiritual phenomena, proved quite useful. Your little group had the perfect range of preconceived notions of God and spirituality, and your diverse areas of expertise lent an air of authenticity. If subjects such as yourselves were fooled, it bodes well for the success of our enterprise."

I stared at him with a sinking sensation. Why should I bother to believe that I had experienced the divine when the most rational and human motive of all, greed, was staring me in the face?

"You can hardly bring a product to market without testing it," he continued. "Although we will, of course, vary the 'quests' for future clients. The Letterbox Scenario, as we like to call it, was merely the prototype."

"Why go to all the trouble?" Asha said dully. "Why not just show us a couple of fake spirits and be done with it?"

"Economics and authenticity. The striving, quest-like nature is designed to promote maximum believability. It also provides a heightened level of emotion. When you solve problems and experience danger, you're more willing to believe in what you see, as well as feel it more deeply. You want to think that you have braved the unknown, solved riddles, conquered dangers.

"And on an economic level, with a multiple-tiered scenario, the client garners more pride in the accomplishment . . . and is less likely to question why he or she has just parted with an exorbitant sum. We're even considering implementing a system where clients are forced to pay at each stage of the journey in order to continue. However," he mused, "that might calculate inversely into authenticity."

Jake crossed his arms. "Do you really believe people are going to pay that kind of money on the chance they might see a ghost?"

The man smirked. "Dr. Fleniken, I believe your exact words were, captured nicely by our recorders: 'I swear to you, nothing on this earth or anywhere else, not the Devil himself, will stop me from discovering its secrets.'"

Jake balled his fists but didn't respond.

"How much would you have given to reach the final choice, to uncover the answers you so desperately sought?"

Chenisdeaux let his words sink in. I gritted my teeth and looked away.

"Look at you. You still want it to be real. Have no doubt: people will pay anything, they will *do* anything, for a taste of God."

"Why are you telling us this?" Lou said.

"As willing but non-paying test subjects, we felt you deserved to know."

"What's stopping us from running straight to the authorities? Do you plan to kill us?"

"You're free to leave, as you always have been. No one forced you to continue the scenario, or to do anything at all."

I waved my arms. "You're a *corporation*. You have rules, protocols."

"S.T., Inc. was a corporate entity created solely for this test run. It has already been dissolved."

"Why not just rob people like normal thieves?" Lou asked in disgust. "Hit up a bank or something?"

The man took umbrage for the first time. "We're no better or worse than any other broker of faith, making promises that can never truly be kept. They are not promises that *can* be kept. People donate billions to churches every year. Where is their assurance that their souls are saved, their futures in heaven assured? Or, as reflected in our moniker, you might liken our corporation to a tourist agency. We provide a grand adventure, the most amazing ride this life has to offer, a journey into the unknown. Just as any tour company or organized religion, we provide the framework for an experience, and you're free to enjoy it in whatever manner you choose. To believe what you wish to believe."

"You can't play with people's lives like that," Asha said. "Use semantics all you want, but what you're doing is evil."

"Evil?" he repeated softly. "I don't think you have any conception, young lady, of the nature of true evil." His visage twisted, for the briefest of moments, into a snarl, a caricature of his bland face. It passed so quickly—like a splice in a movie reel—that I thought I had imagined it. "Did not the prophets of the world, the great religious leaders, give people exactly what we aim to provide? They gave them faith, *hope*. The ultimate gifts. We've done you a service. It's up to you what you do with it."

"So why come clean?" Lou said. "Doesn't that ruin any good your little experiment might've done?"

"Did you not ponder the nature of your existence, experience the wonder of faith?" he asked. "The veracity of the events is irrelevant. Mankind will never be able to prove the existence of God. Even if He were to leave evidence strewn about the world, mankind will never truly believe. It's not in his nature." He grinned and flicked his eyes towards one of the paths. "Not even if God Himself came down from heaven."

"I've heard about enough of this," Jake said. He had a strange smile on his face. "I know who you are."

-81-

"It must gall you," Jake continued, "that in spite of all your clever lies, I still believe."

"I believe a doorway was provided for those with faith," Chenisdeaux said.

"Then you missed the point. She wanted me to stay, said I have things to do. We'll be together again one day."

"That's very touching. I'm glad you liked our hologram."

Jake folded his arms. "You've yet to offer an explanation as to how she knew the things she did. Go on, spin a few more lies."

"Perhaps you should stop talking in your sleep, or be more careful to whom you give confession. If you still don't believe me, there's not much more I can say. Some people can never face the truth. You will hear what you want to hear, believe what you want to believe. Now, let's conclude our business. You provided us with a great service, and we're well aware of the time and effort you've put forth. In compensation, and as a token of our appreciation, we've procured a gift for each of you. Further, we offer another item our team found buried close to the letterbox. You'll find it quite valuable; we thought you should have it for your troubles."

He pointed at the burlap sack lying at his feet. "If you'll please return our property, you may claim your rewards and return to your lives."

Jake reached into his backpack and took out the letterbox, keeping his eyes on Mr. Chenisdeaux the entire time. "This is what you want?"

"We can hardly have the evidence of our scenario floating about."

"Is that right?" Jake said.

"I assure you the contents of the sack will more than compensate you for your trouble."

"Maybe I don't want compensation. Maybe I want the letterbox."

He stared at Jake. "It's not your choice to make."

Jake's slow grin was like the opening of a curtain.

"Leave it on the hill if you prefer," Chenisdeaux said. "I'll pick it up when you leave."

"Nope."

The man took a step closer. I walked over to stand behind Jake.

"What's going on?" Lou asked.

"Commie, just stay where you are."

Mr. Chenisdeaux took another step forward.

"Not one more inch," Jake said, holding up the letterbox.

"You must understand, we can't have our operation threatened by publicity. The contents of the sack are invaluable. Take them. You earned them."

"I feel the need for a memento," Jake said. "I want the letterbox."

"It's our lawful property."

"Feel free to discuss it with the authorities, *Mr. Chenisdeaux.*"

"I'd rather not resort to force," he said calmly.

"I think if you could've taken it from us by now, you would have. Aren't quite *yourself* here without it, are you? I'm also thinkin' you had nothing to do with those doorways and was sweating it out, hoping I wouldn't carry it through." He held up the letterbox. "You're in luck."

The man opened his mouth, but Jake pressed forward. "I think as soon as the sensors struck the box, you started the ball rolling. Outside of this place, and maybe at the points of intersection, I'm guessing you couldn't do much. I don't know how, but you managed a few phone calls to start S.T., Inc. and buy the land around Cranmere. You weren't working with the Druids; you didn't want them to have the box. You couldn't carry it here yourself, and you couldn't tell anyone what the box was, because they'd use it against you or bury it at the bottom of the ocean. You hedged your bets and had a flunky purchase Chateau Donn, in case the Druids got their hands on the box and wouldn't cooperate."

"Really, Dr. Fleniken, now you're just being obstinate," he said. "The scenario is over. None of it was real. Perhaps," he mused, "we went too far."

Jake smiled. "You needed someone who had no idea what the letterbox was, and who'd be compelled to discover its origins. Lucky us. You gave us some nudges from your domain along the way, and trumped up this whole Spirit Tour story to trick us into turning over the box, because you're not strong enough to take it until it's in your hands. I'll give you credit, you make a clever argument, but that's of course what you're good at. And I'm sure whatever's in the bag is a nice distraction. The whole thing is pretty damn impressive." Jake flashed another wicked grin. "Bet right about now you're regretting I came along, aren't you?"

"You still wish for this to be real? So be it," he said softly. "I'll give you one last thrill." He took a step forward, his face shimmering and contorting into a monstrous visage. This time he didn't regain his composure.

I took a step back, staring at him in shock.

The timbre of his voice deepened. "I'm not one of the lowly spirits you're used to seeing. I'm not going to flicker and disappear. Now give it to me, before I come and take it."

"Why don't you, then?" Jake said. "I don't think you can."

The man snarled and his lips curled back, further than they should go. He made a low, guttural sound that caused a shiver of fear somewhere deep inside me. "*You're wrong,*" he said.

I stumbled backwards and heard Jake say something in a low voice I believed was meant only for himself.

"Get thee behind me, Satan," Jake whispered.

The man lunged towards the letterbox, impossibly fast.

But Jake was ready. As Chenisdeaux reached for him, face twisted into an inhuman sneer, Jake threw the letterbox on the ground and stepped on it, bringing his weight crashing down on the lid. His boot went straight through the antique wood.

The moment it did so, Mr. Chenisdeaux disappeared.

-82-

After a stunned silence, Lou gave a raspy laugh. "Smoke and mirrors until the end," he said, his hand shaky as he pulled out a cigarette. "I guess we got our answers."

Jake walked to the edge of the clearing and folded his arms, his back to us, gazing into the darkness.

Asha inhaled sharply. I turned and saw her bent over the sack. She extracted a tome with a tattered cover, bound with gold leaf and decorated with rune-like symbols, similar to the carvings on the letterbox. Lou reached for it, and she handed it to him.

"Ogham," Lou breathed, gently turning the pages. "This must be what the Druids were looking for." He looked up. "He wasn't lying. This is priceless."

Next, Asha pulled a small jewelry box out of the sack. The box had a green velvet cover, with "Ashritha Rana" written decoratively on the front. She opened the box to find a silver ring inset with a saffron-colored gem, in the shape of a lotus flower that had just begun to blossom.

"It's beautiful," I said.

"In Hinduism, the lotus represents the true soul of an individual." She slipped the ring on her finger and looked at me in shock. "It's a perfect fit."

My head was spinning with a barrage of thoughts as my eyes slipped to the spot where Mr. Chenisdeaux had been standing. With jittery hands, I bent to see what else was in the sack, pulling out a photograph in a simple metal frame.

My eyes widened. "Lou, I believe this one's for you."

The photograph depicted a pretty little girl with mocha skin and black curls walking down a dirt road lined with shacks. Her eyes glowed with an inner light, her radiance shining through the dirty face and tattered white dress.

Lou's cigarette hung loose from his fingers. He took the photo and turned away. With a deep breath, I pulled another object from the sack. I knew the effect it would have on the person it was meant for.

"Jake," I said, walking over to hand him an emerald pendant. He turned it over and traced a finger down a set of initials carved into the silver setting on the back, just below the stone.

"It's hers, Counselor," he said softly. "You see that slight imperfection, the little mark below the *A*? That was there when I bought it."

Jake gripped the pendant and returned to staring off the hill. One item remained in the burlap sack, and I pulled it out.

The circular item had a protruding wooden handle carved in the same style as the letterbox, that curious splaying of the edges.I held it up and gazed at my own weary reflection.

It was a mirror.

We stepped carefully down the last remaining path, the one by which none of us had entered, still wary of running into Nyles or his cohorts. We saw no one, heard no more voices. The terrors of the Hill of Crosses had dissipated into the night.

The trail spilled out at the bottom. We re-entered the footpath through the woods that led back to the main road.

The woods were as calm as the hill, white with the innocence of snow. Asha spoke first, hesitantly, as if afraid to disrupt the spell. "My brother was at the doorway. He told me I should stay and that he was fine." She had a distant smile on her face. "And that he loves me."

She turned to Jake. "What happened up there? What did you mean when you told Mr. Chenisdeaux you knew who he was?"

"I was just talking," Jake said quietly.

She regarded him for a moment, and I wondered what she was

thinking—and if I would ever know. "Aidan?" she said. "What happened while you were alone on the hill?"

"I saw someone I knew, and made a choice."

My tone implied that I didn't want to explain. No one asked me to.

Lou was looking down at the photograph of Kika. "I'd really like to know how they pulled this one off. I bet some journalist did a photo shoot in the favelas and this ended up in some magazine." He looked up. "Their twisted idea will probably make millions, you know. I wish I'd thought of it first. Spirit Tours, Incorporated. Brilliant."

"There's no spirit tour," Jake said, in that same quiet voice. "Even with all that happened, even with your photo of Kika staring you in the face, it doesn't matter. You'll take any out you're given."

Lou stopped walking. "Didn't you hear the man? We were tricked. Nyles is on his way back to England, and Chenisdeaux was some kind of advanced hologram, easy to pull off in this weird light. What'd you think he was going to do, show up in person and stick around to have tea with the four people he just cruelly deceived? It was the last trick, and you fell for it. He got you to destroy the letterbox, so there was no more evidence. These gifts could have all been procured by a corporation with ways and means, and you know it. They duped us. Live with it."

"Commie, I just talked to my dead wife. Do you really think some corporate stooge overheard one of my confessions or found a page from your spiral notebook that's been lost for a decade?"

"Yeah, I do."

Jake waved a hand in disgust.

"You can't blame Lou for his beliefs," I said, "just as he can't ridicule you for yours. We can study and research and speculate, perhaps even experience—but do we really get to choose what we believe?"

"You can open your mind," Jake said.

"Yes," I said, feeling the weight of the mirror in my hand. "That you can do."

Epilogue

It's always in the end that we remember the beginning.

On Christmas Eve, close to a month after we returned from the Hill of Crosses, I stood on the street outside Maison de la Voyageur, peering through one of the small windows. I saw the same table at which Lou and I had been sitting the night I met Asha—the same night I first heard mention of the letterbox and set upon the path that would lead to the whirlwind of incredible events.

Maison was set to close, and only a few stragglers remained. Lou was celebrating Christmas Eve with Fredda, his first girlfriend in years, in her condo in the Warehouse District. I was on my way to join them.

Despite the unusually cold weather, I had felt compelled to stop. To look inside and reflect.

Except for a brief and unsuccessful forage for information, I hadn't spent much time pondering the journey. I had made my peace on that ancient hill, when I made my choice before the old man and the two doorways. As Mr. Chenisdeaux had said, whether or not what happened was real was irrelevant. I had gained all the answers I needed.

Which was good, because no more were coming. Our quest ended on the Hill of Crosses, and we were left with our own thoughts and speculations as to what had really occurred.

Only memories remained.

So I remembered.

As soon as I returned from Lithuania, I researched S.T., Inc. and M.A. Chenisdeaux from every possible angle—all to no avail. Just as Mr.

Chenisdeaux had said, the corporation had dissolved the same day we reached the Hill of Crosses, and no record of S.T., Inc. remained. A blip on a radar screen, gone without a trace.

I finally heard from my P.I. on Nyles Kempthorne. Bobby had found a handful of people in the world with the same name, but no one who remotely fit the description.

What he did find was a Welshman named Gareth Clough, a former history teacher who had joined the Cardiff Theosophical Society under the name Nyles Kempthorne. Gareth had quit his job and dropped off the radar years ago, and Bobby couldn't find a photo. The only other reference was a decades-old microfiche article in the *South Wales Echo* concerning a stage fire during a local middle school performance of *A Midsummer Night's Dream*. Gareth Clough had attended the school at the time, and the article stated that several students had suffered localized burns when a paper forest caught fire.

Could Nyles and Gareth be the same person? If so, why had the sign on the hill not borne his real name? Was it because Gareth Clough had wanted to conceal his identity during the final deception—or because Nyles Kempthorne was who he had become?

It didn't matter. It was finished. I somehow knew that if I tried to track down Nyles Kempthorne or anyone else involved with our experiences, I would find either nothing at all or further ambiguities.

When I asked Lou if he had been presented with a similar choice on the hill, he said he had, and that he had laughed and walked through the regular doorway. He seemed pleased to have a rational explanation to sink his teeth into. His worldview had been unaltered, and he was better off for the adventure: it had given him new confidence, as well as validation to spend untold hours on his couch and at Maison, reliving the journey. No, Lou had not changed very much, as far as I could tell.

Except for the newly framed photograph of Kika hanging on his bedroom wall.

Asha had sat lost in thought during the return journey, contemplating the ring adorning her finger. She said she had decided to become more spiritual and seemed excited about life again. She even talked about her brother, remembering things they had done, laughter they had shared. I was happy that his memory no longer seemed the terrible burden it once had been.

I had not seen or spoken to Asha since we left the New Orleans airport. I hugged her as she stepped into a taxi. She said to call when I was ready.

Nor had I heard a word from Jake after he left for Zagreb. On the return journey from Siauliai, he refused to talk about the events at the Hill of Crosses. When I pressed him about the phrase I heard him utter right before Mr. Chenisdeaux disappeared, he fingered the emerald pendant, grinned, and winked at me.

Maison came back into focus. I pulled my gaze away from Lou's empty chair, regarded my reflection in the window, and remembered some more.

I remembered standing before the two doorways, my spirit crushed almost beyond repair from the terrors of the Hill of Crosses and the visions in the mirror. Stripped of hope, I was left spiritually naked, crumpled at the feet of the old man.

Just as I was about to choose the opaque doorway, he showed me a final image that shook me to my core. It was nothing spectacular, no revelation of unknown answers. Just a simple image.

The face of the mirror had been divided into three parts. I saw Asha, Lou, and Jake in the different sections, each of them standing before two doorways identical to my own, unaware I could see them. I could somehow peer directly into their faces, and that glimpse provided the catalyst for my choice.

For in that moment, gleaned from their agonized expressions, I saw their despair, their questioning, their empathy, their pain, their *humanity*. I realized how much I loved them for it, and knew what I had to do.

I had been focused the entire journey—my entire life—on what I didn't have and was trying to obtain, when purpose and meaning had been in front of me all along, in the lives that had intersected with mine. I realized that stepping through the black doorway and leaving this world behind, even symbolically, would have meant sacrificing everything I held dear.

But I had another realization on the Hill of Crosses. There is a huge and implausible leap between mere being and questioning the *why* of that being. The fact that I had been willing to risk my life to find God—indeed, from the very need to search—told me that something greater than ourselves must exist. I hadn't a clue as to what that something might be, but I did know that faith was not something to be found through a doorway, or at the end of a map, or in a secret room inside some veiled sanctum sanctorum.

It didn't matter if that old man was God, or the head of a corporation, or just a paid liar, because the first true act of faith in my life had been not stepping through that doorway.

The real quest, I knew, had just begun.

The sound of a once-familiar voice calling my name broke my reverie. I turned and saw Asha crossing the street.

She stood before me in a white winter coat, a scarf tucked snugly around her neck. "I'm leaving to see my dad in the morning and wanted to say Merry Christmas. I was on my way to surprise you and saw you standing here."

I hugged her. "Merry Christmas."

She gave me a shy smile and adjusted her scarf. "I resigned from the shop. My last day was yesterday."

"Good call," I said. Judging by the shadows behind her gaze, I knew that she knew.

"Mr. Sofistere told me everything, but that's not why I left. He's a good man, Aidan, regardless of his past. I left because I'm going back to design school, and his encouragement was a large part of my decision."

"Congratulations," I said, sincerely. "I think that's a great idea."

She hesitated. "I also wanted you to know that I'm sorry. For the way things ended. For a lot of things."

"Don't be. It all happened for a reason, whether that reason was good or bad, right or wrong. We both felt the way we did and acted accordingly."

"It's not that simple. I—"

"Asha," I interrupted gently. "We've all had choices to make over the last few months. We've all had paths to follow. I don't accept your apology because none is needed. I could've walked away at any time."

She took a step forward. "It's more than that. I know I told you to call when you're ready, but I wanted you to know that after what happened on the hill . . . I've realized my emotions, my ability to love, were tied to the pain of my brother's memory. And now—"

This time I put a finger to her lips. "I'm going to Lou's place tonight," I said. "Why don't you come with me?"

She pressed her lips together and looked to the side.

"I want you to come," I said.

She looked back. "You do? I was afraid—"

"I do."

I watched her for a moment and couldn't tell what she was thinking, but that was okay. She had her thoughts and I had mine.

"Walk to the streetcar?" I said.

"Sure."

As she took my hand, I caught a glimpse of my reflection in the mirror of her eyes, and was pleased by who I saw. I was beginning afresh the game of life, ready to go forth and sample its offerings, wonder at its mystery, tremble at its sadness and beauty, once more. Onward I went, as do we all.

Yes, I smiled, recognizing myself at last.

Yes.

Author Note

The Hill of Crosses is an actual place. Whenever I use existing locations in my novels, I try to depict them as accurately as possible. However, I would like to note that with the Hill of Crosses, while it is a remote site and the origin of the crosses remains shrouded in mystery, I took a few liberties with the positioning of the hill within the surrounding forest. In reality, it's much closer to the road and not buried within the trees.

Yet perhaps those same liberties were taken by M.A. Chenisdeaux during that fateful night on the hill, either for Spirit Tours, Inc. or for another purpose, minor but necessary adjustments to the events of the evening....

Acknowledgments

This is a tough one. This novel has taken so long to come to fruition—almost decades in the plural—that when I sat down to make a list of who I wanted to thank, I became paralyzed both by the length of the list, and the thought that I might leave someone out. So let me first acknowledge a few people in the trade: my amazing editors, Richard Marek and Rusty Dalferes and Mabs Morris and Jen Blood, all of whom helped bring this novel to life. I also want to say a special thanks to Jan and Nena and Marty, of Dupree Miller & Associates, for boosting a young writer's confidence and seeing the potential in this story so very long ago. To everyone else, all those incredibly gracious family members and friends and even strangers who have given their time and selfless support over the years, I can only say, with as much sincerity as words allow, thank you.

LAYTON GREEN is a mystery/suspense/thriller writer and the author of the bestselling Dominic Grey series, as well as other works of fiction. His novels have been nominated for multiple awards (including a finalist for a prestigious International Thriller Writers award), optioned for film, and have reached #1 on numerous genre lists in the United States, the United Kingdom, and Germany. His previous novel, *The Shadow Cartel,* was a #2 bestseller on Amazon UK.

Please visit Layton on Amazon, Goodreads, Facebook, and at his website (www.laytongreen.com) for additional information on the author, his works, and more.

Made in the USA
Middletown, DE
09 March 2017